ZOMBIE
APOCALYPSE!

Also available

ZOMBIE APOCALYPSE!

Created by Stephen Jones

With

Peter Atkins

Peter Crowther

Paul Finch

Christopher Fowler

Tim Lebbon

Paul McAuley

Kim Newman

John Llewellyn Probert

Mark Samuels

Pat Cadigan

Scott Edelman

Jo Fletcher

Robert Hood

Tanith Lee

Lisa Morton

Sarah Pinborough

Jay Russell

Mandy Slater

and Michael Marshall Smith

ROBINSON

RUNNING PRESS
PHILADELPHIA · LONDON

Constable & Robinson Ltd
3 The Lanchesters
162 Fulham Palace Road
London W6 9ER
www.constablerobinson.com

First published in the UK by Robinson,

UK ISBN 9781849013031

1 3 5 7 9 10 8 6 4 2

First published in the United States in 2010 by Running Press Book Publishers
All rights reserved under the Pan-American and International
Copyright Conventions

9 8 7 6 5 4 3 2 1
Digit on the right indicates the number of this printing

US Library of Congress number: 2009943396
US ISBN 978-0-7624-4001-6

Running Press Book Publishers
2300 Chestnut Street
Philadelphia, PA 19103-4371

Visit us on the web!
www.runningpress.com

Printed and bound in the EU

Designed by Basement Press, Glaisdale
www.basementpress.com

This is a work of fiction. Any resemblances to actual companies, organizations
or people, either living or walking dead, is purely coincidental.

the essential Saltes of an
ingenious Man may be prepared
and preserved in a Drye and
Secr't place, without any
criminal Necromancy so that,
when expos'd to pure humours,
his Shape may defie the worm
and be rais'd up from whereinto
his Bodie has been layed, to walk
amongst his fellowes again.

                        Thomas Moreby

Hello Mum,

It feels strange to be e-mailing you, not least because I realise now that it's something I should have done far more often in the past. The phone's all very well but I always finish a call feeling I've got side-tracked and missed the chance to say anything in particular; and also that words, when they've been said aloud, have a way of falling apart and dissolving afterwards, becoming lost and left behind in ways that thoughts set down on paper never do.

Perhaps that's just the lawyer in me talking. Get it down, make it binding, make it *real* (and then bill by the hour, naturally). But I don't believe so. I think this is why we started to paint and write in the first place, why we treasure old letters and notes, why the idea of a person's signature still means something even now so much has become virtual and digital. We trust in the things we can reach out and touch. We try to make our ideas and emotions as concrete as things are in real life, to stop the past breaking apart like a flock of birds. Maybe that's what I'm actually missing, if I'm honest. When you and dad told us you'd decided to retire to Florida, Karen burst into tears but I was all, "Yes, what the hell, go where it's warm, play golf, drink margaritas, you've earned it . . ." — because I felt that's what you *needed* to hear — and maybe I didn't think hard enough about what *I'd* be losing, looking back. Yes, we talked every week, of course, and I've been out to Sarasota many times, but it's not the same, is it? I'm old enough now to understand that the house near Dulwich was just one of several to you and dad, part of a progression, not the forge of life and crucible of childhood it was for me and Karen. However, I also now realise that we can Skype all we like but it's never going to be the same as turning up at that house, chucking my coat on a chair and strolling straight into the kitchen to find you already warming the pot — ready for us to pick up the same old conversations in the same old places, drinking tea from the same old mugs. Perhaps by the age of forty I should have moved beyond the need for those kind of physical comforts, but I haven't. Maybe no one ever does, and it's just that we all grow up and move and die and there comes a point where you can't do those things any more — and so you pretend it doesn't matter because no one wants to start every day in tears.

But . . . anyway. I'm writing to you now.

This whole New Festival farrago was supposed to honour the past, of course, as well as treasuring the present and looking forward to the future. That was the sell, the spin. But I remember dad explaining to me a long time ago (during the slog towards O-Level History, I assume) what the expression "bread and circuses" meant, and that's all the "New Festival of Britain" actually is, or has ever been: smoke and mirrors, a cynical attempt by the government to pretend the country wasn't sinking into the swamp; that the recession + the sodding coalition hadn't effectively bounced us back to the 1950s. I'm not even sure *who* they were trying to kid. The Americans? Europe? People on Mars? If you're living in the UK there's no way you can miss what's been happening — from the pushing through of the Police Special Powers Act to the subsequent deaths in Trafalgar Square. That is unless, of course, you're really, really stupid — which sadly, a lot of people are. The papers have been full of it since the day the New Festival was announced. Some days it's the only story in town (which, of course, was the point of it in the first place). Furrow-browed analysis of how much celebration there'll be of "our boys" in the armed forces, in newspapers pandering to middle-Englanders whose minds and horizons are too small to be seen by the naked eye. In-depth exposés in the "qualities", pontificating about who's taking back-handers and creaming profits off the top (politicians and building contractors, you'll not be surprised to hear), and whether sufficient attention will be paid to off-setting the bloody carbon debt . . . Posturing to their demographic, in other

words, while making no real difference
to anything at all. And, of course,
endless breathless speculation
everywhere over which "celebs" might
deign to take part — not to mention a
special "reality talent show" to pick
who sings the national anthem at the
opening ceremony (for God's sake!).

Bread and circuses, smoke and mirrors.
An endless "silly season". An attempt to
generate enough white noise to mask the
sound of the country crumbling to dust
all around us. I once described it to
Zoe as fiddling while England burned. It
was funny then. I can see the skyline
through my window as I type this letter.
It's not funny now.

I was making a concerted effort to tune
the whole bloody thing out until about
three weeks ago, when Zoe came stomping
into the kitchen one lunchtime ranting
about something she'd just caught on
Radio 4 — a breezy piece mentioning that
pre-construction work was starting on
one of the New Festival's South London
sites — which basically boiled down to
cheerfully destroying the grounds and
graveyard of All Hallows Church. I
suppose I must already have been missing
you and dad more than I'd realised,
because — even though I'd totally
forgotten the church existed, if I'm
honest — suddenly it all came back. I
remembered how you used to bring us up
to take us on walks across Greenwich
Park on day trips to mooch around the

Royal Observatory, and then north in a cab over the river, with lunch always in that Garfunkel's near Leicester Square and a toy from Hamleys if we were good (and on days like that, we generally were).

It all seems like a very long time ago now — but when I heard about the destruction of the graveyard it came crashing back, along with another memory (one which I'd revisited more recently, in fact): that of dad explaining to me about death one morning on one of these walks, standing looking through the railings at All Hallows, at the graveyard with its old and tilted stones. I think it was pretty soon after Nana had died. I'd always got on well with her, and so dad explained (as best you can, to an eight-year-old child) why I would never see Nana again except in my mind, and how sometimes that just had to be enough. He crouched down next to me to explain this and he was calm and measured and (I realise now) very, very strong, given we were talking about *his mother*, and she was only about two weeks dead. Even Karen seemed to absorb the ideas in a positive way, when (as you know) my darling sister had a tendency to stomp on the melodrama pedal even way back then. I recall glancing up to see you standing behind him, your hand gentle on his shoulder as he spoke.

And standing there in the kitchen with Zoe I remembered, too, what it had felt like years later when I went away to college. Being away from home, finally having to lift my head from the meadows of childhood to take a look at the adult world with its long roads and dark alleys and mountains and broken bridges and rainbows and big skies. Alone for the first time in my life — with no one standing behind me, hand on my shoulder, letting me know I was looked after. And yet . . . I knew that you *were* still there, both of you, and that I need never look through any of life's fences alone.

Anyway. I found myself suddenly furious. I couldn't believe that the government and their familiars were allowed to just start digging up a churchyard — *our* churchyard, as I now thought of it — and I decided Zoe and I had to do something, and do it right away. That's something else I got from you and dad, I suppose, for better or worse — from the CND marches you hauled us on, the anti-apartheid protests, all that. The belief that everyone *can* do something about *everything*. Not anything big, perhaps — but *something*. A conviction that although it's easy to think the world has become too big and complex to affect, that it's been turned into an unstoppable train travelling too hard and fast through the night for any individual to stand a chance of making a difference . . . actually we still can.

So we got our coats on and went over

there. We found nothing in the way of organised protest when we arrived: a few old codgers hanging about in a vaguely indignant way — the kind of people you'd *expect* to see protesting at the digging up of the grounds of an old, forgotten church in South London. (Sorry, no offence meant, I realise you probably reached "codger" status quite some years ago, technically, but you know the kind of oldsters I mean. The dusty kind.)

I got talking to a middle-aged academic type. Some kind of professor. She had a bee in her bonnet about something to do with the history of the All Hallows site, and got very excited when I let slip that I was a lawyer. She seemed to have more indignation at her disposal than actual evidence, however, and warning bells went off for me when she started banging on about plague pits and some disciple of Nicholas Hawksmoor (you remember, the 18th century architect, a pupil of Christopher Wren, all that). People have got it into their heads that Hawksmoor was one step away from a black magician (the Ackroyd novel is partly to blame, and the admittedly odd architectural style of Hawksmoor's churches, but it can't just be that) — and as soon as you hear someone conjure the guy's name then it's a fair chance you're dealing with a nutter, or at the very least someone who's put two-and-two together to make five. That's what I thought, anyway, and so I made my excuses and backed away, and she pretty

quickly understood I was going to be no
help and shook her head and hurried off.
Just before she turned the corner I saw
her glance back, and in her face I
thought I saw the look of someone who
was on the verge of becoming very gently
unhinged.

I was wrong. I realise now that it was
fear. I think back and wish I'd read the
woman's face better at the time, but
sometimes, you just *get things wrong*.
The past is not some idyll where
everything was simpler and better and
blessed with the soft sunlight of
childhood afternoons — creatures with
big, sharp teeth live back there, too. I
had a brief affair a few years back, for
example. (I know this is *way* too much
information in a mother-son e-mail, but
I'm putting it down anyway. There's no
point skirting full disclosure now.) It
didn't last long and I ended it myself,
before I'd even had to admit to Zoe what
was happening. Why? Because though the
"now" of it was fun, I knew it would
never stack up against all the
yesterdays — and tomorrows — of the
relationship I already had, and which I
wanted to keep. For one night and a few
afternoons I forgot myself, that's all.
I forgot myself, got lost in time.

I *got something wrong*, is what it boiled
down to, but on that occasion at least I
had the chance to put it right. Zoe and
I had our problems at the time (it
happened soon after our fifth failed

IVF, when the curtain came down on all that and neither of us were sure what the hell we were going to do with our lives); but "now" is not the only game in town, just like the "truth" is not always the thing that must be told. What's gone before is still here. The past hangs around us, inside us: like our clothes; like our lies; like our bones. The past is what holds you up to face the future, too, but when you find you can't have children — what do you do? Where's your road to what's coming up? How do you keep being part of *something*? You do it through trying to keep staying part of the flow, I suppose, though trying *not* to be one of those middle-aged buffoons who stop understanding anything or liking anything new; who step off the moving walkway of the now and retire to yesteryear, to carp and moan about all the things they don't understand now.

Anyway. Zoe and I hung around the church for a while, looking disapproving, but it didn't seem like much was actually *happening*, and there was no one to give a piece of our mind too, so in the end . . . Well, we left, and went and had a nice ploughman's lunch at a pub on the Thames. Not exactly a protest to be celebrated in legend and song, I'll admit, hardly the '68 Paris riots or Greenham Common II . . . but there didn't seem much else we could actually *do* — on that day, anyway. And it got us out of the house and having lunch together, at least, which was nice. Remember the first time you met Zoe? I'm sure you do. That was a pub lunch too, up in Highgate. Dad took to her immediately, but I could tell from your body language when we left that you didn't quite approve, or weren't convinced . . . Yet. But you'd been that way with girlfriends before (admit it), and I was never sure whether it was a genuine take on the girl in question, or merely you being generically protective. You came round to Zoe pretty quickly in the end. How could you not?

Ten days passed. More crapulent newspaper coverage of the New Festival, and amidst the fluff and nonsense, I spotted a tiny piece about a patch of Hampstead Heath (which has been protected ground for centuries, bear in mind, the biggest patch of wild countryside in any city in the world) that had somehow been co-opted to the event and was about to have a huge, permanent statue of Winston Churchill built on it. I realised then that All Hallows was *not* a one-off, that the government truly was prepared to stomp all over London's history for their fifteen days of New Festival Fun, and it infuriated me to realise how people just don't understand the past any more. Attention spans have shrunk to nothing — but not just in the obvious way, the kind of thing dad and I have happily moaned about since I became old enough to realise the Younger Generation isn't

just a phrase but a fact. I don't mean
all the usual guff about MTV and video
games and information being cut up into
tiny chunks for tiny minds. I've watched
the children of our friends playing
video games, for hours upon end, and I
know they *can* focus on something when
they choose to. It's more that history,
time itself, has become truncated,
advert-breaked, atomised. People simply
can't understand the continuum of
experience any more. Anything before the
1950s is black and white and I-don't-
know and I-don't-care, unless it has to
do with Hitler or the Pharaohs. So why
would they care about some old church,
and the bodies buried there? Or get
worked up about some patch of
countryside that people just, like, walk
around? Dead, dusty words blown away in
the wind. People don't honour the past
because they don't understand how *real*
it was, how *written down in acts*, that
it was as genuine and rich and dangerous
as today. That the people in that
shadowy dream we call the past ate and
drank as we do, that they slept with
each other and loved and murdered and
lied, and that they did other things
whose echo still sounds, hundreds of
years after they've died.

And that made me angry, and galvanised
us both. The funny thing is that maybe,
if we *had* been able to have kids, we
wouldn't have gone back that last time.
Maybe little Ethan or Madeline (the
names we'd chosen, but didn't get to

use) would have needed picking up from
school or driving to some after-class
activity and we wouldn't have been there
when they started digging up the bodies.
Wouldn't have seen the shards of ancient
coffins, or the skeletal shapes in
tatters of shrouds yanked
unceremoniously from the ground.

The second time Zoe and I went to All
Hallows it was early in the morning,
although this time there were a lot more
people. It was obvious straight away
that half of them were recreational
protestors — people who'd seen something
on the news and thought it would be fun
to shout and throw things: the kind who
turn up at G18 summits and rant and rave
about naughty capitalism before
returning to their homes to enjoy the
benefits of Western industrialisation
and a globalised economy. There were
those *other* people, too, the ones who
can't seem to care deeply enough about
anything in their own, real, lives, and
so instead latch onto the flavour-of-
the-month issue, or Lady Di, or Big
Brother. The culturally lobotomised.

But there was also a third group —
people like us, people with banners and
placards, who were seriously unhappy
about what was happening and what it
represented. Unhappy . . . And maybe
even disturbed. There were also a lot
more police and army, forming a

defensive cordon around the excavations. Many of them were armed, despite looking little more than teenagers. I noticed they appeared nervous, as if something had already happened that had them spooked.

The contractors had erected wooden fencing around the site by then, of course, but some bright spark had managed to jam a tiny webcam through a knot-hole and was feeding live video to anyone with an iPhone. We saw the cloud of what we assumed was red dust, floating up from the dry ground and up over the top of the fencing. We saw the bodies taken away towards the under-crypt of the church. We saw a declaration, in effect, that history only flows in one direction, and that the living were allowed to do whatever they liked to the remains of the dead.

The bizarre thing was that there was *cheering* while this was happening, while somebody's great-great-great-great-great grandmother was yanked out of the ground like ancient landfill, or the remains of someone else's forgotten pet. On both previous visits, amongst those vaguely protesting, we'd seen these cheerleaders for the New Festival. The kind of people who go to Wimbledon to bellow the name of whatever no-hoper currently represents the feeble best that Britain can do. The ones who string up St George flags whenever England is about to go down the pan in some international football competition. The ones who reduce the idea of being English to some jingoistic farce. They were there that afternoon, and they cheered, not knowing they were hooting and laughing in the face of the end of the world. There's probably a metaphor for something or other to be found in this, but I don't think I have the energy to look for it.

Or the time, either. We've had no power here for nearly two days, and only 8% of the laptop's battery is left now. There's probably not much else to say, really, or at least little that I can face re-living. More mistakes to list, that's all. Like thinking that the government would do more than posture and prevaricate and debate, until it was too late. Like thinking that the man who attacked Zoe and I, when the trouble kicked off at All Hallows, was just a drunk. That thinking that all the love in the world was somehow enough to stop what happened next, or that the sentences of civilisation possessed a glue that would stop the world falling apart quite so quickly.

There's all that and more, but it's all compacting down to a black moment in my head and I find it increasingly hard to distinguish individual words. I've lost track of time too. Perhaps everyone does, towards the end. I've wasted all my time in remembrance and haven't got much said. Maybe a phone call would actually have been better this time, impossible though it would have been. I was on the phone to Karen when she died. I'm pretty sure she'd had a drink. A lot of people have had a drink now when you talk to them — often a great many drinks. I myself haven't been entirely sober in over a week. It doesn't help, but we do it anyway. Karen and I had been talking for over an hour, gathering up our memories like fallen leaves, before the wind blew them away, and then I heard them breaking in through her front door. I heard her shouting and screaming — say what you like about Karen (and you'll be happy to hear that she and I got on much better over the last two years), she gave as good as she got, always.

But in the end I heard her voice break. I heard it stop. I put the phone down before I could hear what happened afterwards. I've heard enough of these things now.

There comes a time when you have to put the phone down forever, and love means hard decisions. Love means remembering everything that has occurred between people, respecting it and honouring it as best you can — and in whatever way makes sense. Like when you gave the nod to dad's morphine being ramped up at the very end. I remember shambling out of that hospital into a numbingly humid Florida night, after he'd finally died,

and standing alone in the parking lot
listening to cicadas and having
absolutely no doubt about the rightness
of what you'd done (and I had tacitly
enabled) — nor about the unspoken
decision that it was something Karen
need never know about. I stood in a
wide-eyed kind of peace, remembering the
man who now lay dead in a bed four
floors above me, back when he had
crouched down with me to look through
railings into a graveyard and told me
that though Grandma was dead, I would
always be able to see her in my mind.

When I close my eyes now, I can still
see dad. The odd thing is that I suspect
a lot of your friends looked at the pair
of you, and saw dad's straight back and
bullet-proof bearing and assumed all the
strength in the partnership came from
him, that you were just the (charming,
and attractive) hostess and mother and
cook. But people don't know anything, do
they? People get things wrong. People
probably had similar thoughts about me
and Zoe, too, over the years. They'd be
just as wrong there — though lately, in
the last few weeks, I have stepped up to
the plate. I was the one who said we
should build a barricade at the end of
the street last weekend, and talked our
neighbours into helping. Okay, it hasn't
held, but it gave us a couple of extra
days. It was me who boarded up our
house, too. You do what you can do, and

then in the end you have to have the strength to admit it failed, and that time has run out.

On which note, Zoe sends her love. She hasn't explicitly said as much, but I know she does, or at least would have done if the opportunity had arisen. So I'm making that decision for her, doing it on her behalf. That feels odd, too (far more bizarre than sitting here writing an e-mail to you, though you've been dead for two years, and are, I truly hope, lying flat and decayed beyond desecration in Florida soil). You know what Zoe's like. She's very like you, in fact — a woman who makes up her own mind. That mind is no longer there, though, at least not as it was. As Karen and I used to say when we were children, the "lights are on but there's nobody home".

And actually, from the glimpse I got before I managed to trap Zoe in the basement yesterday, there's no light left either in those blue eyes now.

I don't think you ever actually made it down into our basement. Dad had a quick peek just after we moved into the house, but there's not a lot to see. Just two rooms, bare; the back one separated from the front one by a door which can be locked — and which is also, thankfully, very thick. I won't falter. I know there's nothing left for me outside the house, and that the remnant of the only

thing I *do* care about is trapped
stumbling and lurching in the dark
beneath the house. She doesn't breathe —
I've tried listening through the door —
but she moves. Slowly, irrevocably, like
the things outside in the street. The
things that pull at the planks I nailed
up, the things that bang their faces
against them until heads break apart and
another thing comes up from behind to
take their place.

When the computer screen finally goes
blank, I'll stand up and set fire to a
few bits and pieces on this level of the
house (it's going to have to be books, I
think, which I know would scandalise
dad, but the bloody EEC made just about
everything else fire-retardant).

Then I'm going down to the basement to
sit and listen to Zoe and be as close to
her as I can, until we both burn.

It's the best plan I can come up with,
and I know you'd do the same, or
something like it. You always believed
the best of people, of our species. You
marked the good times and made them
special, and were fierce and resolute
against the bad — the periods when
unreason and violence and mindlessness
won their temporary (you hoped)
victories. You made the world better for
those you loved, and I'm glad you aren't
here to see what it's becoming, now that

unreason and death has become timeless
and permanent, now all that is wrong and
dark is rising swiftly to the surface.
In about half-an-hour, I won't be here
to see it either.

I'm glad, too, that you're both buried
on the other side of an ocean, so there
is no chance we'll ever meet; shambling
down the same street with no light in
our eyes.

We will never see each other again, but
that's okay. I'll always have you in my
mind.

I lo

-
{
<u>DOCUMENT ENDS</u>:
FILE RETRIEVED FROM HARD DRIVE OF FIRE-
DAMAGED LAPTOP [ref # 46007];
LOCATION WITHHELD IN ACCORDANCE WITH
SECTION 19 OF THE NATIONAL SECURITY ACT;
<u>RECORD ENDS</u>:
}

**British Media Corporation
Internal Communications**

From:	Internal Communications
Sent:	29 April, 08:52 AM
To:	All London Staff
Subject:	Traffic Congestion on Blackheath Road

This email is going to all staff

London staff are advised this week to avoid travel in and around the New Festival South London site, due to possible protests in the area. Congestion is expected to be especially severe around All Hallows Church and Blackheath Road.

Check the BMC's Emergency Information channels for further updates:

Phone: 0800 0666 999

Online: bmc.co.uk/999

Gateway: 999 Emergency Information

Ceefax: page 999

Internal Communications

Dear William,

The department is insisting I use e-mail now, citing the fact that it's faster and conveys more urgency, which is fortunate as I have something rather urgent to discuss with you.

Sorry you couldn't make it over to the conference at St Alpheges. Just as well though, as all the usual imbeciles were there, blocking any progress that might be made. The members of the Catholic Council were barking up the wrong tree as usual, exercising themselves about birth control and women priests when they should have been commenting on the problem at hand, and the CoE synod weren't much better, wittering on about gay clergy, so little was achieved. Put a bunch of priests in a room together and they'll start planning the music programme for the orchestra to play as the *Titanic* goes down. The fact that church attendances have all but disappeared in these troubled times seems to have completely escaped them. Don't get me started on that. I caught the PM's speech last night about how we must all pull together to overcome our economic adversities, and how Britain can teach the rest of the world how to survive this latest recession. He was speaking from a fact-finding trip to Texas. The GBP is now worth less than the Rand and he's hobnobbing with oil barons.

I attended the one-day event because I wanted to raise a question about All Hallows Church, but there was no time left at the end of the meeting to even touch upon the subject. Do you know the building? It's a rather unlovely early Victorian pile in stained and moss-covered Portland stone, with flying buttresses and a collapsing spire, on Blackheath Hill at the edge of Greenwich Park.

I went there last month because there's an odd story about the diocese that keeps surfacing (in my world, at least; you know how much time I spend researching for the London Archaeological Society at the British Library). The architect Nicholas Hawksmoor had a raft of apprentices who took his more controversial views rather too much at face value. It's known that one apprentice, Thomas Moreby, worked on All Hallows, and while it's certain that he oversaw the construction of the crypt and undercroft, nobody knows how much of the above-ground part of the building he finished. It's a bit pointless to wonder now, because the upper section was completely rebuilt around 1850.

Anyway, as I arrived, I noticed a row of bright yellow JCBs lined up in the car park. There were also about a dozen protesters (mostly senior citizens) in rain-hoods hanging about looking cold and bored. One of them had a sign that read KEEP THE COUNTRYSIDE GREEN, like we were in the New Forest or something. Blackheath is the suburbs, for Heaven's sake. I know they mean well, but I think they enjoy being victims.

So I pulled over, hopped out and took a look, and sure enough they'd started to excavate the grounds immediately behind the church. Apparently, the idea is that the New Festival of Britain site is to have a tram-link to the refurbished Virgin Dome, which I suppose is one reason for the site's selection. Which brings me to the urgency of this note; you're a cartographer and know about these things better than I, but isn't there a long-standing government order not to dig up the east side of the park? Can they simply override it without consultation?

I'd appreciate it if you could get back to me as quickly as possible. I came past the site again yesterday and it looks as if they've already started digging.

Best as ever,
Prof. Margaret Winn

To:	William Barnsley, Cartographic Institute, Madrid
Cc:	Dr Daniel Thompson, Dept Head UCH London
From:	Prof Margaret Winn, UCH London
Subject:	All Hallows Church

Dear William,

Thanks for your prompt reply. That's what I thought. But I've checked, and no such consultation has taken place. On Saturday I visited the Museum of London and met with your old colleague Diane Fermier, who by the way sends her regards. Down in that dimly lit basement we pulled out the original mapping grid of the Blackheath area. The 17th century boundary lines surrounding the park and church are surprisingly unchanged from those of the present day. It seems pretty obvious to me that no one has bothered to check up on this, a fact I find simply amazing.

Actually, the area between the park and the heathland has been disturbed on at least three occasions. Most recently, the largest ditches along Ladysmith Crescent were filled with rubble from houses and factories bombed during the Blitz in 1940. Before that, George III ordered a number of grand houses to be pulled down, and their remains were buried on the site in 1803 (this was at a time when the king was suffering from one of his lapses into madness – I imagine he thought the property belonged to raving Papists). Before that we find an estimated figure of almost 11,000 people buried on the site in the months directly preceding the Great Fire of London.

Now, although parish records do not extend to recording the deaths of London's poorest citizens, I'm pretty sure these were the earliest victims of the Bubonic Plague that swept the city in the year preceding the fire. Of the 100,000 who died, it would seem that over 10% of the total were placed here on one site because the soft clay soil was easily removable. According to Diane, some of the rich were buried in lead coffins, but all the rest were placed in winding cloths or sacks, and here is my point – if they were then put in wet clay, surely this would act as a preservative?

I checked with an opposite number in Brussels, because – as you know – the Belgian government has been heavily involved in the disinterment of animal remains from peat bogs on the borders of Northern France, and they have found that not only is skin and hair remarkably well-preserved, but in many cases DNA sampling has shown that diseases we thought long-eradicated remained in stasis within animal carcasses.

If this is the case, what happens when the diggers reach London's dead? The sites in the centre of the old city have never been disturbed on this kind of scale. Do you know any epidemiologists who could offer advice about this? Clearly the government doesn't care to delve this deeply into the subject, but I think someone should make sure that there's no risk of contagion.

Best as ever,
Prof. Margaret Winn

To: William Barnsley, Cartographic Institute, Madrid
Cc: Dr Daniel Thompson, Dept Head, UCH London
From: Prof Margaret Winn, UCH London
Subject: All Hallows Church

Dear William,

I was surprised by your email yesterday. Can you really be so sure? I appreciate the point that centuries of low-core temperature should have killed off the hardiest microbes, but no one has ever tested a single site of this magnitude before. Now it emerges that the dig is to extend over forty metres down in order to incorporate several lift shafts and a large underground car park. This means disturbing a vast quantity of bodies.

I spoke with the site foreman, and he told me that he has been instructed to shift any "debris" he finds into separate containers so that an archaeological expert can sift through it, but he has not been told about the potential health risk posed by any finds, and has not been asked to quarantine any human remains. Indeed, he seems to have no knowledge about the history of the site.

If you really feel this is an overreaction on my part, then I shall leave you to your work and seek advice elsewhere.

Prof. Margaret Winn

To: Professor Margaret Winn, UCH London
From: Dr Marcus Hemming, Wellcome Institute

Dear Prof. Winn,

Thank you for your inquiry about the current excavation of the site at Blackheath designated for the New Festival of Britain. I had read about this in the press, but was surprised to hear that the land was formerly used as a plague pit. I must say I'm rather skeptical about this, as the distribution of the victims has been outlined in a number of historical records starting as early as 1667, and no one has ever singled out this site in particular. It seems especially unlikely as we know the pathogenic route of the plague, from which this area is far removed.

Are you sure about your facts?

Dear Dr Marcus,

Let me set out my case. I hope you'll be able to understand my concerns after reading this.

In 2004, the London Metropolitan Archive in Clerkenwell received a set of large hand-drawn maps from the estate of one Oliver Whitby or Whichby (the spelling differs in different texts), who was the former Justice of the Rolls at Lincoln's Inn Fields. These items were found when the deceased's possessions were unparcelled from a lot sold but never examined by his great-grandfather. One of the problems faced by the LMA is the microfiching of material prior to disintegration, and as the maps were not deemed of sufficient public importance to receive preferential treatment they have sat in the basement of the LMA awaiting scans since their arrival.

In my researches, I met a young woman in charge of scanning these documents, and when she showed me the maps pertaining to the S.E. London area in question, extending across Blackheath to the edge of the church and Greenwich Park, I made copies because I knew I had seen their outline somewhere before, but could not remember where.

I'm sure you know that the architect Nicholas Hawksmoor built six complex churches to his personal design, the nearest to the excavation site being St Alfege's Church at Greenwich. While attending a seminar in that building recently, I was shown a layout dating from the period immediately following the Great Plague, which bore exactly the same borders.

Now, this is where it gets interesting; the Whitby family built and maintained a number of private burial sites around London. The first was constructed in 1642 at Blackheath, and the LMA's maps show a shaded section of the heath which, according to a coda found in Oliver Whitby's notes, had been set aside for the burial of plague victims.

So far as I know, this is the only evidence that has ever been uncovered pertaining to the burial of victims in this area, although it has long been theorised that the area derived its name from its use as plague pit in the 14th century. If it can be proven that these documents are real and not forgeries – and why would they be? – I think I have a case to stop the excavations before any real damage can be caused. What I need from you is some kind of testimonial which acknowledges the possibility that plague bacilli might be able to survive at low temperatures for long periods of time. Would that be possible?

I must point out that as the excavations are now well under way, time is of the utmost essence.

Yours,
Prof. Margaret Winn, UCH London

_ _

Dear Prof. Winn,

This is very worrying news. I can't provide absolute proof of what you want, but I can at least tell you what I know. To begin with, nobody has actually identified the Great Plague as definitely stemming from the Bubonic bacillus. This was always assumed to be the case because the disease was thought to have originated in the Netherlands, from Dutch trading ships carrying infected bales of cotton. Bubonic plague is so-called because it causes swelling of the lymph ducts into "buboes".

The first areas affected in London were down by the docks. It was assumed that the plague was carried in miasma – poisoned air – and most London dignitaries beat a hasty retreat to the countryside, leaving their subjects to fend for themselves. The Lord Mayor, Sir John Lawrence, remained, but carried out his duties inside a specially constructed glass box. We now know that the disease was spread not by air but by blood.

The dead were buried beyond the city walls, one of the largest plague pits being situated in the so-called "Dead Ground" at the Priory Hospital of the Blessed Virgin Mary Without Bishopsgate, known as "St Mary Spital". Burial here stopped when it was discovered that the plague bodies were being placed on corpses from earlier graves, and there was a fear that this denseness of humanity under the ground might cause a return of the contagion. It was a long-held belief that sheer weight of numbers could somehow cause diseases to multiply even among the dead. If the site at Blackheath had previously been used to bury the sick, it could well have been exposed and used again for plague victims – but why carry corpses across the river for burial?

The number of deaths in South London was quite small, so if, as you say, a sizeable percentage of the dead ended up at Blackheath, a proportion must have been moved from the North side of the Thames. Bodies were only shifted after dark – it was commonly said "Grief by day, death by night" – and the journey would have required a great number of carts. But if the sites at St Mary, Charterhouse and St Botolph were full, the City officials may well have hired private contractors to rid themselves of the diseased under cover of darkness. I must say it has always struck me as odd that so many bodies could be placed in just three main sites, and I have wondered before whether alternative arrangements were made for their disposal without public knowledge.

I don't suppose the nature of the site at Blackheath was pointed on any maps of the time. The area grew extremely wealthy during the time of the slave trade, and it would have made the building of local property undesirable.

If this was indeed the case, and this Mr Whitby hired men to transport the dead to his pits, I start to share your concern, because the water table at Blackheath is surprisingly high given its elevation, and the preservation of the bodies requires two main factors, dampness and pressure (to create a vacuum). With both of these requirements being met, it starts to seem foolhardy to simply break open deep ground without expert advice.

There is something else that I am more loathe to mention, simply because it seems so damned peculiar. Two centuries after the Great Fire eradicated the plague (actually the plague burned itself out by killing off everyone in London with weak immunity – the fire merely acted as a cleanser) the Victorians hired a team of Romanian boys to dig up the bodies at Charterhouse. They chose Romanians because this race was thought to be naturally immune to plague; their nation had no history of coming into contact with the pandemic. When the pit was opened and examined, Queen Victoria's royal physician was summoned and he ordered the immediate resealing of the enclosure, but no official reason was ever provided for this act.

I've always wondered if he saw something there that disturbed him, something he could not make known to the general public.

I'm not in a position to make any further investigation into this subject, as you know. But I think you should continue to be concerned – for all our sakes. Do let me know how you get on.

Best,
Marcus

To: Michael Brooks
     Site Manager, New Festival of Britain Project
From: Prof Margaret Winn, UCH London

Dear Mr Brooks,

I have tried repeatedly to contact you by phone about the excavation of this site (to the East of All Hallows Church) without success. I understand you were offered the services of an epidemiologist who could advise you about the safe removal of any human remains you might uncover in the ground. Apparently you turned him down and continued digging prior to receiving EEC health & safety clearance. If this is the case, might I enquire on whose authority you made this decision?

To: Prof M Winn
From: M Brooks
Site Manager, NFOB Construction Ltd.

Dear Ms Winn,

If you have any objection to this
company's code of practice, may I
suggest you take it up with the Home
Office, as they granted us permission
to continue with the excavation in
order to meet the construction
deadline set out by the Home
Secretary.

Yours, etc
M Brooks

INTERVIEW TRANSCRIPT

Conducted April 22, 11:30 am
Marek Schwarinski
Prof Margaret Winn, UCH Health Advisor

WINN:
Could you state your name and position please?

SCHWARINSKI:
Marek Schwarinski, excavation worker, NFOB.

WINN:
This is the planned site of the New Festival of Britain?

SCHWARINSKI:
That is correct.

WINN:
Can you tell me what you saw at the site last—

SCHWARINSKI:
Thursday. We was digging out part of the site known as Quadrant 3 – we're divided into teams to work on different quadrants—

WINN:
And yours is where the lift shafts will be?

SCHWARINSKI:
Yeah, that's right. We're down about twenty-three feet and the going suddenly gets much easier. The ground is softer, like. There's a lot of water down there, and we've got pumps in to drain it, so I'm thinking maybe we've hit an underground river, but there's nothing marked on any of the site maps. I talked to the lads, but they couldn't see nothing.

WINN:
What did you do?

SCHWARINSKI:
Got out of my digger to take a look. The ground under my boots was really soft and wet, it's deep brown clay, and – this was like a horror film, this bit – I see what looks like a bundle of squashed rags pressed into the soil, so I turn over the nearest bit with my foot. And it's a face. But really squashed, like, and the eyes was gone, but definitely a face, even with some wispy bits of hair on the skull. A girl I think.

WINN:
That must have been a shock.

SCHWARINSKI:
You see all kinds of shit on this job but yeah, I bricked it. Now, we'd levelled out a good sixty square feet of soil at this depth, so I had a look across the area, and there's more of these brown lumps. It's wall-to-wall bodies, crushed in together, head-to-toe.

WINN:
What did you do then?

SCHWARINSKI:
I went to see Mike, the site manager, and told him what I'd seen.

WINN:
And what did he say?

SCHWARINSKI:
He told me to keep digging.

WINN:
He didn't suggest that you should stop work until an expert arrived?

SCHWARINSKI:
No, nothing like that. He told me not to say anything to the other workers.

WINN:
You didn't think of removing the bodies and setting them to one side?

SCHWARINSKI:
It ain't my job to do that. I only do what the site manager tells me.

WINN:
How long did it take you to clear the site?

SCHWARINSKI:
About three days, 'cause it was just me and two other blokes. The rest was taken off to another quadrant. When we got to the next level—

WINN:
How deep was that?

SCHWARINSKI:
About another ten feet – when we got there, the bodies stopped appearing and the soil was just clay again.

WINN:
What did you do with the corpses you'd found?

SCHWARINSKI:
They got dumped in with the rest of the outfill.

WINN:
They didn't go into special containers?

SCHWARINSKI:
No, nothing like that.

WINN:
And what happens to the outfill?

SCHWARINSKI:
It gets taken to the Thames estuary and dumped in the water. There's a land project going on down there, a lot of building.

WINN:
Did everything get dumped?

SCHWARINSKI:
No, there was some stuff—

WINN:
Stuff?

SCHWARINSKI:
Bodies. The most complete bodies. They got removed and taken to a skip at the back of the church.

WINN:
Who decided to do that?

SCHWARINSKI:
I don't know.

WINN:
How many bodies were there, would you say?

SCHWARINSKI:
A couple of dozen, maybe. They was all covered in mud, so it was hard to tell. The rest of the stuff, well, it was all mashed together, so it was hard to tell what all the bits were. I mean, there wasn't nothing worth saving. No valuables or nothing.

WINN:
They were incomplete bodies. So the complete ones were removed. Do you know what happened to them?

SCHWARINSKI:
No. When we came back to work the next day, the skip was gone.

WINN:
Did Mr Brooks tell you not to speak about this?

SCHWARINSKI:
No, not really. He just said there used to be a graveyard there – a long time ago, like, and the land got built up over the years – he said it wasn't anything to worry about, but it's been bothering me, like. And then when you turned up—

WINN:
Mr Schwarinski, thank you.

From: Dr Daniel Thompson, Dept. Head, UCH London
To: Professor Margaret Winn, UCH London

Dear Prof Winn,

I have received a letter of complaint from a Mr Michael Brooks, the Site Manager employed by the construction company of the New Festival of Britain, saying that you have been entering his site without permission, and have attempted to conduct interviews with the excavation crew. Apparently you've been citing the health concerns of this hospital, and have made all sorts of wild accusations about what might happen should the construction workers find human remains while they're digging. You've upset them so much that several members of their workforce have threatened to seek union representation over what they now see as breaches in the Health & Safety laws.

May I remind you that you are technically an employee of this hospital, and that your actions must be made justifiable to our board of governors? There are proper channels for this kind of complaint. If you need advice about how to handle the situation, please come to see me and we can discuss the matter in private. I have no doubt that your intentions were for the best, but next time please talk to me first, before acting rashly and endangering a massive public project which – I'm sure I have no need to remind you – is of primary importance to the survival of this government and to the spirit of the nation.

Daniel Thompson

Dr James MacMillan
Royal Archaeological Institute

Dear James,

I can't believe you're still not on e-mail, although given what's been going on lately, maybe it's a good idea that you don't keep a record of our conversation.

Since we spoke on the phone, my office has been ransacked and someone has broken into my car. Luckily, the most important files pertaining to this situation were not in my briefcase at the time. I actually had them with me. You know why I'm pursuing this, but I must admit that so far all I have is proof that Health and Safety regulations were breached.

However, you can help me on a related but slightly different matter. Are you aware that an architect called Thomas Moreby was responsible for constructing the crypt and undercroft of All Hallows Church?

I need to know about this because Moreby was a man of strange beliefs – he thought the body lived on after death, that it was somehow inhabited by the spirits of those who had died of the plague – and that these undead beings would rise again if "expos'd to pure humours". In other words, if they were disinterred and exposed to fresh air. We have a situation where plague victims have been removed from a pit and – well, I can't tell you what happened to them, as nobody seems to know – I just wondered if you had come across any of Moreby's architectural writings?

I'm dropping this off at your house, but perhaps you could call me when you get this.

Ever,
Margaret

April 25

Dear Margaret,

Forgive the scribble, and yes, I'm sorry about the lack
of e-mail but perhaps it's for the best in this case.
I tried calling you but got your machine - hate the
bloody things. To answer your question, Thomas Moreby did
indeed allow his beliefs to affect his buildings. His
convictions concerning resurrection can readily be seen in
outlines for a City of London crypt (thankfully never
constructed) which could be opened from the inside by
its inhabitants. He died in Bedlam, although it's
rather hard to work out if he was mad or whether he
just annoyed the wrong people.

Moreby believed that the newly revived would inherit
the Earth because, despite having been inhabited by
the contagious dead, they would have purer souls (having
seen the Other Side, I presume). Quite where he got
this belief system is a mystery, although I detect the
influence of Hawksmoor in his Papan outlook. According
to a colleague of mine, he left instructions in his
personal effects to build such a crypt for himself

beneath All Hallows church, but I suppose you already know that. I assume the idea was that when the time came, he would be resurrected along with his fellow pure souls.

In his hand-written notes to the publisher of <u>Journal of a Plague Year</u>, Daniel Defoe - a dreadful writer, of course, but an invaluable witness to history - points out that there were a great many strange beliefs among the survivors of the Great Plague and Great Fire of London. It's hardly surprising, given the circumstances. What's particularly interesting is that Moreby was also a closet Catholic with some highly influential friends in parliament. A conspiracy theorist would no doubt start to feel uneasy here. If, as you say, the remains of the burial victims were secretly removed (for a second time!) under the instructions of the Committee for the New Festival of Britain project and interred inside Moreby's crypt, it would suggest they were working within the guidelines set out by the Catholic church.

All Hallows is Church of England now, but the earliest building was not. Therefore, it's not such a wild surmise to guess that Moreby's crypt (if it still exists) has recently been opened and filled with the intact bodies of plague victims according to longstanding instructions lodged with the church. History has taught us that state and church are willing to collude openly when circumstances prove mutually beneficial. In this case, the government gets to expedite its plans for a feel-good event to improve national morale, and the church gets to keep taxes accruing from the property owned by Moreby which is still held in trust by the Duke of Leicester. Everybody wins.

This is of great academic interest, but hardly any help to you if what you most want to prove is that the health of ordinary citizens has been compromised by the exhumation.

Sorry not to be of more assistance. If there's anything else I can do to help, please don't hesitate to get in touch.

Best,
James

Dear Janet,

Congratulations on your promotion. I hear the paper is going from strength to strength. I know you are no fan of the PM, and have a story lead for you that you may find interesting. There's a health scandal brewing over the Home Secretary's decision to waive public safety rules on the construction of the New Festival buildings. I didn't want to drop the details in this e-mail, so I've mailed them to you under separate cover. When you get the envelope you'll find a number of interview transcripts I've recorded with the concerned parties. I have used false names in the document to protect their identities, as they would be at risk of losing their jobs should their views be made known. And in the current climate, who knows how long their opinions would stay on security files?

I also spoke to a friend of mine at the Royal Archaeological Institute, and it seems likely that the NFOB site managers removed bodies from the site and re-interred them under longstanding Papal instructions. What intrigues me most is that all of this information is on public file and readily available. It's just that no one has bothered to fit it all together. Do you remember a time when we used to have proper investigative journalism in this country? The great hacks of the past all seem to have been replaced by celebrity children writing about shoes, restaurants and handbags. God, it's depressing.

I spoke to my superior here at the hospital, but he is a welcome caller at Downing Street and has basically warned me to leave the matter alone. I have spent eighteen years fighting ignorance and spin in matters of public health – my feelings about political interference are no secret, God knows – and I am damned if I'll stand by while risks of this magnitude are taken, simply to make the nation feel good about itself again.

Best,
Maggie

Janet,

Sorry. I've only just found this so it didn't go in the envelope. I'll post it separately. You should be able to see the relevance without comment from me.

Best,

Maggie

BIOSECURITY RULES WERE BREACHED AT DEVON FARM: OFFICIAL

THE DEVON TURKEY farm at the centre of the latest Avian Flu outbreak had been repeatedly warned about breaches in biosecurity, it emerged today. The latest World Health Organisation report is calling for a new international disease surveillance system to track mutating strains of Avian Flu, after it emerged that the virus has once again jumped species into humans, although in a relatively non-lethal strain.

The report states "While there has not been a pandemic since 1968, another one is inevitable. Estimates are that the next pandemic will kill between 2 million and 50 million people worldwide and between 50,000 and 75,000 in the UK. Socio-economic disruption will be massive".

Seventy-five percent of all new human diseases originate from animals, but experts have warned they are currently identified only after infection has spread to humans. The committee chairman, Lord Wentworth, said: "The last century has seen huge advances in public health and disease control through the world, but global mobilisation and lifestyle changes are constantly giving rise to new diseases and providing opportunities for them to spread rapidly. We are particularly concerned about the links between animals and humans. This is why a universal biosecurity code of conduct needs to be enforced on a global scale". ●

April 27

Janet,

Just time for a quick note – call me as soon as you've had a chance to go through everything. I'm going to the site tonight to gather further evidence. My inside contact has arranged to get me admitted to the church grounds. The boy is taking quite a risk, but is willing to make a stand so that we can bring this matter to the attention of the public. Thank God there are a handful of people left with genuine moral convictions. I'll need to be sure of my facts before going public, but if I'm right, there is a very real danger to us all. I'll let you know how I get on.

Best,
Maggie

"YOU HAVE REACHED THE ANSWERPHONE OF PROFESSOR MARGARET WINN. PLEASE LEAVE A MESSAGE AFTER THE BEEP."

"Maggie, if you're there can you pick up? I've been trying your mobile all morning but it goes straight to Voicemail. Where are you? I've been going through the contents of the packet you sent me, and we're going with a front-page splash. But there's something I still don't understand - the stuff about church architecture? This guy called Thomas Moreby, the apprentice of Hawksmoor who designed All Hallows. I couldn't make a connection with what you were telling me about the public health issue, and I need to sort out - well, I need to know if all of this is on the level because it all sounds a bit crazy to be honest. Look, call me when you get this, okay?"

"YOU HAVE REACHED THE ANSWERPHONE OF PROFESSOR MARGARET WINN. PLEASE LEAVE A MESSAGE AFTER THE BEEP."

"Maggie, I still haven't heard from you, and I need to fact-check if I'm going to run with this piece. I've been through everything now, and what you've sent me is potential dynamite. I'm not kidding, this could bring down the government. But I have to be absolutely sure of the facts. What did the police say when you reported the break-ins? We can't afford to make any mistakes if we're going to run all the way with this. If it's a deliberate cover-up, if the Home Secretary has given specific instructions to ignore guidelines and bypass safety checks just so that they can get the poor, dim citizens of this country whipped up in some kind of patriotic frenzy, then I think we have to cover our asses every step of the way. And I'll need photographic evidence, because great blocks of copy aren't going to shift papers. Hey, I'm still a hack at heart, what can I tell you! Call me now, the second you get this."

[This recording was copied from the hard drive of a PDA belonging to J Ramsey, Head of Current Affairs, *Hard News* online newspaper, and is the property of MI6.]

SFX: (Background noise has been removed in order to clarify recording. Voice has been legally identified as that of the above user.)

"Well Maggie, you're always complaining that there are no real investigative reporters left, so I'm doing this for you. And for myself, obviously. Although strictly speaking, our advertisers don't want to see any hard news on our site. They'd be much happier if we stuck to reports about handbags, restaurants and shoes, as you always put it. Let me turn the engine off.

"Okay, your Schwarinski guy appears to be waiting for me outside the church.

1 There's no sign of the supposed police
2 patrols and the main site lights are off.
3 I spoke to him on the phone earlier and he
4 told me that the new EEC law covering
5 light pollution in built-up areas means
6 they have to switch off the power at
7 midnight. It's – let me see, half-past one
8 in the morning. Let me go and see what he
9 has to say. He looks quite cute. I might
10 get a date out of it, if nothing else.
11
12   "All right, Mr Schwarinski has gone off
13 now. I was kind of hoping he'd stick
14 around because it's bloody dark and I'm
15 wearing heels. Not high ones, but the
16 ground is really rough. He's given me his
17 torch and spare batteries, but he took off
18 like a shot as soon as he saw me through
19 the gate. All I have to do is pull it
20 behind me when I leave. I get the feeling
21 his papers weren't exactly in order. He's
22 taken a big enough risk just by letting me
23 in.
24
25   "I'm approaching the church. I think
26 it's safe to wave the torch beam about
27 because there's just the wall of the park
28 on one side and the heath on the other.
29 It's raining lightly and I can't see much

traffic in the distance. The far road has
been closed to vehicles in order to
provide a works entrance to the site, so
it's very quiet here and kind of peaceful,
like being in the countryside. Not that I
know much about countryside, unless you
count the outdoor smoking area at the
Sanderson Hotel.

"I can see mechanical diggers lined in
a long row like huge yellow beetles, all
the way down one side of the churchyard.
The main church door is locked –
Schwarinski warned me that he wouldn't be
able to get the key. But apparently
there's a separate side entrance down here
on the right, which he's left open. It
won't take me into the main part of All
Hallows, but I don't need to go there.
This should – the door's stiff, but – hold
on, there's a stone caught under the door.

"I'm in. There's a small stone
vestibule and a staircase leading down.
Kind of narrow – like the staircase in the
Monument. I hope it doesn't have as many
steps. Very muddy underfoot – someone's
been up and down these stairs a lot from
the main site.

"Okay, let's see what we've got here.
Shit, I just bashed my head on the
ceiling, which is really low. Hang on.
Right, I'm in a brick-lined storage room
that appears to run the width of the
church, but not the length. Pretty boring
so far. It's wet underfoot. Let me just –
that's better. I can see more clearly now.
Not much down here, some blue plastic
crates, a bale of wire, a hosepipe, a
stack of plywood against the wall. But
there's another short corridor at the end,
which, according to your Russian pal,
leads to a second chamber. He thinks this
is where they took the bodies, although if
they did, they cleaned up afterwards as
the floor here looks like it was recently
washed down, and I can smell disinfectant.
Yeah, there are puddles of the stuff all
over the floor. I'm wearing Marc Jacobs
shoes because I was out at dinner earlier.
What an idiot.

"Okay, nothing to report here except
. . . hold on.

"Interesting. Big wooden door rather
like a miniature version of the famous
'Gate of Judgement' from St Stephen's

Church, the one that was destroyed in the
Blitz. This one has the same markings, the
skulls and weeping putti, but it's in
lousy condition. One side has been
completely rotted through with fungus and
woodworm. So much for the Catholic church
preserving its antiquities for future
generations. Smells bad, too.

"Just so you don't worry, I've put on
an anti-bacterial face mask, like the ones
Japanese girls wear. I got it from someone
on the travel desk. Not that I think
there's anything down here to worry about.
Maybe I should try to get the door open.
Oh, it's not even locked. The hinges
aren't attached on the other side. I can
probably just push it out of the way . . .
I have to put down the PDA to do this, so
back in a minute. This is where gym
classes come into use.

". . . Right, I've shifted it a little
to one side, enough to squeeze through.
It's actually a lot heavier than it looks,
and I don't think I'll be able to get it
back in place by myself. I can't believe
I'm doing this. Behind is – let me hold
the flashlight up – a bit disappointing

really. What we've got here is another
room, about thirty by forty feet, the back
of which appears to be unfinished - it
looks like packed earth at the end. The
smell is very bad now. I have to say it
smells like something rotting. No sign of
any bodies, though. If this really was
Thomas Moreby's much-vaunted crypt of pure
souls, it's pretty unspectacular.

"There's something about the end wall
that's interesting, though. Going in for a
closer look. It's bloody freezing in this
part, and I can see my breath. Ah. Okay.
Maybe I got a little too close. This is -
yup, these are bodies all right, stacked
floor-to-ceiling. All pretty squashed,
dark brown and flat, just like the ones
they pull from peat bogs. They're not
going to be following Moreby's creed
anytime soon, getting up and moving to
their higher plane, mainly because I can't
imagine that any of their bones are strong
enough to support them. They're pretty
intact, though. No smell from them - seems
to be coming from somewhere else. Weird.
Something down here smells - kind of
alive, but rotten. Let me - no, definitely
not the corpses.

"Well, they've been moved here now so presumably the church will be happy about that. Not much else to report. I'm going to take a few shots of the body stack for the article, but I have to say I'm starting to wonder if this isn't much ado about nothing, Maggie. Okay, security protocol was breached but, as we know, these days that sort of thing happens all the time.

"Something . . . I just saw something in my camera's flash. Shadows jumped. I probably imagined it. I'm going for another shot.

"*Christ.* There's something in here – it moved really fast, just across the back of the camera frame. Okay, I'll just fire off the flash.

"Jeez-*us.*

"Fuck. Have to get back to the doorway but I can't see the gap. Fuck, fuck, fuck . . .

"Oh. Oh God.

"Oh God Maggie, I'm talking to you and I'm looking right at you.

"How many days have you been in here? You poor . . . what's wrong with your – oh fuck! – I can see your arms moving even though you're slumped against the wall so I know you're alive, but why don't you . . . what is that . . . What is that? There's something all around you, like a red-brown mist. Shifting in and out of your skin. Oh Maggie, you have no eyes.

"Something has half-eaten your eyes and there's something reddish-brown inside your mouth and you're still moving, what happened–?

"Fleas. They're fleas. Thousands and thousands of the fuckers. Christ, I've been an idiot. The Great Plague was caused by fleas that infested the Dutch cotton bales, then travelled on rats and jumped to humans. They bit into the flesh and spread the disease by sucking and transferring blood. Fleas. Simple organisms that are still evolving.

"Everything you said makes sense now.

No wonder Moreby believed the dead could walk again. They're not truly alive, just infested with fleas that have existed in a state of suspension until released into the air once more. But look at you. There's something more I can't see. You're moving almost as if you remember who I am. I can see the fleas shifting underneath your skin, but you look like you're in terrible pain . . . let me see . . . let me—

"Oh God, your ears, there are thousands of them. They're sucking the blood from your brain, gorging themselves on your flesh, it must be a living nightmare for you. I'm going to go for help. Shit, the little fuckers can really jump. I can't see any on me but I feel itchy and you – you can just stay back there while I go back upstairs and make a call.

"Christ, you made me jump, Marek. I didn't see you standing there. I'm glad you came back. I need to go upstairs and phone for an ambulance – what are you doing?

"Don't put the door back! What are you fucking doing?!

1 "The son-of-a-bitch Russian fuck-bastard
2 has shoved the door back in place. Let me
3 out of here, you fucker! How much is he
4 paying you? How much is your slimy boss
5 paying you to do this? Open it, goddamn you!
6
7 "Well, Maggie, it looks like you and
8 me, old pal. Yeah, you can just stay over
9 in that corner where your little parasites
10 can't reach me. Do you even know what I'm
11 saying? I can see you're dead, you're just
12 not lying down. They own you now, your
13 parasites have taken over their host. But
14 what are they going to do once they've
15 finished their food supply, eh? It's a
16 pretty dumb parasite that kills its host.
17 Fuck it, this was going to be the story
18 that made my entire career.
19
20 "Oh. So that's how it works. Just for
21 the record, if anyone ever gets to hear
22 this, my friend Margaret is coming towards
23 me, and I think she means to drain me of
24 blood in order to feed her parasites.
25 She's cold and dead but the fleas are
26 keeping her alive, so that she can feed on
27 others. It looks like I'm about to join
28 the pure souls, but I'm not going down
29 without a fucking fight.

"Not going down.

"Christ, that hurts. Jesus, you bitch.

"You living dead bitch.

"Fuck, I'm down.

"Down.

"This would have made . . . a great
. . . story."

<u>RECORDING ENDS</u>

To:
Dr Daniel Thompson, Dept Head UCH London

Wednesday, May 1

Dear Dr Thompson,

This file has been watermarked and licensed to you only. Please read the contents, then destroy. We think our contact Mr Schwarinski returned last night and attempted to collect the recording from Janet Ramsey's PDA, which he found on the floor of the crypt beneath All Hallows Church. However, he must have also discovered both Ramsey and Professor Winn in a state of revived life. It appears that as he removed the door, they attacked and bit him, making their escape. We are not sure of their current whereabouts.

Mr Schwarinksi died of his wounds this morning, but subsequently revived, attacking a hospital orderly. He has not been seen since.

I have to warn you that you may face prosecution for failure to pass on information vital to national security. This situation is getting out of control.

MESSAGE ENDS.

British Media Corporation
Internal Communications

From: Internal Communications
Sent: 30 April, 09:15 PM
To: All London Staff
Subject: Traffic Congestion on Ladysmith Crescent /
               Blackheath Road / Elliott Park / Greenwich Park

<u>This email is going to all London staff</u>

Due to increasing traffic problems in and around the New Festival
South London excavation site, it is recommended that all staff avoid
the area unless absolutely necessary.

Check the BMC's Emergency Information channels for further
updates:

Phone: 0800 0666 999

Online: bmc.co.uk/999

Gateway: 999 Emergency Information

Ceefax: page 999

Internal Communications

LCalvin
        (LC23 1/2)

- -

New Festival of Britain excavation site -
        G Division / 01-05

- -

FAO *Chief Superintendent Julia Kay (Borough
        Commander, Greenwich, MPS).*
cc *Chief Superintendent John Donnelly (Borough
        Commander, Southwark, MPS), Chief
        Superintendent Adam Shawcross (Borough
        Commander, Bromley, MPS).*

            * * * * * * * * * * * * * * * * * *

I am PS 1649 Liam Calvin, assigned to 5 Relief, G
Division, based at the Blackheath Road MobComm unit
(SE1). It is 04:14h on May 1st.
        As per the "G Division" requirement, this is my
interim shift report.
        I regret to recount a series of developments,
which over the last few hours have got completely out
of hand. Since the shift began, 5 Relief has incurred
several casualties, one apparently serious and, as of
this moment, has an officer unaccounted for. This is
due, in no small part in my opinion, to the new "need-
to-know" nature of the operational activity
surrounding the NFOB excavation site, and to the
incompetent leadership of Inspector Michael Makewaite
from Greenwich Police Station, who I now feel
compelled to make an official complaint about.
        As per the new G Division regulations, this will
be as accurate an account of the shift as I can give,
including "all detail, no matter how seemingly
mundane". Forgive me, however, if this log is later
and lengthier than usual.

- -

30-04

At 21:55h I paraded 5 Relief for night-shift duty at
the Blackheath Road mobile command unit. It comprised
myself and five constables: PCs 1701 Ken Stopford,
5829 Charlotte Gatewood, 9824 Dawn Fletcher, 2315
Stuart Mackintosh and 1357 Vince Barkworth. As "G

Division" was specifically formed for the temporary but primary purpose of controlling public order and providing anti-vandal patrols in the vicinity of the New Festival of Britain excavation site, we have no regular senior command, and to date a different duty officer has been appointed on each shift. At present, we are under the supervision of Inspector Michael Makewaite.

When we arrived for duty yesterday, the "Special Security Team" — we are guessing they are either MI6 or Special Branch — were in their usual position, parked in an Audi A4 Saloon at the front of All Hallows Church (which is about 200 yards from the MobComm caravan). Yet again, they made no effort to communicate with us or update us on any developments.

The Police Special Powers Act, which was rushed onto the statute book earlier this year, and which, as you know, I and several other senior members of the Police Federation Committee made clear in writing that we abhor, may well have given us greater powers of arrest and interrogation, and may deem even raw probationers trustworthy enough to carry firearms on routine duties, but it does not apparently trust us to know the names and ranks of the many non-police personnel who suddenly seem to wield authority over day-to-day police operations in London. These last two weeks, we've been reminded repeatedly by priority notices in force bulletins that we "must defer to the Special Security Team in all matters relating to the NFOB". And yet none of the pairs of Special Security officers who've rotated this duty between them over the last fortnight have felt it necessary to identify themselves to us either by name or rank. I therefore have no alternative but to refer to the two officers on this occasion as "Spook One" and "Spook Two".

I organised the relief as follows:

PC Stopford, being the oldest officer present — he's three months from retirement — was left to staff the mobile unit. PC Gatewood, being my most effective officer, was allocated the FRV, with a remit to answer all emergency calls and provide immediate support as and when necessary. PCs Fletcher and Barkworth were allocated a panda car each. This left PC Mackintosh, who frankly I regard as inadequate for the demands of modern policing. He's young and inexperienced, but he's also incompetent in terms of his procedural knowledge and his dealings with the general public (it's not for nothing that his nickname at Plumstead was "Bungle"). I placed him where I thought he could do least harm — on foot patrol around the perimeter fence of the excavation site. I myself took the Area car, intending to move between the units as the night progressed. As usual, I was given to understand that, if necessary, I'd have access to Dogs and CID night-cover.

If you'll pardon a personal observation here, there's been a strange reversal of the street-policing experience in recent years. At one time, night turn was regarded as less busy than day turn yet significantly more dangerous. Now, while it's not quite the other way round, things have changed noticeably. Recent trends in criminal activity, particularly with regard to public disorder issues, have increased numbers of injuries to police personnel during the day. At night, though crime still occurs, the streets are much quieter than they used to be. The volatile atmosphere of modern Britain, which the NFOB seems so determined to ignore, appears to have dissuaded all but the most hardened offenders from venturing out after dark.

At **22:07h** we received our first call of the evening. A Council employee returning home from work had found his flat in Croxley Court burgled. PC Fletcher attended.

At **22:14h** we received a call to Gornall Street, where three men were reported to be fighting. I responded, but on arrival found PC Gatewood already in attendance. She had placed three vagrant males under arrest for being drunk and disorderly.

At **22:22h** I was notified that PC Barkworth was attending an RTA on Morden Hill.

At **22:38h** Prisoner transport arrived at Gornall Street. PC Gatewood then drove to Greenwich Police Station to process the paperwork for the arrests.

At **22:47h** I attended Cumberpatch Avenue in response to information that two youths had been trying the doors of parked vehicles. PC Fletcher also attended. She arrived at the south end of Cumberpatch Avenue. In doing this, she surprised two youths, who ran west along Frith Lane. PC Fletcher pursued, but because of the numerous wheelie-bins scattered there she had to follow on foot. I drove around to the west end of Frith Lane, only to find that the suspects had scaled a fence mid-way along and climbed down the embankment into an area known locally as Heath Vale (an abandoned railway cutting, now overgrown).

PC Fletcher and I attempted to follow, but she became tangled with barbed wire. I searched the Vale bottom, but found no trace of the suspects. I called CAD to request a dog van, but, as no actual crime had been reported (it was later ascertained that no cars had been damaged or visibly interfered with), I was informed that canine support was unavailable at that time.

PC Fletcher had by now managed to release herself, but had incurred several deep lacerations to her arms and legs.

At 23:13h I dropped PC Fletcher at University Hospital Lewisham.

With two men down, 5 Relief was now significantly weakened. However, thus far this was a routine midweek shift, and I saw no purpose in requesting extra manpower from Borough Command. Instead, I brought PC Stopford out from the mobile unit, and allocated him PC Fletcher's panda car.

At 23:20h, I locked and secured the MobComm caravan, and recommenced patrol.

At 23:25h CAD informed me that PC Stopford had attended a domestic disturbance at 15 Redwood Grove.

At 23:29h I contacted CAD, requesting a progress report from PC Mackintosh. There have been protesters around the excavation site in recent weeks, though nothing in the last few days (possibly owing to the rumours that certain people have "disappeared").

At 23:30h CAD informed me that PC Mackintosh was not answering his radio. I asked them to keep trying.

At 23:33h CAD informed me that PC Stopford had requested support. I replied that everyone else was engaged, but asked what the problem was. I was told that the domestic incident at 15 Redwood Grove was a violent fight between a man and his young wife, as a result of which the interior of their Council maisonette had been destroyed.

The young couple in question are Cory and Freda Dunhill. They are known to us as petty thieves and prolific drinkers, who regularly fight when they've been "partying" together. Cory Dunhill has been arrested several times for assaulting his wife, though Freda Dunhill has also been arrested for assaulting her husband. Neither usually press charges. They have been warned about wasting police time on multiple occasions, and have been advised to seek marriage guidance counselling.

CAD reported that PC Stopford had spoken to the couple regarding possible breaches of the peace, but that they had rounded on him and put him out of their house.

At 23:41h I attended 15 Redwood Grove, where PC Stopford was waiting in a dishevelled state, with visible bruising on his face. He informed me that he'd been assaulted by both the Dunhills in the front room of their maisonette. There'd been a struggle before he was pushed outside.

I knocked on the door, and it was answered immediately by Cory Dunhill. Under caution, Dunhill admitted that he and his wife had continued to argue in PC Stopford's presence, and that Freda Dunhill had used foul and abusive language. PC Stopford had intervened and - somewhat unhelpfully in my view - said that "if his daughter were ever to speak like that, he'd give her the best good hiding of her life".

There is "old school" and "ancient school" in the modern police service. PC Stopford is strictly the latter. He's nearly fifty but looks closer to sixty. I doubt he's driven a patrol car, much less walked a beat, since the pre-PACE era, which has not equipped him to deal with the undisciplined, temperamental youth of today. Having been so admonished and, in their words, "threatened with violence", the Dunhills thus joined forces against him and threw him out of their home.

It is possible that PC Stopford, who, for all his shortcomings, is an old hand, provoked the confrontation and allowed himself to be overpowered and brutalised because the "facial injuries" regulation means that he'd have to remain indoors for the next fortnight at least. But this wasn't a line of enquiry I was able to pursue at that time.

It was now 23:48h and I heard from CAD that PC Mackintosh was still not answering his radio. Evidently I would have to go and look for him.

Regardless of my feelings about PC Stopford's approach, I agreed with his assessment that the Dunhills had assaulted a police officer. PC Stopford thus placed them under arrest. I called for prisoner transport, but was told that this would take time as a gang brawl had occurred in Greenwich, and that a number of bodies were being taken into custody there. I thus opted to transport the prisoners myself.

At 23:59h I arrived at Greenwich Police Station, and PC Stopford took his prisoners into the custody suite. I advised him that, once he'd charged his prisoners, he too should seek hospital treatment.

- -

01-05

At 00:06h I returned to the vicinity of All Hallows Church.

Spook One and Spook Two were still parked at the front of the building. They were inside their car, sharing a take-away pizza. I made a point of speaking to them.

Spook One is a large, burly man, heavily bearded. On this occasion, as on previous occasions when I've seen him, he was wearing a leather bomber jacket. He looks more like a biker than a government agent. Spook Two is younger than the other, fair-haired and well dressed. He has something of the "public schoolboy" about him, but he carries an air of authority.

I asked them if they'd seen PC Mackintosh making rounds of the excavation site. They responded in the negative, though Spook Two advised me that just because they hadn't seen PC Mackintosh, that didn't mean he hadn't been around. He said they'd had other more important things to concentrate on. I asked them if they were enjoying their pizza and if they'd ordered garlic bread with it, to which they chuckled and offered no further comment — until I told them that I was going to look around the church. This appeared to sober them up a little. They warned me that I mustn't try to enter the building itself as it had been locked up. I reminded them that nowhere was locked to police officers when it came to preserving life and limb.

At **00:10h** I commenced a lone foot patrol of the All Hallows grounds.

I didn't go onto the excavation site itself, as it is unlit at night and little more at present than a sprawl of mud, digging machines, Portakabins and piles of equipment covered with rain-soaked tarpaulins.

The church has a strange aura. I suppose one word for it would be "Gothic". It's a very old building, covered in moss, with strands of dead vegetation hanging from its gutters. The grounds are like something from a Hammer film - all mist, bracken and rotted, ancient gravestones. However, there was no sign of PC Mackintosh, and the Spooks were correct: I checked the front, side and rear entrances to the church, and all had been sealed with planks and corrugated metal. Each one bore a notice that unauthorised entry would be prosecuted under the Police Special Powers Act.

At **00:21h** I resumed mobile patrol, driving around the circumference of the excavation site, though some parts of it have now been closed to vehicles to allow for works access.

At **00:29h** I returned to the front of All Hallows Church.

Spook One and Spook Two were still in their car, watching me. I'd seen no trace of PC Mackintosh.

At **00:30h** I again asked CAD to try and contact PC Mackintosh.

At **00:33h** CAD replied that there was still no answer.

At **00:34h** I requested CAD put me on a talk-through channel. They complied and I tried to contact PC Mackintosh personally - but received no response.

If my reaction to this seems calm, I reiterate that PC Mackintosh is an undependable officer - not exactly lazy, but slow-thinking. It may have been that he'd turned the volume of his radio down to speak with a member of the public, and had forgotten to turn it up again. Alternatively, he may have forgotten to put a new battery into his radio when checking it out at the start of his shift. Both of these things have happened before. I made the decision that it wasn't worth raising an alarm at this stage.

At 00:37h CAD informed me that a resident on Ladysmith Crescent, Mrs Joan Akuma, had complained about hearing noises in her attic. Given that Ladysmith Crescent is just across the road from All Hallows Church, I opted to take the job myself.

At 00:38h I attended the address in question.

It's worth mentioning that Ladysmith Crescent was one of the streets at the centre of the controversy when the government first aired its plans for the South London exhibition site. It is a single row of terraced properties dating from just after the Second World War. They are not in good condition; for the most part quite dilapidated. But at the time they were all in private ownership. When a compulsory purchase order was issued for the entire row, there was uproar. All legal challenges have now been exhausted of course, and most of the residents have moved out. Mrs Akuma, who lives at No.12, the house at the very end of the row and the one directly facing All Hallows Church, is one of the few remaining.

Mrs Akuma, though she's quite elderly, is a spirited, bubbly character, who emigrated to Britain from the Gambia in the early 1970s. She made her living for many years as a piano teacher, though she's now retired. She's a pleasant lady, very respectable and pro-police, and many of the beat lads who normally work this area know her house as a reliable brew-shop. She offered to make me a cup of tea there and then, but I declined as I was still concerned about PC Mackintosh.

Mrs Akuma told me that, all evening, she'd been hearing scraping sounds in the attic, as if somebody was hiding up there – though she was more worried that it might be a ghost. Mrs Akuma is a very religious person, and has long been concerned about her home's proximity to All Hallows Church, which she says has a sinister reputation. Apparently, it was first constructed by a man who had black magic connections. Consequently, an evil atmosphere pervades the church and its grounds – or so Mrs Akuma says. She also told me that, as this was May Eve, "mysterious forces are abroad". She was about to elaborate on this peculiar statement, when she had an unexpected visitor. The doorbell rang and, when she answered, Spook Two was there.

It seems that, while we know nothing about the "Special Security Team", they know all there is to know about us, including having full access to our radio transmissions. Spook Two asked me if he could be of help. I regarded this as odd. You may recall the armed robbery on Deptford High Street not five days ago. A young police officer was shot and wounded. Support units not only responded to the call from neighbouring sub-divisions, but from neighbouring boroughs. A unit even crossed the Thames to try and assist. However, the Special Security personnel, who were less than five minutes' drive away, made no effort whatsoever.

I advised Spook Two that I didn't need any help. As a police officer with over twenty years' experience, I was perfectly capable of handling a complaint regarding nuisance neighbours. He left me to it, but I noticed that he continued to loiter outside.

I say that this was a case of "nuisance neighbours" because that is what I believed it to be. Mrs Akuma thought she had a ghost in her attic. I suspected it was either rats, bats or, more likely, something to do with the house next door, which is now empty. It seemed possible that squatters, if they'd found shelter next door, may have forced entry to this property via the adjoining attic wall. I volunteered to go up and look.

Mrs Akuma's upper room is actually more of a loft than an attic. However, her son, Stephen, who is a builder, has installed a floor up there and a loft-ladder, so I was able to ascend with ease. Inside, it was stacked with the usual junk, but quite spacious. Her son had done a good job for her. The floor was solid, there was electric lighting, the underside of the roof was lagged and wooden interior walls had been added to the west-facing wall, the east-facing wall and the gable wall, to provide insulation. The wall adjoining the house next door was neither double-skinned nor insulated, but was still made of sturdy brick. No one had tried to break through it. There was no sign of rodent or bat droppings, so I reassured Mrs Akuma that what she'd probably heard was birds roosting in the eaves, an explanation she seemed only partly satisfied with.

By 01:01h I was back on mobile patrol, and again contacted CAD to see if there'd been word from PC Mackintosh. CAD confirmed that there hadn't, but informed me that PC Barkworth was on Hicks Avenue, having requested prisoner transport. I queried the circumstances, and was told – by a CAD operator clearly struggling not to laugh – that a man had approached PC Barkworth and complained of having "his penis assaulted".

At 01:07h I attended Hicks Avenue, where PC Barkworth had a single male in custody.

I recognised the prisoner as Wayne Devlin, a drug user and alcoholic, who has multiple convictions for violence and dishonesty. Barkworth told me that he'd arrested Devlin on suspicion of attempting to cause criminal damage, at which point Devlin began struggling and swearing, so much that, even though he was already handcuffed, it took both of us to restrain him. I reminded Devlin that, under the Police Special Powers Act, we have greater discretion to use force with prisoners who resist. He kicked out at me, so I drew my firearm – at which point he calmed down.

Devlin insisted that he was the one who'd been offended against. He explained that he had an ongoing "situation" with his next door neighbour, an octogenarian war veteran called William Herbert, who'd made several complaints to the Council about Devlin's loud music. Devlin boasted that, every night when he comes home from the pub, he now stops to urinate through Herbert's letterbox. On this occasion, the elderly neighbour was waiting on the other side, and as soon as Devlin inserted his penis, slammed the letterbox closed. Devlin, in his own words, "can't piss any more, and probably can't wank either". He said that he was on his way to Lewisham Hospital when he spotted the panda and flagged it down. He'd made the complaint about his neighbour in good faith, but had now been arrested himself by "some dozey twat copper, who doesn't know his arse from his truncheon".

I had no problem with this arrest. Attempted criminal damage was the very least we'd charge Devlin with. Most likely we'd go for full damage, indecency, and probably Public Order offences as well in case the CPS pulled their usual trick and knocked it down to something more "cost-effective". But I made the decision that I couldn't spare PC Barkworth at that moment. He wanted to take a witness statement from William Herbert, and then accompany Devlin to Greenwich. I told him to radio the circumstances of the arrest to the custody suite at Greenwich, and to have a quick meeting with Herbert, telling him that we'd interview him properly first thing in the morning.

At **01:25h** Wayne Devlin was removed from Hicks Avenue via prisoner transport.

I resumed my search for PC Mackintosh, having advised PC Barkworth that I needed his assistance as soon as he'd made the appropriate arrangements with the AP.

By **01:30h** PC Mackintosh had been off the air for three-and-a-half hours.

I officially notified CAD that one of our constables was missing, and requested that this information be passed to Inspector Makewaite so that he might take control of the situation and summon support units from off-division.

At **01:35h** CAD informed me that Inspector Makewaite was not in his office at Greenwich and was not answering his radio, but that messages had been left for him.

At **01:36h** I received word that PC Gatewood had charged her prisoners and was back on patrol. I immediately put her on the search for PC Mackintosh.

At **01:48h** I received word from PC Barkworth that he was also available to help with the search.

At **01:55h** I received a call from CAD about Mrs Akuma at 12 Ladysmith Crescent. Apparently "the ghost was at it again".

At **02:03h** I again arrived in the vicinity of All Hallows Church. I observed Spook Two standing outside his car. There was no sign of Spook One.

At **02:04h** I knocked on the door at 12 Ladysmith Crescent.

Mrs Akuma answered immediately. She was tearful, and wearing a coat and carrying a handbag. She insisted that she couldn't stay in the property because she could still hear noises from her attic. I assured her that when I'd looked before there was nobody there. She told me there was no point in looking again because "souls are invisible". Instead, she asked me — though maybe "begged" would be a more accurate term — to give her a ride to her son's house in Catford. She'd already contacted him, and he'd agreed that she should come over and spend the night, but had said that he couldn't collect her as he'd had several drinks during the evening.

Mrs Akuma was understandably upset about her predicament. It wouldn't be safe for her seeking public transport at this hour. Nor did she want to use a taxi. The taxi-driver who carried out the series of rapes in Bexleyheath last autumn has put many women off using cabs late at night. I thus agreed to give her a ride.

That may seem like an abrogation of duty given that I had a man missing, but there seem to be so few decent, law-abiding people living in this part of London now that to abandon her in her hour of need was next to impossible. As we passed All Hallows Church, Mrs Akuma regarded it with open fear. She muttered something like: "the centre of everything that's wrong".

At 02:19h I was *en route* to Catford, passing through Hither Green, with Mrs Akuma in the passenger seat, when I overheard a CAD message to PC Gatewood concerning a naked woman who had been seen walking close to Eliot Park.

I again detected amusement in the voice of the CAD operator, which irritated me. "Doggers", "swingers" — whatever the Internet these days calls the late-night gang-bang crowd who congregate in certain London parks — are not something you hear a lot about at present. Increased levels of crime tend to have put an end to these nocturnal revels, so I couldn't help wondering, and worrying, what this naked woman signified.

At 02:25h I was entering Catford, when I received a call on my mobile phone. It was from Sergeant Buchanan, the custody officer at Greenwich Police Station. He informed me that Wayne Devlin's detention had been authorised, but that Devlin was complaining of injury and demanding hospital attention. Sergeant Buchanan advised me that, with a large number of suspects from the gang brawl in custody, none of his staff were available to accompany Devlin, so the arresting officer would have to do the honours.

At 02:26h I sent a message to PC Barkworth to abandon the search for PC Mackintosh, and told him to go to

Greenwich Police Station, where he had to baby-sit his prisoner on a hospital trip. I also contacted CAD, asking for an update on the whereabouts of Inspector Makewaite, in response to which I was told that he still could not be contacted. I requested that they make an official note of his unavailability and go over his head to ask Borough Command for assistance, as we were now badly short of numbers.

At 02:32h I arrived at Culverley Road in Catford, and left Mrs Akuma in the care of her son, Stephen.

At 02:44h I was returning along Lee Road, when I overheard CAD contacting PC Gatewood to inform her that a second sighting had been made of the naked woman, who had now entered Eliot Park by its north entrance. Apparently, the woman was not just naked, but covered in blood and dirt. I immediately contacted CAD and asked them to put me on talk-through with PC Gatewood.
     I told her that I would join her. If she entered the park via the north entrance, I would enter via the south, and we would work our way towards each other.

At 02:48h I passed All Hallows Church *en route* to Eliot Park when I was flagged down by Spook One. He asked me if I knew where his colleague (Spook Two) was, as he wasn't replying to messages. Spook One explained that he'd been making rounds of the church premises, but on return had found the Audi empty. I told him that I didn't know where Spook Two was, but that he'd been showing interest in the house across the road - 12 Ladysmith Crescent.

At 02:53h I arrived at the south entrance to Eliot Park. I radio checked with PC Gatewood. She was already at the north entrance, and about to enter.

At 02:54h I entered Eliot Park by its south entrance, moving along the row of fences behind which the groundskeeper's huts are located.
     There is no natural light in the park, so I was forced to keep my torch on full beam. This didn't reveal much. As you may know, Eliot Park, while less than a quarter the size of its "bigger twin", Greenwich Park, has extensive areas of natural and very dense woodland.

At **02:58h** I received information from PC Gatewood that she had located PC Mackintosh.

Still at the north end of the park, she'd ventured some fifty yards along the park's central avenue until reaching the benches ranged opposite the War Memorial. Apparently, PC Mackintosh was sitting on one of these, asleep. She admitted to knowing that he's often had trouble adjusting to night duty, and has never been averse to nipping off his beat to grab forty winks.

I asked her if there was any sign of the naked woman. She replied in the negative. I told her to wait for me and prepare PC Mackintosh for the verbal equivalent of a nuclear assault.

At **03:00h** I was a quarter of the way through the park, passing the football pitch on my left, when PC Gatewood notified me that she was having trouble waking PC Mackintosh. She now wasn't sure whether he was asleep or ill.

At **03:01h** PC Gatewood notified me that she'd found an injury on PC Mackintosh's neck. She said that it was a deep gouge, which had bled profusely – mainly down the inside of his uniform, hence she hadn't noticed it previously. She confirmed that he still couldn't be woken, and that his breathing was shallow and his pulse worryingly slow. I hurried through the park, breaking from talk-through to ask CAD to send an ambulance ASAP. I also asked them to locate Inspector Makewaite ASAP and fully appraise him of these serious circumstances.

By **03:03h** I'd reached the cafeteria in the centre of the park, when CAD informed me that PC Gatewood was in pursuit of a suspect. I immediately requested that we be put back on talk-through.

Contact was difficult to maintain as PC Gatewood was running, but she said that she'd been attempting to revive PC Mackintosh when she'd spotted a figure fleeing across the lawn in the direction of the wooded area containing the park lavatories. Before I could reply, she added that the figure had now veered to the right of the wooded area as though to cut around the cafeteria and along the avenue passing the tennis courts and the park playground.

I circled the cafeteria to try and head the figure off. There was nobody in sight, so I took a short cut through the flowerbeds towards the tennis courts.

At 03:05h I reached the avenue alongside the tennis courts, and saw the light of PC Gatewood's torch approaching. She wasn't comfortable about having left PC Mackintosh, and was relieved to hear that an ambulance was *en route*. She expressed a belief that he'd been asleep on the bench, and was attacked by someone walking past – possibly the naked woman, who she surmised might be some kind of escaped mental patient. At this point, we heard what sounded like splintering wood. It seemed to come from the direction of the park lavatories. We immediately headed over there. PC Gatewood had lost sight of her suspect during the foot chase, and felt it possible that whoever it was had now doubled back.

I again contacted CAD and requested supervision and support.

At 03:07h we arrived at the patch of woodland surrounding the park lavatories.

The access path winds into it for about fifty yards between dense rhododendron bushes, so the undergrowth is thick and leafy. We listened before entering, but heard nothing. I was tempted to wait until support units arrived, but, as PC Gatewood said, if the woman was herself the victim of an attack – which was still highly possible, given her bloodied state – she might need immediate help.

We ventured in side-by-side. I kept my torch trained ahead, while PC Gatewood scanned the surrounding undergrowth. Neither of us saw anything untoward, though there was a faint but pungent smell, like the scent of dirty clothes, stale sweat, bad breath – the aroma of a drug addict who's been living on the streets for too long.

At 03:08h we entered the central area where the lavatories are located.

These are basically a single block of grey cement, and look more like a World War II bunker than a public convenience. The Gents' entrance is located on the south side, the Ladies' on the north side. The local authority boarded both doorways up some time ago, as there'd been several cases of public indecency. Entry has since been forced to the Gents again – the Vice Squad still have occasion to visit this place — so it was therefore no surprise that this entrance stood wide open, though of course there was pitch-blackness inside. We'd been working on the basis that a woman who may have been assaulted or even raped might be seeking a public lavatory in which to wash, but it was difficult to imagine that anyone, no matter how traumatised, would enter a place like this. Nevertheless, we called a warning before we went in, to which there was no response. We drew our firearms, levelled our torches, and entered the building in standard "room clearance" fashion.

It was a derelict shell. Our torchlight showed nothing but wreckage — broken washbasins, shattered mirrors, the usual graffiti and cockroaches. However, one of the cubicles had been closed, and the stench, which was now slightly different yet far more overpowering, seemed to be coming from inside it.

We again called out a warning, but no one replied.

We steadied our nerve before I kicked the door open.

There was no one on the other side, though the toilet had been trashed, and excrement filled with wriggling maggots had been smeared all over the cubicle walls. We then heard a noise like a clatter of masonry from the Ladies next door. We hurried outside and circled around the toilet block in different directions.

It was approximately 03:10h, and I'd been separated from PC Gatewood for no more than fifteen seconds when I heard her shout for help. I also heard the report of her firearm.

I ran to the other side of the building, where the boarding over the entrance to the Ladies had also been torn away — in this case quite recently. Alongside it, PC Gatewood was getting to her feet. It may have been the strong light cast by my torch, but she looked pale and appeared badly shocked. She said that the woman had loomed at her out of nowhere and, yes, that she had been naked and was streaked with blood and dirt. The woman had then attacked. They'd struggled and PC Gatewood's firearm had discharged by accident. PC Gatewood had tried to hold onto the woman, but had been bitten on the base of the thumb. I examined her hand. The bite had penetrated the leather glove in several places. When PC Gatewood removed the glove, I saw a gruesome wound, bleeding freely but swollen and badly discoloured.

I told her that she had to go to hospital. We then heard movement in the rhododendrons close by - heavy movement, like a body pushing its way through. I made to give chase, but PC Gatewood tried to stop me - in uncharacteristically panicky fashion.

It was only now dawning on me that something very peculiar was happening.

PC Charlotte Gatewood is one of the more glamorous female officers in the borough. She is a tall, striking blonde, very athletic. She is also highly professional: quick thinking, firm in her dealings with the public and fearless in the face of danger. But she seemed more shaken by this incident than I had ever seen her. She told me that she'd only caught a glimpse of the woman before her torch was knocked to the ground, but that there'd been something "wrong with her".

I didn't have time to discuss this. I told her to go straight to Lewisham Hospital, but to check on PC Mackintosh first and make sure the ambulance was *en route*. I then forced my way through the rhododendrons. Beyond those, I came out onto open grass, and saw a figure maybe thirty yards ahead, limping towards the bandstand.

I say "limping", but that's not quite the correct word. "Lurching" might be better, or even "see-sawing". It was very ungainly. Though it may sound ridiculous, it reminded me of a marionette with some of its strings cut.

I followed, shouting that I was an armed police officer, ordering whoever it was to stand still. The figure kept moving, circling the bandstand. I had no clear shot, and certainly no justification, so I continued in pursuit. Despite its awkward gait, the figure was moving quickly. When I circled the bandstand, it had increased its lead to about forty yards. It rounded the corner of the cafeteria and started along the park's central avenue. When I reached that spot myself, it was at least fifty yards ahead, heading towards the groundskeeper's huts and the park's south entrance. At this point the moon came out, and I had a clearer view of the person I was chasing.

I could tell by the shape that it was a middle-aged woman, and by the way the moonlight glinted on her pallid flesh that she was naked. I could also see that she was coated in blood, grease and other filth. I detected that pungent odour again - sweat and dirt, mingled with something like bad fish. The stench of faeces in the lavatories had temporarily masked it. I ran to catch up with her. Whoever the woman was, she would leave the park before I got close. But now, just ahead of her, I saw light spearing into view. A vehicle was pulling up on the parking area just beyond the entrance. I also heard the yelping of a dog. It seemed that a support unit had finally responded.

Reacting to this, the woman veered sharp left across more open grass, toward the playground on the east side of the park. As you may know, this area is kept locked at night, and is divided from the rest of the park by a twelve-foot wire mesh fence. However, the woman scaled it - slowly but quite easily. She dropped down on the other side, landing badly, but got to her feet again, crossed the playground, scaled the fence on its opposite side, and climbed the embankment towards the overland railway line.

It was now 03:24h and PC 3947 Les Khan entered the park.

PC Khan is one of the Greenwich Borough dog-handlers. He had his Alsatian, "Alfie", with him on an extended chain lead. I explained what had happened. PC Khan felt sure Alfie would pick up the woman's trail - as he said at the time, he could smell it himself. But first we had to get through the playground. The gate in the mesh fence was padlocked, so I had no option but to break it open with a gunshot.

Alfie was released and had no trouble following the suspect. When he reached the playground's opposite fence, he found his own route through it - part of the wire netting on that side had become detached at the base, and he scampered underneath. PC Khan and I also climbed under the fence and clambered up the embankment. This was a difficult ascent. Not only is it heavily treed, but it was muddy from the recent rain, and deep in thorny bracken. Our progress was slow, and we were only part way up when we heard what sounded like Alfie yelping in pain.

At 03:28h we reached the top of the embankment, where spiked railings prevented us from trespassing on the railway itself. There was no sign of either Alfie or the woman. PC Khan, who was baffled and not a little alarmed, whistled. At first there was no response, but then we heard a whimper. It came from about thirty yards to our left. We moved along, having to sidle between the fence and thickly tangled thorn bushes, before we found the dog impaled sideways on the top of the railings. Three steel barbs penetrated his torso, and one his neck. The one in his neck had emerged through the top, completely transfixing him.

In my opinion, there was no possibility the dog had accidentally skewered himself while attempting to climb over. He had been forced down on the spikes by someone of considerable strength. It took the two of us to loosen the poor creature and lift him down. Alfie's head had also been brutally gashed; his left eye was missing, as though clawed or - dare I say it, *chewed* - from its socket.

PC Khan tended him, but the dog died less than a minute later, still licking its handler's hand.

It was now 03:36h and I received a call from CAD, putting me on talk-through with PC Gatewood. She sounded tired but very concerned. She said that PC Mackintosh was missing again. Apparently, she'd passed the bench where she'd found him unconscious, and it was empty. She'd assumed the ambulance had already been and collected him, but then continued to the park's north gate - and saw the ambulance only just arriving. Its crew hadn't seen or heard anything of PC Mackintosh.

I had no option but to leave PC Khan, who, though very upset, said that he would take care of Alfie's body.

At 03:40h I attended the north gates of Eliot Park, where the ambulance was waiting and there was still no sign of PC Mackintosh.

PC Gatewood's injured hand was being treated by the paramedics. She looked much worse than before: trembling, sweating, white as a sheet. She asked the paramedics to step away so that she could have a quiet word with me. When she spoke it was in a nervous tone and in curious, disconnected sentences. She said again that there'd been something "wrong" with the woman who'd bitten her - that she wasn't just naked but that patches of skin had been flayed off her, in some cases so deeply that the musculature underneath was exposed. PC Gatewood had the impression that these were drag marks, as if the woman had been hauled over rough ground or along a very narrow passage. However, the woman's face had been the most shocking thing. PC Gatewood described eyes "like two black pits sunk in rotted flesh", and "a gaping mouth with a reddish-brown tongue lolling out". PC Gatewood likened it to the effect of hanging. She also said that the woman had two cavernous wounds — "like carnivore bites" — one on her right shoulder, and the other where her right breast used to be.

While she was telling me this, PC Gatewood fainted.

The paramedics managed to revive her, and she continued to speak, but it was incoherent. It sounded as though she was describing a spider emerging from the naked woman's gaping mouth. One of the paramedics said that he thought PC Gatewood was going into shock, as her temperature and blood pressure were dropping alarmingly. I agreed to have her removed to hospital by ambulance, and said that I would arrange to have her panda car collected later.

By the time PC Gatewood was placed in the back of the ambulance, she'd lapsed into deep unconsciousness.

At 03:45h the ambulance set off to University Hospital Lewisham and I reported the incident to CAD. I was then told that Inspector Makewaite wanted a meeting with me.

At 03:52h, I met Inspector Makewaite at the junction of Blackheath Road and Greenwich South Street.

I think it's fair to say that he and I don't, and never have, seen eye-to-eye on everyday policing issues. Possibly this is due to a preconceived prejudice on my part, and it may be something to do with him planning to register a grievance about me at the end of this shift. But I don't think I speak solely for myself when I say that he's an uninspiring presence.

I don't object to Inspector Makewaite looking young enough to be a school-leaver (which he near-enough is). I don't object to him wearing his uniform like a male model. I don't object to him using politically correct phrases all day to win brownie points with his supervisors. I don't object to him being, in every sense, a plastikit Bramshill bratpacker. What I object to is that he isn't a policeman. He's an administrator, a careerist. He spent almost no time on the beat before he was promoted. As such he's never really acclimatised to this job, and, in my opinion, had no intention of ever acclimatising because the reality of policing the streets of Britain doesn't concern him. To Inspector Makewaite, it's all about seminars, in-trays, cups of tea and meetings with the Top Brass. The only victims he ever sees are those defaulting officers whose broken wings he's used to feather his own nest.

I first met him while working section on 3 Relief at Woolwich. That first day he introduced himself to his new team with the belligerent statement: "Be warned, I am an absolute stickler for paperwork". Paperwork, he said, was "the life-blood of the modern police service, that a strong, unobstructed flow was essential" - and that he'd have "no hesitation at all in canning anyone whose incompetence hampered this". I later found out that he was also a stickler for extra-marital affairs, in particular with one of the secretaries at Woolwich, whose house he regularly visited - and still does - sometimes for several hours at a time during night-shift. I've never reported this in the past because, frankly, I preferred it when he was out of the way, though I'm drawing the line at his no-show tonight.

At the junction of Blackheath Road and Greenwich South Street, Inspector Makewaite gave me a severe dressing-down.

He reminded me that G Division had been specifically created to provide security for the NFOB excavation site; and that this was the prime duty of all section sergeants based there. Routine criminal matters were of secondary importance - and yet the site had been bereft of police officers for most of the shift. I replied that when incidents are reported to us via CAD, we have a duty to respond. This notion of responding quickly when the public need us seems to be a new concept to him, which he appeared to have trouble grappling with, though he eventually asserted that I should have been focussed enough to refuse all but the most pressing calls and insist that the others be handed back to Borough.

He also berated me for my handling of the Wayne Devlin arrest, claiming that, thanks to my negligent supervision, the job had only been half-completed. He had now issued orders for the arrest of William Herbert, the World War II veteran, on suspicion of wounding.

I was stunned when I heard this.

"It's about accountability," Inspector Makewaite said. "It's about the letter of the law." Wayne Devlin had needed ten stitches in his penis. It had been an unnecessarily vicious assault, and defence of William Herbert's front doormat was no excuse. As the police, we couldn't possibly ignore such an incident.

Of course, this is all palpable nonsense. In his twisted way, Inspector Makewaite might genuinely believe that William Herbert is an equal criminal to Wayne Devlin, but the real motive here was to cast me in a bad light. I know for a fact that Inspector Makewaite resents my Federation activities because he feels that it undermines the authority of the "officer class" of which he's proud to be part. But there is another reason too — when I asked him what we were going to do for extra man-power, he replied that it was all in hand because "apparently some jackanapes" had "leap-frogged the chain of command". When I asked how many extra bodies we could expect, he told me that I should be thinking about how many disciplinary charges he'd be logging against me. Perhaps that would teach me to go over his head.

Before he drove off, he wound his window down, and said, and I quote: "Given your length of service, Sergeant Calvin, I'm surprised that you're still such an idealist. Haven't you realised yet that there's no longer any room for morality in police work? I'd have thought the Police Special Powers Act has made that clear. We haven't been here to serve the public for several years now. We're here to serve the state."

I replied that the Police Special Powers Act is only supposed to be temporary.

He laughed and said: "There's nothing temporary about the state, Calvin. The state will last forever."

Please pardon my verbatim account of these latter events, but I genuinely feel that Inspector Makewaite's pompous attitude and prolonged absence at a time when we desperately needed supervision and support have been key contributors to the major problems we've faced during this shift.

It may also be that the current arrangements regarding the NFOB excavation site are proving unmanageable. Even disregarding the reality that it will be yet another "white elephant" set up to honour a vacuous and vainglorious government, there is no obvious necessity for the recent high security measures which are now causing so much disruption to normal police activities in this district. That said, however, if there *is* some necessity — and if, for example, the more bizarre events of this shift are in some way connected with the excavation site (which I'm increasingly starting to suspect) - I'd say it was doubly important that we should be appraised of *all* the facts. We are the people on the ground dealing with this situation. The "need to know" nature of this operation is only alienating those having to apply it and, dare I say it, putting them at increased risk because they're having difficulty treating it with the seriousness that it maybe deserves.

04:38h - Interim shift report concludes (completed shift report to follow later).

#

         * * * * * * * * * * * * * * * * *
         * * * * * * * * * * * * * * * * *
         * * * * * * * * * * * * * * * * *

- -

New Festival of Britain excavation site –
        G Division / 01-05

- -

FAO *Chief Superintendent Julia Kay (Borough
    Commander, Greenwich, MPS).*
cc *Chief Superintendent John Donnelly (Borough
    Commander, Southwark, MPS), Chief
    Superintendent Adam Shawcross (Borough
    Commander, Bromley, MPS); Commissioner Jane
    Ronaldson (New Scotland Yard); Detective Chief
    Superintendent Marcus Howell (Major Incident
    Command, New Scotland Yard); Lady Margaret
    Hinton-Speer (chair, London Assembly and
    Metropolitan Police Authority); Deputy
    Assistant Commissioner Tony Rutherford (DPS);
    PC Derek Entwhistle (chair, Police Federation
    of England and Wales).*

            * * * * * * * * * * * * * * * * * *

I am PS 1649 Liam Calvin, assigned to 5 Relief, G
Division, based at the Blackheath Road MobComm unit
(SE1). It is 06.35h on May 1st.
    As per the "G Division" requirement, this is my
completed shift report.
    You'll notice that I've now taken it on myself to
publicise this report beyond the Borough Command,
using all direct channels. I apologise for this
breach in protocol, but I think that, on reading it,
you'll agree that speed of communication is now
essential. For this reason, and because I don't know
how long I actually have – as I write, I can hear
automatic gunfire from the vicinity of All Hallows
Church – I must decline to recount the more mundane
details and concentrate on key incidents. If some of
these seem fanciful at first, I suspect they won't do
for long.

At 04:50h I returned to All Hallows Church, to await
the additional man-power that Inspector Makewaite had
implied would shortly be arriving. Almost
immediately, I spotted a figure leaning against the
gatepost at the front of 12 Ladysmith Crescent.

It was Spook One. He was suffering from extensive head and facial injuries, which again looked like bite-marks. He was groggy but, when I attempted to summon an ambulance, he stopped me, assuring me that he was "okay". I asked him what had happened, and he said something like "Gregson", which I suspect is the name of Spook Two. He indicated Mrs Akuma's house, which was still closed-up and standing in darkness.

I took him to the Area car, where I had a medical kit, and placed him in the rear seat. I patched up his wounds, which, on closer inspection, looked superficial, though he was shuddering and displaying similar symptoms to PC Gatewood.

At 04:53h, despite his protestations, I contacted CAD and told them that I'd found Spook One in a collapsed state and that there was no sign of Spook Two. I added that I wasn't sure whose jurisdiction these two men came under, but that someone ought to be informed.

At 04:54h I approached 12 Ladysmith Crescent.

Instinct, or "hunch" as we used to call it, is not appreciated in modern police work. Inspector Makewaite certainly wouldn't approve; he'd once referred to it as "dinosaur coppering". Nevertheless, though I didn't share Mrs Akuma's belief in ghosts, I now — as you may have gauged from my interim report — had developed a strong hunch that, whatever was happening in this district, 12 Ladysmith Crescent was central to it.

At 04:55h I commenced a property check at 12 Ladysmith Crescent. The front seemed secure. The windows and doors were closed and locked.

At 04:56h I circled around to the rear of the property, and found the back door wide open, though the interior was still in darkness. Ordinarily I would never enter an insecure property late at night without support, but with no support to call on I had no option.

Not wanting to alert any burglars who might still be on the premises, I didn't switch the main lights on, and went straight upstairs. The attic/loft is accessible by a trapdoor in the landing ceiling. This trapdoor was now open and the loft ladder had been lowered. I listened but heard nothing, so I climbed the ladder, and, on entering the attic, switched my torch on.

Initially I thought nothing was amiss, but then spotted what looked like damage to the gable wall. I approached it and saw that a hole had been smashed in the wood panelling, approximately four feet wide by three. By the angle of the splinters, it had been smashed inward, as though force had been applied from the other side. I stuck my head through and shone my torch down a narrow, letterbox-shaped shaft, which seemed to drop to ground level and maybe beyond that into the house's foundations.

I thought about the noises Mrs Akuma had been hearing. Had they been caused by some object slithering its way up this gap between the interior and exterior walls, having first gained access from underground? On reaching the attic, had it finally encountered a flimsy interior wall, which it had been able to break through? I now heard a noise myself. Again, I shone my torch down. Something was moving at the base of the shaft, though I couldn't see for sure what it was. There was a scuffling, scraping sound, as if it was inching its way upward. There was also a foul and very distinctive smell.

I ran from the attic, dropping my torch in the process.

It's an embarrassing thing for a police officer to admit, but an overwhelming sense of dread had taken possession of me. I'd reached the bottom of the stairs before regaining control — at which point I found myself gazing directly through into the living room. It was dark in there, with only a dim radiance leeching through the drawn curtains, but I realised that someone was sitting in the facing armchair. I couldn't see any detail, but I suspected it was a man. I had the idea - again, call it "hunch" - that this was Spook Two. I also had the idea that he was wide-awake and watching me intently. Perhaps it was an effect of the filtered street lighting, but his eyes gleamed like two luminous pebbles.

Before I could say anything, I heard the sound of vehicles arriving, and went quickly outside.

It was 05:07h when I left Mrs Akuma's house, to find four or five armoured TSG wagons parking outside All Hallows Church. "Heavy weapons" teams from SO22 disembarked from them. I'd asked for support, but I'd never expected this.

SO22, as you're no doubt aware, was formed under the Police Special Powers Act to provide overwhelming force in emergency situations. I've never quite been able to accept the notion of police officers in Britain carrying automatic firearms. When I was a "shot" in SO19, our primary weapon was the MP5 carbine with a repeating but non-automatic capability. The Kurtz sub-machine gun was only available to specialist units and was almost never seen in public. But with SO22, weapons of this nature seem to be the rule rather than the exception. (Their role in the Trafalgar Square atrocity is of course well documented.)

I spoke to the Heavy Weapons OIC, a Chief Inspector Bertelli. I tried to explain what had been happening, but he wasn't interested. He told me to clear the area.

His men were already deploying around the church in a cordon. Other Trojan vehicles were arriving at selected points around the excavation perimeter fence. I told him that I thought there was a problem at 12 Ladysmith Crescent, but he didn't want to listen. He had a job to do, he said, and I was getting in the way.

It was now 05:09h, and before I could argue I received an urgent message from CAD.

It was a Code XXX, with a telephone number attached.

Code XXX is yet another innovation of the Police Special Powers Act that we in the Federation objected to very strongly. However you may dress it in euphemistic language - "threat removal", "surgical solution" - we're all fully aware that a Code XXX is a shoot-on-sight order. We were assured at the time that it would only ever be invoked in the event of extreme peril to the nation. We were also assured that it would almost never be required and that, if it was, it was inconceivable that ordinary street coppers would be utilised.

Needless to say, I was astonished to receive such an instruction - though not quite as astonished as I would have been on any other night-shift.

The ruling with Code XXX is that you must immediately call the telephone number attached on a private line, at which point the target will be revealed to you. No explanations are given, and no questions permitted. It is a duty that must be prioritised above all others. I climbed into the Area car and called the number on my mobile. It was answered almost immediately by Superintendent Hobart at Greenwich, which didn't surprise me, as a Code XXX cannot be authorised by any rank lower than superintendent. But what followed was a massive shock - in fact it wouldn't be going too far to say that it rocked my world.

The name of the target was PC 5829 Charlotte Gatewood.

Superintendent Hobart advised me there'd been no mistake and that, if it would clarify my thinking, I should know that the three-man ambulance crew who took PC Gatewood had now been found dead in an alley in Lewisham. PC Gatewood was believed to be in possession of the ambulance, which was last seen heading south towards Plaistow. Before he hung up, I broke the cardinal rule and asked him why I'd been given this task when there were so many shooters from SO22 on the plot. Perhaps sensing that simply to say nothing would in this circumstance do more harm than good, he replied that first of all I had my original SFO credentials, and secondly, "and more importantly", of all the officers on duty in Southeast London at this moment I probably had a better idea than most what we were dealing with.

That may have been true, though it's just as likely that the real motive was deniability. If, during the course of my shift, I'd been exposed to something that was supposed to remain a secret, wouldn't it be convenient if I then murdered a fellow officer, for which I could be tried and hanged, and my embarrassing knowledge buried along with me? Wouldn't that be killing two birds with one stone?

It used to be said of us street bobbies that the brightest thing about us is our buttons, but there are times when I feel the high command should really credit us with more intelligence than they do.

At 05:13h I commenced pursuit of PC Gatewood.

At 05:14h I remembered that I still had Spook One in the back seat when a groan alerted me to his presence.

He was wan in colour and apparently delirious - no longer in any fit state to insist that we didn't visit hospital, though there wasn't time for that now.

At 05:15h I took him into the mobile unit on Blackheath Road, and placed him in the refs armchair. I made him a flask of tea and, from the first-aid cupboard, gave him a packet of Paracetamol. I told him that I would be back as soon as possible, and that, if I could, I would send help in the meantime.

At 05:16h I resumed my pursuit.

At 05:18h CAD informed me that I was to switch my PR off, and that all conversation regarding this matter was to be conducted via a private channel on the Force radio.
    I acknowledged and said that I would comply, but I freely admit now that I had no intention of XXX'ing PC Gatewood.
    The bewildering and horrifying events of the last few hours had been capped by the most bizarre order I'd ever received. The whole thing had become too surreal to comprehend. Though clearly, whatever was happening, PC Gatewood needed to be apprehended.

At 05:21h I received information that the target vehicle was heading south along Burnt Ash Road.

At 05:23h I received a message that I had to expedite the mission. Early-morning traffic levels would soon be picking up.

At 05:25h I received information that the target vehicle was now on Bromley Road, heading north again through Catford. I swung out of Glenbow Road, and saw damage to a number of parked cars. Fragments of bodywork littered both carriageways.

At 05:31h I turned left onto Lewisham Way, and saw the target vehicle about forty yards ahead. This too was showing extensive accident damage, and was being driven erratically, swinging from one carriageway to the next, colliding with numerous objects. At least one of its tyres had burst, because it was dragging a trail of sparks behind it. Despite this, it was pushing 50 mph, maybe more.
    I was about ten yards behind it when I applied the "blues and twos". The ambulance made no effort to slow down, let alone stop. I was uncertain what action to take next. Under Code XXX, I couldn't surrender the pursuit. Neither Traffic nor aerial support would be called. Stinger units would not be deployed.

At 05:36h we incurred our first casualty of the pursuit, as the ambulance mounted the kerb while swerving from Lewisham Way into New Cross Road. It struck a homeless woman pushing a supermarket trolley, and sent her somersaulting through a pub's plate-glass window. With Code XXX carrying the highest priority possible, I could not stop to attend the injured party, though I relayed the incident to Force HQ.

I maintained pursuit, but for the first time now it began to occur to me that maybe a XXX solution was the only real option.

At 05:38h the target spun right from Deptford Church Street onto Creek Road, in the process sideswiping a Ford Focus emerging from Deptford Green. It was a heavy collision. The Focus spun around on its axis, though its single occupant appeared to be unhurt. Knowing that I couldn't risk further civilian casualties, I drew my firearm and accelerated until I was alongside the target vehicle, intending to shoot out its remaining tyres. At which point, whoever was driving the ambulance lost control. It veered sharp left, crashing through a barrier and down the embankment towards Deptford Creek. There are concrete bollards at the bottom, and a massive impact resulted, at which point the ambulance's petrol tank exploded.

I braked and parked, made a call for a fire brigade turnout — which I knew would be slow given that this was a Code XXX — and scrambled down the embankment towards the creek.

The ambulance was already an inferno. The heat from it was so intense that I couldn't get close enough to affect a rescue. However, what happened next is almost impossible to describe. The wrecked vehicle was hard up against the bollards, its driving cab crumpled like an accordion and burning fiercely — presumably the ruptured fuel tank had sprayed its contents all through the interior. And yet a figure clambered out from it. Though engulfed in flame from head to foot, this figure walked towards me. And it wasn't the helpless stagger of someone in their death throes. It was a purposeful stride. I backed away, but the blazing form had now got close enough for me to see that it was PC Gatewood.

Her features were clearly recognisable even as they blistered and peeled and shrivelled, even as her eyes distended in their sockets until they burst. I levelled my firearm, intending to execute my mission — for pity's sake if nothing else. But I was too mesmerised to pull the trigger. She was literally a human torch. Her hair had completely gone. Fatty tissue streamed from her face like melted wax. The stench of burning meat was nauseating. Yet she was completely unaffected. She moved steadily towards me, only at the last second veering sideways and falling into the creek.

It took several moments for me to recover sufficiently to move.

I scanned the water, but it was too dark and smoky for me to see anything. And then I heard a splashing at the far bank. I looked over and saw that PC Gatewood had clambered out and was standing there, swaying. She was black and crisp all over, and hissing loudly. Steam poured off her. As I watched, she pivoted around and strode jerkily away, vanishing into the night.

I laughed — rather crazily. I couldn't help wondering who had the "special powers" now?

It was 05:49h, and a good ten minutes had passed since I'd lost sight of PC Gatewood, before I was able to contact Force HQ and lie that my mission was accomplished. There was no congratulation, no request for detail. Just a simple: "Roger, received."

At 05:54h, I arrived back at the MobComm unit on Blackheath Road.

It seemed almost inconsequential that Spook Two was lying beside the armchair. I checked for vital signs, but they were absent. Though I'm not qualified to pronounce, he was quite clearly dead. I covered his head with my anorak, and sat down to key in this final report.

It will soon be time for the rest of 5 Relief to sign off, but I don't expect that any of them will. Since I've turned my PR back on, I've overheard radio messages concerning a young man in a police uniform "behaving strangely and attacking passers-by" near Eliot Park. One of these victims was apparently admitted to Casualty at Lewisham, where she promptly became violent with the nursing staff, and had to be restrained by PCs Fletcher, Barkworth and Stopford, all of whom sustained injuries in the struggle. Inspector Makewaite has also had a busy shift. I heard that he'd made a complaint about a dog van left insecure and unattended. The gist of his annoyance concerned the poor animal, which was in the rear compartment, "apparently hurt and bouncing around in a stressed condition". Even though it's only late spring, Inspector Makewaite was mindful that another scandal surrounding police dogs dying from heat exhaustion would damage our reputation. If I'd thought about it, I'd have sent a message via CAD to warn him. But instead I was thinking about PC Les Khan and whereabouts in London he now might be, trudging through the darkness with Alfie's chain pulled taut between his gnawed and bitten hands. Inspector Makewaite apparently said that he was going to let the poor dog out so that it could get some air. He sent no more messages after that.

It's a consolation, I suppose. But only a minor one.

I've been twenty years in the police service. It took my marriage away. It even took my daughter away — five years ago she became an opinionated student, and hasn't spoken to me since. I don't regret this. What's the point in regretting something you had no control over? What I do regret is what I've seen happen to my country in that time, the way it's simply gone to Hell — quite literally, I now realise — and that all of my efforts as a law-enforcement official have made no difference.

I can still hear sustained gunfire from the vicinity of All Hallows Church. I'm going to have to go down there and assist. In some ways it'll be against my personal philosophy — though perhaps not totally. I've always striven to be an affable and even-tempered police officer, to be firm but fair. When I first qualified to carry a firearm on duty eight years ago, I prayed that I would never have to fire a single shot at another human being, and to date I never have.

And even at this moment — as the rustle of fabric behind me denotes that my anorak is shifting — technically, with regard to the "human being" bit, that principle won't be compromised . . .

* * * * * * * * * * * * * * * * * *
* * * * * * * * * * * * * * * * * *
* * * * * * * * * * * * * * * * * *

British Media Corporation
Internal Communications

From: Internal Communications
Sent: 1 May, 08:32 AM
To: All London Staff
Subject: Traffic Congestion on Ladysmith Crescent /
                Blackheath Road / Elliott Park / Greenwich Park

<u>This email is going to all staff</u>

Due to the deteriorating situation around All Hallows Church and
the Blackheath Road area, concerns are growing today over safety
of BMC staff.

It is recommended that all non-essential production staff stay in
their homes and lock all doors and windows.

Essential staff are advised to contact their line manager for further
information.

Check the BMC's Emergency Information channels for further
updates:

Phone: 0800 0666 999

Online: bmc.co.uk/999

Gateway: 999 Emergency Information

Ceefax: page 999

Internal Communications

SUNDAY, APRIL 28

OMG! I'm 13. Finally! At last! A teenager!! I wonder if I look any different? I sooo feel different, even if I'm not having a great big grown-up party like Emma Bolton and Charlotte Partridge had last month. (Joint of course, cos like the Barbies could ever do anything apart.???). I don't even really want a huge party but if I had one I wouldn't invite them anyway cos they never invited me to theirs even though they invited George – but that was probably just to get Alex to go. (Alex – sigh.)

Oh god, I'm just ranting already! Deep breaths . . . start from the beginning. My name is Maddy Wood and I live in London with my parents. Today is my 13th birthday and as you can tell I'm pretty excited about it!

You, diary, are new today – a birthday present from George, who's my best friend in the world and has been since we started Woodlands Primary together. George was 13 last month and he didn't have a big party either, but we did all go bowling just before the leisure centre was closed down which was great fun. Alex was there too which meant my bowling was total rubbish but he didn't seem to mind and he winked at me three times!!!

Sorry, should say — Alex is George's brother. He's seventeen and a TOTAL hottie. Even Emma and her lipstick gang go funny if they see him and they spend most of their time mooning over Mr Eyre the new Maths teacher (like a teacher is ever going to look at them like that? Purleease! They just sooo need to get over themselves.) But back to Alex (sigh). Lewisham College closed last year so he had to stay on at Lewisham Secondary for sixth form. Total result! It means I still get to see him most days. Maybe now I'm 13 he'll start to notice me as a proper girl rather than his little brother's best friend. Arghh! Can't even think about it, it would be too good! He doesn't have a girlfriend and I don't think he'd want one like the Barbies. I mean yes, they're pretty and everything but I don't think Alex is fooled by that stuff. I think he'd want a woman with brains. A woman. Wow. Feels weird even writing that word, but 13 nearly is, isn't it?

I'm going to have to go in a minute because I can hear mum's just got back from picking gran up, and I know she's made a big chocolate cake that we're going to have with tea when Uncle Jack and dad get home, so let me tell you about my birthday so far in case I don't get a chance later.

Its been brilliant! Mum woke me up with my present which was my first ever bra!! A proper one – not a stupid training one. This has little flowers on it and everything. It doesn't exactly fit yet, cos my chest is being boringly slow at growing, but I wore it anyway. I think just having it on under my school shirt made my boobs look bigger. I think George maybe noticed, cos I'm sure I caught him looking when he came to walk to school with me – or maybe I was just subconsciously sticking my chest out more – whatever – I'm pretty sure he looked.

When we got to school on Friday the gates were locked and there was another big sign up on them saying it was a strike day. That's three since half-term!! At least we haven't got exams this year. Most of the kids love the strikes that keep happening and yeah, its great we're getting extra holidays, but if it keeps going on then we'll never know enough for when we have to take our GCSEs. (That just made me sound really dull, didn't it? I'm not dull — but I like school, especially English, and I really don't want to fail anything.) BUT last week it was great, cos I had double PE in the afternoon and I hate hockey and I was going to pretend I had my period to get out of it, but Miss Mather never believes that and always makes you go out on the field and freeze on the sidelines anyway.

Yesterday me and George went and hung around the clock tower for a while and he gave me my present! This notebook! You! George is so good at things like that. He's the only person that knows I want to be a writer when I grow up. A proper author with my books in the supermarkets and everything. I haven't even told Miss Turney at school, and she's always telling me my stories are really good. Maybe I'll write a story in you. Maybe not. You're even red, my favourite colour, and your paper feels really soft. George gave me a really nice black pen to write in you too — which of course I'm using. I've never kept a diary before but I think I'm going to like it already. George is great but I can't really talk to him, and since Ella moved away last month I've missed having another girl to share my feelings with. That can be you!

Anyway, we hung round the shops for a bit, but didn't have any money and all the good ones seem to be closing and then went back to George's to watch a film. And guess what? ALEX WAS THERE!! It was brilliant!! He stayed in the sitting room with us and wished me happy birthday, and although I can't say I saw him looking at my chest, you never know, he might have done!

Mum's calling . . . time for birthday cake I think! I'll write again later!!

MONDAY, APRIL 29

Things are so boring since the curfew. I mean, its not as if mum and dad have let me out much in the evenings anyway, not since the riots started (even though we never had one in Lewisham, but you know what parents are like – <u>GOD</u> they worry!! its like I'm 5 or something!!) George used to come over here and we'd sit in the stairwell of the flats and muck around. Now, that doesn't even happen. I know he and Alex sneak out cos he came over here once, but mum had a go about it and now he's nervous of coming in case she gets mad at him. Its crazy – I didn't speak to her for two whole days after that. I mean, surely I'm allowed some kind of social life – I'm 13!!!

I've just read that back and I sound like a right cow. I don't mean it like that, and I know its not mum and dad's fault that he's lost his job and she can't get any extra shifts at the bakery, its just that its all so annoying. Its typical of my luck that I become a teenager and the stupid government or the army or whoever is in charge now decide that no-one under 18 can be out after 6:00 pm. We can't even text that much because apparently "money's tight" whatever that means and now I get so little credit for my phone I might as well not bother having one and I'm not old enough for a Saturday job even if there were any! We seem to spend all our time after school (if its ever open!!) with one eye on the clock tower and waiting for the soldiers to magically appear and clear us off the streets. I know when the curfew started I said it was exciting, but now its just dull. The soldiers don't even smile. I tried talking to one once and he wouldn't even look at me! How rude!

Mum won't listen either. She just says stuff like "you don't understand". Or "its for your own good". Sometimes she even shouts, which to be honest really freaks me out, cos mum and dad aren't shouty people. But then they've both been different since gran moved in. Maybe its cos the flat really isn't big enough and so dad is now sleeping on the sofa and gran is in with mum. To be honest, I don't even know what gran is doing here. I don't see why she can't be in her own flat cos, yes she's pretty old, but its not as if she can't walk or anything and her own flat down near the High Street is probably more practical because at least its on the ground floor. I took her to church on Sunday (SOOOOO boring . . .) and it took us nearly the rest of the day to get back up the stairs to our fourth floor flat.

Mum says she feels happier with gran here, but as far as I can see everyone's just really miserable. They sit around and mutter at the boring news and no one seems to care how I'm getting on at school although dad does make me do maths and comprehension from my text books when school's closed. I guess I should be glad about that, because I DO want to go to Uni and stuff, but now there's the curfew the times that the strikes are on are the only relaxed time we get to hang out, and instead I have to be home by lunchtime to study. I feel like I haven't seen Alex in AGES - at least a week. DULL, DULL, DULL. But, on the upside, I think my boobs have been inspired to grow since the arrival of the proper bra - I think I'm filling it better, (Either that or mum's shrunk it in the wash but I'm sure they're

looking bigger!), so maybe next time I
see him he'll realise I'm not just a little
girl anymore. (Alex - sigh.) (in fact,
Alex - double sigh.)

Hang on - teatime. Yesterday's stew
reheated and with a couple of cans of
beans and some potato chucked in to
make it look like its worth eating. I
can't wait. (Heavy sarcasm, diary, in
case you hadn't noticed!!)

TUESDAY, APRIL 30

Well, I didn't get back to you last night because it was nearly midnight by the time I went to bed. Uncle Jack came round and we had a power cut that lasted all night! I think that's the longest one we've had. Gran said that looking out the window was like the blackouts when she was a little girl in the war. At least for once it meant that the TV was off and they all actually talked! (Oh — stew was total rubbish by the way — as expected. Ate it though, like a good girl . . . yawn.) I think they forgot I was in the room, and for once I stayed quiet and just listened.

It wasn't that difficult because I'm normally pretty quiet when Uncle Jack comes round now. I still love him and everything but he's changed since his friend Mark was killed during the riots in Trafalgar Square. That was probably only a month or so ago but it seems like AGES and its hard to really imagine that all those people died. I mean, its not as if it was on the telly or anything. Only one news channel showed it and that was late at night and I think they stopped broadcasting soon after that. The only thing on the TV these days seems to be STRICTLY COME DANCING ON ICE and THE X-TRA FACTOR or loads of old comedy programmes. Uncle Jack told dad that the only place you could hear anything true any more was on the radio or on some Internet sites, but as dad sold our PC a while back that's not really an option, and like mum says, sometimes its better NOT knowing.

The teachers didn't even talk about what happened. Miss Turney's eyes were all puffy as if she'd been crying, I remember that, and for a minute it looked like she was going to answer our questions, but then she just told us to get our books out for our spelling test. She looked kinda funny. Like she was scared or something. It made me feel weird and I was pretty glad that what happened that day all kind of got forgotten. I mean, it was nearly my birthday and I didn't want to think about stuff like that. But now that I'm 13, I probably should pay more attention, (and no, I'm not just saying that because the last time I went to

George's, Alex was there with some of his sixth form friends and they all looked really serious and were talking about the government and the strikes and riots and stuff).

If I'm honest, and there's no point in having you diary if I can't be honest with you, then I guess I've just avoided thinking about everything that's going wrong because it scares me. Not in a scared of the dark way, but kind of scary because everyone else looks scared. I'm not making any sense. I guess its just that everyone seems to be so serious and angry all the time at home and sometimes over stupid things that I can't for the life of me see as anything horrible.

Like all this fuss over the New Festival of Britain. It sounds way more fun than the Olympics would have been if they'd ever happened, and from what the posters and TV adverts say, there'll be street parties and big events as well as the actual show itself, but according to Uncle Jack and dad you'd think it was the worst thing <u>EVER</u>!

Uncle Jack lit a cigarette and said, "They think we're stupid. They think they can fob us off with some fireworks and we won't see just how shit everything has got."

He said that. The shit word, and mum didn't even shh him. That's how I knew they were all totally weirded out. It was dark by then with only the candles dotted around the sitting room. Mum didn't light them all. She said the last time she'd been to the shops, they'd sold out of candles. That made her shake her head and tut, but I didn't see why it was such a big deal. I mean, who cares about candles?

"Have you seen the slogans?"

I couldn't even see Uncle Jack's face properly, just the angry gleam in his eyes behind the steady wisps of smoke. It made my nose itch. I didn't need to see his face to know that his mouth would be tight and mean. I could hear it in his voice. He never sounds much like Uncle Jack anymore. Uncle Jack is someone who laughs a lot. This man

doesn't. It makes me a bit sad but I
don't really know why.

"Yeah." My dad snorted. He was
drinking whisky. "Let's Put the Great
Back Into Britain. Who are they
kidding? Where the hell is the 'Great'
supposed to come from when no one's
got a bloody job and we're all just
struggling to survive?"

"Even the price of potatoes has gone
up." Mum was still sitting at the table
and trying to sew something in the bad
light. Maybe a rip in one of my school
shirts. I wish she'd just buy me a new
one. The sleeves on the two I've got are
well above my wrists now. Apparently
that's another thing we just have to
"make do" with for now.

"And potatoes are something we grow
here." She ask'd again.

"They want us to have the Blitz spirit."
It was the first thing gran had said.
She was smoking too and a small grey
cloud was filling the room. "But back
then we had an Outside Enemy. Then we
had to all stick together and make the
best of it. I remember the night

Ladysmith Cescent was hit. Terrible, it was. Nearly 100 people died that night. Everyone lost someone. Its the silence I remember the most. The silence the next day as we all stood looking at the rubble, me holding my ma's skirt and her crying. Bloody awful it was, but we got through it because we had each other and our hatred for those German bombers. But this time . . . " she paused and pointed over at Jack, ". . . this time, son, the enemy is within. "

Normally, gran just talks about her books and her radio plays and her friend Erma who's been dead forever (well, longer than I've been alive, and 13 years is a pretty long time!) and all the stuff they used to do when they were young (which totally freaks me out to imagine). The thing is, no-one usually listens. Not properly — they just do that nod and smile thing. I know cos mum does it to me sometimes when I'm talking about school, and we ALL do it to gran. But last night, it was like they were actually listening.

"I know, mum. And lots of us want to do something about it. "

"Mark was a lovely boy," gran said, and I could see all of her thousand wrinkles in the shadows of the candlelight. "But I'm glad you weren't with him that day."

"I should have been. I should have been right beside him."

"And if you had been, you'd be gone too." Mum didn't even look up from her work.

"You know they're still intending on putting this farce of a Festival on, don't you?"

Dad shook his head. "Are they?"

"Jesus, Graham, haven't you been listening to the radio?"

"I've been looking for a bloody job, Jack. I've got a family to feed."

My heart was thumping hard in my chest at that point and I could feel it making my skin hot. Dad and Uncle Jack never argue, and no, this wasn't exactly a big shouty argument but it was SOMETHING.

"Well, they've restarted the digging at All Hallows. Can you believe it? There's another protest planned for early tomorrow morning, before they can start excavating the bodies."

This time mum did look up. "You're not going are you?"

"Wish I could. I'm working shifts and I can't risk not showing up. They fire you for nothing these days." He stubbed the cigarette out. "But I'm letting the protesters use my flat as a base. They've been storing some stuff there. Nothing radical, just banners and spray paint. They can walk to the site from my place in Brookmill Road."

"What's the problem with them digging up an old church?" Mum frowned. "I mean, god knows I could cry at them throwing that money away, but they're not knocking down homes or anything."

"I wish you'd listen to that bloody station." Jack lit a second cigarette. "Its not the church that's the problem. Its what's UNDERNEATH. They had this professor woman on the radio talking about it. Its a bloody plague pit.

Medical experts are up in arms about it.

"Why?"

"There are hundreds of bodies that went into that ground about four or five centuries ago, and they were full of the plague virus. Who knows what kind of noxious gases will come out? It should never be opened up."

"Its just not respectful, neither." Gran shook her head. "You leave those who have passed, be. That's the way it should be. No good ever came of disturbing the dead."

"I just don't see why you need to be involved at all," Mum said. I could see she was worried about Uncle Jack. Her forehead did that funny almost-frown she uses on me when I say I want to do something she thinks I'm too young for (like when I wanted high heels for last year's disco! HA HA!).

"The police won't care that you just hid banners. They'll come after you too. They don't seem to care who they hurt these days."

"I know what's right and what's wrong and I can't just sit back. Someone's got to at least speak up. That professor woman tried, but nobody's heard again from her recently. It won't be like last time though. The diggers will probably have armed protection after all the fuss that's been made. But its still important that people show they care."

"He's right." Gran glared at mum. "Do you know what Lewisham's motto is?"

"Does it matter?" Mum shrugged.

I didn't even know we had one, but then I'm never exactly sure what the school's motto is, never mind the whole borough's!

"Its Salus poluli suprema lex. I remember when they put the new plaque up. It means 'The welfare of the people is highest'. Its Latin." She smiled at Uncle Jack. "Your dad and granddad would be proud of you, son. You're looking out for the people. Someone has too and we all know it won't be the bloody government."

I was getting tired, and after that I kind of drifted off a bit while they talked about other stuff like the strikes and dad's job hunt and all that other grown-up stuff, mainly about people I didn't really know. I think Uncle Jack mentioned someone called "Hawksmoor". Cool name, but it wasn't half as interesting as thinking about all those dead people getting dug up. That was really creepy. We did the plague at school back in Year 7 and its weird to think that they died all that long time ago and tonight they're going to be out in the air again.

Anyway, seems like I've been writing for ages. There's no school again tomorrow (surprise, surprise!), so I'm going to go over to George's for a bit before dad makes me do more work (yawn.). Hopefully Alex will be in!!! Going to wear a skinny T (well it wasn't skinny when I got it, but its so old now its too tight - HA!!) and maybe he'll look at my chest and realise that I'm growing up!!! (Alex - sigh!) (LOL!)

WEDNESDAY, MAY 1

I don't even know what time it is. Maybe six or seven in the morning? Its still nearly dark outside anyway. Mum thinks I'm asleep but I'm writing this under my covers with the little book torch I got at Christmas. I feel a bit sick. Uncle Jack turned up half-an-hour ago. Mum sent me back to bed, but I sat by the door instead and peered out through a small gap. Uncle Jack was shaking - I mean properly shaking, and he kept pacing up and down in the hallway muttering, "What have they done? What have they done?" His arm was bleeding like he'd cut it and he was sweating as if he'd run all the way from his flat to here. Maybe he had. What could have happened that was so terrible to make him run five miles this early in the morning?

I can feel my heart pounding in my chest so hard I'm sure the mattress is vibrating under me. My mouth tastes funny all of a sudden. I wonder if something happened to all the protesters. But I don't understand because Uncle

Jack said he wasn't going down to the church. He was working. Maybe something happened when he got back to his flat? God, I just want to go and ask mum. I know that she and gran and dad are still whispering away in the lounge even though the lights are off. I heard Uncle Jack leaving about 10 minutes ago and I think mum was crying. That scares me. She didn't cry when Mark was killed. Why is she crying now? Ugh. The battery is flickering. I'll write more in the morning when I've found out at least a little bit of what's going on!!

MAY 1 (LATER)

Well all I've found out is that mum says I'm not allowed out at all today!!! How STUUUPID is that??? Sometimes I just can't believe her!! She's never been exactly a cool mum but now she's just totally retro. There's nothing on the news saying anything's wrong and if I have to stay in THE WHOLE DAY then I'll just go crazy or die of boredom. I only want to go to George's house, and that's barely a five-minute walk away if I go fast, but NO, I can't. Dad even shouted at me when I tried to argue and gran shhh'd him, but she didn't exactly stick up for me!! And after all those stupid stories she told me about her and silly old Erma and how they used to sneak out to go dancing — you'd think she'd at least understand!! God, its like I'm still a baby or something.

All mum would say was that Uncle Jack said something went wrong at the protest and lots of the police got injured and some of the protesters came back coughing from some red dust or mist,

and one of them attacked Uncle Jack.
She didn't make a lot of sense. I
mean, why would one of the protesters
hurt Uncle Jack?? I just don't get any
of it. All I know is that its only 11
o'clock and I'm stuck in my room.

This is just the worst day ever.

British Media Corporation
Internal Communications

From: Internal Communications
Sent: 1 May, 11:14 AM
To: All London Staff
Subject: HRV – Update to Managers – your role in the cascade of information to line managers

<u>This email is going to HRDs, HRDMs, Internal Communications Specialists and key divisional representatives including Partner communications areas.</u>

We continue to assess the situation regarding the apparent outbreak of HRV at the New Festival South London site. To avoid unnecessary panic, but to keep all staff informed, it has been decided that cascading a daily **"HRV – Update to Managers"** email, via the distribution list above, is the best way to get cascade information to relevant staff in your areas.

Remember, HRV is a mild, flu-like virus and there is no cause for alarm.

Check the BMC's Emergency Information channels for further updates:

Phone: 0800 0666 999

Online: bmc.co.uk/999

Gateway: 999 Emergency Information

Ceefax: page 999

Internal Communications

DEAD DI
AND THE
ZOMBIE KING

Princess Di, the People's Princess, _WILL_ live again!

A *HARD NEWS*
EXCLUSIVE

by Janet Ramsey,
Head of Current Affairs

London, April 29

CRAZED MOURNERS have dug up the body of Princess Diana from its final resting place in her ancestral home and reburied her on the New Festival of Britain site in South London – in a bid to reanimate her decades-dead corpse.

Hard News investigators have discovered the super-secret cabal has an even sicker plan: to use a 150-year-old secret crypt built by the "Zombie King" Thomas Moreby to put Dead Di on the throne of England!

Sources at the heart of the conspiracy revealed the shocking truth: the high-powered cabal of Di-lovers – who call themselves the "Royal Resurrectionists" and are said to include her still-grieving sons, Princes William and Harry, media emperor Rupert Murdoch and football legend David Beckham – are secretly planning to infect the princess's corpse with the so-called "Zombie Virus".

Princess Di was mourned by a shattered world when her car was mysteriously forced off the road in a high-speed chase in Paris on August 31, 1997, and billions wept as she was buried on September 6, 1997 on a private island called The Oval, within Althorp Park, the Spencer family home where she grew up.

But our investigators, posing as medical experts on re-animation, infiltrated the evil conspiracy and discovered:

- Princess Di's body has already been dug up, and on Wednesday night it was taken to All Hallows Church, near the Greenwich Park site of the New Festival of Britain project, as part of the cabal's warped plans.
- The church was built by black magician Nicholas Hawksmoor and his apprentice Thomas Moreby, the "Zombie King" – and it has a hidden crypt with magical properties where Moreby planned to bring the dead back to life.
- Princess Di's body is to be re-buried in the crypt amongst hundreds of corpses while her re-animators wait for the virus to infect her.
- Once Princess Di is restored to life, the Royal Resurrectionists have a list of other influential candidates for their special Zombie treatment – including Winston Churchill and Lord Wellington!

(see pages 4 and 5)

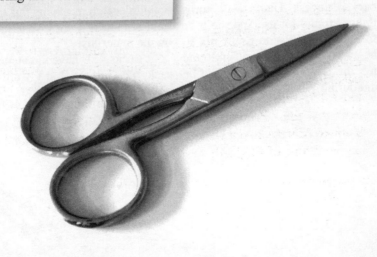

(continued from page 1)

Hard News infiltrated the Royal Resurrectionists after a tip-off from a worried insider. JCB operator Marek Schwarinski revealed the depths of the evil conspiracy when he realised the crazy cabal intended to deliberately infect famous corpses with the Zombie Virus – with no safeguards in case of disaster.

Mr Schwarinski, a Georgia-born native who came to Britain illegally in 2001, had been working on the New Festival of Britain site when he was recruited by the Resurrectionists to help them carry out their foul plan.

He told our investigators, "They've no idea what they're playing with. They think bringing back Princess Diana will turns things around for us. And she'll be followed by Winston Churchill, so he can reunite the country; do the job the government can't, like he did during World War II.

"But it isn't right. I know we got problems, but they're desecrating a plague pit – they think just because those bodies were buried three, four hundred years ago that the virus is safe. They think they can pick and choose who gets infected – and they think they have a way to control the virus, so the 'Resurrected' are just like normal people again. But in my country we know about these things.

"I went to my bosses first, but they just want the job done. They don't care what goes on behind their backs as long as it doesn't screw with their schedules. We've had health investigators here, and the bosses don't listen to them either – all they care about is getting this New Festival site built – they cut corners all the time. You wouldn't catch me riding this tram-link, not the way they've skimped on the materials.

"It's true NFB have threatened to sack me – they don't want me blabbing about the hundreds of dead bodies we already dug up and secretly disposed of, which is what the bosses told us to do. But decent people are going to end up dead, just so the PM can have this big festival that no one cares about. That's not patriotism: it's going to be suicide once the Zombie plague gets lose and no jumped-up 'Resurrectionist' is going to be able to control it."

The Home Office has refused to comment officially on Mr Schwarinski's allegations of three-hundred-year-old corpses being dug up and dumped, despite the evidence our investigators passed to the Minister. Off the record, a source close to the Home Office admitted, "Some crazy Russian comes out with a story like this and I'd have called you crazy myself if I hadn't kept hearing odd whispers myself. My boss says it's as true as a James Herbert story, but I'm beginning to get some weird calls; you're not the only people worried about weird things happening in Greenwich. And coming up to Beltane – hell of a coincidence, if you ask me, but that's what my boss says it is."

We could get no response from anyone connected with the Royal Resurrectionists; and the Spencer family refused to confirm or deny that Princess Di's body had been moved.

New Festival of New Britain site manager Paddy O'Shaughnessy told us, "Yes, we found bodies – this is an old church, and we're digging up what was probably a graveyard – but we didn't dump the bodies anywhere. They have been decently stored in the church crypt, which is just what it was originally built for.

"Mr Schwarinski is no longer with us, after a disagreement about working conditions, and the discovery that he was in this country illegally. Obviously he has a grudge and he has come up with this imaginative way to stop work. "It's the twenty-first century – who believes in zombies these days? I have no knowledge of Princess Diana or anyone else being buried anywhere near our site."

The New Festival of Britain project managers referred us to the Home Office, who have so far refused to respond to our requests now that the Freedom of Information Act has been repealed.

Christian Church

ALL HALLOWS CHURCH stands on Blackheath Road, on the edge of Eliot Park, a grand old example of Victorian church architecture. The rector, Canon Terence Abercrombie, 68, has been leading the protest against the New Festival of Britain development that threatens to destroy his churchyard forever.

As the Canon explained, "This scarred old building has a secret past."

The church looks like a pretty standard Victorian pile, and from the ground up it is. But below ground level it's another story – for the "Zombie King" architect Thomas Moreby, an apprentice of the great baroque architect Nicholas Hawksmoor, built the crypt and undercroft, all that is left of the original church, after a mysterious blaze nearly destroyed the whole building in 1850.

Canon Abercrombie, who has done a lot of research into his parish, told us, "Nicholas Hawksmoor himself was apprenticed to Sir Christopher Wren, and worked on rebuilding the churches damaged in the great Fire of London, as well as St Paul's Cathedral. But he got this reputation as a master magician when he designed six churches and two obelisks, which he claimed formed a 'power matrix' over the London landscape.

"In fact, some experts claim that Hawksmoor's churches formed a pattern consistent with the forms of Theistic Satanism – better known as Devil Worship.

"Hawksmoor believed this 'power matrix' attracted to itself many dark and dreadful deeds that happened within the shadows of these church sites – which include the murders of Jack the Ripper – all nonsense, of course," the Canon said with a laugh. "His followers believe that if you mark out the buildings and obelisks on

or Zombie Revival Hall?

a map you will find the Eye of Horus. The hawk is the bird of Horus, and 'moor' is the old-fashioned name for a North African or Middle Eastern person.

According to the Egyptians, the god Horus is the child of Osiris, who represents fertility, and Isis, who represents magic, and his eyes represent the sun and moon, and both orbs are connected with the death-rebirth motif. And the idea of rebirth fascinated Hawksmoor and his apprentice Moreby.

"All Hallows Church is not a Hawksmoor church; but it's not very far from St Alfege's, which is – and conspiracy theorists believe Hawksmoor sent his apprentice Thomas Moreby to build All Hallows for a reason. Hawksmoor and Moreby thought they were involved with some very powerful magic; Moreby wrote that he believed

the body would rise after death if 'expos'd to pure humours' – if it was dug up and exposed to fresh air – and he left instructions that he himself be interred in a crypt he had designed for that very purpose beneath this very church, so when the time came he would be resurrected along with his fellow 'pure souls'. He died in Bedlam, of course."

The Canon admitted he believed this was just a good story to attract tourists to his otherwise insignificant church, but it was part of London's history, and as such, should protect the church and churchyard from unseemly development. "Of course, as a good Christian, a man of God, I think this is all just make-believe. All the trouble around here has everything to do with the parlous state of the economy and nothing to do with some 260-year-old architect playing with higher – or lower –

powers; anything else is just coincidence. No one really believes there's a plague pit beside the church, or that the dead will rise again – other than Jesus Christ, of course. The myths surrounding Moreby and Hawksmoor are just superstitions handed down from days before television.

"But that doesn't mean our venerable churchyard should be turned into a tram-stop for the New Festival of Britain. That is a sacrilege, and I and my parishioners continue to fight to stop the development."

Shortly after this interview Canon Abercrombie was found dead in the rectory by his housekeeper. The inquest will be held on Friday at the Coroner's Court in Devonshire Drive, Greenwich. A candlelit memorial service will be held outside All Hallows tonight.

"THERE ARE VICAR FOUND

by *Hard News* staff reporter

THE MUTILATED BODY of the Right Reverend Terence Abercrombie, 67, Canon of All Hallows Church in Greenwich, was found yesterday by his devoted housekeeper, who had a heart attack when she discovered his abused corpse.

Mrs Enid Stella, 58, wiping away tears, spoke of the traumatic discovery from her hospital bed. "I was bringing the Reverend his afternoon tea, just like I always did, but the door to the study was stuck. The rectory's an old building and there's no central heating, so it gets damp.

"I called out, but when the Reverend didn't answer I thought he'd dozed off over his sermon again. I had to put the tea tray down to push the door open. It felt like something was blocking it, and when I got it open enough to look in I saw it was the Reverend – he looked like he'd just fallen over.

GNAWED PRIEST FOOD FOR FLEAS

"I managed to get the door shifted enough to slide it, and then I saw that his clothes were all ripped, and his arms looked like they were covered in bite-marks – I swear to God, it looked like someone had been *gnawing* on him! And there were fleas everywhere too – any stray he found, he'd bring back for a meal, so we did get fleas in the house once in a while. But this was really scary. I checked his pulse, but there was no sign of life."

Mrs Stella, who worked for Canon Abercrombie for 37 years, called the

NO ZOMBIES" CHEWED?

Emergency Services. "I know they're very busy these days," she said, "and there are the lay-offs and everything, but I didn't expect to have to wait for five hours. I was terrified. I wanted to wait with him, but I couldn't; those bite marks were creeping me out."

The former gospel singer described how she tried to jam the door shut and waited in the hall. "I know it's stupid – he was definitely dead – but I thought I could hear these noises. So I pulled a chair over by the front door, where I could look out for the police or ambulance.

"I must have dozed off because suddenly there was this dreadful smell and I heard the door upstairs being pushed open. I know I screamed – my throat is still sore – and I must have caught my arm on the doorknob to get this gash and these bruises. Thank God

the ambulance finally arrived because the next thing I know this nice young man is doing CPR and telling me I'm going to be all right.

"But it was too late for Canon Abercrombie. They say it was just my overwrought imagination, but I'll never forget his face. He looked like he'd seen one of them vampires from the horror movies.

"I'm thanking God my heart attack was minor otherwise it could have been me too, lying there next to the Reverend. I feel pretty dreadful, but at least I'm not dead, thanks to that paramedic."

George Bear, 29, the paramedic who saved Mrs Stella's life, is currently off work sick, but his crewmate, Brenda Brookes, said, "We're all very proud of George, but that's what our training's for. It's great when we can actually help people."

British Media Corporation
Internal Communications

From: Internal Communications

<u>This email is going to all staff</u>

HRV – Q & A's

Q1: I am worried about catching HRV. Do I have to come to work?

A1: Should the situation change, then updates will be provided through "all staff" emails, 999 and your line manager.

Q2: I have been bitten by someone with HRV. What should I do?

A2: Staff who may have come into close contact with an infected person should monitor their health for any signs of illness in the 7 days after contact and if they start to develop symptoms, they should stay at home, go online and check their symptoms on the following sites:

<u>www.nhs.co.uk</u> (England)

<u>http://www.nhsdirect.wales.nhs.co.uk</u> (Wales)

<u>http://www.nhsdirect.gov.uk</u> (Northern Ireland)

<u>http://www.nhs24.com/content/</u> (Scotland)

Alternatively, call the HRV information line on 0800 000 0666. If appropriate, call your local GP.

Q3: I have been diagnosed with HRV. What should I do?

A3: Stay at home. Follow any medical advice you have been given. As soon as possible, notify your line manager and your local HR team and don't forget to keep your local HR team and line manager updated.

Q4: What will the BMC do to protect me from a HRV pandemic?

A4: The BMC will follow official advice given by the Government and will, as necessary, provide information to all staff, via email, posters and in the UK, via the 999 Emergency Information Service, on the best action to take. This will include additional hygiene measures and advice on how to avoid spreading the illness to others.

The BMC will publish guidance on the myRisks information site: http://explore.gateway.bmc.co.uk/myrisks/myriskshome/ safetynews/HRVlatestnews.aspx

Q5: Is it true that some staff are being provided with antiviral drugs?

A5: No antiviral drugs are being issued at present, though the BMC continues to look at the potential future requirements.

Q6: Is there any connection between "HRV" and what everybody is calling the "The Death" or "Beltane Plague"?

A6: Staff have no need to be concerned. The BMC has assured us that there is absolutely no connection between HRV and these, frankly unsubstantiated, other diseases.

More Q & A's will be added and this document will be updated as required.

The following notes and documents pertaining to the clinical manifestations of the outbreak of the condition now being referred to as the "Zombie Virus" or, more colloquially, "The Death", were compiled by Dr James Lancaster of University Hospital, Lewisham, and have been edited with explanatory notes for a non-medical readership in view of subsequent events.

1. Symptoms

<u>Source: Accident and Emergency Case Notes</u>
<u>748939/01/05/</u>

2:33 am: Anna Carstairs – 26-year-old girl brought in to accident and emergency on the first of May by her boyfriend Peter James who claimed she had taken an overdose. Patient was aggressive in the reception area and had to be restrained by Mr James while Miss Carstairs' details were taken. In view of the severity of the disruption she was causing to other individuals the patient was fast-tracked through to A&E major end by the triage nurse (Staff Nurse Susan Jenkins) because of concern of the possibility of ingestion of toxic substances, possibility of brain tumour, exacerbation of epilepsy (boyfriend denied any history) or possible combination of two or more of the above. While waiting for the attending doctor the patient refused to keep still to allow for routine measurements of pulse, blood pressure and temperature, and was physically

S.L

and verbally aggressive, further adding to the suspicion of ingestion of toxic and / or hallucinogenic substances. Following Staff Nurse Jenkins receiving a bite from the patient to the medial aspect of her right forearm (see case notes 759303/01/05/) members of security and the on-call senior house officer (Dr Marcus Blackstock) were asked to attend immediately and the patient was restrained using three sets of body straps around the ankles, waist and neck. Procedure deemed necessary for her own protection.

History: Patient uncommunicative. History taken from boyfriend but unreliable. Conversation between Dr Blackstock (MB) and patient's boyfriend (PJ) reproduced below from eyewitness accounts:

MB: So what has she taken?
PJ: I don't know. Pills.
MB: What kind of pills?
PJ: All sorts. Does it matter?
MB: Yes it does. In fact it could be very important. That's why I'm asking you.
PJ: Paracetamol.
MB: OK. Anything else?
PJ: Aspirin.
MB: Anything else?
PJ: Some antidepressants, half a packet of contraceptive pills, some other painkillers I think, all washed down with half a bottle of vodka.
MB: Everything in the medicine cupboard then?
PJ: And the drinks cabinet. Look, she was like this when I got home. I don't think she even knows who I am, and I could barely keep her off me in the car on the way here.

S.L

3:13 am: Ipecacuanha prescribed. Patient repeatedly refused administration of this emetic agent.

3:45 am: Decision to perform gastric lavage.

[Explanatory Note: The standard equipment held by an accident and emergency department for gastric lavage, or stomach pumping, consists of a six-foot length of hollow plastic tubing which is passed via the mouth into the stomach. A broad plastic funnel is then connected to the end protruding from the mouth and a volume of between 100–500ml of sterile water is poured down the tube. Once the stomach has sufficiently filled, the funnel is then placed upside down into a bucket on the floor to produce a siphon-like effect, thus facilitating the evacuation of the stomach contents.]

3:55 am: Five members of security called to aid in restraining patient to allow gastric lavage to be performed.

4:07 am: Gastric lavage ceased as patient vomiting of own accord.

4:25 am: Vomitus noted to consist of numerous undigested pills, green bile, a large quantity of blood from a presumed tear in the patient's oesophagus due to prolonged emesis, and a collection of teeth, bone fragments, flesh and fur that, according to the patient's boyfriend, could represent the remains of their pet cat.

Following induced emesis monitoring equipment was presumed to be failing to work properly as both the patient's pulse and blood pressure monitor readings fell to zero despite clinical observations to the contrary. Replacement equipment also apparently malfunctioning as patient still active and in fact more aggressive than ever. Attempts to draw blood after only a very small quantity obtained for laboratory analysis abandoned owing to uncooperative subject and inability to find suitable venous access despite the use of tourniquets.

Attempts to find patient a bed under admitting teams documented as follows:

- On-call physicians – refused. Degree of bleeding from suspected oesophageal tear suggests referral to surgeons.
- On-call general surgeons – refused. Patient unfit for surgery and too uncooperative to allow any form of anaesthesia. In view of patient appearing haemodynamically stable despite obviously malfunctioning monitor readings suggest referral to psychiatrists for assessment and possible sectioning.
- On-call psychiatrist – uncontactable after two hours.
- On-call physicians (second attempt) – in view of apparently stable state will try to admit when bed becomes available but unlikely in next four to six hours.

10:00 am: Still no bed available under physicians. Patient much calmer but attempts to examine still spark weak acts of aggression. Skin has taken on a yellow-grey hue with mottling. On moving her left arm the skin covering the brachialis muscle tore and the tissue beneath was noted by Dr Blackstock to be in a state of partial liquefaction. Physicians called again. Advised to refer to surgeons with diagnosis of potential necrotising fasciitis.

11:45 am: No breath sounds and no heart sounds over one minute. No response to pain. Pupils unreactive to light. Patient certified dead. Possible case of necrotising fasciitis or atypical Fournier's gangrene. For referral for Coroner's Post-Mortem.

[Note: Post-mortem unavailable as body never received by mortuary.]

2. Signs

Source: Accident and Emergency Case Notes
759303/01/05/

Staff Nurse Susan Jenkins reviewed by Dr Marcus Blackstock approximately thirty minutes following trauma to right forearm received while treating Anna Carstairs (see notes 748939/01/05/). When examined, Staff Nurse Jenkins claimed the appearance of the wound had changed considerably from the initial trauma, which, according to the patient, resembled a minor bite. Lesion examined by Dr Blackstock and its appearance recorded as follows:

Wound on the medial aspect of the right forearm consisting of two semicircular bite marks, all of which have broken the skin. Each puncture wound deep (in fact deeper now than they were when she was bitten, according to the patient), and the skin edges of each exhibits a pronounced acute inflammatory response with yellowing suggestive of cell death already taking place. Necrosis could be responsible for increased depth of wound. Bite marks encircle a central maculopapular erythematous rash which appears to consist of several areas of slightly differing redness.

Next to Dr Blackstock's attempted rendering of this lesion in his notes in diagrammatic form is the scribbled comment "?Similar 'Ring Around the Rose' Sign as seen in two previous cases brought in earlier".

Microbiologist unavailable for consultation so broad spectrum antibiotics prescribed: intravenous co-amoxiclav 1.2g tds, metronidazole 400mg tds and loading dose of gentamicin 7mg/kg in view of severity of infection. IV access impossible in affected arm so cannula sited in left antecubital fossa.

Two hours later primary lesion not noted to have changed but marked alterations distal to location of bite. Veins of distal forearm and hand now noted to be considerably more prominent and "almost black". Dark yellow discoloration of skin most marked closest to these prominent vessels. Skin noted to be breaking down in places with associated offensive mucopurulent discharge. Swabs taken.

Subject's mental state at this stage stable but patient obviously and understandably distressed.

Thirty minutes later process appears to be accelerating. Skin of distal forearm now much darker. Multiple areas of skin breakdown. Muscle tissue visible beneath, the appearance of which is distinctly plum-coloured, suggestive of ischaemia. Loss of sensation over these areas. Of more concern is the progress of the disease process proximally, extending above the patient's elbow.

Urgent surgical opinion sought (on call consultant Mr R Masters). RM's opinion reproduced below:

"Right upper limb shows advanced state of necrosis. Significant distal ischaemia and evidence of 'wet' gangrene in all fingers and both dorsal and ventral aspects of hand. Skin appears viable above elbow. Good axillary pulse.

Impression: Extremely aggressive necrotising fasciitis.

Advise: Surgical debridement, likely amputation.

Please obtain consent from patient. I will advise theatre staff and arrange anaesthetic assessment."

Patient unable to sign consent form owing to:

a)   Disease process affecting dominant hand.
b)   Mental state now such that patient unable to appreciate process, implications or possible complications of procedure for which she is signing.

Close relative unavailable. On-call psychiatrist uncontactable to provide advice as regards sectioning. Discussed with on-call surgeon who advises to proceed anyway.

Patient now becoming extremely aggressive. 5mg diazepam administered through IV cannula. No effect noted. Dose doubled. Subject more disorientated and now becoming violent. Increasing doses of haloperidol given intravenously until 200mg administered and subject sufficiently sedated to be transferred to operating theatre. Anaesthetist informed of all administered drugs and dosages.

3. Surgical Management

<u>Source: Operation Notes written by Mr Robert Masters
MD FRCS (Gen Surg)</u>

Date: 01/05/
Patient Name: Jenkins, Susan
Date of birth: 25/03/81
Hospital Number: 759303

Procedure: Attempted Surgical Debridement and Subsequent Through-Shoulder Amputation of Right Upper Limb

Surgeon: R Masters
Anaesthetist: D Srivastava

Indication for Procedure: Extensive suspected necrotising fasciitis affecting right upper limb. Procedure as follows:

Patient Position: Supine with right arm abducted at ninety degrees.

Chlorhexidine and Betadine mix used to clean skin and prep for surgery. No pre-operative antibiotics administered in view of loading doses given in A&E.

5.6 During skin preparation the application of the Betadine-soaked gauze to the patient caused a large segment of skin to be stripped from the arm as far up as the elbow, in the same manner as a degloving injury. Muscle beneath noted to be necrotic and cavitating with significant secretion of tissue fluids. Decision made to proceed directly to amputation. Transhumeral amputation initially considered but for safety it was decided to perform a glenohumeral amputation to allow complete removal of the upper limb at the shoulder.

Incision: Circumferential around right shoulder joint.

Procedure: Axillary vein and artery identified, ligated and divided. Muscle attachments divided (details here omitted). Nerve endings divided and electrocautery applied to reduce neuroma formation.

Closure: (Details omitted). Muscle layers closed over bone with non-absorbable sutures. Skin closed with mattress sutures.

Drains: None.

Post-Operative Instructions: Continue IV antibiotics.

4. Post-Operative Considerations

Source: Clinical notes made by Dr D Srivastava, the last few lines of which are spurious conjecture but which have been retained for information

Patient Susan Jenkins admitted to the intensive care unit (ICU) following surgical debridement and amputation of right upper limb. Observations stable but admitted to ICU after difficulty in extubating *[Explanatory Note: i.e. removing the endotracheal tube used to administer anaesthetic gases]*. This is not uncommon but is noted here because of the patient's subsequent post-operative course which was as follows:

Thirty minutes after admission to ICU Miss Jenkins was noted to become agitated, tachycardic (pulse of 290), hypertensive (blood pressure of 290/179) and tachypnoeic despite being on the ventilator (respiratory rate of more than 100). Decision made to again attempt extubation, but *[here the words THE PATIENT BEAT US TO IT! have been heavily crossed out]* almost immediately this was deemed unnecessary as the patient somehow achieved this herself, followed by removal of the intravenous and arterial lines that had been inserted pre-operatively. No blood loss from the puncture wounds as would have been expected under normal circumstances and in view of the vastly high blood pressure. Patient became more agitated and screamed as she attempted to lever herself out of the bed with her single good arm, which was now also noted to be displaying similarly worrying discoloration as the limb which had just been amputated. Sister Parkhurst attempted to restrain her but must have slipped because otherwise the only explanation for what was next observed is that the patient must have grabbed her by the throat and with her single viable arm thrown Sister Parkhurst across the room. Miss Jenkins' dressing leaking a profuse volume of serosanguinous fluid – a mixture of blood, pus and something a dark green colour that looked like bile but obviously couldn't be.

Patient swung herself out of bed, took hold of the steel drip stand and somehow managed to bend it with the force of her grip before throwing it at advancing staff who immediately retreated with me into the office located in the middle of the ICU, from where it was possible to observe her progress. Security called and informed of the situation but they were busy dealing with problems elsewhere and said there might be a considerable delay to their arrival. The two staff nurses and Sister Parkhurst expressed concern for the other intensive care patients but it was a decision made by the group as a whole that to leave the office at that point would be to possibly fatally endanger ourselves with no guarantee of being able to prevent what was happening in the ICU.

[Several attempts at starting the next paragraph crossed out.]

Staff Nurse Jenkins came over to the office and hammered on the glass in an extremely aggressive way that suggested she intended us harm rather than because she was seeking assistance. When it became clear that the glass was unbreakable, and that the office door was securely locked (and barricaded from our side with two swivel chairs and a filing cabinet we had managed to push across in front of it) she—

[Several more crossings out here, most of which are illegible.]

Staff Nurse Jenkins turned to the nearest bed with a patient in it – a 73-year-old man named Mr Albert Long being ventilated for a severe exacerbation of COPD *[Explanatory note: = chronic obstructive pulmonary disease]* and was observed to take his right hand in her left and tear the flesh from his forearm with her teeth. Nurse Jenkins noted to take several more bites before pulling the sheet back to expose the patient's abdomen, proceeding to consume more of the patient before moving on to the only other patient on the unit at the moment. Holly Paterson, a 15-year-old female RTA victim, was then similarly attacked and mutilated. Staff Nurse Jenkins was then observed to come back to the window of our office and hammer on it again before leaving the intensive care unit, but not before spitting a mixture of blood, flesh and hair onto the glass that could quite possibly pose an infection risk.

Sitting here writing this account for both clinical and medico-legal purposes, and having reviewed all that I have set down above, I would add the following:

The patient exhibited remarkable strength totally out of context with her height, weight and build. The fact that she had undergone major surgery and was exhibiting the symptoms and signs of overwhelming sepsis makes her actions all the more unbelievable and has given me all the more reason to feel the need to document them here. The patient has now left the unit and security has been informed, but actually I hope they don't find her as I dread to think what she might do to them. She *cannot* possibly remain mobile, or even alive, for much longer. As for what has caused her to act like this I cannot venture to say. Perhaps she never had necrotising fasciitis at all, or if she did perhaps she had it in combination with a virulent Ebola virus strain. Or perhaps rabies.

Oh God what if it's ALL of them???

Sister Parkhurst has just directed my attention to the fact that the torn and mutilated bodies of both Mr Long and Miss Paterson are starting to move.

Which is impossible.

S.L

5. Post-Mortem Findings & Histopathological Studies

POST-MORTEM REPORT

PM No.: 759303/01/05/
Hospital Clinician: Mr R Masters MD FRCS Gen Surg
Pathologist: Dr James Lancaster
Name: Susan Elizabeth Jenkins
Date of Birth: 25/03/81
Race: Caucasian
Sex: Female
Occupation: Staff Nurse
Date and Time of Death: 01-05- @ 14:50
Date and Time of Post-Mortem: 01-05- @ 17:30
Body identified by: Identification tag on left wrist.
Observers: Nil .

HISTORY: 31-year-old woman with history as documented
in preceding case notes. Following her self-discharge from
the intensive care unit of this institution she made her way
out into the grounds, attacking a number of members of
staff and the general public. Her mental state was obviously
in considerable disarray and she failed to notice an
approaching ambulance as she crossed the road in front of
the hospital main entrance. Death was confirmed at the site
and the body brought to the pathology department where
blood and tissue samples were taken for analysis and the
body prepared for post-mortem.

S.L

EXTERNAL EXAMINATION: Weight 63kg. Assessed age: mid-thirties. Hair: brown. Nutrition: Normal. Development: normal female. Rigor mortis: established. Hypostasis pattern: posterior. Cyanosis suggestive of oxygen depletion present but no jaundice. The deceased was pale and anaemic. Evidence of surgical amputation of right arm through shoulder. Numerous interrupted sutures holding the wound closed although at the inferior aspect there is evidence of the wound having been torn open (eye witness account claims patient did this to herself). Both lower limbs exhibit evidence of multiple compound fractures with several splintered bone fragments exiting from skin which has a peculiarly soft texture to it. Heavy bruising over breasts and abdomen consistent with blunt trauma. Left upper limb exhibiting signs of minor trauma except for left hand which has been crushed, as has the left side of the skull and face.

ADDITIONAL HISTORY (Added later): Despite extensive injuries consistent with significant blunt trauma sustained in the accident described above, and despite these injuries being of such severity that they should be incompatible with life, after thirty minutes the subject was observed to move. Initially this was thought to be due to the admittedly highly unlikely possibility that her reflex motor neurone arcs were displaying some residual function, but when the subject opened what was left of her mouth and screamed the emergency department was contacted. Apparently a Major Incident Situation had been declared over there and no one was able to provide any advice or assistance as to the appropriate course of action. In view of the fact that the quality of life which the patient would likely have were she to survive this episode of trauma would be very poor indeed I therefore took it upon myself to end the subject's life in as sympathetic and caring a manner as possible. Unfortunately venous access for the administration of a high dose of morphine was impossible and therefore it was decided to stop the patient's heartbeat with a high dose AC electric shock. When the monitor was connected it was observed that the subject had no heartbeat, this finding being corroborated by direct observation of the organ through the subject's open chest cavity. Despite the fact that the heart was obviously not beating, the lungs not inflating, and indeed there being absolutely no blood flow whatsoever, the subject was observed trying to get off the post-mortem bench, albeit unsuccessfully.

After a number of other methods were attempted death was finally achieved by the severing of the head from the body through the atlanto-axial joint of the cervical spine using an oscillating bone saw. I have yet to alter the time of death on the appropriate paperwork.

INTERNAL EXAMINATION:
(Only relevant sections have been reproduced)

Cardiovascular System: Heart: 375g. The pale myocardium suggests rapid overdistension with blood causing rupture of the left ventricle which should have led to the patient's death but evidently didn't. Venous system filled with clotted blood of a much thinner consistency than would normally be expected.

Respiratory System: Larynx and trachea show evidence of trauma due to recent intubation. Trachea filled with aspirated gastric contents. Right lung: 430g. Left lung: 395g. On sectioning both lungs exhibited marked congestion with blood and gastric contents and should not have been able to function.

Alimentary System: Mouth, teeth and tongue had to be scraped clean of adherent tissue prior to examination. Tissue possibly human, possibly patient's own, but also quite possibly belonging to the individuals she attacked in view of history above. Tissue isolated in view of potential infection risk. Stomach contained a large volume of undigested flesh and skin suggesting that while the patient's appetite had remained normal or excessive the ability of the stomach to produce digestive acid had ceased. The small intestine was also clogged with semi-digested human tissue most of which was muscle, but also noted were some identifiable scraps of skin and, in the descending part of the duodenum, a human eye (blue). Large intestine was mildly dilated and contained firm faeces. Distal colon and rectum normal.

Lymphoid System: Marked lymphadenopathy *[Explanatory Note: enlargement of lymph nodes]* throughout the body consistent with widespread systemic infective processes. Bone marrow examined and found to be of a much thicker consistency than normal.

Central Nervous System: Scalp and skull injured as described above. What remained of brain weighed 630g. On sectioning there was evidence of profuse haemorrhage throughout the cerebral tissue, suggesting a severe cerebrovascular *accident [Note = a major stroke.]* This could possibly explain the above observations related to the patient's poor responsiveness and regression to baser instincts.

Haematology: The blood smear prepared from the patient is fascinating. The patient's red cells have clumped together into a discernible pattern. Oddly enough this is similar in appearance to the central part of the skin lesion described by Dr Blackstock in his notes. The constituent cells are overlying each other forming a shape and pattern not unlike the petals of a rose. Whether this finding is significant, and whether or not the suspected infective agent is responsible for it I cannot yet say. What is interesting is that only a few of these "roses" could be found in an undamaged form. Most showed evidence of deterioration, with some having collapsed in on themselves and others being in the process of fragmentation. Presumably the red flecks between them are the remnants of cell complexes that have already completed this self-destructive process.

6. Commentary

I feel qualified to comment on the above reports as it is now some time since I sought out and compiled them, slightly longer since I performed the post-mortem on Staff Nurse Susan Jenkins, and most importantly for this part of the record, slightly longer still since Staff Nurse Jenkins took a bite out of my left hand, depriving it of the little finger and part of the hypothenar eminence of muscles that serve as its attachment to, and form the lateral border of, my left palm. This bite was inflicted shortly before I was able to end her undead existence as described in the "History" section of this post-mortem record. The failure to mention it at that time was deliberate as I felt it irrelevant to that part of the document. It is however extremely relevant to this section which is why I intend to describe the effect of her attack on me in a little more detail.

The injury produced a considerable amount of pain, far more than one would anticipate, and I wonder if the toxins present in the girl's saliva were particularly stimulatory to the afferent sensory neurones that mediate pain. Bleeding was as profuse as one might expect, and within an hour-and-a-half the wound had began to suppurate and leak the fluids described in the case notes above. This release of pus occurred along with the concomitant darkening of the veins around the bitten area that has been previously noted in other affected individuals, presumably indicating the spread of the communicated infection around my body.

My temperature reached a maximum of 43 degrees centigrade, which should be incompatible with life. I have little memory of the episode when my pyrexia was at its greatest, but before I became too unwell to function I attached myself to as much monitoring equipment as possible in the hope that it might aid whoever found my records. Of course I think it is unlikely they are going to be of use to anyone now, but the academic within me still demands closure and hence these few paragraphs of comment that I am adding as a conclusion of sorts to this document.

Once I had recovered from the acute pyrexial phase I was able to take blood samples from myself and prepare specimen smears, all of which have demonstrated some of the changes I noted in Nurse Jenkins' blood. Having subsequently had the opportunity to review her case notes and the testimonies of the various clinicians involved with her care I now find it remarkable that I have felt no desire or urge to act in an uncontrollable or aggressive manner. Instead I have been able to observe with dispassionate clarity the gradual but sustained fall in both my pulse and blood pressure. I may append the graphical representation of these data as when plotted each vital sign follows a perfect parabolic curve from what would be my normal physiological measurements down to zero.

And yet I am not dead.

Neither am I, for want of a better term, a raving lunatic. Indeed, once the fever and the burning sensation that flooded and then racked my body for a number of days (I am afraid I am unable to report the exact number due to my state at that time) had finally subsided I felt . . . not exactly my old self, but certainly not unwell. I therefore think it would be of interest if I were to set down here the observations I have made as regards my "new" and presumably what one might describe as "undead" self.

Despite the intense agony I experienced as a consequence of the bite, I now have no response to either pain or temperature. Gradations of pain have been tested in terms of the variously sized surgical clamps I was able to find up in the operating theatres. The application of a small Poirier tissue clamp produced no pain at all, and therefore larger clamps were then applied to the flesh of my left forearm. However, pressure was not exerted to the extent that the skin was broken as I am still unsure as to my current ability to heal. My body's response to temperature was assessed using ice that had formed on the inside of one of the mortuary doors, and by placing my hand inside one of the ovens used to prepare histopathological slides that require tissue to be stained with certain preparations. In all instances I felt nothing. From these observations I can hesitantly conclude that the disease must in some way obliterate the spinothalamic pathways to the brain that mediate both the sensations of pain and temperature, perhaps by overloading them in the acute phase of infection so that they literally "burn out".

Following my acute phase of disorientation and my experiments above, I have now repeated my blood tests to note an interesting new phenomenon not observed in the blood of the post-mortem specimen. Whereas her red blood cells had formed the aforementioned "rose" shape which appeared to be inherently unstable, the groupings of my cells in this manner have acquired a coating around them similar to the basement membrane observed in more complex tissue. These "Rings Around the Roses" (how bizarre and yet apt a description!) seem to confer a greater stability to my cell complexes, as confirmed by their ability to withstand abnormally great extremes of temperature, as well as other toxic environments, when tested.

I am beginning to suspect that I am now far from normal.

I am still highly reticent as regards any attempts to cause trauma to myself to observe its effect as I am still concerned that my healing abilities may be poor, or possibly non-existent. I know from laboratory analysis that my clotting factors have all but vanished and so if I were to bleed the activation of the normal coagulation cascade would be impossible. In fact I would have less chance of clotting the wound than the most severe case of haemophilia.

One final observation. My "emotions", for want of a better word, have also changed since I recovered from the acute phase of the disease. While my critical and intellectual faculties seem unaffected and perhaps even improved, I have become far more detached and dispassionate as regards the fate of my "fellow man". This reduction in my emotional capacity may be the reason why my other faculties have improved, as the moral and ethical dilemmas which may have previously left me in a quandary are no longer an issue.

S.L

7. Implications

What do my findings imply for the prognosis of individuals affected with "The Death"? As I write these notes it is becoming increasingly likely that by reference to the above group I am now referring to the majority of individuals resident within the United Kingdom, and since in this age it is almost impossible to confine a disease to a single country, or island, I may even be referring to the majority of the world's population. I appreciate that the following may be dismissed as conjecture but seeing as it is highly unlikely that anyone other than myself, or others like me, will get to read it, and that writing this document has assisted me considerably in making deductions and formulating hypotheses as regards "The Death", I see no reason not to include it.

My colleagues and I used to "joke", for want of a better word, about the need for a solution to the world's population problem. In the past wars, plagues and famine have wiped out vast numbers of individuals and kept the population down. In recent times the sterling work of numerous charitable organisations has meant that despite the best efforts of any number of Third World despots the number of people living and being born in the poorest parts of the world has increased. I used to wonder privately about the need for some form of catastrophe to solve the problem of over-population, and the nutritional and healthcare demands made by a multitude far too great to be able to be supported by the already limited resources this planet has to offer. It was always a source of ironic amusement to me that the very people who wanted to save the "starving millions" also happened to be the same people who were concerned about the consumption of global resources and wanted to "save the planet" as well. But they never seemed to appreciate the basic problem with that.

Everything is a balance, from human blood being a mixture of clotting and anti-clotting factors held in equilibrium so you can heal if you need to but not die of a thrombosis otherwise, to the fact that too many people living on this planet means that it simply cannot sustain itself.

But, my old science master used to say, nature is always capable of intervening in the evolutionary process when it becomes necessary.

Well this time, as well as the credit crunch, and governmental impotence, and political greed, now we have The Death.

Most of all The Death.

Consider the delicious irony – the starving millions will indeed be able to feed, but on each other. Their bellies will finally be full for the short time before they truly die – for the second time. And once this acute phase is over the planet will be able to recover from all the damage wrought upon it by twenty-first century humanity.

And so we have a powerful, voracious, all-consuming disease from which only a few have any chance of survival, coupled with a government whose lack of funds, lack of control and lack of willpower means that such an infection can run riot without let or hindrance of research that would have been carried out by departments so appallingly underfunded that the chances of finding a cure are zero.

I know there are people out there trying to fight this disease, trying to produce vaccines, develop antibiotics, and moderate the kinds of drugs we used to devastate people's bodies with in an attempt to kill their cancer but not them.

Let them. It won't work. I know. There's too much evidence in the pages of this document to suggest that they will fail.

Let them carry on.

Let the dead feed and then let the dead die.

Or become like me.

But most of them will die, I think.

Almost all.

And that's a good thing.

8. Postscript

I wonder if I am capable of communicating "The Death"?

This statement consisting of (23) pages each signed by me is true to the best of my knowledge and belief and I make it knowing that, if it is tendered in evidence, I shall be liable to prosecution if I have wilfully stated anything in it which I know to be false, or do not believe to be true.

Dr James Lancaster BSc MB ChB FRCPath
Consultant Histopathologist,
University Hospital, Lewisham

J. Lancaster

British Media Corporation
Internal Communications

From:	Internal Communications
Sent:	2 May, 08:32 AM
To:	All London Staff
Subject:	HRV – Update to Managers #2

<u>This email is going to HRDs, HRDMs, Internal Communications
Specialists and key divisional representatives</u>

Dear All

This is the latest managers' update on the HRV outbreak
in London.

Please forward the message below to line managers. It can be sent
out immediately/

Title: HRV – Managers' Update #2 – Date: 2 May

We continue to monitor the situation in terms of staff members who
have contracted HRV. Remember, HRV (in most cases) is a mild
virus and there is no cause for alarm, but we must ensure we take
reasonable precautions to further limit the spread of the disease.

In line with health agency advice, staff who develop HRV should
stay at home, lock their doors, seek medical advice from the NHS
advice line and contact their line managers, who should inform their
HR representatives.

If a member of staff develops symptoms while in the workplace, line managers should use common sense and discretion and send their staff home to seek medical advice, or else lock them in a secure room until help arrives. Violence is only advisable under extreme circumstances.

All managers should ensure they are familiar with the latest Q & A's regarding HRV on the BMC website, which is continually being updated.

Further information can also be found on the myRisks website.

If you are being asked questions about HRV which these websites do not fully cover, or you feel unable to answer, please forward the query to the Internal Communications email.

Check the BMC's Emergency Information channels for further updates:

Phone: 0800 0666 999

Online: bmc.co.uk/999

Gateway: 999 Emergency Information

Ceefax: page 999

Internal Communications

Subject: Event
From: dow@secure.ironplate.dhs.gov
Date: 05/2/ 06:23 (GMT -5)
To: cap@secure.steelglove.dhs.gov
cc: blind@secure.steelglove.dhs.gov
— —

Cappy:

Bricks are being shat enough to build a pyramid. We're all
dancing as fast as we can but nothing is fast enough for
this beat, I know.

Lapida's been trawling Twitter trails all night (Jesus,
does she ever sleep? I know, I know: who with? tee-hee)
and found this, as attached in original form. There are so
goddamn many of them now that I really don't know what to
think. But I'm passing everything up to you. Just. In.
Case. (Of course, I don't get paid to think, do I? At
least: not enough.)

But I don't know — there is something about this one which
is making me itch and twitch in my rectal region. The
username on this is BooBooBoy - what a prick, eh? We've
realized an unofficial ID on BooBooBoy's true name — and
he pans out as authentic, matching flight records (also
obtained "unofficially") — but making all this official
will take god knows. You know what the limeys are like
when it comes to paperwork and snappy movement. I'll have
Lapida follow-up herself to play it safe. I mean: no one
knows nothing, ain't it the truth?

Don't say I never learn, at least. Which isn't to say
that I don't hate this shit. Not to mention my ongoing,
very bad ass-itch.

—Diamond

PS: Lapida flipped the Twitter chronology to make
it more readable, but it is otherwise unedited.
Tweet-tweet . . .

BooBooBoy

Effing black cab a no-show! Anyone you can count on, anywhere? Knowledge my ass. What's wrong with GPS? Called a local mini. Tick-tock . . .

6:38 AM May 1st from Twhirl

G-D protesters. Every street in south London fucked! Heathrow far, driver brown and smelly. And practically coughing up a lung. Bastard.

7:04 AM May 1st from TweetDeck

@SumBitch So happy I amuse you. At least I'm not facing heap big pow-wow with God and The Lady. Deal with it yourself, tosser.

7:06 AM May 1st from TweetDeck in reply to SumBitch

@SumBitch Awwww, poor ickle boy. Count her cleavage wrinkles to stay awake! Uh-oh, you don't think she tweets, do ya?

7:08 AM May 1st from TweetDeck in reply to SumBitch

@SumBitch He out sick, too? It is seriously going around. Better be better in NYC. Major partying IS engraved in this lad's diary.

7:10 AM May 1st From TweetDeck in reply to SumBitch

Bollocks! Dead-looking cyclist at Chiswick. Hope she's dead, anyway. No other excuse for delaying me more. Fuck, that's a lot of blood.

7:33 AM May 1st from TweetDeck

Terminal 5. Designed and built by twats for lemmings. Wouldn't put up with this in any decent city. Bloody government!

8:01 AM May 1st from TweetDeck

Does everyone in this country have the effing flu? Can't we just kill all those poxy birds once and for all and save ourselves some bother?

8:09 AM May 1st from TweetDeck

@Bigtop DOUBLE-STARRED: Remind CJ to fax me revised warrants. Can't go into JPM meet holding only my Johnson. Big and tasty as it is . . .

8:22 AM May 1st from TweetDeck in reply to Bigtop

Airport lounges not what they used to be. No brioche?!?

8:46 AM May 1st from TweetDeck

@Cristalslut Thnx. Tell him I'm go for wifi on the flight so I'll do it then. Too much grief to use iPhone now. Boarding in 10 anyway.

9:17 AM May 1st from TweetDeck in reply to Cristalslut

Why oh why do they let coffin dodgers and crumbsnatchers board early with the first classers? Justice in this world? I don't think so.

9:34 AM May 1st from TweetDeck

Ah, seatbelts off, netbook on, drinks cart a-rattling. Sweet, sweet sound of alcohol. Screwdriver, please, hold the OJ. Make it a double.

10.12 AM May 1st from web

@soppyfeline Hey sexy thing, you're up awfully early – dirty dreams? Can't wait to see me, might a boy suggest . . .?

10:22 AM May 1st from web in reply to soppyfeline

@soppyfeline Whew! You're getting me in a lather here. Say more!

10:24 AM May 1st from web in reply to soppyfeline

@soppyfeline Ummm . . . other people can read this you know.
10:26 AM May 1st from web in reply to soppyfeline

@soppyfeline You utterly, disgustingly filthy thing. Can you really do that?
10:28 AM May 1st from web in reply to soppyfeline

@soppyfeline Wouldn't that scar?
10:29 AM May 1st from web in reply to soppyfeline

@soppyfeline What if I made you . . .
10:30 AM May 1st from web in reply to soppyfeline

@soppyfeline OK, OK: begged you?
10:32 AM May 1st from web in reply to soppyfeline

@soppyfeline Fuck. That even makes me blush. Promise me you will. I have cash and lots of it if that sways your thinking . . .
10:34 AM May 1st from web in reply to soppyfeline

Mile-high smile from City bimbo on aisle. Those tits'll float if we ditch. Must remember to grab hold in event of water landing.
10:41 AM May 1st from web

@soppyfeline Relax: just looking. I break it, I bought it. I know. Oh, how I know.
10:44 AM May 1st from web in reply to soppyfeline

Whatever happened to sexy stewardesses? Or young stewardesses? Or stewardesses full stop? Cabin crew! Cabana boys, more like. Sigh.
11:15 AM May 1st from web

@SumBitch Worry not: shiraz already in hand. Awfully rude of you to interrupt, dear boy. Hit KK-S up for access. She'll oblige ;-)
11:22 AM May 1st from web in reply to SumBitch

@SumBitch You're just a jealous guy. She's mine mine mine, and she's strictly a one-woman man.
11:25 AM May 1st from web in reply to SumBitch

@soppyfeline You wouldn't! (would you?)
11:27 AM May 1st from web in reply to soppyfeline

@soppyfeline And do I get heads or tails?
11:29 AM May 1st from web in reply to soppyfeline

@SumBitch OK, clearly I stand corrected. And I do stand. Lunch coming. Need the distraction (long as it's not a roast). Damn!
11:31 AM May 1st from web in reply to SumBitch

@soppyfeline I don't think you can say things like that on here.
11:33 AM May 1st from web in reply to soppyfeline

@soppyfeline I swear to god they're gonna ban our accounts at this rate.
11:35 AM May 1st from web in reply to soppyfeline

@SumBitch I know. Some of us just born lucky. But I'd need more than 140 characters to describe *that* to you . . .
11:39 AM May 1st from web in reply to SumBitch

Criminy! The slop they serve on high now. Like Wormwood Scrubs with wings. & no proper steak knives. Thank you, Osama. Cunt.
12:15 PM May 1st from web

After-lunch VSOP does take the edge off. That's better! Cabana boy nearly sneezed in it, though. Air in here ranker than usual, too.
12:40 PM May 1st from web

60+ movies on the teeny screen and Nicolas Cage in every fucking one of them. Apparently he's Hannah Montana now, too.
1:03 PM May 1st from web

Natives in economy sound restless. Must not like their chix in grey sauce. Cabana boys all look flustered. Heh! Fetch, you gay dogs.

1:11 PM May 1st from web

@SumBitch I'm at 30K feet fer chrissake – IMDB him yourself! I gave up after Police Academy 4 anyway.

1:17 PM May 1st from web in reply to SumBitch

Maybe those pussy Greens are right: too much travel, too many proles in the air. Noisiest flight ever. Can barely hear Nic Cage grunt.

1:31 PM May 1st from web

Shit! Entertainment system out. First Class? We will hunt you down and kill you, Richard Branson and eat your liver (without a steak knife).

1:52 PM May 1st from web

@soppyfeline That most definitely would entertain me instead! Looking at yr pix right now on my phone. Hummina-hummina.

1:55 PM May 1st from web in reply to soppyfeline

@soppyfeline That's the very one I'm ogling, o buxom vixen. Wood alert!

1:57 PM May 1st from web in reply to soppyfeline

@soppyfeline No probs, doll. Go do what you gotta do. I'm not going anyplace, am I?

1:59 PM May 1st from web in reply to soppyfeline

Seatbelt light on. Pilot says turbulence ahead. Don't feel anything. Could perform circumcisions it's so smooth. What gives?

2:08 PM May 1st from web

@Cristalslut You do know that I am on an airplane over the ocean. Can you just deal with it there? For once? PLEASE!

2:14 May 1st from web in reply to Cristalslut

@SumBitch Cause something funny's going down. Captain asked for doctor twice. More ruckus from cattle class, too. Bad chow? Please not.
2:16 PM May 1st from web in reply to SumBitch

@SumBitch Thank you I have seen Airplane (and don't call me Shirley!). Seriously, I think there's a real problem here. Me no like.
2:18 PM May 1st from web in reply to SumBitch

@SumBitch Where did you hear they shut the airport? What are they saying?
2:31 PM May 1st from web in reply to SumBitch

@SumBitch Nothing on the net I can see. You sure about this?
2:33 PM May 1st from web in reply to SumBitch

Captain asking if any medical personnel on the flight. Doctor, nurse, paramedic. Vet?!? Can't be good, can it?
2:39 PM May 1st from web

@SumBitch Yeah, I see it now. It's even on the beeb site. Claiming Heathrow and Gatwick closed for security alert.
2:44 PM May 1st from web in reply to SumBitch

@SumBitch ALL of them? No inbounds either? The whole goddamn country? Fuuuuck.
2:46 PM May 1st from web in reply to SumBitch

@SumBitch So who is this friend? Is he for real? How does he know this stuff?
2:53 PM May 1st from web in reply to SumBitch

@SumBitch Shit shit shit shit shit.
2:56 PM May 1st from web in reply to SumBitch

@SumBitch Ask him what I should do. What would he do if he were stuck up here?
3:02 PM May 1st from web in reply to SumBitch

@SumBitch You there? Ding-dong.

3:04 PM May 1st from web in reply to SumBitch

@SumBitch HULLO????? Need help here.

3:08 PM May 1st from web in reply to SumBitch

@SumBitch That's not funny. I'm not laughing. I'm fucked and not in the way I had planned. Where would be safest he think?

3:16 PM May 1st from web in reply to SumBitch

@SumBitch Fuck you.

3:19 PM May 1st from web in reply to SumBitch

I think I am trapped on an airplane with terrorists.

3:23 PM May 1st from web

@soppyfeline Not shitting you, doll. Shitting myself plenty. Everyone is. Panic buttons getting pushed.

3:28 PM May 1st from web in reply to soppyfeline

@soppyfeline The cabin crew are going apeshit. Won't answer any questions. Just running around like crazies. Wait . . .

3:31 PM May 1st from web in reply to soppyfeline

@SumBitch Cool dude. Kind of scared here, though. Savvy?

3:37 PM May 1st from web in reply to SumBitch

Screaming from the back of the plane. What the fuck?

3:45 PM May 1st from web

Cabana boy covered in blood!! Can't understand him. Eating? Eating what?

3:51 PM May 1st from web

Gunshots. Fucking gunshots.

3:55 PM May 1st from web

@SumBitch Call yr friend. Ask him for fucksake. NOW!

4:01 PM May 1st in reply to SumBitch

I am on Virgin flight 001 London to NY. Terrorists on plane. If u can read this call police, air force, SOMEBODY. This is NOT a joke.

4:06 PM May 1st from web

@SumBitch Air marshals on board. Fired the shots. One dead, other with us. No bullets left. Not terrorists! Some fucking crazy shit lik

4:14 PM May 1st from TweetDeck in reply to SumBitch

@SumBitch twitter only thing that works using iphone now wifi still on. They coming through again nothing to

4:15 PM May 1st from TweetDeck in reply to SumBitch

@SumBitch Creature mosnters cant be tho. Biting tearing kill. Bigtit blonde guts ripped out EATEN

4:16 PM May 1st from TweetDeck in reply to SumBitch

@SumBitch PLEASE yr friend say anything? Few us made it upper deck blocked stairs. Don't think will last tho

4:20 PM May 1st from TweetDeck in reply to SumBitch

@SumBitch THEY KNOW? fuckers fuckers fuckers

4:23 PM May 1st from TweetDeck in reply to SumBitch

@soppyfeline I love you for true. They coming

4:24 PM May 1st from TweetDeck

THEYRE KILLING US ALL EATING US THI PLANE FULL OF DEAD HELP ME PLESE GO

4:31 PM May 1st from TweetDeck

---

kkljbcbbaafded7jkasdho iasdjajknsdjkbasdpaisdjfnakjsd kasjjkjhsakjoasikskjdkcnskkajshkjcoasidjknfkjasdn9is eoljiosijskjnflsisjskslsnlkusdhsuhva

4:33 PM May 1st from TweetDeck

---

*

4:34 PM May 1st from TweetDeck

Subject: Re: Event
From: cap@secure.steelglove.dhs.gov
Date: 05/2/ 08:12 (GMT -5)
To: dow@secure.ironplate.dhs.gov

- -

Diamond:

Tell Lapida to continue tracking down all relevant
references no matter how obscure or bizarre. This looks
like a valid one, I concur. If she finds any more like
this, mark them urgent and forward to me immediately. DO
NOT COPY TO BLINDMAN.

This log does support some of the other immediate
documentation of the Event our teams have unearthed. The
time line in particular is proving very useful here.
Your pal BooBooBoy's obsession with tweeting every
minute of his life was sad, to be sure, but it is
turning out to be very handy in these unusual
circumstances.

(I'm still old school — or just old — but why do people
need to document their lives like this? Does anyone
really want to read about it? Is this what passes for
entertainment with you kids? Give me an episode of *The
Rockford Files* any day and twice on Sunday.)

As you know, the last official ATC contact with VS001
flight deck occurred at 16:38, so BooBooBoy's trail
takes us almost right up to Captain Prado's final
exchange with ATC. The (currently) official version
circulating has the second USAF F-15 Strike Eagle
downing VS001 at 17:11. If Lapida or anyone else in your
unit can locate a tweet, email, text or anything else
off the plane authenticated between 16:38 and 17:11, it
would be most helpful. We're desperate here, boy, and
the big cats upstairs are sharpening their claws. We
need answers and we need them fast. So do that voodoo
you do so well.

—Cap

PS virtual Preparation-H attached for case of itchy-ass.

Subject: Re: Re: Event
From: cap@secure.steelglove.dhs.gov
Date: 05/2/ 09:35 (GMT -5)
To: dow@secure.ironplate.dhs.gov

- -

Diamond:

Thanks for that follow-up. Very interesting.

All agencies are moving as quickly as possible.
"@soppyfeline" is already in custody courtesy NYPD. MI5
promise (yeah, right) that "@SumBitch" will be in their
hands by 11:00 (GMT -5). I agree that the others on the
list look to be of secondary importance at best, but
we'll apprehend all of them to be sure. UK is still
under effective lockdown. The chaos there is making
things hard info-wise.

I've got something else for your crew to chase up ASAP:
BasalNode has been monitoring local radio on Long
Island. They have multiple reports of non-stochastic
violent incidents near Massapequa, NY. Most likely just
morning drive-time nonsense, but this proximity formally
lies within the constituted debris cone of VS001, so
let's dot every I and cross every T on this, yes?

—Cap

PS: what do you mean you never heard of *The Rockford
Files*? How fucking young are you? Do you know anything
at all?

British Media Corporation
Internal Communications

This is an Automated Reply

<u>BMC Automated message</u>

Due to staff illness, the Internal Communications email is currently not being monitored.

Check the BMC's Emergency Information channels for further updates:

Phone: 0800 0666 999

Online: bmc.co.uk/999

Gateway: 999 Emergency Information

Ceefax: page 999

Internal Communications

SATURDAY, MAY 4

Sorry I haven't written for a few days, but everything's got a bit freaky and I didn't really know what to write. And when I say freaky, I mean REALLY freaky. I'm writing this at George's. I finally got let out of the house 'cos mum's sick and dad said I could come round here so she could have some peace and quiet, which normally would be GREAT, but today just feels kind of odd. Part of me really wants to be at home and I don't really know why. Maybe 13 isn't that grown-up at all.

George has gone to the shop for his mum, but I stayed here. Its too quiet out there, like everyone's asleep or something. Its like that weird time just before a thunderstorm when the air gets really hot and you're just waiting for the rain to start and break the tension and make all those itchy black bugs disappear, but this time I'm not sure exactly what it is I'm waiting for. I'm not even sure George's mum wants me here. She's not smiley like she normally is, and her face went funny after I said mum was sick. Apparently – according to George – a lot of people are getting sick. He said his mum's totally freaked by it, and by the fact that Alex keeps going on about how maybe some kind of plague did really escape when they started digging up that old church. Yesterday she wanted Alex to find them all some of those facemasks like decorators wear, but George said Alex just laughed at her and said that wouldn't help. He said this was going to be worse than bird flu and all that other stuff and even worse than the plague itself according to what they were saying on the radio. He said that the presenter said people started eating each other when whatever it was came up out of the church, but that can't be right.

Alex (sigh– still – I can't help it!) has got really serious. He barely said hello when I got here and was rowing with his mum about going out to see his college friends who were going to try and "do

something about it". Whatever it is.
He's reminding me of Uncle Jack a
bit and I wish he wouldn't. Still,
there is something about the fact
that he's so willing to go out there
and take on the government and the
army that makes my tummy go
funny, and he's still just the best-
looking boy in the whole town and I
still wish he would notice me!!

George's mums sounds like she's
crying, and the door just slammed.
I guess Alex has gone out to see his
friends after all. Surely, they can't
be right about this sickness. I just
can't believe it. I don't want to
believe it. And anyway, we learnt
about that stuff, and the plague gave
people big boils and blisters, and
mum doesn't have anything like that
so even if it is true, then she
definitely doesn't have the plague,
but somehow that thought doesn't
make the knot in my stomach go
away. I just want everything to go
back to normal. I don't want to
think about the sick people.

Even though I'm pretty sure everyone's exaggerating this bug thing, I can't help being a bit worried about George out there and I keep looking out his bedroom window. About ten minutes ago I saw three men go and stand outside the bookies opposite. They just stood there, like they'd forgotten why they'd gone in the first place. They weren't talking or anything. They looked pale like mum and one of them had a tatty bandage wrapped round his hand that looked like it should have been changed.

My mouth tasted funny again. Mum's sickness started with a cut. Well, she said it was a cut, but it looked more like a bite to me when I caught her cleaning it. It was on her shoulder when she got back from visiting Uncle Jack the other day. She said he'd done it accidentally because he had a fever and that she'd rung an ambulance for him, but it was an army truck that came to take him away. I don't think she told the army people about the cut or bite or whatever it is. She looked really scared. So did dad. She said it would be fine, but I think maybe its got infected or something because last night she was just wandering round the flat and today she's all pale and sweaty. Her eyes looked funny too. Like she was there but not there. I wish she'd just go to the doctor and get some antibiotics or something. Why would Uncle Jack have bitten her? He had a cut when he came to ours the night of the protest. I wonder if that was how he got sick. OMG, I just wish I knew what was going on.

When George gets back from the shop I think I'll ask him to walk me home. Its not far, but its just too creepy out there and its nearly curfew time. I've just realised what's spooky. The streets are deserted, but its more than that. There aren't even any of the army out there. There's normally always a truck in sight these days. Where are they all?

SUNDAY, MAY 5

Back at George's. Its been nearly twenty-four hours now since I went home and I can't stop crying. I can't breathe properly. My hand is shaking too much to even write. I'm scared that if I don't write it down I won't believe it, and if I do write it down then that will make it true. I don't want to make it true. While George and his mum were blocking the door up, Alex told me I should write it down. He said it might be important one day. That made me cry some more, and I'm not really sure why. But Alex asked me to, and so I will. And I have to. You're a diary.

Everything's quiet here. George's dad isn't home from the factory yet. He didn't come home last night and I can see George's mum is frantic. She can't help thinking about what happened at mine yesterday too. I can see it in her eyes. Still, she's packing some bags. I don't think she's expecting him to come home, not really, and that's making me feel a bit sick too. What's going on? Why aren't the army stopping it? It seems like everyone is trying to leave London. Its getting dark outside and there are fires burning in the distance and car horns blaring. People keep shouting angrily at each other and then there are the screams. Those are the worst. Not the screams themselves, but the way they stop suddenly. I just want to curl up under the duvet and wait for it all to go away. But I can't. I have to at least try to be grown up. I'm thirteen.

Deep breath. And write. I'm just going to tell what happened. Try not to think about it being mum or gran or dad. Just other people that look like them.

When George got back from the shops yesterday, his mum made us both a sandwich and then he walked me home. We didn't talk much. I asked what he knew about the protest, and he just kind of shrugged and said that Alex had said that everything just went crazy and something attacked the army and the protesters. He said that some people swore that the dead got up and walked, but he figured that was probably just some kind of hallucinogenic effect of whatever toxic gas came out of the church and drove everyone mad. It made me think of Uncle Jack who hadn't gone on the protest but had let the protesters use his flat. It made more sense now that he'd been injured if some gas had made the people go crazy.

When we got to the flats, George came all the way up with me. He doesn't normally, and I don't really know why he did yesterday, except maybe he had some kind of instinct that something was wrong. Sometimes I think George thinks a lot about things but doesn't say anything. Sometimes I wonder if maybe he's cleverer than Alex underneath it all. Looking back, I can't help but wonder if he half-expected what we found, especially after what I'd said about mum being sick. He can't have expected what we actually saw, no-one could, but I think he knew something would be very wrong. He went quiet as we came up the stairs and his face kind of tightened. He looked older.

We were probably only in the flat about a minute before George dragged me out and we were running back down and into the street. That minute seems to be about a year in my head. I keep seeing it. I try not to, but its always there behind my eyes and I can't even cry it away.

We opened the front door and I think I shouted hello. Something smashed in the sitting room and I looked at George but he didn't look back. He went ahead and pushed the sitting room door open. I must have been speaking because I remember stopping. I remember thinking this is totally wrong. This is totally fucking wrong. I remember the thought clearly cos I just don't use that word very often. The Barbies use it all the time and it makes them sound cheap. But it just came in my head.

There was a lot of blood. My gran was in her chair but her head was tilted over to one side and her mouth was wide. At first I just couldn't understand what was the matter with her. Her clothes were soaked red and she was just staring at me. My fingers tingled and I think I tried to say something but instead I just took a step forward so I could see better. I don't even remember trying to move my feet. I didn't want to look closer, I really didn't, but there was a funny noise coming from the other side of the sofa and all I could think was that maybe a wild dog had somehow got into the flat and attacked my gran. I don't know what I saw first. Maybe I saw them both at the same time. My gran's throat was ripped open, with a flap of loose skin hanging to one side. A thin stream of smoke rose up from the carpet and stank of burning. Maybe that's what made me look down. It must have been. She'd dropped her cigarette and it was burning a black hole in the carpet. It stank like plastic. I remember thinking that mum wouldn't like that and then I saw dad's shoes sticking out from behind the sofa and his feet were kind of shaking. There was a wet sound too, something slick and horrid and

greedy, and then George gasped and
started pulling me back. I remember
his hand was hot and mine was
cold. I remember peering over the
back of the sofa and seeing dad.

Mum was straddling him. She
looked funny with her skirt all
hitched up and her tights torn.
Mum's neat and tidy. She likes to
look presentable. But this wasn't
mum. It just looked like her. There
was a knife in her shoulder. It was
one of the ones from the block in
the kitchen and it was right in to
the hilt, but she didn't seem to
notice it.

The vase from the coffee table was
smashed around her and her hair
was soaking wet and a daffodil hung
loosely across the back of her untidy
bun. The base was still in dad's
hand, but his grip had gone. Water
ran down mum's face and made
pink paths through the crimson that
smeared across her mouth and
covered her chin. She didn't look at
us, but buried her head back into

dad's shoulder with a hiss. She sounded like a snake. It was yuk.

Dad let out a soft sigh. No scream or anything. But it was enough to make us run.

I'm crying again. I can't help it.

MONDAY, MAY 6

Alex went out with some of his
friends from college today. When
they came back they had guns that
they'd found in an abandoned army
truck. They said that it was chaos
out there and that all the main
roads out of the city were blocked
and none of the trains or tubes or
anything were running. It made me
want to cry again, but I didn't. It
didn't really surprise me either.
George's mum said that we could
walk out of the city and head to
Kent or somewhere less crowded. Her
eyes were all red and puffy from
crying so much and she kept twisting
her hankie between her fingers until I
just wanted to grab it from her.
Alex and his friends all kind of
looked at each other a bit then,
before he sat his mum down. He
talked to her like she was a child,
which was totally weird and maybe
scared me more. I wanted her to
stop crying. I wanted her to act like
a grown-up.

"They're attacking people out there, mum. It isn't safe."

"Who's attacking people? The army?"

One of Alex's friend's sniggered at that but shut up quickly when Alex glared at him.

"No, its this virus. It changes people. The infected are attacking everyone else. Even in daylight its not safe out there. If they don't tear you apart then all it seems to take is a scratch or a bite to make you like them."

"Where's the army? What are the government doing?"

Alex shrugged. "I don't know mum. Maybe they're trying to find a cure or something. But for now I think its safer if you hide in the city."

"Hide?"

"Uncle Simon converted the eaves above his shop into a small flat last year. He was getting a bit of extra money renting it out to a couple of political protesters, but you still have to get to it up a ladder."

"Simon's been doing what? He's been . . . How did you know?"

"Don't worry about that now, mum. Even if they break into the shop, they won't know you're up there, that's the point. And we'll bring you food and stuff and make sure you're okay."

That was when she stopped squeezing her hankie. "What do you mean? Where will you be?"

"Don't worry mum. We've got places to stay, and we're going to try and fight this thing."

My stomach felt really funny then. I know that its wrong and with everything that happened with mum and dad and gran I totally shouldn't even have been thinking like this, but a part of me had kind of liked the idea of being hidden in the flat with Alex. He'd have to notice me if we were locked away together. I'd have had time to make him see that I wasn't just a little girl and then he'd realise that we were made for each other and when all this was over and I was older we'd get married or something. Its crazy isn't it? I must be the most selfish girl in the whole world. But when he said he wasn't coming too, my heart twisted.

"You have to come, Alex. It isn't safe, you said so yourself." She gripped his arm.

"They only have room for three, mum." Alex's voice was really soft as he peeled her fingers away. "You, George and Maddy. I wouldn't go anyway. I want to try and help out here. Someone's got to."

His mum cried some more then, and begged and pleaded with him but he wouldn't change his mind. George pulled me into his room and we packed a small holdall of his things and some extra T-shirts that I could wear. He didn't say much and his face had that funny grown-up look on it like he'd had when we went to my flat. Once we'd packed, we went into the kitchen and filled another bag with all the tins and things from the cupboards. It didn't look like so very much when we were done. Alex says he'll take us over there first thing in the morning. At dawn. When things quieten down. He's not going out with his friends tonight, but said he'll spend the evening with his mum. I think I'll stay in George's room. This is their night, even if they're all I have left now.

I miss mum and dad and even gran with her stupid stories about her dead friend. I want everything to go back to how it was. I want to cry.

TUESDAY, MAY 7

OMG, I don't know where to begin. I feel so out of place and I'm sure George's mum is blaming me somehow but it wasn't my fault and I wish he was here too. Things were bad and now they're so much worse and this place is tiny and I don't know anyone. I honest to God don't think I could feel any worse.

Sorry, I need to backtrack. I'm at the secret flat. We got up really early which wasn't a problem because I don't think anyone had really slept much. There was too much noise outside and George's mum kept crying. Me and George chatted a bit about people from school wondering if they were okay, but in the end we just lay there in silence. I was glad he was there though. He isn't like Alex (sigh), but sometimes I think that maybe when he's grown up, I'll see him properly. I think he loves me a bit in a kind of boyfriend/girlfriend way, but he's never said. I've just caught him looking at me occasionally (not at my chest, despite my new bra!), and I can see something soft in his eyes. If I wasn't so in love with Alex, then maybe one day I'd see George differently, but as it is, he'll never be more than my best friend. But I'm ever so glad he's that. Especially now. He's the only person I've got left.

Writing that has made me miss him even more. George isn't here, you see. He came with us, but didn't stay. We crept out of their flat and Alex made us almost jog all the way to the High Street. It was scary. Some of the houses had their doors wide open. Bins were overturned in the streets and the rubbish had blown everywhere. I saw blood too. I don't want to think about that. Some of the big windows of the shops were broken as if they'd been looted. It was really quiet too, as if the whole world was asleep. London's never quiet like that. You can normally hear a bus or a car or something, but this morning it was just us and our footsteps. I was really scared.

We went in the side door that led up past Mr Drake's (George's Uncle Simon — he insists I call him and his wife Mr and Mrs Drake — how old-fashioned???) shop and then through the solicitor's office on the second floor to the small hallway at the back. Alex stood on a chair and did a funny knock on the small hatch. Mr Drake opened it. He didn't look overly happy to see us, and I could see him scanning us. Maybe he was checking for bites or something.

"I hope no-one saw you" he whispered. "Come up quickly!"

He lowered the ladder and George's mum went up first and then me, and then Alex and George passed up our bags and the food.

"Come on, George," his mum said. The air in the flat smelt of sawdust and the boards that cut into my knees were bare and untreated.

George stayed at the bottom of the ladder. "I'm not coming. I'm going with Alex." He was already backing away, and I could feel tears stinging the back of my eyes. His mum started crying and begging him to not be stupid and she leaned through the hole as if she could somehow grab him but Mr Drake pulled her back in.

"I'll come every other day. I'll bring you and Maddy and everyone food stuff. I'll be fine mum." He vanished then. And I think he was crying a bit. I was, I know that.

Another man, who I now know is John Meckan (I supposed I'd better call him Mr Meckan just so Mr Drake doesn't think I'm one of "those rude children" (I'll tell you about <u>that</u> later!)) appeared from a door on the left and pulled the ladder up as Mr Drake tugged George's mum away. It was weird seeing Alex standing at the bottom and looking up. I suddenly felt like he was in a different world to me. Maybe he is. Maybe "out there" and "in here" are two different universes. It already feels a bit like that and I've only been here a day. I can't help but wish I was "out there" with George and Alex. I feel so alone in here.

Okay, enough whining. Let me tell you about a) the flat and then b) the people.

Number one: The flat is SMALL. Especially for the number of people in it!! There's a little kitchen and a small bathroom with a shower but no bath and a sink and a toilet (which Mr Drake says we can only flush if we really have to and never at night!!! How yuk is that?....), a bedroom and the small sitting room. Mr Drake and Mr Meckan are having the sitting room to sleep in, and Mrs Drake, George's mum and me are in the bedroom. I have to sleep in a sleeping bag on the floor and they have the bed. There's barely room for the double bed and with me on the floor at the end the door won't open properly. There is going to be NO privacy at all!!! I just hope we don't have to stay in here long. It smells a bit funny already.

At least from the bedroom window, if I peep out under the curtain (another of Mr Drake's rules – <u>NO</u> looking out the windows – Yawn. He should have been a teacher he has so many rules!) then I can see the clock tower and all the shops. Not that much is happening out there, but I like to see the clock tower. It makes me think that despite everything, when all this is over, we'll all hang around it again, and I promise that when that happens, I won't ever moan about being bored or wishing there was more to do in Lewisham and I won't even care if the Barbies still look down their noses at me, I'll just be happy that they're safe and that things are normal again. I try not to remember that mum and dad and gran won't be there. That doesn't seem real despite what I saw. In my head that's just part of this nightmare and I'll think about it when I have to and not before. Maybe that's silly, but its the only way that I can really cope with this.

To pretend its just a nightmare. I thought that it made me childish but I heard Mrs Drake say she felt like she was living in a nightmare earlier, so I figure maybe 13 isn't so far from being a grown-up after all.

Anyway, since I've mentioned Mrs Drake I may as well talk about the people. Well, there's me and George's mum, Sylvie. (I'm still calling her by her first name and if Mr Drake thinks that's going to change then he can . . . well . . . he can shove it up his you know what!), Mr Meckan, and Mr and Mrs Drake.

Firstly, Mrs Drake is fat. I know that's rude to say and mum would shh me for it, but mum isn't here and this is my diary, so I'm going to be honest. She's REALLY fat. Like American fat. I can't help but feel sorry for Sylvie having to share the bed with her because I probably have more room on the floor. I haven't decided if I like her or not yet to be honest. She grabbed me and hugged me, but it felt like she squeezed me too tight and her perfume smelt awful and I could smell sweat under it too. She kept saying how lovely it was to have a little girl to fuss over, but I get the feeling she doesn't really know a lot about children — and especially teenagers. I've been really polite to her because after all this is her flat and I'm lucky to be here (and mum would hate it if I was rude), but so far she's just a bit loud and over the top. A bit like Mrs Swain, the drama teacher at school who makes everything about her rather than us when we do a play. That sounds mean, and maybe Mrs Drake will turn out to be great. Maybe I'm just comparing her to my mum, or Sylvie. I should be nicer. That's what mum would say.

Mr Drake is the complete <u>TOTAL</u> opposite to his wife. If things weren't so serious you'd laugh if you saw them. He's like a flipping stick and has this stupid beard that is in a strip down his chin which he's <u>WAY</u> too old for. He must be forty at least!!! It looks so wrong, especially when he's so serious and expects to be called "Mr". Maybe that's how solicitors or lawyers or whatever have to look, but it just seems silly to me and he tucks his T-shirt into his jeans too which is such a fashion fail. Anyway, Mr Drake is definitely in charge in the flat. He made us all sit in the sitting room and he went through all the rules. I didn't really listen to be honest, I was still in shock at George not coming in, but he kept staring at me so I figure most of them were aimed in my direction.

Mr Meckan seems quite nice so far. He hasn't said much but he made us all a cup of tea and winked at me in a way that reminded me of Alex (total sigh) and he has really nice blond hair. I don't think he's all that old. He's much younger than Mr Drake anyway. Mr Drake doesn't seem to talk to him much, but Mrs Drake does. She seems to make more of a fuss over him than she does her husband. Sylvie says he worked in the solicitors' office with Mr Drake so he knew about the secret flat and that's why he's here too. Anyway, I'm glad he's here. He's nice.

Anyway, I'll write more later. I've got to go and do the washing-up. Apparently that's one of my jobs, according to Mr Drake. I bet they're all my jobs! And I have to do them quietly! I have to do everything quietly! What does he think I am — a baby elephant???

**British Media Corporation
Internal Communications**

**999 Emergency Service
for BMC Staff**

This is information for people who work at the BMC.

This information has been updated at 09:30 AM Wednesday 8 May. There are no further incidents at any BMC buildings.

Service Status:

Following the unfortunate incidents in London, there are currently no further outbreaks reported at key BMC buildings. For information during an incident please call 0800 0666 999.

Introduction The BMC's "999" Emergency Information Service is designed to keep people who work at the BMC (a private company formed when Channel 4 and the British Broadcasting Company merged) informed during emergency situations such as major security alerts, fires or power failures at all key BMC buildings which might prevent them from reporting to work as normal. 999 provides up-to-date information for staff who have either been evacuated from, or hear media reports about an incident involving, a key BMC building.

For information updates please keep checking the usual BMC Emergency Channels:

Phone: 0800 0666 999
Online: bmc.co.uk/999
Gateway: 999 Emergency Information
Ceefax: page 999

MINUTES OF MEETING, PARLIAMENTARY SELECT COMMITTEE SUPERVISING THE EXTREME CONTINGENCIES PLANNING GROUP

Present: Sir Kenneth Smart, Minister With Responsibility; Frances Sheil, Junior Assistant Planner; Millicent Trevor (Recording Secretary).

Absent: Alastair Garnett, Permanent Undersecretary to the Minister (apologies – sent by text message, from Mustique); Maureen Trenchard, M.P. (no apologies – reported seen at Gatwick); Tony Jones-Bates, Lead Planner (no apologies); Gemma Pulsford, Deputy Lead Planner (no apologies); James McKay, Junior Planner (no apologies); Dieter Heidl, Department of Logistics and Statistics (no apologies); Deputy Chief Constable Wilfrid Palmersdale, Metropolitan Police (no apologies); Colonel Tom Ouedrago, Armed Services Liaison Planner (no apologies – obituary notice in *The Times* online); Dr Raj Dass, NHS Liaison Planner (no apologies); Reg Briscombe, NALGO (no apologies); Sandra Derbyshire, ECPG Secretary (no apologies); Graham Gorham, Small Business Association (no apologies).

Ms Sheil: Minister . . .

Sir Kenneth: . . . Shush, I'm reading.

Ms Sheil: . . . You must understand the *circumstances*.

Sir Kenneth: All too bloody well. Now shut up, and let me read this through.

Ms Sheil: You've read it, Sir Kenneth. You must have. You *implemented* it. It was . . .

Sir Kenneth: . . . My bloody decision. Yes. It was. Bollocks.

Ms Sheil: Sir Kenneth?

Sir Kenneth: Bollocks. This report, this *contingency plan*. Bollocks.

Ms Sheil: I couldn't comment.

Sir Kenneth: Your name is on it woman. At the bottom. With Garnett and that idiot Trenchard woman and all the others.

Ms Sheil: We all signed it. Unanimity was a requirement. It's in the planning regs.

Sir Kenneth: Ah yes, the regs.

Ms Sheil: You have to understand . . .

Sir Kenneth: . . . The circumstances, yes. So, as the sole representative who was able to make it to this meeting – sorry there's no tea and biscuits, by the way – what would you say was the purpose of the Extreme Contingencies Planning Group?

Ms Sheil: It's not for me to say. I'm very junior.

Sir Kenneth: Not now you're not. You're very senior. Taking into account those who have Gone With the Wind Up or are otherwise unavailable, you are the Extreme Contingencies Planning Group, Miss Sheil. At this rate, if you stay alert and avoid bloody draughts, you could be Prime Minister within the week. So, I repeat, what would you say was the purpose . . .

Ms Sheil: It's there, on the folder, in the name. Planning for Extreme Contingencies.

Sir Kenneth: Thank you. Clarity at last. Extreme Contingencies. Now, this report, this plan . . .

Ms Sheil: . . . Which you *implemented*.

Sir Kenneth: . . . Which I *implemented* . . . What were the circumstances of its compilation?

Ms Sheil: I beg your pardon?

Sir Kenneth: How did you come up with it, woman? When . . .?

Ms Sheil: The date's there.

Sir Kenneth: I can see the bloody date.

Ms Sheil: This particular contingency plan was developed at the last biannual seminar session . . . no, at the one before that, the one in Leeds.

Sir Kenneth: So it's out of date?

Ms Sheil: Not necessarily. Many contingency plans remain the same from year to year. They are reviewed regularly, of course. Codicils are added. Revisions made. This report was compiled, from start to finish, eight months ago. Our contingency plan for a Russian invasion goes back decades. We had to change the name of the country from the Soviet Union. Similarly, plans for a reaction to a flood which overhwelms the Thames Barrier were drawn up before the Thames barrier was even put in place . . .

Sir Kenneth: Ah, a brand-new plan, then? Cutting edge?

Ms Sheil: You might say so, Sir Kenneth.

Sir Kenneth: Bit of a wash-out, then?

Ms Sheil: Uh . . . well . . . you might say so, Sir Kenneth.

Sir Kenneth: She might say so. Millie, are you getting this? Nod your head. Thank you. Miss Shiel of the Extreme Contingencies Planning Group admits the plan was a bit of a wash-out. I'd take that to both houses, if anyone would turn up to listen. This seminar session . . .?

Ms Sheil: In Leeds.

Sir Kenneth: Bit of a bun-fest, was it?

Ms Sheil: I'm not sure I understand.

Sir Kenneth: Five-star hotel, drinkies in the evening, big lunches, jaw-jaw all day?

Ms Sheil: You've attended the seminars, Sir Kenneth. Very serious work is done, in – I might say – a hothouse environment. The best brains of the civil service, and the top representatives of the police, the armed forces, the national health, the fire service, disaster relief, trade and industry. Every branch of government is represented. It is our brief to think the unthinkable.

Sir Kenneth: I've read the hand-out.

Ms Sheil: I'm sorry, it's just that . . . it's been a trying week.

Sir Kenneth: For all of us. I'm sure Millie would rather be home with her cats, but she's here, working. Doing her job. Which is more than I can say for the Extreme Contingencies Planning Group.

Ms Sheil: Sir Kenneth, I resent . . .

Sir Kenneth: I'm sure you do, girlie. I'm sure you do. But, in the meantime, if you could cast your mind back.

Ms Sheil: . . . To Leeds?

Sir Kenneth: Yes. What can you tell me about the formulation of this particular contingency plan which – before you bring it up again – I have implemented?

Ms Sheil: It was on the last day of the final week. Friday, after lunch.

Sir Kenneth: A big lunch?

Ms Sheil: I don't see what that has to do with it, but yes, a big lunch. It was Colonel Tom's birthday. We'd worked hard all week – fifteen contingencies were fully assessed and planned for – and . . .

Sir Kenneth: . . . And the wine flowed?

Ms Sheil: A little. You have to understand, fifteen contingencies . . .

Sir Kenneth: Terrorist attack with conventional weapons on the Channel Tunnel. Terrorist attack with depleted uranium "dirty bomb" on the New Festival of Britain. Nice. An outbreak of smallpox in Birmingham. Collapse of a high-street bank. Military coup by a separatist party in one constituent of the United Kingdom . . .

Ms Sheil: Scotland.

Sir Kenneth: I know we mean Scotland, but we can't – couldn't – say so on an official document. Don't suppose it matters now. Anyway, another great fire of London. Forty nights of rain. Virulent strain of foot and mouth disease. Riot and race war in Manchester. Co-ordinated strikes in the vital services. Assassination of the sovereign or Prime Minister – I can see you enjoyed that one. Nuclear strike by a rogue state. And so forth . . .

Ms Sheil: Yes.

Sir Kenneth: Fifteen contingencies. Considered in depth. Resources allocated. Initial and long-term responses framed. Speeches written for the PM to deliver solemnly – or the Deputy PM in the case of Contingency Ten. Standing orders to the emergency services, the armed forces. Everyone down to the postman and the gas-meter reader would have a sealed envelope to open, which would tell them exactly what to do.

Ms Sheil: You are familiar with the remit of the Extreme Contingencies Planning Group, Sir Kenneth.

Sir Kenneth: Yes, all too familiar. Do we have one of these Leeds plans here . . .

Ms Sheil: . . . The folder, Sir Kenneth.

Sir Kenneth: Not this one . . . not this *thing* . . . the one we implemented. One of the other ones. Contingency Three, say . . .

Ms Sheil: That would be . . . the smallpox contingency. Smallpox was only an example. Any other epidemic disease is covered. Yes, on the shelf, Sir Kenneth. The yellow volumes.

Sir Kenneth: I see. Four thick, bound books.

Ms Sheil: It is – was – a major contingency, Sir Kenneth. We had to be very thorough.

Sir Kenneth: Two thousand pages.

Ms Sheil: Yes, sir. Two thousand pages. There's another volume of footnotes and references.

Sir Kenneth: That's typical, is it? The length.

Ms Sheil: For a major contingency, yes.

Sir Kenneth: And how many pages are in this folder? Come on, you can see it. It's on the table.

Ms Sheil: Two, sir.

Sir Kenneth: And one of them is this . . . doodle. A stick figure with bug-eyes and a speech balloon reading "aaargh . . . brains" . . .

Ms Sheil: Dieter did that.

Sir Kenneth: So, you spent all month on Major Contingencies. Fifteen of them. Four volumes each. That's, uh, easy sum. Thirty thousand pages. All signed off on. Ready for implementation.

Ms Sheil: Contingency One to Contingency Fifteen.

Sir Kenneth: But that's not all that came out of the seminar session. There were Twenty-Five Contingencies.

Ms Sheil: . . .

Sir Kenneth: Speak up.

Ms Sheil: Yes. Twenty-five.

Sir Kenneth: The Friday afternoon contingencies. Contingency Sixteen: Attack by the Evilerons from Planet X . . . to Contingency Twenty-Five: the Return of King Arthur from Avalon in England's Hour of Greatest Need?

Ms Sheil: Yes.

Sir Kenneth: Shame we can't use the last one. How was the Friday afternoon agenda decided?

Ms Sheil: We all chipped in.

Sir Kenneth: Did you? Did you personally chip in . . .?

Ms Sheil: Yes.

Sir Kenneth: And were you responsible for . . .?

Ms Sheil: . . . Oh no, Sir Kenneth. Not that. Mine was, ah, Contingency Twenty-Two.

Sir Kenneth: Invasion of Gnomes and Pixies from Fairyland.

Ms Sheil: . . .

Sir Kenneth: Speak up.

Ms Sheil: . . . Yes, that was me, but . . .

Sir Kenneth: No buts. The purpose of the Extreme Contingencies Planning Group is – or, rather, was – as you say, planning for extreme contingencies. Pixies would count.

Ms Sheil: It wasn't . . .

Sir Kenneth: It wasn't what?

Ms Sheil: Serious.

Sir Kenneth: A bit of a laugh, then.

Ms Sheil: Yes. At the time. It had been a long month, a very demanding session. Quite depressing, actually. Contemplating death tolls. Deciding who would live or die, sometimes – knowing that decisions made in the Group might be very hard to live with. So . . . on the Final Friday . . . it was a bit of a tradition.

Sir Kenneth: I understand.

Ms Sheil: It was Jimmy McKay. Contingency Twenty-Four. He played a lot of those computer games . . . and he had a *Shaun of the Dead* T-shirt.

Sir Kenneth: *Shaun of the Dead*?

Ms Sheil: It's a film, Sir Kenneth.

Sir Kenneth: Really? I haven't been to the cinema since *Chariots of Fire*. Don't see the point. Films are all made up. You can't learn anything from them. Not like *Chariots of Fire*. That really happened, you know.

Ms Sheil: So did . . .

Sir Kenneth: . . .

Ms Sheil: . . .

Sir Kenneth: Speak up. I shan't tell you again.

Ms Sheil: So did *Shaun of the Dead*, Sir Kenneth.

Sir Kenneth: If you say so. I shall download it from the Internet, if there is an Internet any more. So, Contingency Twenty-Four . . .

Ms Sheil: *Which you implemented* . . .

Sir Kenneth: Which, and I can't stress this enough, I implemented. As soon as the news was in, it was automatic. The services were ready for the word, for the response that was needed, that would have to go out. I didn't panic, Miss Sheil, I came into this room. I looked at these shelves. I knew we had a contingency plan . . .

Ms Sheil: Contingency Twenty-Four: In the Event of the Zombie Apocalypse . . .

Sir Kenneth: Yes. Bit dramatic that. No shilly-shallying. No double-talk about reanimated citizens with anthropophagous tendencies. No, the plan has it on the front. What it means: Zombie Apocalypse.

Ms Sheil: You did read it . . .?

Sir Kenneth: It wasn't my job to read the Plan, woman. It was my job to implement it.

Ms Sheil: Good lord . . .!

Sir Kenneth: Yes, good lord. Indeed, Jesus F—k. I see you've not written that down in full, Millie. I quite understand. But Jesus Creeping F—k on toast.

Ms Sheil: The generals, the police, the hospitals, the emergency services . . .?

Sir Kenneth: They were ready. They were waiting for their orders. For the precious plan. Which we developed and paid for. It wasn't cheap, you know. Jimmy McKay probably got a whacking bonus. So, what do you think we transmitted? What went out by e-mail, text, courier's letter?

Ms Sheil: Jimmy's plan?

Sir Kenneth: Yes, Jimmy's plan. You saw it.

Ms Sheil: Yes.

Sir Kenneth: You read it.

Ms Sheil: Yes.

Sir Kenneth: I didn't, of course. I trusted the Extreme Contingencies Planning Group. More fool me. Can you remember Jimmy's plan?

Ms Sheil: Yes.

Sir Kenneth: All three words of it?

Ms Sheil: Yes.

Sir Kenneth: They were . . .?

Ms Sheil: . . . Run away screaming.

Sir Kenneth: Anything to say for the record? Are you satisfied with the performance of the Extreme Contingencies Planning Group? How would you self-assess your contribution to this crisis?

Ms Sheil: . . . Inadequate?

Sir Kenneth: Millie, pass me my golf clubs. Thank you.

Ms Sheil: Minister? Sir Kenenth?

Sir Kenneth: *Run away screaming!* How's that for a plan, girlie! *Run away f——g screaming!* Are you listening now? Are you satisfied? Was it a laugh? Was it?

Ms Sheil: . . .

Sir Kenneth: The bloody woman's not answering. Not surprised. Are those brains, Millie? All that cleverness on the table. Wasted. RUN AWAY F——G SCREAMING! Fat load of good that was. I think we could have come up with it on our own without bloody consultants and committees and expense accounts and all that waste. I'm declaring the Extreme Contingencies Planning Group dissolved. In fact, bloody defunct! It is a dead Group. It is no more. It is deceased. Its battered-out brains are spilled on the table.

. . .

Sir Kenneth: Millie, what are you doing? Don't eat that. It's disturbing. Millie? You're still writing, so . . . no, Millie, don't eat those. Millie . . .

MONDAY, MAY 6
2:26 P.M.

I saw my first zombie today, and it was brilliant.

It was one of those really old blighters; I'm dubbing them "Templars" because they're skeletal like the knights in De Ossorio's TOMBS OF THE BLIND DEAD. So old its skin was grey, bits flaking away here and there; nose, eyes, ears, and lips all completely gone. Slow as fuck, could barely gimp along. Just a few shreds of some brittle cloth left draped around it. No noise, no smell. Have no bloody idea how it knows where anything is. But its rotten fucking head turned towards me when I laughed.

I reckon that means one of the barricades has been breached. Strange that this divvy was alone.

Well, if truth be told . . . I didn't wait to make sure it was solo. It was a bit of fun, yeah, and I might have danced right up to it for a second and called it something mum would have belted me for, but then I realised: There was blood all over it. Fresh, bright red claret, totally Fulci. This Templar had noshed recently, and something told me the meal had been human. By himself, it was hard to believe he could catch a fucking thing, but if his mates showed up . . .

So I had it away on my toes and now I'm back in me diggs again. That was five minutes ago.

I know what some of you are thinking right now: Mark, you wanker, two days ago you were telling us this was nothing but a flu outbreak, more H1N1 kind of shite. Tabloid cack, you said. Yellow journalism, inspired by whatever zombie flick the writer'd just watched on the telly. Mark, you said this was as likely as alien probes up your arse, or as Uwe Boll making a good movie.

Well, kiddies, I'm a big man, and I'm here to tell you I was dead fucking wrong. Or rather – they're dead and I was wrong.

The filth wouldn't let us close enough to the barricades to get a look at them before, so fucking right we thought they were just sick. Maybe some publicity gig for this Nude Festival of Britain shite. Or a hoax, like that thing somebody pulled online a year ago where they hijacked a BMC News web page and claimed the flu was reanimating the dead. I didn't believe that, and there was no reason to believe this.

(Yes, I know I'm living in one of the new quarantined areas so there was no reason really to suspect a hoax, but it made more sense than the alternative, dinit?)

So it's bang on, all of it. Thousands of real, unalive Templars are loose in the city. And since they're covered in blood, I'm going to take the next leap and say they eat us, you and me, mates. And after they eat us, we come back as them – mindless, fucking shambling monsters. Dunno yet if they're true Romeros all the way – do they die if you damage the brain, or is it something weird like that Japanese flick STACY, where they had to be cut into 165 pieces?

Whatfuckingever. What it boils down to is: This is it. The big one. The Apocalypse. The final battle. Us vs. them. The movie no one ever had the nadgers to make: WAR OF THE DEAD.

In fifty years, Romero will be considered a prophet and his movies will be training films.

Game on.

TUESDAY, MAY 7
10:37 A.M.

(FRIENDS-LOCKED POST)

So I had to bag off quickly yesterday because Julie was coming over, yeah? And me, I thought, Well, Mark, here's where she lays it on the line and says she needs you to protect her, to see her through this, you're the action man and nobody knows the zombies better than you. She'll say, Mark, you've seen it all, from WHITE ZOMBIE up through ZOMBIELAND, and nobody knows more about the walking dead than you. Of course she'll throw in, I was wrong when I said THE BEYOND was a bag of wank and you're wasting your time on that cack. And then she'll rip my clothes off and we'll be having it off like we're in DELLAMORTE DELLAMORE, in the living room, in front of my window, so that barking mad Henry across the way can see every lick and thrust. It'll probably be the closest to real sex that window licker's ever had.

Except . . . it didn't exactly go down that way.

She dumped me.

Over, done. I can't fucking believe it. Said that if things were going seriously bad, I wasn't who she wanted to be with. Said it'd been fun, but she's going to try to get out of London and probably won't be back.

Didn't even kiss me goodbye. Just turned and walked out.

Well, you know what? Fuck her, and her university, and her Masters dissertation's twaddle on Lacanian and

Marxist theory in European horror films of the 1970s and all that pretentious arty-farty shite she liked to go on about. Fuck her and "Mark, you need to get a real job and get out of that video shoppe" and only liking flicks that are subtitled. I'm glomming she's really a todger dodger anyway. Fuck her.

Except I won't. Not anymore.

After she left I nipped on down to the corner shop for vodka and crisps. The streets are strange hereabouts – no cars. Quiet. Everyone's got the abdabs, they're all holed up inside. Naff, the lot of 'em.

Fuck 'em all. I put on DAWN OF THE DEAD (1978 original, bollocks to the remake) and started on the voddy. By the time I got to DIARY OF THE DEAD, I was arse-over-tit. Christ, I must've been, because I even put on that Bollywood disaster MY HUSBAND THE ZOMBIE at some point.

That was yesterday. Today I've got a headache that could split open your grandmum's quim, no bird, and a notice taped to my door telling me that I'm now under food rationing and giving me the address of where I can go to pick up my daily dole.

Fuck me. Suppose the corner store's closed. Shouldn't have been so anxious to put the booze away last night, because I might very fucking well not get any more for a while.

The vid shoppe's closed for now, so I guess I'm temporarily out of work. At least the Queen – if she survived the attack on Buck House – is providing my food. Maybe she'll pay my rent, too.

In the meantime, I'm going to log off and go start up Bianchi's BURIAL GROUND. I think I'll fast-forward through the sex (which'll just make me want that gash again) and just watch to see how they bust all those zombie heads. So far my streets are still empty, but I should brush up . . . just in case.

▶ **FROM CHIRP.COM**
@THEZOMBIEKING
2:11 PM MAY 7TH FROM CHIRPOUT

Standing in line now for rations 2 hours.
Lines 3 blx long & patrolled by coppers w/guns drawn.
Dont come to St Bodolphs unless yer starving.

TUESDAY, MAY 7
4:26 P.M.

So they sent us to St. Botolph's for our rations, stood in line for four hours while twitchy boydem walked next to us fingering their guns, and what I got out of it was one brown paper bag with a loaf of bread, some nasty smelling cheese, two litres of water, a couple of tins of some veggie or other, some apples so mushy I can push a finger through 'em, and some other shite I can't even identify.

A boy could waste away on this diet. Hope the apocalypse ends soon so I can eat some decent takeout again.

The coppers were strange, too. Looking around all edgy, full of aggro, like they were expecting an ambush. For fuck's sake, the Templars are so slow and papery that one swing from a stick could take down three of 'em, so what's with all the nerves?

When I got back to me gaff, peeped that nutter Henry is nailing boards up over his windows. He's on the second floor, like I am. Boy's daft. Or hasn't seen enough movies, because if he had, he'd know they can't fucking climb.

For me tonight it's RETURN OF THE LIVING DEAD 3, the one where the girlfriend gets killed and comes back as the zombie with the torn clothes and the pins stuck all through her flesh because she needs pain and a lot of it. Best part of all: Her name's Julie.

WEDNESDAY, MAY 8
12:03 P.M.

Got pissed last night with the last of the voddy. Ended up passing out to old skool PLAGUE OF THE ZOMBIES. Hammer horror and zombies as slave labour. Absolutely no one gets eaten. They had no idea, did they?

Woke up a few minutes ago, went to my window, looked down . . . and there they are.

Zombies. Gimping about in my street.

Not all of them move like they're solid monged, though. Some of them seem to be getting about well; in fact, I'd think they were friends and neighbours just recovering from a night at the afters if they weren't trailing their intestines behind them.

As if I had any friends and neighbours. Aside from you lot, that is.

The ones who can amble piss-easy seem to be new; even from up here I can tell they aren't colourless and flaky like the Templars. They don't walk with their arms extended, like cheap zombies (ZOMBIE HOLOCAUST, anyone?), and I don't know what they're doing down there. They just kind of stroll along. Looking for a bite, I reckon.

I've got to see one up close.

Done

WEDNESDAY, MAY 8
12:22 P.M.

Awright, Mark – that was a bad idea.

I went down the stairs and up to the gaff's front door. It's a heavy one, with a little window inset and solid locks. Somebody had brought a heavy chest into the hallway and it stood nearby; I guessed they'd used it recently to block the door, but had left. Since it wasn't in place, they obviously hadn't come back.

I went up and looked through the window. The nearest of 'em was a Templar, maybe 50 feet up the street. Looked safe, in other words.

So I unlocked the door and opened it.

I hadn't made a sound, but somehow that fucking old wanker knew I was there. It turned towards me, and made this kind of whispery hiss, I suppose that was the most it could manage with its rotted vocal cords. That one microbudget thing from '87, THE DEAD PLACE, the one about the tourist trap that's turned zombie, got the sound bang on.

And then I heard something else, off to my left. I turned, and two of the newer ones were coming at me, not running exactly but kind of almost dancing towards me. One was slower, thrown off balance by a missing arm. The other had chunks missing from cheek and neck. Blood was still oozing from the wounds, so that one at least hadn't been dead that long. They were dressed like me, about my age. Could've been drinking mates.

Could've been me.

They wanted to eat me.

I yelled at them, then stepped back into the building doublequick and slammed the door just as they hit it. I turned the lock and put my face up to the little window just to taunt them, fuck with them a bit.

Fortunately I saw the fist drawn back just before it hit the glass. If I hadn't jerked to the side when I did, it would have been goodbye Marky. As it was, a shard hit my chin and carved it up nicely. But I didn't have time to notice. I got my weight behind that big chest and moved it on over to the door. If whoever'd left the chest there was coming back, they'd be SOL. I didn't wait to see if it'd hold, but jogged straight back up here.

It's holding . . . but barely. There must be a score of them down there now, a mix of old and new. All pounding on my door. One of them looked around and saw me up here, and that at least got them away from the door. They actually tried to climb the bricks, stupid fucks. I watched one tear its fingernails off, not that it cared. They won't get up here.

Naff bastards. Try to get me, will they? It'd serve them right if I yanked the window down, took a wazz on the lot, and screamed, "Have some of that!"

Not that I'd do that, mind you. <G>

WEDNESDAY, MAY 8
6:22 P.M.

They finally moved on a few minutes ago. Persistent buggers.

Me, I'm feeling contemplative tonight, like I want to prove Julie's not the only one who can formulate the big thoughts.

First, a few questions: Dear readers, what's it like where you are? I notice no one's commented on my last two entries. Where are you, especially joss_manders and zombielurv? You mates are always right there with the witty fucking repartee in the comments. Are you on the run, or just decided I'm completely daft? Seen a zombie yet? Still got power?

On the telly, some BBC reporter I've never seen is urging us all to stay inside, to keep the doors and windows locked and barricaded. They're not coming right out yet and saying what we all know, but keep talking about "the victims of The Death" (always got to give it a fucking name, don't they?), like they're just sick and can be treated with a shot and a pill.

Well, a shot, maybe . . .

There's quick footage of some kind of crowd, looks like maybe the protests around All Hallows. Sawhorses and sandbags, coppers, army, people looking frantic. It's night and dark, so it's hard to make out, but there are screams somewhere in the distance, and gunfire.

Pretty fucking spectacular. DIARY OF THE DEAD could've used this. Except this is a lie, too, because I know for a fact this footage is a week old now.

Back to Miss Earnest BMC Reporter telling us to stay inside until the "situation is under control".

Ha. That's a larf.

Which is why tonight's entertainment will be Jackson's BRAINDEAD and SHAUN OF THE DEAD. Possibly the two finest entries in the zom–com sweepstakes, although as most of you know, I'm also a big fan of the 1975 German Nazi parody DER UBERTOD. Later I might even toss in Hong Kong's BIO–ZOMBIE and cheer on Woody Invincible.

If there are any of you still reading this out there, maybe you're sitting in front of your computer right now wondering why I'm still watching zombie movies when I've got the real thing outside. Mark, you're saying, shouldn't that be the LAST thing you'd be wanting to watch?

Let me put it this way: Ever hear of how birds, after a bad breakup, will watch nothing but romantic comedies for weeks after? (I work in a video shoppe, mates – I can always tell when a girl's just been dumped, because it's about the only time we can rent all those bloody Sandra Bullock and Katherine Heigl flicks.) Well, this is the same kind of thing – except without the bird and the romantic comedies. I've been watching these movies for near 20 years now, ever since I figured out how to operate the remote on mum and da's telly. I've seen everything from ARMY OF DARKNESS to ZOMBOID (the best science fiction/horror zombie crossover ever, and fuck you, zombielurv). I'm the A to Z zombie man. I love these movies because they reduce life to its simplest, most basic terms: Human survivor versus shambling, mindless consumers who only want to eat that which they once were. The moral of a zombie movie is this: Are you human or meat? Good enough to avoid becoming one of the sheep, or will the same neuroses that killed them bring you down? Will you freeze with your finger on the trigger? Will you trip and fall when you run? Will you just cower and offer up a free lunch?

Are you one of the fighters? Or are you just another zombie?

Is that why none of you have commented for a while? Too busy hiding in corners, crying, whimpering, stumbling, splitting up at the wrong moment, running out of ammunition, hiding behind a door that's not strong enough, stupidly standing in front of a wall made of rotten balsa wood?

Not me. I'll be Peter in DAWN, shooting their ugly brains out and flying off into the rising sun with a blonde; I'll be Shaun with a cricket bat, or Henry the Red in ARMY, riding in on horseback to bash zombie skulls with a whirling mace. I'll be Jimmy "General" Washington in BLACK ZOMBIE, I'll be Woody Invincible.

Before this is over, the rest of you just might wish you'd watched a few more zombie movies.

THURSDAY, MAY 9:
1:14 P.M.

Tried to call Jules today. I admit it. Didn't matter anyway, because there was no answer. I have no fucking clue as to whether she wouldn't answer or couldn't answer.

And you know what? I'm fine with either option. Because frankly it doesn't exactly tear me up to imagine her surrounded by zombies, their grotty half-chewed fingers pulling her down, ripping chunks of flesh out while she screams. I like to imagine that they'd eat most of her, but leave just enough to come back as half a zombie, maybe nothing but a head and a spinal column. And some last little part of her – some little part even deeper than that R complex Dr. Logan talks about in DAY OF THE DEAD, the reptile brain – knows fucking well what's happened to her, but all she can do is lay there in some stinking gutter and feel the hunger burn and hope to fucking Christ that somebody shows up with a nice iron bar and puts her out of her misery.

THURSDAY, MAY 9
8:53 P.M.

Old Mrs. Morgenstern from down the hall just knocked on my door, asking if I could spare some food. Told her I didn't have any, but maybe we could go out and get her some tomorrow. She left looking pretty beat, the ropey old slag.

Of course I've got three tins of veggies and half a loaf of bread left, but she's what – 75, 80? I've still got most of my life in front of me, I need this food more than she does. It's just plain common sense.

Watching RESIDENT EVIL tonight, and imagining myself side-by-side with Milla Jovavich. Not that I'd mind if she wanted to make the beast with two backs, either.

FRIDAY, MAY 10
9:35 A.M.

Ate the rest of the bread for brekky, down to two tins now.

After I finished the loaf, I watched someone die. For real, I mean.

I was gnawing at the heel (waste not want not, my mum always said), when I glanced outside and saw Nutter Henry step out of his door. He's always been off his noggin, mind you, but this was the barmiest thing I'd seen from him yet: He was dressed in about three heavy sweaters, gloves, and what looked to be at least two pairs of trousers, and he was carrying a stack of lumber.

WTF? Lumber?

Of course the zombies started towards him right quick, with two fresh ones – a fat middle-aged man and a young bird – leading the pack. Henry, he just sees them coming, and – calm as you like – lays down those 2 by 4's. He must've had at least 20 there, each about four feet long. Henry picks one up from the pile, and just stands there. Then those first two zombies arrive, hands reaching for him, moaning like they do, and Henry just turns right to them and whaps fatso as hard as he can on the head. Fatso's skull crushes like a seedpod, and he's down, but the board's broke clean in half.

So Henry just dives down, grabs the next board, and lets the gash have it. Her skull must be made of metal, because Henry has to whack her twice, and she gets a fistful of sweater before she falls.

Now I get it. Weapons and armour. He may be a window licker, but he's a smart window licker.

I cheer him on, even though I know he can't hear me two stories above him and across the street, and besides, he's focused on the zombie mob growing around him. THWACK! CRUNCH! Four more boards quickfire, and now Henry has to kick bodies away. He sees an opening, and he grabs the boards and runs to his parked car, which is an ancient old battleship that just might be able to plow through a mass of zombies. He sets the board down and digs out his keys, but he's gone eppy, he's jangling them too much, trying to pull out the one key he needs to unlock the door—

—and three of them rush him. He takes out two, but while he's doing that the third one grabs his arm and yanks. It rips out a fistful of sweater, and even though Henry's not injured I can see he's shook up. He grabs another board and really lets that wanker have it, splatters blood all over his own face and doesn't care.

He's also made a lot of noise, and I guess that's attracted more, because there must be at least 50 moving towards him now, some will reach him in seconds . . .

I'll give the naff bastard credit, he used up those boards and held his own for a few seconds, but then they were on him and it was tits up for Henry and I never even heard him scream.

What happened next, though, was . . . interesting. Not what I expected.

Henry disappeared under their backs, so all I could see was arms, heads moving. I knew what they were doing, of course . . .

But they stopped. They hadn't been at him more than a few seconds when they all just stopped and got up, all stained with Henry's claret, some of them with bits of Henry still dangling from mouths and fingers, but they were done. Turned away, already looking for the next one.

And Henry got right up – as a zombie. With chunks missing, of course, tatters of three different sweaters flapping around great bloody holes, but not enough so he couldn't move with the best of them.

It'd happened that fast. No anxious wait over the victim's body, like in DAWN when Peter sits over Roger for what seems like fucking forever. Almost instantaneous.

That was when it struck me, something only hinted at in the movies but never quite extrapolated, never quite got right:

It's why they're always hungry. Because the transformation sometimes happens so fast that they don't have time to really eat. Only a few bitefuls before their meat becomes something they can't munch. It's like someone constantly yanking the banger out of your mouth as you're trying to finish your meal.

Poor fuckers.

There was one final, curious thing to see, though, before the Tale of the Death of Nutter Henry had finished:

One of the zombies – in fact it was a Templar, an ancient fucking monster who'd chomped part of Henry's head – stopped and looked down where Henry had been. It looked like it was trying to work out something in its decaying old head, and I watched, wondering what the fuck it was on about.

It stood there for a while, then finally it bent over, slow, like its joints didn't really work. After a few seconds it came up with something shiny in its nasty paws.

Henry's keys.

Now, I'm thinking about then: It's like a cat, or a baby, it likes shiny things. It can't know what those keys are, or understand what they do. It's over 100 years old, for fuck's sake, they didn't even have cars when this thing went into its coffin.

But fuck me if it didn't put those keys in the car's door lock, and wrench that door open. It fiddled there for a few seconds, then took the keys and climbed in. I couldn't see exactly what it was doing then, but I heard the car's motor crank. Then – the door was still open – the car lurched forward and went 20 feet before it slammed into another car. After a second the motor stopped rumbling and the Templar climbed out from inside and shambled off down the street, as if nothing strange had happened at all.

WTF had I just seen?

I guess it's no different from Big Daddy in LAND OF THE DEAD, picking up a jackhammer and kind of knowing what it does but not figuring out that it needs juice to run . . . but Big Daddy's probably used a jackhammer before. There was no way this thing had ever ridden in anything that wasn't pulled by a horse. Or maybe a serf.

Oh, and one other thing: Big Daddy won that war, didn't he?

SATURDAY, MAY 11
10:15 A.M.

I now officially have no food.

The people on the telly are fucking useless. "Stay in your homes!" they say. "Ration your supplies – it could be several more days before help arrives."

Fuck that. I'm not one of the sheeple. I know there's no help coming, Bob's yer uncle.

I'm not completely alone, either. There are Chirps from blokes in the streets, letting us know how to get around, which streets are relatively clear, where there's a market that hasn't been picked clean, where to meet other righteous warriormen to protect each other.

I'll be fucked if I wait here in this apartment, slowly starving until I go as barmy as Henry, or Mr. Jello in DAY, clutching a fucking cross in my teeth while I let them tear me to shreds. I won't wait until I'm too weak to fight them off when they break in. Because they will get in, sooner or later.

No, today's the day.

I'll probably be on Chirp from now on, mates. Look for @thezombieking. Tell me what it's like where you are, and I'll tell you mine.

Ass-kicking, cue-the-heroic-music time.

SATURDAY, MAY 11
12:32 P.M.

Sorry, all. You haven't heard me on Chirp yet because I haven't left the gaff. Here's why:

I haven't got anything to use as a weapon.

I know how that sounds. Mark, you're saying, you're The Zombie King, you must have something, even if it's not a gun.

Look, I'm not some sporty chap with a closet full of bats and paddles and bows and croquet mallets. Haven't played any of those fucking games since I left school. Don't own a car, so I haven't got anything like a nice hefty crowbar. I live in an apartment, so I don't have the usual house tools. Crikey, I don't even cook. The biggest utensil I've got is a steak knife.

I've got a screwdriver, and yeah, I've seen screwdrivers driven into a few movie zombie brains . . . but those were usually courtesy of Tom Savini, and Mr. Savini's not fucking here, is he? It's just not realistic in the here and now, in the New Millennium (long time since you heard that fucking term, I bet). How many brains can I drive a screwdriver into before they start screwdriving teeth into my arm? I need something with length and heft.

SATURDAY, MAY 11
2:17 P.M.

Well . . . I'm tooled up.

Got a spear.

I went to that utility closet that Marvin, the building manager, sometimes uses up on the third floor. Door was open. There wasn't much in there – buckets, rags, bottles of cleaning chemicals – but Marvie did have this ancient mop he loved that feels like it was hewn from God's own thigh. I brought that and a few rolls of heavy duct tape I found back down to my place. I figure Marv won't miss them, especially given that I think I saw him wandering around in the street this morning with one eyeball hanging down a cheek.

So first I got the mophead off, then I used that steak knife to whittle both ends of the heavy wooden handle into nice sharp pointy ends. Wrapped duct tape all around the whole thing, just to make it even tighter. Tried a few practice jabs with it, and it feels good in my hands. Fucking good, mates. I even impaled a couch cushion. I'm ready for a little aggro meself.

The street looks light below – can't see more than ten in any direction. I figure I'll just outrun the Templars and give the rest a brain massage with a sharp stick. I'll try to Chirp if I find anything useful.

Any of the rest of you up for meeting at St. Botolph's in Aldgate, see if we can't roust some munch? No? Didn't think any of you had a bit of bottle.

I'm off.

▶ **FROM CHIRP.COM**
@THEZOMBIEKING
2:32 PM MAY 11TH FROM CHIRPOUT

Made 2 blx. Hiding in Thai shop near Haydon & Minories. Cant make Botolphs. Spear lost. Dont come here. Overrun. Fucked.

SATURDAY, MAY 11
5:15 P.M.

Jesus H. Christ.

In case you didn't catch that the first time, let me try it again: Jesus H. Christ.

They're everyfuckingwhere.

The spear performed like a champion for five minutes or so. Two of the newer ones rushed me almost as soon as I got out the door. The first was a blond bird what took the business end right through one eye (reminded me of ZOMBI 2, it did). But I barely had time to yank that wood out before the second came up, and my first thrust caught him in the neck. It was enough to keep him from reaching me, but I had a bit of a dilemma: If I pulled the spear out for a proper jab into his ugly topper, he'd be on me before I'd even aimed. As it was, that fucking waste was actually pulling himself along the spear, sliding it further and further through his own self, so desperate to reach me he was.

Well, Mark, how did you get out of THAT one, I hear you asking. Did you have a movie for that? Nothing came to mind – so I dropped that spear and legged it.

Fortunately having a five-foot long spear centred in his neck slowed my would-be consumer down, and the rest of the nearest bunch were Templar, old crusty buggers who could barely turn to look at me as I dodged past.

When I reached Minories, the news wasn't good: There

were dozens in every direction, new and old. Looking at myself as a nice steak with legs, I did the only smart thing and ducked through the broken doorway of the Thai restaurant (where I'd eaten my share of curries). A quick survey showed it to be empty, but I carefully checked behind the counter (I've seen DAWN and LAND OF THE DEAD, mates, I know about zombies popping up from behind counters). Then I crouched behind a table and peeped out.

It looked safe, so that's when I Chirped like a good little explorer should.

When I looked up, there was a Templar lumbering out of the kitchen.

He was frail enough that I could probably have stopped him with a sneeze . . . but then some of the others might have heard that sneeze, too.

So I gave up on all thoughts of a nice meal acquired from St. Botolph's and took to my feet.

I made one stop on the way at a busted-in shop and grabbed two bottles of water and a crushed packet of biscuits, then it was home again, jiggityjig.

Because I sure wouldn't want to be out there after dark.

SUNDAY, MAY 12
6:32 P.M.

Fucking hell I'm hungry. I can't Adam and Eve we've still got power in this area. What fucking good is power when you're starving? I'd trade all these discs for the world's worst bowl of rice right now.

Been following a few other Chirps from the locals. One bloke (fucker had an axe) did make it to St. Botolph's, but said it was empty. No people, no fedz, no food. No indication as to where anyone went, or should go.

Just lots of fresh new zombies.

Chirps from other parts of the city make it sound just as bad everywhere.

No food's coming. Our fearless leaders have undoubtedly locked themselves away with steaks and wine and left us wretches out here to fend for ourselves. There will be no last minute appearance from the cavalry. No SWAT team, no Army men, no Dead Reckoning. This is a zombie holocaust, but unlike the film of that name there won't be some native tribe showing up at the last second to put the zombies down like so many insects crushed underfoot.

Ladies and gents, I'm afraid we are well and truly fucked.

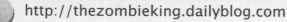
MONDAY, MAY 13
8:57 A.M.

Third day without food. I'm up early because it's fucking
impossible to sleep when your interior regions are in
revolt.

Fuck this. All of it. Fuck Julie. Fuck the government.
Fuck the movies that lied to us all these years. This is
what it's really about – an empty belly and no one to tell it
to.

Fuck you.

Fuck me.

Done

TUESDAY, MAY 14
3:02 A.M.

No more. No more hunger. No more pointless attempts. No more fucking movies that it turns out don't know shite.

And after this one, no more words.

Because I'm done. Laying here in the night, feeling myself wasting away, it's suddenly become crystal clear what my real destiny is:

I'm the monster now.

Time to claim my true legacy and accept it.

From now on, I'll be the one scratching at your doors and windows. I'll be the one just out of sight around the corner of the building, waiting to jump out at you and tear a bloody chunk from your shoulder. I'll be the one you can't stop, always right behind you, reaching out for your neck. I'll be Johnny, your brother; Stephen, your boyfriend; Cholo, your enforcer. Those cold fingers you'll feel will be mine. Mine will be the last face you see, stained with your blood. Pray now, if you're so inclined. Enjoy a last smoke, a last pint, a last shag, a last wank. Soon you'll be my meat.

I'm coming to get you.

British Media Corporation
Internal Communications

---

999 Emergency Service
for BMC Staff

This is Information for people who work at the BMC.

This information has been updated at 03:40 PM Thursday 9 May.
There are major incidents at all BMC buildings.

Service Status:

There are currently major incidents reported at all key BMC buildings. Official government advice is to "run away screaming". For information during an incident please call 0800 0666 999.

Introduction The BMC's "999" Emergency Information Service is designed to keep people who work at the BMC (a private company formed when Channel 4 and the British Broadcasting Company merged) informed during emergency situations such as major security alerts, fires or power failures at all key BMC buildings which might prevent them from reporting to work as normal. 999 provides up-to-date information for staff who have either been evacuated from, or hear media reports about an incident involving, a key BMC building.

For information updates please keep checking the usual BMC Emergency Channels:

Phone: 0800 0666 999
Online: bmc.co.uk/999
Gateway: 999 Emergency Information
Ceefax: page 999

Monday, 13 May

Dear Laura,

          I hope you're well, and happy. Of course, I know
that you are probably neither. To be happy you'd have
to be insane. To be well you'd have to be
You'd have to be alive, and

                    yourself. I don't want to visualise the
          alternative. But then anyway, I
haven't seen you for over twenty years, not since you
and Jean moved to France. So I don't know what you'd
look like now even if

          Even if.
I've still got that picture Jean took of us, you and me,
at Brighton. He was a very good photographer, wasn't
he, Jean. And poor old Ken, well, he and I had only
known each other a week or so, and he used to get so
jealous. Stupid really. Ken was the biggest flirt all
the time we were together. He had three or four
things with other women, too. I always knew, he used to
be so nice to me. Well.

          In the photo you and I are standing on the
pebbly beach against a blue-green sea. You were about
33, and I was just on 37. We both look a good five years
younger than we were - admittedly my reading/close-
focus glasses need renewing, and no chance of that,
but I've looked at the picture often over the years. We
were good-looking girls, Laura, you and I. Maybe you
still are. Were. Not me, I'm afraid. I went grey and
never bothered to colour it. And I got so thin. But I
was lovely then - oh, surely I can say it. That me is
another person, that slim, curvy young woman, with
her naturally blonde hair and those large green eyes
that didn't need glasses at all. And you. You were
beautiful. Your long auburn hair.

          Do you remember when we were really young, in
our teens, when we used to go to Blackheath in the

summer holidays, and end up in the park eating ices and singing songs from West Side Story, and we were so good when boys picked us
up. Just a soft drink in the pub and a kiss, then the bus home. I remember that hot day you and I just sat on the grass on the heath. I think the fair was there - yes, it was - and we went on the carousel and had our fortunes told - can't remember what they said - and then we sat quite near that old church. It was so peaceful even with the noise of the fair and the cars, the hot green grass, the blue sky, everything sort of working out as it should. That church.

That's where it started. I expect you know. Or you did know

before.

The graveyard by the church. There. At Blackheath.

I remember being told once, the whole heath had been a burial pit - I think in the 14th Century, during the Black Death.

When they did it this time, I mean moved the bodies from by the church, Ken kept on grumbling. They "shouldn't be digging up the dead". He wasn't worried about anything medical, mind you, let alone anything religious. Just the ethics. Everything the government did by then - any government - was "wrong - mental - deranged". My God, the way he went on about the Olympics - waste of money, make a mess of it and ruin the economy, etc; and then about losing the Olympics, and then about that other ridiculous Festival they decided we had to have. He was right, of course.

Of course he was, wasn't he.

But when I look back now, you know I get this weird feeling, as if some awful Power - I don't think I mean God, or the Devil - was deliberately and relentlessly driving everything, all of us - people,

governments, countries, the whole
world — towards an abyss.

This isn't a religious conviction either. I don't
mean pre-destined apocalypse, occasioned by the sins
of mankind. Christ, Laura, you know I'm a sort of
hopeful agnostic. I've no idea if anything is out
there, or wherever. But if it were — it would be
neutral and benign. It wouldn't want to punish us —
and certainly not for sins it had itself designed into
us!

This is so bloody depressing.

I didn't want to write to you and start moaning.
I

I wanted to

I just wanted

to talk to you.

So, well, hope you're OK, darling, if I could
wave a magic wand you would be. But we all would be,
then.

All my love,

Ruth.

Dearest Laura,

      The best thing is, I think, just to say how it was for us. It's a very common story. In 2008 Ken's book business started to go down the drain. We lost the shop. It had been a bit rocky for some while. He said, nobody wanted to read any more. But, that wasn't true, of course. He said it was all the free downloading available via the Internet, and later on he said it was the big Google controversy, that would put so many really good writers on the ropes. And kids' minds being poisoned against reading by the remorseless school Curriculum. And the Credit Crunch. And so on. Only in our case, really, it was just the shop had never been in the best place, down that side street. And our customers had got old and died or moved away, and new customers had found everything was cheaper with the big chains. So we folded. We lost the house next. It still upsets me. Those two lovely trees in the garden, and the birds I used to feed in winter. We lived in some rented place a while but then we were in real trouble, and by then too Ken was a pensioner and I soon would be. So eventually we got "housed" up here.

      I call it the Tower.

      Oh, it's not the worst place.

      It's only ten storeys, and the lifts used to work. They don't now, of course.

      We were on the top floor. Typical, he said. Put a couple of arthritic doddery old rejects up on the highest floor and leave them there to rot. Hope they'll fall down the stairs and break a hip, and not inconvenience the useless NHS too long because they'll get inevitable pneumonia, and the nurses will creep in at night and lie them flat so they suffocate. Yes, Ken did get worse as he got older. He was a sort of self-fulfilling prophecy. Do you remember how he was

when you and I first met him? Kenneth Stanton, that
lean handsome guy with his dark hair and black-brown
eyes, and talked like a radio actor, oh yes. He was
lovely then. But life beats it out of you. Or out of
some of us. And then death
                  really beats it right out.
        The first thing I did when we got here, and the
grumbling removal people had left, I went to the front
windows and out on the little private balcony. We'd
been there once before, but it had been driving rain
then. Now I said, "Ken, come and look, you can see
right over London. I can see as far as the river!"
That day it was sunny, a day in autumn. Cold gold
light soaked down, and in the little gardens and parks
laid out among the buildings and roads, trees were
yellow and magenta and red - auburn as your hair,
Laura! And the river glittered like a silver smile.
        But Ken just sat on the old sofa and he started
to cry. Oh God, Laura. Poor Ken. Poor, poor Ken.
        But I began to call this place the Tower. I
lived atop a stately tower, and saw for miles, like a
Queen in a fantasy novel by someone who could really
write, like Angela Carter. Aaabxcd
                  Sorry about that mistake, Laura. It
        happened because somenone just
knowcked on my doorr. Sorry.
        I mean knocked. No one does. No one gets up here
now. The whole building is empty, apart from rats and
insects, and the pigeons or gulls that sometimes still
visit, though I haven't any scraps left to spare for
them. But there was a knock.
        That's terrifying in itself, except, it's
daylight still and normally nothing - they - don't
seem to be about down there and when they were, it was
only at night. Anyway. Would they knock?

The knocking happened only twice. Then I heard a girl's voice. It called out, "Anyone there? Don't be scared." She didn't sound like

       them. They don't talk to you. Not so far as I've

       Not that I know.

She sounded human, and very young. 16 tops. The way I was once, and you. 16.

I sat still as stone, as they say.

She's gone now.

Well, I'll just have to be extra careful. Ken and Roger saw to it the door was well boarded, the letter-box welded shut, all the extra locks and everything, before

       before. Just as the cupboards and the fridge were well-stocked, yes even the fridge now it doesn't work since the power went off, only crammed with dry stuff now. But even cold food lasted quite well at first after we pushed the fridge out on the balcony for the chilly nights. Thank god for English summers.

I used to have a few plants out there before. They were doing quite well. When the water stopped and we couldn't spare any from the bottles, they died. And do you know this is the most fucking stupid thing of all when I think of the trees in my garden and those plants and the birds I start to cry I cry and when I think of Ken and what must have happened I feel so sorry and I dont cry at all and I think I must be a terrible woman a madwoman and

Dear Laura,

Two days since I wrote to you. Just so you know,
I'm putting these messily-typed letters — Ken's
computer obviously can't run without power, but I
still have some supplies for my faithful old
typewriter — into what used to be my "jewellery box".
Not that it ever was a proper version, only a biscuit
tin with a reproduced Pre-Raphaelite girl on the lid
— some beautiful nymph, with hair a lot like yours.
There used to be my aunt's pearls in this box, and an
emerald ring Ken bought me for my 40th birthday, a
couple of other things. But they all got sold when we
lost the shop. There's only my gold wedding ring in
there now. I took it off after Ken came back. The
little pistol used to be in there too, but it seemed
wrong to leave it with the ring, so that now lives in
the cutlery drawer. As I go gradually more dotty, I
expect I'll take it out one day and try to eat pasta
with it.

What did I eat for lunch today? Some rather
good, out-of-date tomato and roast bean soup. I cook
in a saucepan over two candles. Takes a little while. I
sometimes have a glass of wine as I wait. Just one. I'd
kill for a rasher of bacon, fried or grilled, or a
fresh apple. Well no, I wouldn't kill. I can see the
ruin of the small supermarket just down there, from
my high window. All its windows are gone, and trolleys
and other stuff still lying out there on the pavement
from five days ago. And a wild orchard in that garden
right over there, less than a mile away. I can
remember often seeing that when I walked by, and
marvelling, all those red-green apples and the yellow
pears, and blackberry bushes clawing out over the
wall.

I've seen people fight over them, from up here.
The battles at the supermarket and the other local
shops were worse. Much closer. The off-licence was the
first to go. All that smashing glass and screaming. I
can remember thinking, My God, it really is like this,
the way writers like Wyndham and Christopher had it.
World's end.

I didn't mean to go on so much about that.
I wanted to tell you about her.
I mean the girl.
I suppose inevitably people were going to come
back into this building. Most families got out.
Perhaps they had somewhere more safe to go. Roger's
wife and two sons took off after

what happened that time. They invited me to go
with them. But she, and obviously the boys, are much
younger. She's only about 50, which used to be the new
40, didn't it. I'd have slowed them down, and they'd have
bullied me. I said no. They were gone by next morning.
Later on, when the building was empty, a couple of
times new tenants, for want of a better word, moved in
on the lower floors. Once a man and woman came up to
this floor, but they didn't knock, only swore and ran
down again. There was then a strong bad smell out
there. I think it's more or less gone now.

Whoever was in the building downstairs either
left or

whatever. The horrible assaults when
they
---
tried to

in the beginning
That hasn't been repeated. Of course
there are
the fires, terrible fires, like November 5th gone mad.
Some go on and on. Or die — then spring up again. Or
it doesn't. They're worst in the dark, like the weird
troughs of urban light where electric street-lamps

still work — but all this is distant, on the horizons.
You only smell the smoke now when the wind blows this
way.

I'm rambling on again. I talk to myself aloud
half the time too. Who else do I have? Well, you, my
dear. My Laura.

So then, today I went out on to the balcony to
get some muesli from the old fridge. I'm always
careful. I go when the sun's behind the building, or
the sky is overcast. And I don't stand upright, I crawl.

The air has such a strange smell now, do you
find that? Up here it isn't often any smell of decay.
No, it's more a bizarre inevitable freshness. No cars,
no buses, no trains. No planes even crossing the sky
with their vapour-trail spiderwebs. Nothing electric.
Nothing mechanised. A leafy smell. And something
cindery, rainy cement, concrete, brick. And the river,
which can still smell pretty nasty, has a faint
fishiness now, like the sea. Did it always? It's tidal
after all —

So there I was, and I suddenly heard a step.
Right there on the balcony with me it sounded.

I gave a sort of grunt and froze. Images
without words raced through my mind. Things climbing
up the sides of buildings like Dracula. Stupid. I don't
think they can do that, can they? Or why would they
ever use the stairs?

Then I thought, it wasn't a footfall, but a bird
landing — pigeon, or river gull, or one of those
bigger birds that escaped from the zoo when

When

I turned round and so I saw her.

You see, each of the balconies was originally
closed in either side by a brick wall, and each
balcony shared the wall either side with the adjacent
two neighbouring balconies. So you could only ever
talk to the neighbours, if you ever wanted to, by

leaning out at the front and craning round. But part
of next-door-on-the-right's balcony, and both its two
side-walls, have partly dropped away, leaving a
perilous half slice of ledge and some uneven
brickwork. There had been a fight out there. Somebody
fell right over. Next day you could see the body lying
there below. Then it vanished. In the later rain the
balcony and parts of the walls went. Since then you
can see over the top of the broken wall, and across
the broken ledge, and right into the balcony the far
side.

And that's where she was standing, about 14 - 15
feet away, about four and a half metres, is it? It was
her. The girl.

"Hi," she said.

She didn't look frightened. If anything she
looked a bit amused.

Perfectly visible herself, she'd just watched
the very top of an old woman's grey-haired head, as
she crawled out to take a package from a fridge that
didn't work.

"My name's Gee," she said.

I kneeled there, staring across and up at her.

"Don't be scared," she said again, and so I knew
her. She was the one who'd knocked twice on my door
those couple of nights before. "I'm not," she said, "one
of those things. None of us," she added proudly,
holding up her head, "are like that fucking rubbish.
Oh," she added, looking at me concerned. "Sorry." She
was apologising for using the F word. Forgetting my
generation practically relaunched it.

I edged back so she could see even less of me,
and said, "What do you want?"

"Just t'say hello," she said. She had a soft
London accent. She didn't talk, or didn't know, the
rappy yappy slurry street-talk, the "lingua yucka", as
Ken had called it, of sub-culture teens. But she was

about 18 in fact. Or else recent times had aged her a
little. Her hair was wild and very blonde.
Surprisingly clean. No roots. Her eyes were
splintered-beer-bottle green. She reminded me of
someone. I thought it was you, Laura, but you have
blue eyes, red hair.

"Really sorry," she said. She stretched
suddenly, all that fluid unstiff cat-like stretching
one can manage when one is 16, 18, 25. She wore torn
jeans and a sleeveless T-shirt, greyish or just dirty.
She had a human smell.

It would be impossible, or only impossibly
dangerous, unless she was super-human limber, which
they are not, so far as I know, to spring right across
the space from her balcony to mine.

I eased back off my knees, frankly I had to,
they were hurting, and stood up awkwardly, pressed
into the fridge. From the street below, or any distant
occupied windows, I wouldn't be very noticeable. Not
like her.

I said, "So you're here with some friends, or
your family?"

"My Mum's dead. She came back. Stew took her
head off with the spade. Then we ran." She said this
quite impassively. But from her green eyes some
gleaming tears flowed down her cheeks. She rubbed
them off, as if to free them of sweat or rain, with the
back of her hand.

"Who is Stew?"

"My bloke."

I said nothing.

She said, "There's only five of us. We thought
we could hole up here. Till it stops. Or someone sorts
it out."

I thought, who do you think is going to do that,
you bloody little fool — the US Cavalry? But her

generation don't rate the American military. Come to that, neither does mine. Maybe she thinks the rescuer will be Batman, or Watchman.

She doesn't look crazy. She looks — I like this expression — together. Sad and together and not unkind. She looks like me, Laura. Me when I was young. When you and I really knew each other, before Jean and Ken.

I said, "Look, Gee?"

"Yeah Gee."

"I don't think there's much point in our talking. I haven't got much food — I mean—"

"Oh, we've got plenty of food," she said, proud again. "Would you like some? It's OK," she added, reading my tired old mind, "it's not a trap or anything. I mean, we've gotta look out for each other. We're the survivors."

"Thank you. Gee. I don't need anything. Except I need to go in. Don't stay out on that balcony too long. You shouldn't let yourself be seen."

"Oh, s'OK," she said airily. "Wayne and Stew have got it all covered."

"And don't," I added, "speak to strangers."

She laughed. Laura, her laugh. She laughs like I used to, as you did too. Girls' laughter. Poor little child.

"Take care," I gracelessly and coldly told her, and withdrew into the room and shut the windows. Locked them. They're double-glazed.

If only we could protect our minds like that, cold-proof, shock-proof. Our hearts, of course, it wouldn't be possible. But hearts don't matter any more.

Oh Laura. Sorry, my dear—

Dear Laura,

It gets cold at night. I have a lot of covers on the bed, and also make myself two hot-water bottles by the saucepan and candle method.

I miss Ken. He was always warm. Even when we stopped having sex, he'd warm the bed. But he was often not there. Book hunts or pub nights with male friends. Or his girlfriends. Later he was absent on forays with Roger. Roger's van still ran. He had a hoard of petrol, the kind already frowned on by then. But it worked. That's how all these stores were assembled. God, it's bats putting Evian in a hot-water bottle.

Last night however I was frozen. I had to get up twice to renew both bottles, which ends up with me getting even colder while I wait. And I have to be careful now as well. Even though I re-use it till it's gone, the bottled water and the candles aren't inexhaustible. I could recycle my pee, boil that. But it's bad enough getting rid of all that stuff off the balcony. And the acid could destroy the rubber maybe.

I sometimes thank God I stopped menstruating before we had all this — what did she say? Fucking rubbish. How on earth do young women manage every month? But how does anyone.

The thing was, at 2:00 am, when I was in a sort of sickly doze, I heard loud rock music, down below in the flats.

They must have a battery CD player. Gee and her friends, her bloke. Stew.

Years ago I used to hate loud music played like that, at unsocial hours especially. Though Ken, who could be so vitriolic, would snore happily through it all.

Last night though, it warmed me. It — warmed me through.

There were these young people in the Tower. And they weren't them. They were human still. And — I wasn't all alone.

I did think, of course. My God, they'll be heard for miles. It'll be like a beacon. And no doubt they have some sort of cheery fire burning, incredibly dangerous, candles alight too, and no boards or curtains at windows, as I always, scrupulously, do.

Yet these admonitions some part of my brain just simply flipped aside.

There always are fires anyway, big fires. Maybe this one won't notice.

I lay in my cocoon and gradually relaxed, my feet warmed like toast even as the bottles cooled. My thoughts stopped scrabbling around each other. When I slipped asleep, my dreams stopped trying to find my husband, who was adulterously elsewhere, or doggedly surviving elsewhere, or dead elsewhere for ever and over amen. Or

only just downstairs and dead. Dead twice over — rotting and stinking.

And then I slept through to the morning, dreamless maybe. The best night I'd had in months. Or years. Perhaps since I was 18.

Dear Laura,

About one minute after I woke up, I remembered the music and went into a panic. I sniffed after smoke. A fire! They could have burned the bloody Tower down. There was a time before, but Ken and Rog had gone down and sorted it out. And the building is so damp and leaky by now, full of actual ponds of water from a pipe that burst. Could fire now take much hold?

There was no immediate whiff of smoke anyway. And I was still alive, so far as I could tell.

I was making tea, which takes about twenty minutes, when she knocked on the door.

I knew it was her. Who else. And then her voice: "Mrs Neighbour," she called, sweet and playful, "Don't jump. I'm going to throw something on to your balcony."

I did jump. I jumped up, ricking my back, never at its best first thing — then froze again in bewildered panic. What would she throw? Why?

"I'll be back this afternoon. Kind of midday, if you've got a clock still going. When the sun's right overhead."

That was all. I heard her light footfall go away.

Then I cowered until about five minutes later I heard something land outside, beyond the boarded window I hadn't yet uncovered — I'd had the candlelight from making tea.

After the little thump and patter the thing — whatever it was — made, I wouldn't go and see. After half-an-hour more though I had to get the window clear.

Outside, lying by the fridge, were a couple of chocolate bars. Green and Black's. A favourite.

I stood gaping at them, then undid the window and raked them in.

Then I sat and held them on my lap and I started crying. I cried for the chocolate bars. As if

I'd just found my two lost kittens, or the lost baby I'd
never wanted or tried to have.

But I said about me, didn't I. Ruth, the
unnatural madwoman.

"Thank you for the chocolate," I said, when she
appeared outside just after 12, by Ken's old wind-up
watch which, for some reason, he left behind and which
still goes. "Can you spare them?"

"Oh sure. Thought you'd like it."

"Can I offer you something in exchange?" I
said. "But only this once. I haven't got much."

"You said," she said. "I didn't do it for that."

"Why did you do it?" I kneeled by the fridge on
a cushion, and she, now sitting, looked across the
remaining brickwork and the gap.

"Oh, just." She glanced away, calm as you like.
Even her profile is like my profile, before my nose
got bony and my chin full of strings. "Doesn't it smell
clean now," she said. "The air's really pure. Eco-
friendly." She gave a hard little yap of laughter.
"What's your name, Mrs Neighbour?"

"Ruth."

"Hi, Ruth. My Mum called me Giselle, so I cut
that down to Gee." Her face was bleak.

"Look," I said, "Gee, this probably isn't the best
place for you to hole up. Maybe you should all try to
get right out of London. I don't know, but I don't think
it's safe here. I haven't seen - any of them, but, well,
it can't be safe, can it? And we still don't quite know
how it works - the infection. The Death. Whatever it
is. But you're all young and healthy, so-"

"It's OK," she said. She flashed me a radiant
smile. Her smile is much better than mine. She has
perfect teeth too. She's prettier than I was. Like a
twin sister who just has the edge. Or a daughter,
maybe. The new improved model, Ruth Mark 2. "Wayne
says the countryside's no good. Had some mates in Kent

near the sea. Bad there. This is fine. Anyway, it'll get
sorted. Then everything'll start up again."

Blind faith. Like an early Christian. Oh, it
won't be a problem, that lion eating
me alive. I'll be in Heaven five seconds after, on the
right hand of God.

"We've got a radio with working batteries. We
check for signals twice a day. When they start to
broadcast, we'll know."

"What happens when the batteries fail?" I heard
myself ask, and thought shut up, you wicked old cow.

"Stew says we've got enough for another year.
It'll all be sorted by then."

I thought, yes, it'll all be sorted.

I said, "Won't Stew or Wayne, or one of the
others, mind your giving me the chocolate?"

"No. It came out of my share. I'll bring you
something else when I can."

"That's kind, but no. Keep it for you."

"Can't stop me," she said, flirtatiously. The way
you used to, Laura, when you'd say, oh, we'll split the
bill for lunch. And then you'd pay it.

I sighed. No, I can't stop you. And I don't want
to spoil your faith game: if it's all going to be all
right, of course you can afford to be generous.

"Last night," I said, "your music-"

"Sorry, did it wake you?"

"No, no, it's fine. Only - you might attract
attention, Gee. Both from desperate people who need
food and don't care how they get it, or from-"

"They don't hear music. They're zombies."

Into the cliche of that word, such scorn was
poured.

"We don't know if they can hear, or reason. But
perhaps they can. Just a rudimentary amount. They can
certainly see in some way. And are you lighting a
fire or anything after dark? If you do, you need to be

in a closed space with all holes and windows blacked out."

"Tony," she said, "saw to all that."

Troubled, so troubled, I heard the glib confidence in her voice. At least three tough guys, then, and presumably all of them young. They can hack it. No undead cretin is going to get the better of them.

We sat there a while not saying anything. Why had she sought me out? A mother substitute? No. Poor decapitated Mum must have been at least twenty years — more, almost certainly — younger than me.

I wanted to stay with her though. Looking at her face that seemed like my face when I'd been her age, and her life so unlike mine then, so unlike anyone's in recent times. Except perhaps the Second World War years. But even then the disgusting evil terror had been human in origin. That terror had been — legitimate.

But I was already exhausted. I hadn't spoken to another person for a while.

"I have to go in now. Gee. Thanks again for the chocolate. I'll really enjoy it, make it last. Please, please do take care of yourself."

"You too, Ruthie," she said, standing up, smiling at me, ducking back into the derelict flat behind her balcony. "See you."

Dear Laura,

          Ken and Roger went out that night to pillage a
place near the Elephant and Castle. It was a big old
house, long made over into slummy flats, but word had
got around there was a lot of stuff there, either
hoarded or the result of burglary prior to the
catastrophe: dry goods, books — Ken always wanted
those — weather-proof clothing, alcohol. When Ken and
Rog had done this twice previously, they would always
be gone most of the night. He warned me this time he
might not get back until late morning.

          I hated it when he went out on these forays. I
mean, I knew it was necessary. It was why we still
could hope to have coffee and tea and wine and whisky
and lavatory paper — the luxuries. It was less I got
scared for him than that I felt the night close in. I'd
hear things that weren't there. Well, they were, but
they were rats, nothing worse. Rog's wife was fine
with it. She said to me it was nice when they got the
place to themselves, that was her and the boys. They
never asked me down, I wouldn't have gone anyway. They
were helpful people but very limited and loud,
sometimes cras. They used the N word a lot — they
claimed not meaning "anything", but Christ — that
kind of shit. So I stayed upstairs and tried to sleep
in the empty, jet-black boarded-window dark, to which,
by now, I'm so accustomed.

          It was Rog's wife who came up next day. It was 2
o'clock by then. "He isn't back. Is your Ken back?"

          "No," I said. "But Ken said they'd be extra late."

          "Rog said he'd be back by eleven in the morning.
He's never wrong on that, my Roger."

          She didn't stay but went down again.

          Later, when it started to get dark, I heard her
below, weeping and screaming, having hysterics. The
boys went out looking that night. Never found him. He
never came back, either. I mean he didn't, nor did the

thing he might have, and probably did become. Which is
odd because from all I've heard, they really do have a
sort of — homing instinct. They do tend to try to get
— home. Which had made me think maybe they could
still reason. Something left in the cavity of their
decaying dehumanised brains. Some memory, lonely
hankering after the one they were
                    even when they were shambling wrecks,
        with
        pieces gone from their bodies, their organs
laid bare or partly hanging out, their eyes rotting
in the sockets, their tongues dangling, disconnected,
out on their chins.
        That was how
        That was how
        He
        Ken
        That
        He came back like that.
        In
                those days I sometimes used to open the
        door,
        obviously, even go down a flight to carry
messages to Rog.
        That night and the next day went, and I knew. I
didn't cry. I just paced about. I couldn't eat. I drank a
whole bottle of water from some Scottish spring. And
then I drank three glasses of wine in half-an-hour
and threw up. What a waste.
        It was when I walked down to ask Rog's family
if there was any news, knowing there wouldn't be, and
there wasn't, and then I trudged back up. I ate some of
the very last stale crackers. I had this awful thought
of how very much longer the stores would last, with
only me to use them up. And then the even more awful
thought that nothing new would ever arrive to replace
them. Ken, though by that time approaching 70, was

still quite strong and able. But even by the year I
was 61 I'd stopped being at all able. My back — ankles
— all of it stiffening and aching. Domestic tasks were
about all I could — can — manage. Certainly poor old
decrepit Ruth could not negotiate ten flights of
stairs down, a swift canny search outside for
anything worth having, let alone lugging anything,
even herself, ten flights up again to her flat.

I'd shut the door and locked it. The door was
already boarded over, strengthened with sheets of
metal — panels off old washing machines, that sort of
armoury. Over the fused-shut letterbox Rog had welded
a steel plate.

It was the middle of the night. I don't know
what time. Pitch black. I'd fallen asleep in a chair.

Something outside.

As I said, they don't knock. Not so far as I
know, but for God's sake, I only know from what Rog or
Ken told me.

And Ken didn't. He didn't knock.

It was like

a small elephant perhaps, stumbling and
shuffling and banging against the door, all its body,
as if by accident. Or not an elephant. Not anything
alive. As opposed to animated. Re-animated.

Slump and bang, shuffle and slide and bang. On
and on. Like a shutter or door in a high wind. But
there was no wind.

I knew what it was, who. It wouldn't go away.
And it might have super strength, no longer afraid to
harm itself, intent only on some blind quest to
return.

I didn't love him, hadn't loved him for years, if
I ever even had loved him ever and maybe I didn't but
I knew he was out there and I thought he — it — would
break in the door and perhaps he would have?

He had taught me how to use it. I'd found that
difficult — he was so impatient — but in the end I
grasped the principle. I mean the little gun, the
pistol, which Ken himself had brought back early in
May, with a cache of bullets. He had cleaned it and
kept it loaded, like the other guns and the knives he
and Rog took when they went out. The pistol was in the
box: with the pre-Raphaelite nymph on the lid.

I knew I'd have to undo the door
I must have been in a sort of trance
I remember it so clearly as if
I saw it from high above
I walked to the door with the loaded gun
I opened the door carefully
I could smell
I could smell the stink the deathstink
I could smell it
I could see
     it
I raised the pistol as it swung forward
I thrust the gun straight through its left eye
I squeezed the trigger pulled the trigger
whatever you do

There was an awful sort of crack. Not an
explosion. This insane ghastly crack like a bone
breaking but an instant soggy echo and everything
inside Ken's head, under his hair that was still thick
and glossy, all that tissue and blood and little
spraying fragments like tiny pieces of the stale
crackers all splurged away and hit the opposite wall.

It — the thing — fell down and a gush of air
came out of it — not breath, some gas. the smell was so
terrible it

     didn't matter. It belonged to some other
    dimension and didn't count.

     It flopped on the floor for a while, a
    few seconds. My husband, I mean.

When I was sure I went in and relocked
and bolted the door.

In the morning, even through door and wall, I
could smell it, and I was me again and I was sick
again. Still retching, I got a thick towel and went
out and gripped him by it. I don't know how, I
explained about my back. I lugged him off along the
corridor and let him tumble away downstairs.

I ached for days.

My hand and shoulder hurt for days from the
recoil of the gun. But it all got better. At my age, I
was quite impressed by my powers of recovery.

Soon after Rog's family left the building.

Forgive the X-certificate nature of this
letter, darling.

It's helped me such a lot to tell you, ᴴᴷᴷ.

Christ. Sorry. Not Gee.

Laura, I mean. Laura.

All my love,

                    Ruthie.

My Dearest Laura,

For nearly a week now the girl, Gee, has been coming up most afternoons. I sit on a couple of cushions my side and she sits on the other concrete balcony. We talk. Sometimes she brings me something. Do you know, yesterday she brought me an apple! A real one. It was bruised and withered, no juice left – but wonderful. I dug out the single pip too, and bit it to get that almondy-cyanide part in the middle.

What do we talk about? Well mostly about her, but that's right, isn't it? She's young. I find it interesting and sad, and it doesn't tire me out so much now, though I find I get a sore throat every evening from vocalising to someone else so much, even if she speaks so much more than I do. But she's young as I say, 19 in fact. And she's had the others to talk to all this while, Stewart and Anthony and Wayne and Liane – that's the other girl.

I've never met any of them. I'm glad. It would be too much for me. All that energy and positive belief. Don't get me wrong. Of course I'm so pleased they're like that. They need to be. And maybe they are quite right – oh, God, I hope so – you see, even I've caught it a little – hope. At least for them. But I just don't have the spirit any more. Can't keep it up. Perhaps don't want to.

I think, how could I cope if it did get sorted out, and "civilisation" returned. You can bet it would be an even worse police state, everybody dragooned, and frightened to say or write what they thought. The governments would all have us where they want us, have always wanted us. A slave race. And resistance to be crushed for the Public Good – it was getting that way before.

I sound like Ken, don't I?

But anyway. Gee's told me about her life. The usual. One parent family, "Mum" just 15 – which makes her 14 when Gee was conceived. Then endless more kids, not because the mother wanted them, just didn't bother. Gee disliked most of this. She managed to get to uni, and always took precautions when she had sex — the Pill and condoms. She still has a stash. She said she doesn't want to have any babies until "this mess is put right". But the other girl, Liane, is pregnant already. It's probably Tony's. Or Wayne's. I thought, how terrible if anything — and kept my trap shut.

Of course our generation was so lucky. Any transmittable disease curable, and the Pill worked.

She's never spoken again about her mother and what happened at the end.

And I've probably said more than enough.

A couple of days Gee didn't turn up. I missed her. And I was worried. But both times she called through the door later that everything was OK. They do go out. She's told me. I've never spotted them from up here. I think they really are very careful. And they play music softer now. It doesn't often happen. Well, they have to treasure those batteries.

Yesterday, while I was nibbling at the apple, Gee asked me if I can actually open my front door.

I said I could, if I had to, but it was a bit of a job. Unused, the damp has got at it, everything has just rusted and stiffened up. Like me.

She said she was glad I could undo the door, in case of emergency. I didn't ask what type. One doesn't need to. Anything at all could happen nowadays. I don't just mean them. They can happen any time. We live, if we still do live, in a Sea of Chaos, out of which any fucking monster can evolve.

One day anyway my dwindling stores will be gone. She'll be long gone too by then. Quite right. She should be.

Or maybe she's softening me up so the boys can break in and steal the lot. She's asked about the front door after all.

But you get to a point. I mean. What does it matter? And I like her, Laura. It isn't just she reminds me of me, or you, or our youth. She's a decent kid. She made herself a life. She'd learned what not to do. And then this. All this. Oh Laura, it really isn't fair, is it? So not fair, as they say.

So not fucking fair.

Ruth.

Laura
Laura Laura Laura La
No. I'll stop this fantasy.
There's no Laura. Laura's dead. Or
        Laura's _that_
        Dear _Nothing_, then. Dearest ABYSS, Dear
HELL ON EARTH.
        Oh Christ

I hadn't seen her for 3 days running. She didn't come
up to call through the door either. But then, they
might be busy with something, and they were young.
Don't kid yourself, Ruthie, you're not that important.
OK, she doesn't dislike you. A friendly old grown-up
in the ruined world. But a little will go a long way.
She has more important things to do.
        After the third day I began to admit I was
alarmed. I used to peer over the balcony, taking
chances, as I never had. I used to listen at the door.
Just _listen_. They hadn't made much noise, just the
music now and then. No music now.
        I did something I thought, even as I did it, was
ludicrously unwise. I got the door undone. Eased the
boards and oiled the bolts and locks. I didn't actually
open it — just got it so I knew I could. So what was I
planning to do? Go trotting — crawling more likely —
up and down the Tower, looking for her?
        They'd gone. Perhaps there had been some
amazing chance at something — an old mate turning up
with working transport: "Hey, it's fine down at
Eastbourne or up at Glasgow or in the Hebrides," Some
John Wyndham scenario of survival, a fortified
commune, an old working farm, where the still young
and fit could close ranks and get by. It was that. She
might even have suggested they should take me, and

been outvoted. What could I contribute? I wasn't even family.

She said to me one of those times on the balconies, "Y'know, you remind me so much of someone. Don't know who."

Sensibly I said, "Yes, you do me, too. I don't know either."

But that could mean nothing. Nor should it have. They were gone. I hoped she'd do fine. I hoped.

But by then I'd seen a new fire out there, off towards the river. Something, some houses. But then it rained and the fire died. But it made me think. As if it had only just struck me. However quiet it seemed, out there, in that wasteland, lay the ultimate danger.

I started to feel sick with fear. I pushed a heavy chair against the front door. I kept watch from the balcony once the sun went if there was a moon. Sometimes I was out there hours, fell asleep out there bundled in blankets, so stiff I could hardly get up to go indoors.

She came back last night. I hadn't seen anything. Didn't hear anything until I heard her knock on the door.

It was so cold. I'd come inside, put the boards on the windows. The rooms were black and I'd gone to sleep lying on the bed, but the knock woke me.

I sat straight up - funny, even my back didn't catch. I sat, and I listened to her knock. I knew it was her knock. I knew it was her.

But the knock wasn't quite right. Not quite. And then I heard her voice.

"Don't be scared. Mum," she called softly, "Mum, s'me. Let me in. Mum. Go on. Mum. Please Mum. S'me Mum. Let me in."

It was as if my head were full of tears like a bottle of water. They burst out of my eyes and nose, out of my mouth even. And then they were spent. I got off the bed as quickly as I could, and walked across the little bedroom and opened the wardrobe door.

Outside she was knocking again, and now the knock was familiar in another way.

I leant into the wardrobe and picked up the biscuit tin. I'd forgotten, you see. Forgotten I'd moved it.

It was familiar because it was how he'd knocked. Ken. That last time. Soft bangs and stumbling bumps.

"Mum let me in I know slate let me in Im cold mum."

I remembered where I'd put it. After I put my wedding ring in the box. I went, still quietly, to the kitchen and took it, and the torch, out of the cutlery drawer.

"mumm you are a bidge mumb yare ledmeein-" Her voice had become a squeal.

I held the gun. I was automatically checking it. It was ready.

Where were the others? Also like this? Or did they see it happen and run away?

I thought, she can still speak. Why can she speak still? They can't, not when — they become like
        that.

I thought of her now remembering the way out on to the balcony, somehow springing across, the thump and slide of her against the long windows, all night. Till she broke through.

I went to the front door, with the pistol. I was flexing my hand a little, limbering up.

"S'you?" she asked. Definite upward inflexion. Syou?

I found I spoke to her. "It's all right, darling."

"Wanna cominn led me scold."

"I'll just undo the door, darling."

"S'okay," she said.

And she stopped shoving as I started to shoot the bolts. As if she understood.

But me — I don't know why I did this. It was as if I had to. It was like — that time I had to kill the beautiful little broken mouse, still just living, our last cat brought in. You couldn't just — leave it — you can't just—

Or was it something else? I don't know. I never will.

The last lock undid. The door swung wide.

She stood there in the beam of the solar torch I had charged up every time there was any sun. The thin spear of light struck straight through her left cheekbone, where most of her was missing. What was left of her blonde hair looked green in the light, and her one green eye was dark with rotting haemorrhage. Could she see?

"Gee . . ." I said.

"Gissle," she corrected me, almost primly. "Thas my name."

And her arms flung at me, to rend me or to hug me, and I fired the gun point-blank, as they do in old thrillers, through her broken face. The noise was different. Her head, already so terribly damaged, simply fragmented. It seems to kill them, this form of assault on skull and brain. But maybe it doesn't. Maybe after a while they still get up, what's still left, and move off back into their shambling existence. I never looked, did I, after all to see if Ken's body stayed where it fell down all those stairs. That time, till now, was the very last time I undid the door.

But she didn't move now, as Ken hadn't. There was just a sort of clicking sound for a bit, where her smooth — still smooth and young and white — her smooth young throat ended at the severed jaw.

I went in and shut the door. Bolted, locked. I
didn't have the strength any more to move a body, even
her slim light one. I'll have to put up with the stink.
Till it goes. If it ever does.

This time my hand doesn't hurt from the recoil.
Lucky, that.

I won't say anything else about
              feelings. Pointless. Nothing more.

Dear Gee,

   It'ss been a few days now and the smell is
consistently horrible and so I assume you are still
where I left you.

   Something really strange happened yesterday. I
think yesterday, and then this morning.

   I felt a bit ill yesterday, itchy and achy —
worse than usual. If it was yest— anyway, went to bed
early, even forgot to do blackout. Slept. Really slept.
Woke about 4 in the afternoon by the watch — but felt
like I'd been out days! Sort of hangover sleep.
Deathly. Then when I woke

   I woke up and didn't know who I was. I mean
truly did not know. Didn't know where I was either.
And not long after this I found some of my hair fell
out in the night, and then a little mark on my right
wrist. I put some TCP on but don't really th

   Well the weather is so nice isn't it, after all
that rain. Ken should be back soon. We did talk about
go to Brightone for the day, but there's that smell —
ded rats I think and we'll prob

   abl

   You kno I w

   Well, I said to Lora in my last lett and she and
Jaune an it

   I think you caught me, G, one of your strong
young fingernails. That would be enough, would it?
Infection. Or even just the gassses — only that din
happn with ken, but there and then

   My hand ths od

   my han

   cannt make it walk on the kees it. and no
pressoor cand mak it.

   My

   Hhhhh

   hhnnnnnnnnnnnnnnnnnnnnnnnnnnnnnnnnnnnnnnnn

| News Front Page | Page last updated at 12:22 GMT, 15 May | News Feed |

World

UK

England

Northern Ireland

Scotland

Wales

Business

Politics

Health

Education

Science & Environment

Technology

Entertainment

Also in the news

Video and Audio

Have Your Say

Magazine

In Pictures

Country Profiles

Special Reports

Related BMC Sites

Sport

Weather

Democracy Live

Radio Freedom

CBMC Newsround

On This Day

Editor's Blog

LATEST: HRV outbreak – can failing NHS cope?

Princess Diana's body stolen from final resting-place – Royal Resurrectionists to blame?

The BMC newsdesk confirms that rumours in the tabloid press regarding the whereabouts of Diana's body have now been confirmed...

▶ MORE

ALSO IN THE NEWS

Bravery medal for Zoe, the HRV-sniffing German Shepherd

▶ WATCH

THE GOVERNMENT REPORTS

No cause for alarm. Situation is under control

▶ LISTEN

HAVE YOUR SAY

HRV infected – threat or saviour ?
Tell us your thoughts

▶ MORE

PRODUCTS & SERVICES | E-mail news | Mobiles | Alerts | News feeds | Interactive TV | Podcasts

B M C

News Sources
About BMC News

BMC Help
Accessibility Help
Jobs

About BMC
Contact Us
Terms of Use
Privacy & Cookies

http://news/bmc.co.uk 15/05

17/05 10:20
Patient intubated and fully sedated following surgical amputation of right arm above elbow after HRV-carrier bite. Whole blood perfusion x2, atazanavir (600 mg) and delarviridine (400 mg) via drip infusion. Tests for viral activity pending. Patient status: stable, resting.

(signed) Andrew Wrothsly

Dr Alison McReady's journal, 17/05:
My first and I hope last helicopter ride. Got through three airsick bags, but no other way of travelling safely. Followed M4 part of the way – jammed for miles beyond London, some of it on fire.

It's a big country house the army is doing its best to turn into a fortress. Tanks on lawn, literally. A sandbagged emplacement at gates at end of drive. A helicopter always whomping somewhere overhead. Soldiers moved our equipment in: down to basement, naturally, near kitchens. Didn't see much of place, led up backstairs to Prince's bedroom, a big room hushed and dimly lit, curtains drawn across windows, deep carpets. I'd been prepared, but it was still a shock to see that familiar sad basset-hound face. He was unconscious and intubated on an elevated hospital bed that looked completely out of place amongst the antiques and oil paintings, wired up for EEG and EKG, a shunt in his good arm feeding him an antiviral cocktail, for all the good that will do. So much for my swift etiquette lesson (don't speak to the patient unless spoken to, ask permission before touching the patient, never call him by his first name but call him "your highness" et bloody cetera: my father would have been appalled by the bowing and scraping, my mother over the moon to learn such insider knowledge).

Two sleek middle-aged equerries in expensive pinstripes – Tweedledum and Tweedledee – looked down their noses at me. A third man, much younger, slim and tanned, studied me with frank appraisal. Public schoolboy type but fairly dishy. *Intense* blue eyes. Also Professor D, of course, and a steel-haired man in a tailored safari suit and a red cravat: Mr H, the Prince's jumped-up alt. therapy guru, who started to ask me about the TAB suspension, what was in it? Professor D told me to go ahead and administer it, he'd already discussed the procedure extensively with Mr H and there was nothing more to say. Which didn't stop Mr H questioning my credentials. I told him I was an MD and PhD, asked him where he qualified. Couldn't help myself. Professor D shot me a grateful look; Mr H, stony, said he was the owner and senior practitioner at the Royal Homeopathy Clinic, said he needed to know what the tagged antibodies were suspended in because it might interfere with the remedy he had administered.

"I have already made adjustments for the titanium your antibodies contain, but further adjustments will be necessary if other disruptive elements are present."

"It won't affect the distilled water you gave him," said Prof D, which set Mr H off on one about rubrics and potentialisation. I reckon I'm going to learn far too much about that kind of bollocks if Prof D doesn't find a way of sidelining the charlatan. Anyhow, I asked very nicely for permission to inject the antibodies into the royal blood system and did my work, gloved and gowned and more than a wee bit nervous, and not just because of the potential for infection with HRV. The patient should be just another patient, but I have to admit, laying hands (or gloves, unlike everyone else I was in full biohaz gear) on the royal personage gave me a touch of the heebie-jeebies. Even laid out the way he was on the elevated bed, crisp navy-blue pyjamas, restraint straps on his legs and one good arm, breath mechanically pumped through his orotracheal tube, he looks exactly like his photographs. Tanned. Silvery hair brushed just so.

Nerves vanished when I got to work, I'm pleased to say. Found a vein, inserted the cannula and taped it up and injected the TAB suspension. When I'd finished, I was led straight out, back to my little whitewashed, stone flag-floored and slightly damp cell. I guess I should unpack.

Later:

Prof D found me in the kitchen, where I was looking for an extension lead because there's only a single socket in my cell. Prof D flushed and slightly wild-eyed. Told me that we'd gone through the mirror here. That the lunatics had taken over. That we were the Prince's only hope. According to Prof D, the Prince's doctor – his real doctor, Wrothsly, the man who'd recruited us – had been infected when he'd performed the pointless field amputation after the Prince had been bitten. He'd been a slow converter, Wrothsly. He'd managed to stabilise his patient and arrange transport for Prof D and me, but he'd collapsed with a high fever while we were in the air. Now he was in a cage in a stable block, with the policewoman who'd bitten the Prince, and Mr H had taken over with the connivance of Tweedle's Dum and Dee. The Prince's personal secretary and wife are missing – last seen being driven away at speed from the Royal Free Hospital. She was on a visit to give moral support to the staff and things went pear-shaped. Likewise his sons. We'll have to get some results fast, Prof D said, or else that charlatan will shut us down. Haven't seen him this angry since he lost the big MRC grant last year.

When I went upstairs to concentrate and remove the tagged viral load (riding in a small iron-caged lift with my N45s and the bloodwork gear on a trolley), Mr H insisted on watching very closely while I deployed the N45s. Prof D didn't object – gave him a step-by-step account, in fact. Why not? It's his baby. I'm just the research troll who made it work, and even worse, I'm a woman, and Prof D may be a brilliant research team leader, but he's also one of those old-fashioned misogynists who are still all too common in the NHS.

Got a good sharp focus with the N45s on the patient's cephalic vein (it's easier if I think of him as just a patient) and exsanguinated 200 ml and at Prof D's insistence did a double precipitation test then and there. Recovery >80%, binding a shade over 60%. High, but not unexpected. It will drop when the patient begins to convert – or unless we actually do manage to find a cure. Mr H wanted to know if I'd removed all the virus in the patient's bloodstream; I left Prof D trying to explain antibody binding efficiency, how the magnetic field of the N45s can only capture and concentrate tagged viruses that pass through the vein on which they're focussed, why the procedure would have to be repeated several times, to mop up fresh viral loads shed from infected tissue, etc etc. Good luck with that.

Mr Blond winked at me as I wheeled the trolley out. Only human being in the room if you ask me. Him, and the poor old Prince.

17/05 16:30
Patient in state of morphine-induced unconsciousness.
Low-grade fever (39°C). Stump inflamed around stitching,
no bleeding. Repacked dressings, applied topical antibody
(erythromycin). Tests show active HRV in spleen, small
intestine, liver. Cerebrospinal fluid positive. Bone marrow
(left femur) positive. Tests for conversion of nerve sheaf and
muscle cells pending. Tagged antibodies (TAB batch 6)
injected to clear HRV from bloodstream: >62% binding.
Patient status: poor but remains stable.

(signed) E.M.B. Draper
(note of protest appended: REDACTED)

Dr Alison McReady's journal, 18/05:

Third coffee in as many hours, this one with a dash of
brandy courtesy of Mr Blond, aka Please Call Me Ralph
(he pronounces it Rafe, like the actor). According to one
of the kitchen staff he's some kind of spook, in charge of
security. He's certainly the only one close to the Prince
who knows there isn't much hope. Tweedledum,
Tweedledee and Mr H are all neck-deep in the large
Egyptian River; Prof D is up to his knees, selling TAB as
the wonder cure it isn't, hoping the team back at the lab
will miraculously produce something that will knock out
HRV before the inevitable happens.

It's been a bit of a day so far. Yesterday ended with a
weirdly formal meal, me and the servants in this little
windowless room off the kitchen, arcane rituals reminding
me of the top table at St John's College that time I gave a
seminar at Oxford. Got little sleep on the army camp bed
they've given me. At one point dreamed I was on some
luxury liner with the patient. The Prince. He asked me to
dance but I didn't know how or my feet wouldn't move.
You don't need to consult Great-Granddaddy Freud to
know what that's about. We're in the middle of a fairytale
told backwards here, trying to stop a prince turning into

something far worse than a frog. And not doing too well. Oh, TAB treatment is ripping active HRV from his blood, but the infection is deep in his organs and muscle mass, and we're only capturing what's been shed. We're little Dutch boys running out of thumbs – slowing down the flood but only delaying the inevitable because we can't fix the fundamental cause.

Anyhow, I was half-knocked out by lack of sleep and that weird dream when I walked in on the tail-end of a spat between Prof D and Mr H, who's insisting on keeping the Prince deeply sedated. I missed most of the ding-dong, thank goodness; Prof D stormed out; Mr H, unruffled, told Tweedledee and Tweedledum that "sleep was a fine remedy for sovereigns". Jesus. This is the pompous fool who has managed to take charge. Things aren't much better elsewhere. After Buck House burned down, the massacre at the Houses of Parliament, and the helicopter crash that killed the Prime Minister, the country's under martial law but no one knows who is in control. Ralph told me that the most senior minister left standing seems to be the Home Secretary, who's supposedly cowering in some old nuclear bunker in Wales. Doesn't help that the TV is mostly out now, and all we can get on the radio are repeats of *The Archers*, light classical music, and emergency bulletins that add up to sweet FA.

Later:

Did my thing with the TAB, despite all the drama. Sleeping Prince seems unchanged and binding and therefore viral load well down, which pleased both Prof D and Mr H, who are both claiming credit. Prof D highly pissed off because he couldn't get through to the lab. Mobile phones aren't working, all the networks are down again, and when he finally got permission to use a secure landline every number rang out. He tried to organise a helicopter ride, said it was important to get in contact with his people, check on development of antiviral therapy. No go, even when he said the life of the Prince depended on it. So we're stuck here.

Hope the rest of the team is okay. On the plus side, even before it became clear this wasn't an ordinary pandemic, we were all bunked down at UCL, working 24/7, and the place was locked tight. But by the time Prof D and I left the armed police guards had been reassigned and all we had by way of security were a few porters armed with fire axes. And outside, on the streets . . . Maybe it's only a glitch with the phones. I really do hope they're okay.

18/05 15:00
Atazanavir and delarviridine treatment continued at my insistence. HRV remains active in spleen, liver and small intestine. Muscle twitch test: 10-15% conversion. Second flush with TAB batch 6: >24% binding.
Prognosis: (REDACTED).

(signed) E.M.B. Draper

Dr Alison McReady's journal, 19/05:

From bad to worse. Way we behave, fighting each other, no wonder everything is falling apart. Another row between Professor D and Mr H. At one point expected it to come to blows. The two of them inches apart, hissing like cats. Started when Mr H refused permission to move the Prince to Gloucester hospital for CAT scan – claimed it would undo his work, mess up even pattern of patient's chi. Prof D turned white then red. Told Mr H if he was claiming responsibility for the patient he would lock them both in the room and see who came out after a day. Mr H pale but held ground. Said allopathic medicine could only do so much. That only extraordinary measures would be effective against this "terrible epidemic". Said he welcomed chance to liaise with Prof D, but if D continued to be "uncooperative" it would harm patient. Tweedledee and Tweedledum backed Mr H up, as did Mr Blond, although he said it wasn't possible to move the Prince on grounds of security and safety.

So Prof D stalked off, in high dudgeon. Apparently he tried to contact someone higher up but had no luck. And then it really fell apart.

Still no sign of the Prince's wife, but his oldest son came to visit. In army uniform, grim, smoke-smudged. A definite would, despite early onset male baldness. I was prepping the Prince, getting ready to remove his third dose of TAB, and saw the son kneel and kiss his father's hand as I was leaving. Prof D tried to intercept the son when he came out, weepy but determined, but Mr H and Tweedledee and Tweedledum moved in, and there was A Bit Of A Scene. Prof D tried to throw a punch and Ralph put him in a hammerlock and the son was hustled out by his bodyguards in one direction and Ralph hustled Prof D out in another.

I had to wonder about that kiss. When I finished the TAB rip I asked Ralph what it had meant. He said, very serious, that he couldn't comment because, quote/unquote, her Majesty isn't officially dead. Which either means she is and they're denying it, or the worst has happened to her – the new thing that's worse than death.

Always sided with my dad on the monarchist thing, but it's a bit of a shock.

Later:

Prof D gone. Just like that. Put on a helicopter and taken to an army place in Wiltshire to help at an emergency research centre. Ralph told me about it. Mr H used that scuffle as an excuse to lower the boom.

Mr H wants me to continue using TAB treatment. He likes the instant measurement of HRV blood load. Likes the way the viral load in the prince's blood has been reduced so dramatically. Pointless to tell him it's pointless. Or that my niobium magnets are far more powerful than a mere CAT scan (I tried: he said that they were "focussed" in a different way that made them "resonant"; the great thing about alt. medicine is that you can always find an excuse to discard something you don't like, or to include something you do).

Apart from TAB, there's no other conventional treatment, now, unless you count the heavy sedation. That's been upped to what in any other circumstances would be a lethal load. Despite Mr H's blind optimism, it's clear the Prince is converting. I can clean up his blood, but the virus is solidly established in his organs and muscle mass. Turning them into virus factories that lyse and release floods of active units into the bloodstream. Even if I catch 90% of them with each flush, which is highly unlikely, frankly, that remaining 10% will infect new muscle and nerve cells. And so it goes, step by step. Conversion is inevitable. No matter what we do, we can only put it off.

19/05 18:00
Low grade fever subsided, following treatment with Ferrum phosphoricum 30C potency. First administration of nosode plus antiHRV rubric (acon., am. c., Apis, Arn., Bell., bry., bufo, camph., carb. ac., crot. h., Hyper., ip., LACH., Merc., Nat. m., puls., pyrog., rhus t., sil., stram., Sulph., vip.) at 20C potency. Pulse full and bounding. Permitted fourth flush with tagged antibodies: 4.2% binding. Allopathy useful for monitoring virus load, at least.
Prognosis: hopeful.
(signed) T. Harkover

Dr Alison McReady's journal, 20/05:
The patient more or less came around this morning, struggled against the restraints. Wanted to find the welcoming committee, apparently. Thought he was in hospital to unveil a plaque and open the place. He popped one restraint – his muscle mass is almost at 50% conversion now: as what he once was dies, what he's becoming gets stronger and stronger – and bit Ralph's assistant as he flailed about. And an hour later the assistant shot himself with his own gun.

R told me it's how he wants to go, when it happens. When, not if. He told me that after this tour of duty, he was going on the front line. Very bitter and angry for a moment, before his usual composure rolled over him like a shutter. Asked me what I wanted to do, after. "Assuming there is, you know, an after." I told him I would go where Prof D had been taken, help look for a cure. He asked me about HRV. He's a good listener. Knows no biochem or meds but quick to grasp essentials. I told him how HRV beds into patient's DNA and activates sequences long-dormant, told him that the sequences were analogous to retroviruses that were once virulent but became part of our DNA and sometimes break out to cause sarcomas, and he understood at once. Said that HRV was only activating a potential, yes? Said, we all carry a zombie within us. Like original sin.

He gets a faraway look when he's thinking – got it then. Wistful, resolute, impossibly handsome. I know it's the stress of the situation, but if he'd taken me up in his arms then I would have succumbed. Absolutely succumbed. Like the heroine one of those stupid romance novels my mother liked so much. See now they weren't so stupid after all.

Anyway, of course he didn't take me up in his arms etc. Instead, all business, asked me if it was possible to stop the dormant sequences expressing. I told him about research, the many different failures. He asked me what the chances were of finding a cure. I gave him an honest answer; he shrugged, as if he expected it. Said he didn't expect the Prince to be cured, said that's why he let his man keep his gun after he'd been bitten. I said I'd take an overdose of barbiturates, if it came to it, lights out, no pain.

How easily we talk of death now. I guess it's like this in all wars. Everything stripped bare: the niceties and protocols we use to avoid the reality of existence no longer have a point. Oh, it's the "crisis" or "the ongoing situation" according to the increasingly pointless government bulletins, but war is what it is. Death has changed. It's no longer an end. Something passive. It's coming after us.

So, we talked R and me. An honest-to-God conversation. Him about his tours of duty in Iraq and Afghanistan (he was in the SAS) and a few of the places he's seen, on the royal protection squad. I mostly talked about my work, because, you know – lab geek. Work is mostly what I have. Tried to explain how TAB ripping worked. Almost lost my temper when he said that using antibodies tagged with titanium to bind with viral particles and concentrating them with high-resolution magnetic fields sounded like the kind of thing Dr H was doing. Then realised, ha ha, he was joking.

A nice human moment, but it makes me realise just how much I miss moments like that. I haven't slept for more than 2 hours in each 24 for the past two weeks. Mr H is being a royal pain, you'll excuse the pun. Aromatic oils I can take, might even help the patient if he associates peppermint and rosemary with calm places. And there may be some placebo effect with the homeopathy and the acupuncture, but there's no fucking way any it can be having a placebo effect against HRV, especially with the patient spark-out all the time. While I was doing the last rip, Mr H explained at great length the principles he'd used to concoct his homeopathic treatment. How he'd worked up what he called rubrics that represented symptoms of the worst case scenario, which I'm going to try to set down here as faithfully as I can to show you what I'm dealing with.

"Lachesis came out with the strongest emphasis," he said. "And *Crotalus horridus* repertorised out, too – snake remedies in general are useful for this disease. So I have added Vipera as the 22nd remedy even though it did not repertorise down, but exists in one of the two larger rubrics. All snakes are 'on the table', as it were."

So you see. Resisted temptation to take cheap shot and ask about eye of newt and tongue of bat or whatever. He added what he called a nosode into this mix too – blood from someone infected with HRV. All of it diluted so that not a trace of any original substance remained, of course, and each dilution knocked ten times on his special leather striking board to potentiate them, by which he means imprint them on the molecular memory of water.

He's actually proud of this nonsense. Told me that homeopathic medicines didn't interfere with the natural immune response but worked alongside it by enhancing the patient's ability to fight an infection, thus making him more able to effectively destroy a virus.

Tweedledum and Tweedledee lap it up. The two of them fine examples of my dad's hobby-horse that inbreeding and self-interest in the upper classes has wrecked our country. When I asked R why he stood by and let these idiots kill the Prince, he stuck out his jaw a little and said that he had his duty.

20/05 18:00
Patient resting. Flush with tagged antibodies showed unacceptable levels of binding. This and other signs are definite proof that allopathic Western medicine has failed – has indeed made things worse. However, after treatment with the rubric, whole body photon imaging showed considerable improvement. Chiropractic manipulation of spine recommended to regress changes in nervous system. Treatment with aconite at one hundred dilution to prevent so-called "conversion". Even if that takes place, it may be possible to control subject with traditional hoodan rites. Initial tests have been approved by [REDACTED]. (signed) T. Harkover

Dr Alison McReady's journal, 21/05:

Mr H icy when I told him binding rates had gone up. I tried to explain why, and he turned his back on me. Tweedledee gave me a hard stare; Tweedledum was concentrating on his nails. Nothing to do but leave. Guess I'll be following Prof D. If I'm lucky. Or given a gun if not. Most of staff here being recruited into an amateur defence force, crawling through the vegetable beds and bayoneting sacks of straw.

Later:

God, that was creepy. I was in my lab, working up a new batch of TAB6, when Mr H materialised in the doorway. Entered silently – I was concentrating, had no idea how long he'd been there when I looked up and saw him. He smiled when he saw he'd unnerved me (these days, it doesn't take much). Straight to business. Said he knew the Prince was converting and the TAB treatments weren't efficacious (his word). Told me that I must consider my position. Asked him what he meant – he said that I was a clever young woman, I must realise that allopathic medicine was no longer to the point, that I could come over to his "side". Then he actually closed the door at his back and with a furtive look asked me, was I a virgin. I told him where to put that question and he apologised and said it didn't matter. Also said that as an "African" I must be sympathetic to alternative ways of thinking. I told him I was born in Brixton, just like my mum, and my dad was from County Mayo. Shaking with anger, feeling very cold and no longer frightened of him, this stupid man in his stupid safari suit with his stupid alt. medicine crap, thinking that because I'm a person of colour, I'm completely down with his ongo-bongo back-to-nature nonsense. He studied me, a little smile tucked in the corner of his mouth. Why I didn't kick him in the bollocks I don't know. At last he said, still, you have the right heritage and told me to think about it. Said there was an apprentice gardener with the same heritage as me, he could use her instead. "Although it would be a shame to waste your talents, so please do think about it," he said, and drifted out. An "or else" left hanging in the air.

Later:

R found me outside the kitchen, smoking a cig I'd bummed from one of the cooks. Haven't smoked for three years, tasted vile but hit the spot. R said he knows what Mr H is up to. Voodoo, or something like it. The Prince converts; Mr H and the terrible twins will control him – and the country. My first thought: they're crazy. My second: the world's crazy, so why not join in? After all, hello, we're talking about HRV here – human *reanimation* virus. Otherwise known as The Death, or Beltane plague. We're talking walking dead people. We're talking the z word, which R used, telling me, there are enemies worse than the zombies. R said he knew everything because he had been told everything: T&T trust him: he is in charge of the security side of the operation. Explained what he wanted. I asked him why me of course and he said army is army, blindly loyal, and staff blindly loyal too, or too scared to do anything. I walked about coldly furious. Trapped, knowing it. R waited, patiently. When I came back he took out a slim cigarette case and lit a fresh cig for me, told me that the army wasn't interested in cures. Only in ways of killing them. Poison gas. Another virus. Anything. That was what Prof D had been recruited for. That's what I would be doing, if I went where he'd gone.

R said if you don't do it out of duty, do it for him. For your patient. I called him every kind of name. And said yes, yes I would.

Later:

At the time R told me I looked out of the kitchen window and saw in the courtyard Mr H greeting a man in a Savile Row suit. Black, matt skin, sunglasses, a homburg hat with a leopard skin band. R was there too, following them inside, not once looking towards the window where I stood. So this is it.

Dr Alison McReady's journal, 06/06:
A man came up to me today, told me he'd seen the Prince. Said he recognised me from that time. Said he'd been one of the gardeners. Showed me a creased photo of him with the Prince in a flower garden, in case I didn't believe him.

I believe he worked there. Still not sure that I believe what he told me, although I want to.

That night, the night the witchdoctor came, I snuck into the stable block and let the two zombies out of their cage. The Prince's doctor, and the policewoman who'd bitten the Prince. The doctor was pale and stinking but intact; the policewoman was mostly naked and her torso was riddled with gunshot wounds and she walked with a swirling limp. I used the electric prod to drive them to the back of the cage and unlocked the padlocks and ran for it. Found the ladder outside, where R said it would be, climbed into the hayloft. I was pulling the ladder up when the two of them came out. Both of them sniffing the night air like dogs before heading towards the house. The doctor quickly drawing ahead of the policewoman. A few minutes later the screaming and shooting started – the diversion for what R needed to do.

Worst thing I ever did, climbing down and making a run for the courtyard. Saw the doctor shambling across the big swathe of gravel in front of the house, shots knocking gouts from his body as he plodded towards the lighted entrance. Relentless. That's how they get us. They don't stop. I saw all this in an instant, as I ran. Then someone shot at me. It was like a very fast and angry bee going past my head and made me run even harder. I flung myself around the corner and was almost knocked down by R's Range Rover. I fell to my knees as it braked hard right in front of me and R jumped down and bundled me in and we were off, driving down the service road at about two hundred miles an hour.

The Prince was in the back seat, hog-tied and dead. R had given him the massive dose of morphine I'd prepared. It had stopped his heart. He was dead, but he was beginning to twitch. He was already coming back. As they do.

We drove straight through the roadblock at the service entrance. Big smash, gunshots. That focussed me. Out into the dark countryside. R's face was striped black and green with camo makeup. Tigerish. He looked tigerish. And cool and in control. He told me he had tasered Mr H, menaced the witchdoctor and the terrible twins with a gun and handcuffed them before he dealt with the Prince. I was certain he was lying, certain that he'd killed them, but didn't care. It was treason we were dealing with, after all. So I told myself. So I still tell myself. We did it for King and country.

We lapsed into silence. The thing in the back was becoming livelier. After about ten miles we pulled off the road into a field and laid him out. R cut most of the cords binding him and he sat straight up, looking like nothing on Earth in the headlights, and we ran for the Range Rover before he could get us.

R dropped me off at a Red Cross depot in Stroud. A brisk farewell, a kiss on the cheek. If it had been a film it might have been different, but it was what it was. He used me, I know. Played me. And I went along with it not because I'd fallen for him but because I knew it was the right thing to do. I like to think my dad would have been proud of me. I know my mum would have been.

I put my medical training to use. Now I'm running the field hospital in one of the camps outside Oxford, the centre of the government after what happened to London and Edinburgh. I like to think we're making a difference.

The gardener told me he said he'd seen the Prince two weeks ago. Said he was one of them, but he'd know him anywhere. The proud straightbacked gait amongst the shambling and the lame. That silver hair. That profile, glimpsed by firelight – he was leading a crowd or pack past a shopping arcade alight from end to end. Leading them away into darkness and safety, the gardener said.

The King is dead. God save him, and each and every one of us.

B M C
NEWS

| News Front Page | Page last updated at 10:33 GMT, 17 May | News Feed |

World

UK

England

Northern Ireland

Scotland

Wales

Business

Politics

Health

Education

Science & Environment

Technology

Entertainment

Also in the news

Video and Audio

Have Your Say

Magazine

In Pictures

Country Profiles

Special Reports

Related BMC Sites

Sport

Weather

Democracy Live

Radio Freedom

CBMC Newsround

On This Day

Editor's Blog

LATEST: Wreckage of Queen's helicopter found in North Sea

The Walking Dead – is this the end of humanity as we know it?

While Government authorities are optimistic over the recent turn of events, the UK's religious bodies have a different take on the crisis and many have declared that "The End is Nigh"

▶ MORE

ALSO IN THE NEWS

Cancellation of New Festival of Britain now confirmed

▶ WATCH

THE GOVERNMENT REPORTS

Stay indoors. We are winning the battle

▶ LISTEN

HAVE YOUR SAY

How can you tell that your neighbour is a zombie?

▶ MORE

PRODUCTS & SERVICES | E-mail news | Mobiles | Alerts | News feeds | Interactive TV | Podcasts

http://news/bmc.co.uk 17/05

MONDAY, MAY 20

I can't believe we've been here two weeks now. It feels like forever. Only two weeks, but seems more like a year. Mr Drake is arguing with Joe again (why he won't let me call him by his first name now I just don't get. Mr Mecken lets me call him Joe, so why — after two weeks stuck in this smelly flat together — I still have to call him "Mr" just seems stupid. But then I think he probably is quite stupid. Arghh!). They seem to argue a lot. I think Mr Drake's jealous because we all like Joe more than him — even Mrs Drake. I think she totally fancies Joe because she goes all giggly whenever he speaks, like the Barbies did around Mr Eyre. Its really embarrassing to watch cos he's soo never going to fancy her back. I like Joe. He's funny and I think maybe I have a bit of a crush on him too, although that makes me feel like I'm being unfaithful to my crush on Alex (sigh), even though that's REALLY

stupid because he's "out there" and
I'm "in here".
GOD, ITS SO BORING!

Sylvie's changed too. She lets Mr
Drake tell her what to do like she
just doesn't care that he's such a
rude bossy boots. He talks down to
everyone, but to her and me the
worst. She doesn't seem to notice.
Most days she just sits out on the
floorboards by the hatch and waits
to see if Alex and George will come.

George has been brilliant. Thank god
he brought my clothes so I haven't
had to wear his. Last time he came
he brought me a book too, as well
as some tins of food. We haven't
seen much of Alex. George says he
guards the downstairs while he comes
up. He says its safer that way. I
know its only been two weeks but
George looks different. He's thinner,
but I think we all probably are
(except for Mrs Drake who I'm sure
is getting fatter!!!), because there's

always this horrible tension which
makes us not want to eat, especially
at night and when the power goes
out. But George looks different in
his eyes. It frightens me. He looks
so much older and I don't want to
ask what he's seen that's made him
that way. I don't want to think
about Mum and Dad and Gran.

MONDAY, MAY 27

George didn't come today. And its the first day that we haven't heard lots of fighting in the city. Normally there's at least some sound of something terrible happening to a building or some blast of guns, even in the distance. They used to make me jump, but at least it felt like something was happening to put things right. This quiet is terrible. The radio isn't even working now, so we can't get any updates on what's going on, even if they were a bit vague. None of the mobiles seem to be working, even Mr Drake's which was on a contract.

I opened the window in the bedroom today, just a little bit, and pressed my mouth into the gap. Summer is almost here. The air tasted fresh and cool and wonderful. It made me wonder how things could be getting so much worse and the air was still so beautiful. I almost cried and I wasn't sure why. I shut my eyes so I didn't have to see the clock tower.

I'm worried about George.

THURSDAY, MAY 30

George and Alex came!! I'm so
relieved!! It made all of our moods
better I think — even Mr Drake
managed a smile and all he seems
to do the past couple of days is
glare at us all and mutter to
himself.

Alex's hair has grown but looks even
better than it did before. I'd
forgotten just how totally GORGEOUS
he is! I know I shouldn't be
thinking like that in all this, but
what's the point of all of this worry
and fear if you can't have something
brilliant to think about too! They
didn't stay long and Alex talked
mainly to Mr Drake and Joe but it
was good to see him and of course
George. I leaned over the edge of the
hatch and squeezed George's hand
like I do every time he comes. We
don't talk that much but just smile
at each other. Sometimes its hard to
know what to say. NOTHING changes

in here apart from it gets smellier
and smellier, and George never
seems to want to talk about what's
happening "out there" except to say
that its pretty bad.

He said they hadn't come for a few
days because they had to move.
Someone had been "compromised"
whatever that means, and so their
hideout wasn't safe anymore. I
asked him if the army were still out
there controlling the infected like
when they came to take Uncle Jack
away. He just laughed. It wasn't a
nice laugh. It didn't sound like
George. It sounded like George
without any of the fun stuff. He
said half the army was infected
now. He didn't look at me when he
said that and it scared me. When
he left he gave me his old smile
though, so I know it can't be that
bad. But I'm still scared for him.
If I'm honest, I'm scared for all
of us. If the army can't help what
will happen? Joe seems convinced
that the virus or whatever it is will
pass eventually because that's how

diseases work, but I'm not sure.
This doesn't seem like the flu.
There's too much noise out there at
night. People aren't sick. They're
changing.

I just keep thinking of Mum.

SUNDAY, JUNE 2

Its late. Mrs Drake's snoring in the
bed and Sylvie's sleeping out in the
hallway. She says its so they can
have more space, but I don't believe
her. This flat is full of hate. We're
all wearing it like a second skin. I
like to stay awake at night now,
just so I can have some peace,
although I'm not sure how much
anyone is actually sleeping or whether
they're just hiding behind they're
closed eyes. I don't want to close
my eyes now. Not after what I just
saw. I don't think I ever want to
close my eyes again.

There was a man shouting for help
outside. Really shouting. I haven't
heard anyone NORMAL being so loud
out there for what seems like ages
and my heart started racing. It still
is now. I looked out under the
blind, lifting it just the tiniest bit.
Not all the street lights are working
any more, but enough of them are
still struggling on that I could see
him quite clearly. I think my

tummy came right up into my mouth when I realised who it was. It was Mr Eyre from school. He was standing by the clock tower and just shouting for someone, anyone to help. He looked very young, not in his suit but just in jeans and trainers. At first I couldn't figure out why he wasn't running and what he was shouting about and then I saw them. The Barbies. They used to be the Barbies anyway.

I had to put my hand over my mouth to stop myself calling out and I thought I might be sick. It was Charlotte, Emma and Mandy. They were circling the clock tower, Emma Bolton was wearing that stupid pink dress that's too short, but she only had one shoe on, and the dress was dirty like she'd been wearing it for ages. Her head was at a funny angle. Charlotte's perfect hair was tangled and I'm sure there was blood in a thick dark patch down the back. Mandy was the only one whose face I could see and she was still kind of pretty, but it looked like she was snarling. Her face was kind of twisted. She looked like Mum had.

I've seen the infected from the window before. Sometimes, late at night when the others are in the sitting room and they think I'm asleep, I've looked out when the noises start. I'm not supposed to and if they knew I did, then Mrs Drake would probably get all hysterical again and Mr Drake would call me a "useless child" in that way he does that makes me want to shout, but how can you hear things like that and not want to look? Maybe you have to be grown up or something, but if I hadn't looked it would have driven me mad. And anyway, I don't think THEY look up. They didn't used to anyway. When I've seen them before, they were always on their own. Maybe in groups but still on their own if you know what I mean? Like being in a crowded place but not knowing anyone. And they were slower and clumsier. I'm sure half the rubbish that's all over the streets and the broken windows come more from this weird confusion they have.

I should say <u>HAD</u>. Not have. The Barbies weren't like that when they circled poor Mr Eyre. There was no confusion there. This time they knew what they were doing. This is going to sound completely stupidly crazy, but it was like all those crushes they had on him when they were . . . well, normal were still there but turned into something nasty. They looked at each other before they attacked. They weren't alone anymore. The Barbies had been a BitchClick when they were at school and now they were the same but something different. Like a pack.

Mr Eyre finally made a break for it as they closed in. He pushed between Charlotte and Emma and I'm sure they looked like they were laughing as they tore his T-shirt off. He must have been tired, because he stumbled and I'm sure he started crying then. He was making some sobbing noise.

The Barbies went after him. They were fast, not like the others I've seen. They caught him just at the edge of my view. I didn't watch that bit. But I know he didn't scream for long.

I'm shaking all over. I want to go and sit with Sylvie and have her tell me everything's going to be all right, but even if she did I don't think I'd believe it. Not any more.

TUESDAY, JUNE 4

OMG, why won't anyone listen to me?? Its like just because I'm not all grown-up and STUPID they think what I have to say doesn't matter!! Even Joe looked at me like I was a baby and told me that this was "adult business". Don't they realise this is EVERYONE'S business and I've been stuck in this stupid flat as long as everyone else so I know as much as they do!! Plus, at least I've actually looked outside rather than just pretended nothing was going on out there!! And now Joe's gone!! I can't believe it!!

Okay, - breathe. Must calm down. There's nothing I can do to change things, however weird the flat feels now that he's gone. Its like there's some kind of empty space that no one wants to talk about.

I'm not explaining again, am I? Do I need to? Sometimes I wonder if there's any point. This diary's only read by me and I know what's

going on. Arghh. And breathe again.
I may as well. There's nothing else
for me to do but think and if I do
much more of that while staring at
these walls I really will go mad.

Its been quieter outside the past
couple of days since I saw what the
Barbies did to Mr Eyre. This has
made Mr "I know everything cos
I'm the oldest IDIOT" Drake think
that things must be getting better.
He thinks this means the infected
are dying. I can't believe that Joe
actually agreed! Sylvie and Mrs
Drake just looked all wide-eyed and
hopeful as if Mr Drake was God or
something and just because he said
it and they wanted to hear it, it
must be true. He said one of us
should go and see what it was like
out there and if the army was
coming back. He said that maybe
the Town Hall would be where any
survivors were gathering.

I tried to say that just because
things were quieter it didn't mean
they were better, it just meant they

were calmer. I tried to tell them about how the infected had changed, and what I saw the girls doing, but that just made him explode about me looking out of the window. I can't believe how stupid he is. Does it matter that I was looking out the window when what I had to tell him was so important? ARRRGGGHH. In the end they told me to go to the bedroom while they talked and I slammed the door so hard I think the whole building shook. I don't care if it was childish, it was how they made me feel!

Joe was leaving when I came out. I cried and so did Sylvie. I didn't say anything though. I could feel Mr Drake staring at me and I knew it was pointless. I've grown up a lot in the weeks we've been stuck in here. I've learnt that sometimes its just pointless trying to argue with people when they're so convinced they're right even when you know they're wrong. I think though, that as Joe went down the ladder, he might have wanted to change his mind. His

smile didn't quite reach his eyes. I
kissed his cheek and it was warm.

"Take care, gorgeous." He said. And
then he went down the ladder.

I don't think we'll see him again.

THURSDAY, JUNE 6

Alex is dead.

Even staring at the page I can't
believe it. Alex. Gone. I don't think
I can even cry. I can hear Sylvie
sobbing in the sitting room but I
can't bear to go in there. George
came an hour ago. He brought some
tins, but not as many as he had
before.

"Things are getting worse," he said.
He was pale and trembling. "We got
attacked last night, down by the
river. This time they seemed
organised. Like they're getting ready
to do something." He couldn't look
at his mum. "They got Alex." The
words were barely a whisper but they
were enough to make the world
shimmer at the corner of my eyes.
I couldn't breathe. I didn't think
I'd be able to ever breathe again.
Somewhere in the background this
awful keening sound cut through the
stinking hot air.

"What do you mean _got?_" Even Mr Drake sounded like some of that patronising rudeness had been knocked out of him.

George looked so lost. His eyes welled up and he leaned back against the open hatch. He didn't even come inside. Maybe that's where he belonged now, half—in and half—out. He shrugged. It was the tiniest movement but seemed like it cost him the world.

"They dragged him away. They came after me. I ran onto a roof and got away that way."

Sylvie was sobbing and her breathing was coming in that horrible rushed way that seemed to fill the whole of the small hallway space. Soon she would scream. I could feel it. It was humming unsung in the air between my lack of breath and her breaking heart. Mr Drake must have felt it coming too because he asked George to wait a minute and he and his wife pulled her back into

the living room and closed the door. I
think they were less concerned for her
and more concerned about the noise
she was making drawing attention to
us. She didn't fight them much; she
looked like she had no energy. I think
the worst part was the way her
shoulders sagged in a kind of relief,
as if she'd been expecting something
like this all these weeks.

You'd have thought it would have
been strange to be alone with George
after all this time, but it wasn't.
As soon as the Drakes were gone I
wrapped my arms around his neck
and pressed my face into his skin,
hot tears falling and my nose
running. His skin was clammy and
chilled, but he hugged me back. His
wrist was rough and wrapped in
gauze against my hair.

"Take me with you, George. I hate
it here." My words breathed out in
an angry whisper.

He didn't answer, but squeezed me
tight. It felt terrible and it felt

good all rolled into one. Eventually,
I sniffed and pulled my head back.
Mr Drake would be back in a minute
and I didn't want him to see me
crying. I didn't want him to see
anything that was important to me
and that made me sad too. All of
us trapped in here and with only
resentment and fear holding us
together.

George's eyes were rimmed with red
and his pupils were small as if he
hadn't slept for weeks. He looked so
sad and defeated.

"I love you, you know that don't
you Maddy?"

He was blurry through my tears. All
I could do was nod and I thought
my whole body was going to explode
with the longing for things to just go
back to how they'd been when there
were the Barbies and Me and George
and my crush on Alex, and Mum
and Dad would ignore Gran and her
stupid stories. It all burned in my
choked throat.

His cold hand touched my cheek and then he kissed me.

I'm crying now just thinking about it. It wasn't a kiss like I'd imagined kissing with Alex would be. His mouth was cold and tasted stale. But it was my first kiss and I'm glad it was with George. It was gentle and his lips were soft and his tongue only touched mine once. But it was a kiss. An adult kiss.

"I can't stay, Maddy. Its not safe. I've got to go."

He didn't wait for Mr Drake to come back, but started back down the ladder. I think he was crying too. I grabbed at his hand and tried to pull him back, and I was crying so much I couldn't see properly and his fingernails scratched along the back of my hand. I didn't even feel it at the time. All I could feel was my heart breaking.

Mr Drake came back out in time to stop me following George out there.

"Don't be stupid, girl!" He hissed at me. His hand pinched my arm hard as he pulled me away. He gripped my arms like he hated me. Maybe he does.

The scratch on the back of my hand is stinging. I'll see if I can find a plaster later. When Sylvie's stopped crying. George won't be coming back. I'm sure of it. I suddenly feel completely alone.

JUNE 7

Its still early. Can't sleep. Don't
want to sleep. I'm cold. The world
is grey. I never realised. Everything
is grey with shadows of red. Its
strange. Should freak me. It
doesn't though. Just a bit weird.
Maybe its a fever. I don't feel like
I've got a fever but I think I'm
sick. I think I should be scared.
I'm not though. I just feel . . .
fuzzy. Couldn't remember what Mum
looked like today. I tried really hard
but I couldn't see her face. I just
slept instead. Can't sleep now. Feel
restless. My bra is itching against
my back. Maybe at last my boobs
are growing. I don't think I care.
Why don't I care?

I like the night.

I like the night.

I wrote that twice. See. Fever.
Weird.

Earlier there was the sound of something big blowing up. I think it was over towards Blackfriars.

I've pulled the blind right up to look. I don't care what Mr Drake thinks. They're all next door. They're "out there" and I'm "in here". LOL. Ha. Not laughing really. LOL looks funny. The words look funny. The pen's sweaty in my hand but my skin's cold. They're in there talking about me. I know it. I can hear their whispers. I almost wrote I can smell their whispers but that would be wrong. Can't smell whispers.

Infected.

I'm not scared. They're scared. I'm not scared.

The blind's up. I can see outside. The sky is orange. Its not the dawn. This side of the river the city is burning.

Now I can hear the sound of a plane. It sounds like its right overhead.

I can still see the clock tower. Alex is there. And George. And the Barbies. They're looking up. I think I'm smiling but my face feels numb. Everyone's down there. Not so different from before. They're waiting for me. That makes me feel something. Good. Not lonely. I want to go outside.

I lift my hand so they know I see them.

I don't think I'll write anymore.

I'm hungry.

**Unable to open
http://news/bmc.co.uk/
Cannot locate the internet
server or proxy server.**

DNS error - cannot find server

Oops! This link appears to be ... dead.

OK

Pastor Pat on The 700 Club

Christian Broadcasting Network, 6-7

"Of course, it's a tragedy . . . what's happening in Great England, but you have to understand, Kristi, it's not a natural phenomenon. It's the fruit of a long-standing, deeply-entrenched commitment to Satanic values.

"Something happened a long time ago in England. People might not want to talk about it. After the Romans left, Christianity was beset. There were Pagans, people we would now recognize as Satanists in all but name. They sought, as Satan always seeks, power, and they burrowed into the woodwork of England, just like a boll-weevil eating its way into a cotton plant. They stayed hidden, but they kept in power. The Kings and Queens of England have always been Satanists. They offer up Christian virgins in their Trooping the Color and Coronation, and the Devil said 'it's a deal,' come on over, turn away from CHRIST and be my followers, and Hell will see you all right. Of course, the Devil is a tremendous liar, as we can now see. It gives me no pleasure to say this, but the people of England now know the consequences. The deal is off, you see. The piper must be paid. You know, this is interesting. We've all heard that phrase 'the piper must be paid,' but how many among us knew *who* this Piper is, and what he would be paid in? Few, I reckon. The Piper is the Devil – if you've heard those English bagpipes, you won't be surprised, for their wailing is terrible, like unto the damned in torment – and His payment is in flesh. Rotting flesh!

"The founding fathers knew this, which is why good CHRISTIANS like George Washington were driven to a righteous revolution of the godly. To cast off the Satanic yoke of Jolly Old England. George III, the Black Pope of Beelzebub, sent a demon in the form of Benedict Arnold to stifle this great nation in its crib, just as Herod sent murderers to kill JESUS CHRIST when we was new-born. Like JESUS, these United States were preserved through the intervention of GOD ALMIGHTY, and stands by His Will alone against the forces of Evil. Ever since then, England has been cursed. True story.

"All churches in England are, in fact, consecrated to the Devil. The so-called Anglican Church is a secret society of pederasts, sodomites and all manner of unholy predators. They marry goats, and drown CHRISTIAN babies in their fonts. If you look at it upside-down in a mirror, the signature on this five pound note reads 'Lucifer Himself.' In the 19th Century, when England's power was extended around the globe in an Empire significantly colored DEEPEST SCARLET on their maps, a great cobweb of Satanism spread across the world. The official religions of Great England are Voodoo, Thuggee, Obeah, Druidism, Wicca, Darwinism and Presbyterianism – all the branches of the Great Seven-Headed Serpent of Satanism. You hear what I'm saying, Christie? Satan, the Great Adversary. He's a tricky old one. We all know that. It may come to us in an unassuming, beguiling form, which would seem to be ingratiating – like Mister Bean. BUT IT IS SATAN! It may adopt a comely face and limbs – like Helen Mirren. BUT IT IS SATAN!

"All the works of England are the works of the Devil. The Four Beatles were War, Famine, Pestilence, and Death. Stuart Sutcliffe, a good Christian, knew this and abjured the band. He was killed for it. Hung up by one heel, with his insides cut out and strewn upon the floor in an inverted pentagram. You can read about this in books. It's all true. Winston Churchill smoked that cigar so that

President Roosevelt would not smell the whiff of sulfur when they met at Yalta. Churchill came to that conference direct from Hell, where he had been taking orders from his true master. Months later, Roosevelt was dead. And Great England was not cast out of the community of nations, as Roosevelt intended. Queen Elizabeth is a hardcore feminist, who sticks by a socialist, anti-family political movement that encourages women to leave their husbands, kill their children, practice witchcraft, destroy capitalism and become lesbians. She gives women who do three or more of these things a medal called an Order of the English Empire, and invites them to orgiastic garden parties in the grounds of her Castle of Doom.

"And so, now that England is overrun, the debt has fallen due. The Devil has abandoned his worshippers, and refused to accept any more of them into Hell – and so they wander the country lanes and market towns of their home country. In the Bible, only one can truly raise the dead, and that one is Our Lord JESUS CHRIST! The Devil always seeks to mock JESUS, and – like so many of his works – this is a parody of the true Christian miracle. These English men and women of Satan, feasting on each other, are cast out of our Lord's sight. We must not pity these risen pagan dead, and we must not let our government spend one tax dollar in so-called aid for the ungodly. We are a CHRISTIAN country.

"They need to have, and we need to pray for them, a great turning to God. The only thing that can save them is conversion. Conversion and prayer. They must throw out their Satanic leaders, and come to God, invite God in – on helicopters, by boat, on wings of song – just let God into their borders, and I really believe this could be a Good Thing, that this could be the end of Satan's hold on England, the first blow in the great defeat that will drive the Devil from this world and make way for the establishment of God's Citadel in this Christian country. It is, we must remember, their own fault. We must be strong. Thank you."

FROM: THE OFFICE OF THE HOME SECRETARY, EMERGENCY ASSEMBLY
BUILDING, CARDIFF BAY, WALES.

TO: U.S. STRATEGIC COMMAND, OFFUTT AIR FORCE BASE, NEBRASKA.

*RECORD OF TEXT MESSAGES SENT FROM AND RECEIVED ON
MOBILE PHONES OWNED BY:*

MICHAEL MCCLINTOCK

AND

JANE LUCILLE DEAN

BETWEEN JUNE 6 AND FIRST FINAL SOLUTION.

FOR THE ATTENTION OF AUTHORISED PERSONNEL ONLY. THE
CONTENTS OF THIS TRANSCRIPT ARE CONFIDENTIAL. THE
DUPLICATION OF THIS MATERIAL IS STRICTLY PROHIBITED
UNDER SECTION 19 OF THE NATIONAL SECURITY ACT.

[Thursday, June 6: 10:37am]

Mike: R U there?

Mike: Im runnin

Mike: Better. Bit of calm. This still yr number Jane?

[Thursday, June 6: 10:58am]

Jane: Who is this?

Mike: mike

Jane: Mike who?

Mike: Richards. Remember?

[Thursday, June 6: 11:05am]

Jane: What do you want?

Mike: Help

Jane: From me? Help yourself. You always did. Helped yourself to every tart that came your way

Mike: I apologised. Now I really need yr help. Really

Jane: Where are you?

Mike: south of rvr

Jane: Oh my God. Mike

Mike: sijgf

Jane: Mike?

Jane: Mike???

[Thursday, June 6: 11:32am]

Mike: Sorry. Was running. Hiding now. There R so many of thm. Tried acting like one, but they know

Mike: They can tell lvng
from ded

Mike: I have something here.
The cure. You have to
help me

Jane: The cure for what?

Mike: 4 the Death.
Documents in a bag

Jane: A cure?

Mike: Sure

Jane: How do you know? What
documents? In a bag?

Mike: Later. Now I need 2
get 2 river and cross
— you cn help me

Jane: I'm not sure I can.
Everyone here has to
stay in their homes.
Army are in the
streets - curfew.
Suzy was arrested and
taken away

Mike: Suzy?

Jane: My friend Suzy, the
costume designer. She
was working on Holby
when it all started

Mike: Fuck Suzy. U can help!

Jane: How do you think I can
possibly help you?

Mike: Be my eyes. Still got
net? TV?

Jane: TV channels are all
running advisory
messages from
government. But yes, I
can still access the
internet

Mike: Tell me where 2 go

Jane: What's the cure?

Mike: Dunno. Got it frm dead
guy

Jane: What dead guy?

Mike: Soldier. No time 4
this

Jane: Why me? Last time I
saw you, I told you I
never wanted to see
you again

Mike: fuck sake this not
about U!

[Thursday, June 6: 11:46am]

Mike: Jane?

[Thursday, June 6: 12:10pm]

Jane: What soldier?

Mike: OK. I tell, U help?

Jane: If I can trust you.
The world's in a mess

Mike: Telling me! I'm in
worst of it. I cn hear
thm from here. Growling

Jane: Stay hidden. Tell me,
and while you're doing
that, I'm firing up my
laptop

Mike: mmmmm, I remember yr
lap. Tasted good

Jane: Fuck off Mike

Mike: Your folks still h8 me?

Jane: They're old fashioned,
      that's all

Mike: U?

Jane: I never said I hated
      you

Mike: As good as

Jane: I said you were a
      waster and a bigot and
      unfaithful and a shit
      and a bastard. But
      never said I hated you

Mike: theyre cmng.

[Thursday, June 6: 12:20pm]

Jane: Mike?

[Thursday, June 6: 12:22pm]

Jane: Mike?

Mike: Here. Sorry, turned
      fone off. That was
      close

Jane: I can help. There are
      three sites I need to
      look at, but between
      them I think I can
      guide you through safer
      routes to the river

Mike: & then?

Jane: Then I don't know.
      They've blown all but
      Blackfriars Bridge.
      It's a defensive line

Mike: Ha. They float

Jane: What?

Mike: Doesn't matter

Jane: I can't believe this
      is happening

Mike: You & me both

Jane: It was supposed to be
      so good. New Festival
      of Britain. Restore
      our identity

Mike: Hah! Diversion.
      Government's always
      good at that

Jane: What?

Mike: Look, see how gr8 we
      R, oh and ignore the
      fact that we're fucked

Jane: You're still so cynical

Mike: Events justify

Jane: My parents had hope.
      Said it was time to
      put Great back into
      Britain

Mike: Jane, yr parents read
      the daily mail

[Thursday, June 6: 12:42pm]

Mike: Sorry. So, soldiers.
      Still wanna know?

Jane: Tell me where you are
      first

Mike: Stockwell. Was in
      Brockwell pk. Hiding
      there by lido. Heard
      engine, ran onto
      Dulwich Rd, fckrs
      almost ran me down.
      Drove at me, thought
      that was it. Covered
      in blood, they thought
      I was zombie

Jane: Blood?

Mike: Not mine. So put my
hands up, started
singing. Saw their
faces. Boys, most
younger thn me.
Terrified. Even then,
thought they were
going 2 shoot

Mike: Sergeant jumped from
Saracen. Big cnt.
Pulled his sidearm. I
started on one —
ranting y'know, like
What have you done? He
came at me, punched me

Jane: Not surprised if you
called him a "cunt"

Mike: U got time 2 use
speechmarks in txts?

Jane: I don't like swearing.
It's foul. You're foul

Mike: shhhhhh. Thye hre. im
hidng. Dont txt

[Thursday, June 6: 12:50pm]

Mike: You swore when we
screwed. "Oh fuck, oh
fuck." Notice speech
marks?

Mike: Still like it from
behind? All posh birds
do. Heh

[Thursday, June 6: 12:55pm]

Mike: U can txt now. They
weren't really here.
I'm sitting in sun

Jane: Bastard. Bastard.
Bastard

Mike: Potty mouth

Jane: You're doing this for
a joke. You're in
Scotland somewhere, or
France. Bored, so
decided to wind me up

Mike: I wish. No. I'm in
Stockwell. A bldng's
on fire 2 or 3 streets
away. Choppers
buzzing. 3 kids locked
in a car, all zombies.
One is baby in seat.
Hand bitten off.
Can't see a parent

Jane: And you have the cure

Mike: The sergeant punched
me, shouted, said I had
no respect. Think he ws
mad. His soldiers,
young, more scared of
him than Zmbs. Then he
laughed at me. Patted
shoulder bag, said he
had cure, told me to
wait for it 2 come

Jane: He told you what cure
was?

Mike: No. Got into Saracen
and they went. Kid
soldiers stared at me
all the way, til
turned into side
street. Then the crash

[Thursday, June 6: 1:13pm]

Jane: Mike?

Mike: shhh ... really ...

[Thursday, June 6: 1:29pm]

Mike: Fuck. Hndrds of them. Im in stckwll tube entrnce, ticket booth, can U see if it's clear?

Jane: Hang on

[Thursday, June 6: 1:32pm]

Jane: I don't think the Tube's infested there. I'm checking London Met & official Government websites, and tracking things on Twitter & Facebook. You might find people hiding down there, but no Zmbs

Mike: right. Gotta go deeper, they're cmng in. might lose reception?

Jane: Hope not. Text me when you can

Mike: ok

[Thursday, June 6: 1:55pm]

Jane: Mike?

[Thursday, June 6: 2:23pm]

Jane: Mike?

[Thursday, June 6: 2:54pm]

Jane: We should have carried on. Not listened to my folks. I saw what you were, not what they thought you were. And I liked it

[Thursday, June 6: 2:57pm]

Mike: U also liked it doggy

Jane: You OK?

Mike: Just. That was fckng hairy. In Oval station now, have 2 go up, they're down here

Jane: Hang on

[Thursday, June 6: 3:01pm]

Jane: I think roads are clear above, but go north, not south. NOT south

Mike: What's south?

Jane: Trouble

[Thursday, June 6: 3:19pm]

Mike: Resting. Thirsty. Nice pub. Free ale! So I heard the crash. Heard the explosion, saw smoke. Then the screams. Something made me run towards crash, not away from

Jane: Why?

Mike: Those kids' eyes. That mad sergeant

Jane: And?

Mike: Ironic. Z in road —
      must've swerved to
      avoid it. By the time
      I got there, Z's were
      all over Saracen.
      Burning. Pulling thm
      out. Some shooting,
      but not much. The kids
      were burning while
      they ate them

Jane: Oh God

Mike: Don't think so. Not
      here. I waited til
      they left, then went 2
      check. Most were dead.
      Sarge dead, just
      starting 2 move again,
      doc pouch hanging off
      his arm. Grabbed it.
      He growled, went for
      me. Picked up his
      sidearm and blew his
      head off

Jane: Why did you grab the
      pouch?

Mike: Important

Jane: Yeah right

[Thursday, June 6: 3:28pm]

Mike: OK. Grabbed it cos
      thought it might be my
      ticket over river

Jane: So. Honesty. Let's
      keep it that way.
      What was in the pouch?

Mike: Like he said — cure

Jane: But what?

Mike: I'm no scientist.
      Fuck knows. Get me out

of here I'll bring it
with me

Jane: OK. Where are you now?

Mike: Foresters Arms. Good
      food, real ale, kids
      welcome

Jane: Hang on

[Thursday, June 6: 3:45pm]

Jane: North's OK

Mike: Good. U meant that?

Jane: Yes, north

Mike: No, other stuff. Shld
      have crrd on

Jane: North's good

Mike: Right

[Thursday, June 6: 3:59pm]

Mike: I loved going down on U

[Thursday, June 6: 4:22pm]

Mike: Put yr phone on
      vibrate, I'll keep
      txtg

Jane: Stop it. Hardly the
      time

Mike: When is?

[Thursday, June 6: 4:35pm]

Jane: Maybe when you get out

Mike: Your folks?

Jane: Fuck them

Mike: Would rather not

Jane: Tell me where you are

Mike: shhhhhhhh

[Thursday, June 6: 5:31pm]

Mike: dont txt. 100s of thm

[Thursday, June 6: 5:57pm]

Mike: so close dont txt not
      sure ill get out

[Thursday, June 6: 6:45pm]

Mike: need a piss

[Thursday, June 6: 7:12pm]

Mike: im trapped. Will start
      txtg what's in
      documents, just in
      case. You can answer

Jane: WHAT'S HAPPENING????

Mike: I'm in upstairs room
      of house in vauxhall.
      Z's outside. And
      downstairs. Not coming
      up yet. So here goes.
      Seems 2 be code or
      formula. Write it down

Jane: Can't you get out?

Mike: Emergency Plan AHC.
      Execution protocol.
      Five phase build,
      pyramid structure,
      current initiation code
      as follows: 232-RFD-

566G. Getting this?

Jane: Yes. AHC, could be All
      Hallows Church. They
      say it started there

Mike: Whatever. Phase 1:
      genetic build 765.
      Phase 2: Swiss ops
      build HG-8. Phase 3:
      Batch 77. Phase 4:
      detonation build
      "Home". Phase 5:
      codeword "panicland"

Jane: Panicland?

Mike: What it says. Mayb

Jane: Mike?

[Thursday, June 6: 7:34pm]

Jane: Mike?

[Thursday, June 6: 8:12pm]

Mike: Had 2 get out.
      Jumped. Ran. Fucked my
      foot

Jane: Where are you now?

Mike: Hiding again.
      Kennington rd
      McBurger's outlet.

Jane: Good. They only eat
      real meat. Hold on.

Mike: lol

[Thursday, June 6: 8:17pm]

Jane: OK. East from there
      along Lambeth Road
      might be clear

Mike: Might?

Jane: Can't promise. North
      to river's not good

Mike: ?

Jane: Twitter's down. Net's
      flaky. TV hasn't
      mentioned London in a
      while

Mike: ?

Jane: I think it's been
      written off

Mike: Oh

Mike: I'll try east then.
      Can't stay here 2 long

Jane: I'll keep watching the
      net. Text me any time
      you reach new street
      or junction

Mike: OK sexy

Mike: OK sexy!

Jane: Just stay safe

[Thursday, June 6: 8:29pm]

Mike: Just past war museum.
      I hear them

Jane: Which direction?

Mike: North. South

Mike: East. West

Mike: Fuck

Jane: Mike, can't find
      anything about that area

Mike: Just gonna run

Jane: Tell me when you're
      safe

[Thursday, June 6: 8:37pm]

Jane: Mike?

[Thursday, June 6: 8:56pm]

Jane: I liked it when U went
      down on me 2

Mike: Course U did. Foot
      swollen. Bleeding

Jane: Bitten?????

Mike: No. Don't think so

Mike: No

[Thursday, June 6: 9:05pm]

Jane: You need to be sure

Mike: Am sure! Hurt it when
      I jumped. Foot
      bleeding, nasty.
      Think ankle broke

Jane: You wouldn't be able
      to walk on it. Are you
      safe for now?

Mike: For now. Got 2 rest.
      Take this down, into
      last code on those
      documents

Mike: Zero one + one.
      Radius full basin.
      Make sense?

Jane: No. Mike, don't need
      to text it all

Mike: WTF was that??

Jane: ??

Mike: Explosion. Fckng huge

Jane: Dunno. Heard nothing,
but I'm miles away

Mike: Christ. Can't see
anything. Heard
smashing glass

Mike: I'll carry on. Ready?

Jane: You don't need to

Mike: What if I don't get
out?

Jane: You will. I'll help
you. Need to help you,
got to feel like I'm
doing something

Mike: Do U want 2 run?

Jane: They won't let us.
House arrest,
virtually.
Quarantined area.
Curfew

Mike: U could still go.
Sneak out

Jane: What about my parents

Mike: Don't tell them

Jane: I'll save you. That's
doing something

Mike: OK. But write this
down. Just in case.
What if no one else
has details of cure?

Jane: They will

Mike: But we don't know
that. Write it

Jane: OK

Mike: Almost done. Source at
first vector. Then a
series of numbers: 51N
28' 19.52" -0S 0'
22.73"

Mike: Got that?

Jane: Yes

Mike: Good. Hang on

[Thursday, June 6: 9:57pm]

Jane: Mike?

Mike: Something went by.
Army truck full of
grunts

Jane: And?

Mike: Looks like retreat

Jane: Hitch a ride

Mike: Guy jumped at truck.
They shot him

Jane: Killed him?!?!?

Mike: No. Injured. Z's
finished job

Jane: Oh Christ

Mike: Not good. Don't like
feel of this

Jane: Where are you now? We
need to get you out

Mike: Morley Street
ambulance station.
It's empty

Jane: Hang on

[Thursday, June 6: 10:09pm]

Jane: Parents

[Thursday, June 6: 10:20pm]

Mike: U there?

[Thursday, June 6: 10:44pm]

Jane: Police came to door, told us we have to leave. Had a row with Mum and Dad — they've gone

Mike: And you?

Jane: If I go, can't help guide you out

Mike: I can find own way! You got 2 go!

Jane: No Mike. Waterloo Road north of you might be OK, I found a Tweet mentioning it half an hour ago. But Zmbs R in Waterloo Station

Mike: They must B telling U 2 leave 4 a reason!

Jane: Hurry, then

[Thursday, June 6: 10:59pm]

Mike: OK, outside BFI Imax. Having to dodge Z's. Foot worse — just fell over

Jane: Hang on

Mike: If had to run, couldn't. River not far

Jane: Wait

[Thursday, June 6: 11:07pm]

Jane: River **ked. U should see this. Clogged with bodies of Zmbs trying to swim across

Mike: Told you — they float

Jane: Yeah, and they don't drown

Mike: Oh. Just get me there

Jane: Stamford St looks OK . . . ish. Don't hit river until you have to. Text again when U see Blackfriars Bridge

Mike: It's dark. Should hole up smwhr

Jane: I think you should move. I've checked as many sites as I can think of. That stretch of the South Bank should be OK

Jane: But don't get too close to the river

Jane: OK?

Mike: Right. U were always 2 posh for me

Jane: For a commoner, you're pretty hot

Mike: lol

[Thursday, June 6: 11:24pm]

Jane: How's it going?

Mike: Slow. Being careful. Don't text 4 a bit, phone light is giveaway

[Friday, June 7: 12:29am]

Jane: Mike

Mike: wait

[Friday, June 7: 12:38am]

Mike: Fuck. Thames isn't water anymore

Jane: Mike, I've been looking at the stuff you texted from the document you found

Mike: The cure

Jane: Not sure it's a cure. Think it's map co-ordinates

Mike: Where 4?

Jane: All Hallows church

Mike: Where they say this shit began?

Jane: Yeah

Mike: Thought it was formula, or smthng

Jane: Procedure, all coded. Map co-ordinates. And a time

Mike: Oh. Not good. What time?

Jane: U need 2 get out of there now

Mike: Jane, Blackfriars Bridge is gone

Jane: What?

Mike: Blown

Jane: There's nothing on the net about that!

Mike: Must've just happened. The explosion I heard

Jane: I think they're doing something. That soldier, what did he say about a cure?

[Friday, June 7: 12:56am]

Mike: Not much. Said they had one. Laughed

Jane: You really need to cross river

Mike: Hang on

Jane: Now

[Friday, June 7: 1:04am]

Mike: OK. Might be able to cr. Wait

Jane: I hear planes

Mike: Fuck. Planes. Im crossing. Enough Z's floating, Im crossing

Jane: Across the bodies? What if you slip? What if they trip you?

Jane: Shit, more planes. Run, Mike. Fast as you can. Get the hell out of there, now, and keep running

Mike: Can't wait 2 C me huh

Jane: Careful on the North Bank, they're guarding it

Jane: Mike?

Jane: I said careful,
      they're guarding, not
      cautious, just
      shooting. Seeing stuff
      on the net . . . bad
      stuff. Careful Mike

Jane: Mike?

[Friday, June 7: 1:11am]

Jane: Mike?

Jane: Christ. No! The
      fires! Run Mike. Oh
      the fires . . . all
      of South London . . .
      keep running, babe.
      Keep running wherever
      you are

[Friday, June 7: 1:32am]

Jane: Mike?

[Friday, June 7: 1:56am]

Jane: Mike?

[Friday, June 7: 2:32am]

Jane: Mike. Mike. Mike

[Friday, June 7: 4:45am]

Mum: Janey? Are you there
      sweetie? Tried to call
      but couldn't, and we
      saw the fires

Jane: Mummy. I'm fine

Mum: Oh thank the Lord!
      What about that man

you were texting?

Jane: He must be dead

Mum: Oh dear. You should
      have come with us

Jane: I will now. I

Mum: Janey?

[Friday, June 7: 5:05am]

Jane: Mum. Don't txt. Zmbs R
      outside. I can see
      them from window.

Jane: Oh no. One just looked
      up. I think he saw me

[Friday, June 7: 5:06am]

Mike: Jane.

Jane: Mike!! You're alive!
      That firestorm, like
      the end of the world,
      I thought you must be
      dead!

Mike: Thort so 2

Jane: I'm trapped, don't
      know what 2 do.
      Soldiers gone from
      street. Just zombies
      out there now — must
      have crossed river

Jane: I got to stop crying,
      they'll hear me.
      There was one . . . a
      fucking clown. Can you
      believe that?

Jane: That fire, that
      explosion. All for
      nothing. They crossed.
      What now? Same for us?

Jane: And the fleas.
      Millions of fleas,
      everywhere

Mike: they don't itch

Jane: ?

Mike: U look tastee

[Friday, June 7: 5:32am]

Mum: Janey?

[Friday, June 7: 5:33am]

Mum: Janey?

[Friday, June 7: 5:34am]

Mum: Jane?

NO FURTHER TEXT MESSAGES WERE SENT FROM EITHER PHONE.

MESSAGE ENDS.

"And on the entertainment front, pre-production leaks look set to place James Cameron's *Avatar II* at the numb—"

"I'm sorry, Rosie, we have news just in."

[*Dick Gardener presses his ear mic and stares blankly at the camera. He does not smile. He begins to shake his head. Rosie Cameroon next to him also shakes her head and lets out a brief sob before getting to her feet and walking off camera, her ear mic tugged out and clunking to the floor.*]

"Ladies and gentlemen, we have it confirmed. This is fact. At just past midnight our time, the British government has detonated a nuclear device above the British capital. Much of London has been wiped out. We have no estimates of casualties at this time. I repeat: the British government has exploded a nuclear device above South London. We'll pass along more details as we receive them. Meanwhile, let's go across to Baxter Fielding at the Pentagon. Baxter . . ."

[Newsflash on NewsChannel 5 WEWS, Cleveland, Ohio, June 7]

FILE XL-34528-14

RELATING TO LYNDA RUSSO, SENIOR PILOT,
ROYAL FLYING DOCTOR SERVICE OF
AUSTRALIA (RFDS), SOUTH EAST SECTION.

ITEM 4.
TRANSCRIPT OF VERBAL ACCOUNT OF EVENTS
OF 9 JUNE AS REPORTED TO SECTION DIRECTOR
JONATHON PIKE BY PILOT LYNDA RUSSO, AT
REQUEST OF THE RFDS NATIONAL BOARD UNDER
THE HON. TIM FISCHER. PARTIAL. RECORDED 10
JUNE.

This is bullshit, right? Is it some sort of performance evaluation? Okay, okay, so it's not an evaluation – whatever you say. But an investigation? What's going on, Jon? I understand something happened and it's a matter of national security or some such crap, but we were called in, for god's sake. We don't know anything. Can someone tell me why we're being treated like we're a bunch of terrorists?

Okay, I'll calm down. Promise.

They reckon you are what you eat. Well, that morning I was up early, very early, and breakfast was leftover pizza from two days before. It was cold and loveless. Perhaps it was an omen.

The call came at about 3:05. I wasn't supposed to be on duty for another few hours, but what the hell? Wind was lashing the walls of my bungalow so hard I'd been awake for yonks already. Wretched weather for a joy-flight, so the emergency had better be something important.

This call-out wasn't typical. Seems an analogue distress beacon had been activated off the north-east coast and the Rescue Coordination Centre in Canberra was having a bugger of a time pinning it down. The sea was rough, they said, making visual sighting difficult, and the antiquated nature of the beacon made accurate satellite orientation impossible. At that point they had no idea if the signal was coming from a vessel or from a PLB carried on an individual lost at sea. In the latter case they didn't hold out much hope.

The sea isn't the natural provenance of the Royal Flying Doctor Service, but in this case, it wasn't our medical assistance they wanted. Search and Rescue reckoned our aircraft's on-board directional locating equipment could be useful to them. Their best positioning apparatus was busy elsewhere, it seems, while ours was not only state-of-the-art but available. Dispatch said they needed a favor. Clearly something significant was going down somewhere that morning, but we didn't know what and to be honest, didn't think about it.

No, I don't have the foggiest who rang it in – I received the call from our regional office. Didn't ask who was on the other end. The line was so bad, I couldn't twig to the voice. Does it matter? Surely it's in the daily log.

By the time I got to the field the night duty pilot had everything ready. The bird – my usual King Air B200C – was fueled and we'd received further directional intel from SAR, provided by the border protection choppers that were combing the offshore waters. No doctor was in attendance – not needed as the distress beacon was located well out to sea, but well within the exclusion zone, and I couldn't land the King Air on the water, short of ditching the plane, could I? But flight nurse Barry Chandish was there to keep me company.

Estimated flight time was about twenty minutes. I took her up and we skimmed along the base of some rather nasty-looking cumulous stacks, glad to be away and expecting bugger-all. The weather *en route* dumped light icing on the wings – nothing to fuss about. Clouds and rain and rather furious winds, especially once we reached the coast just south of Kempsey. But I could handle it easy. And by the time we descended to the search area, a few klicks out to sea, it'd cleared up quite a bit anyway. Light showers and some gusting. White tops everywhere, but nothing that would even be likely to swamp a dinghy.

Finding the source of the distress signal proved to be a piece of cake. At about 5400 feet, with Chandish working the DF monitors, we finally placed ourselves pretty well straight above the beacon, though I could see bugger-all of the ocean surface from up there. Too much cloud. With a GPS reading of that position as a fix, I did a few sweeps lower down. On about the fifth, with the waves tickling our arse, I spotted the vessel in the early morning light. It was adrift all right. Listing around like a pollie after a late night at the bar. I circled and Chandish reckoned he could see figures on the deck. They were acting weird, he said. Had to have spotted us, though they were giving no sign of it. Just standing there. He tried to contact the boat on a marine VHF transceiver and got nothing but static.

So I radioed SAR and gave them the position, which as it turned out was about 125 nautical miles north-east of Port Macquarie. They said they'd send a Coast Guard interception boat and in the meantime we should circle and keep an eye on the target.

No worries. It was a good result – or so we thought.

ITEM 4A.
TRANSCRIPTION OF IN-FLIGHT COMMUNICATION BETWEEN RFDS AIRCRAFT CODENAME TANGO DELTA AND RESCUE COORDINATION OFFICER ED FARLEY, 9 JUNE, 5:32AM

SAR Farley: Base to Tango Delta. We've had confirmation that the coast guard is on the way – ETA fifteen minutes. Request that you recon from as close as you can get and report on the condition of the target. Over.

RFDS Senior Pilot Russo: Roger that, Base. We're coming in at about 500 feet now. The air's fairly unpredictable. With the naked eye I can pick out three, maybe four figures standing on the deck.

SAR Farley: What are they doing?

Russo: Not a bloody thing. Just standing there. Hang on . . . Chandish is fetching the field glasses—

RFDS Nurse Barry Chandish: There's four, no, five of them, just standing on the deck staring out to sea . . . toward the coast I think. Which is definitely not visible right at the moment. Their faces look, I don't know . . . "stunned" may be the best way to describe it. Perhaps it's shock. What the hell happened down there? Wait on!

SAR Farley: What's up, Tango Delta?

Chandish: One of them . . . That can't be right. My god! Half his face is gone!

SAR Farley: What?

Chandish: Looks as though the right side of his face, half his jawbone, was . . . well, ripped off. And he's missing his right forearm.

SAR Farley: Are you sure of that?

Chandish: Maybe. I don't know! It's hard to get a clear view. We've passed now. Circling back around. I'll tell you what I *can* see clearly enough. Bodies.

SAR Farley: I didn't catch that, Tango Delta.

Chandish: Bodies, Farley. Or bits of them. There's blood everywhere on the deck – an arm or two, sure looks like it anyway. God! An upper torso. Ripped apart, with intestines everywhere. Were they transporting illegal wildlife that got out of their cages or something? It's a real massacre! Any reports of pirate activity in the area lately? One of the crew appears to be chewing on something. Can't tell what. Hey, they're taking notice of us now we've swung back 'round. Coming in . . . God Almighty! They're screaming at us. Can't hear it, but the look on their faces! I've never seen anything like that before! Their hands are grasping up at us like they want to drag us out of the sky—

SAR Farley: Do they appear to be . . . you know, um . . . fully alive?

Chandish: Fully alive? What d'you mean "fully alive"? Not much sign of life in the ones that are torn to pieces, that's for sure. What're you getting at?

SAR Farley: It's not what we expected here, Delta Tango. But from incident reports elsewhere, it's possible they're *all* dead.

Chandish: But they're still moving. How could they be dead? Oh, Jesus, you mean—

Russo: Not ordinary illegal immigrants, then, Farley?

SAR Farley: We have no information, Tango Delta. This was supposed to be a routine rescue, but from your description—

Russo: Oh, bullshit. Then it's true? There really are . . .

SAR Farley: Tango Delta, I've just had word from Naval Intelligence.

Chandish: Naval Intelligence? You're kidding?

SAR Farley: You're ordered to break off right now, Tango Delta. Under no circumstances are you to stay in the vicinity. The coast guard has a fix on the target and will arrive soon—

Russo: I can see them. But that's no coast guard clipper. Looks like a friggin' naval patrol boat. Armidale Class.

SAR Farley: Clear the area, Tango Delta. Now.

Russo: But surely we could offer assistance—

SAR Farley: Now, Tango Delta. I'm serious, Lynda. Get out of there *now!*

Russo: Okay, relax. I'm banking her away as we speak.

Chandish: The Navy vessel's approaching fast. The target's crew seems oblivious. They're still screaming at us—

Russo: What's this all about, Farley? This got something to do with those bogus reports about some kind of plague sweeping Europe – "The Death" or whatever it's called?

Chandish: What makes you think they're bogus?

Russo: Come on, Bazza. Zombies? It's crap.

Chandish: I've heard that Health Minister Roxon's earmarked a significant sum for research into this *bogus* Death virus—

Russo: Ha! That'd be right. Any excuse. So, is that what we've got here, Farley? Zombies off the Australian coast?

SAR Farley: Can't comment, Lynda.

Russo: Surely it's Internet nerds bullshitting us?

Chandish: There's been no news out of Britain for more than two weeks now. I know, my sister's there.

SAR Farley: Head home, Tango Delta. Head home and forget what you've seen. The relevant authorities have got it covered. Over and out.

There's not much more to say. We were given our orders and I'm well aware of the protocols, so I was out of there. But I was feeling creeped-out and a little curious. I banked high as we headed west toward the coast, to give us a good view right to the boat and the approaching naval clipper while we fled the scene. The naval clipper came in close and then I swear I could hear gunfire, even across that distance. Chandish reckoned he could see the flashes. Those Armidales are well equipped – a Rafael Typhoon 25mm stabilised gun deck and 12.7mm machine guns. That's from memory. God knows what else these days. Can do a fair bit of damage. Before we lost vision in the haze thanks to an unexpected cloudbank, it was pretty clear that the SOS boat was on fire—

Anchor voice-over: A resident of the north-coast township of Sawtell was shocked this morning to find what he believed were drowned bodies washed up on the beach where he was walking with his dog.

Resident [name not given]: It was real early in the morning, you know – sun barely up. The place was deserted. Jasper here started sniffin' around a heap of kelp. I went over and there was this body – a man dressed in what looked like some sorta uniform. He was burnt down one side. Bit further on there was another one. When I took a gander, looked to me like he'd been shot. Well, it sure coulda been bullet holes. There was a third further up the beach.

Interviewer: What did you do? Check for life signs?

Resident: I could see they were dead well enough, no worries. The skin of the one with the holes was startin' to rot.

Interviewer: Were you worried about infection?

Resident: Infection? Na. Just thought I'd better ring the cops. So I grabbed Jasper and headed back across the beach. But the bloody dog took a fit, barkin' like crazy. I could barely hold onto him. When I looked back, one of the bodies was standing up – the one with the bullet holes. Freakiest thing I've ever seen. He was dead, I swear it on my mother's grave.

Interviewer: You didn't try to talk to him?

Resident: You jokin'? I was too busy gettin' the hell outa there.

Anchor voice-over: When authorities arrived about half an hour later, there was no sign of any bodies, though a trail of footprints that suggested three persons walking with difficulty were visible in the sand, leading off the beach in the direction of the township. Police have begun a search of the area for survivors of what is assumed to be a shipwreck at sea.

Archivist note: *This news item was aired only once and nothing further on this incident appeared in any of the normal news outlets. It did cause some Internet chatter, however, especially after the footage appeared briefly on YouTube. That the entire Sawtell area was subsequently cordoned off following a spate of violent acts and murders throughout the township may lead us to speculate that this incident represents the beginning of The Death's entry onto the Australian continent. Little more than four days after it occurred, however, any such speculation had become irrelevant . . .*

ITEM 8.

HF RADIO TRANSMISSION MADE BY PILOT LYNDA RUSSO, ROYAL FLYING DOCTOR SERVICE OF AUSTRALIA, SOUTH EAST SECTION, 18 JUNE, FROM SOMEWHERE NEAR THE TOWNSHIP OF GULARGAMBONE, NORTH-WESTERN NSW. FULL TRANSCRIPT.

I don't know if anyone can hear this. Not even sure how effectively the radio's working. I'm trapped in the King Air halfway down the bank of the Castlereagh River. Hasn't rained for some time and the bed's dry. Lucky, I s'pose. Less lucky is the condition of the aircraft. The whole wing's a goner. At any rate the left engine's stuffed. It's not going anywhere. No sign of fuel leakage though. That's something.

I can't move. Can't really tell how much damage there's been to my lower legs. Reckon I'm stuck 'til they send someone in. *If* they send someone in. If it was up to me I'd be tempted to nuke the place, like it's rumoured they did in London. Not that I believe it.

I've sent out all the regulation distress calls, though there's been bugger-all in reply. That either means the radio won't receive – or everyone's too busy to answer. Maybe everyone's dead. When I'm feeling pessimistic – which is pretty much all the time these days – I'm inclined toward this theory. If this thing's out as far as Gulargambone, it sure as hell's got a toehold on the more populated areas along the coast. I expected I might be able to contact Broken Hill, but no luck there either. Or Dubbo.

Hopefully someone's working on a cure.

Anyway, I figured I'd better send in a report. Everyone wants reports. Some of what happened here should be of interest to someone, I guess, if anyone's listening. If anyone's left to listen . . .

At least it keeps me occupied.

My team didn't connect the search mission off the coast with the job we were given three days later. Why would we? A boatload of illegal immigrants that turned out to be way more illegal than anyone had imagined? At heart we all knew what it was about, but I'd pretty well convinced myself we hadn't really seen what we thought we'd seen. It's so easy to rationalize, to come up with alternative explanations – anything's better than the truth. Sure, stories about violence in the Coffs Harbour area were jumping out from behind every media bush. But there'd been nothing official as yet and it sounded like the work of rumormongers, to be perfectly honest. The anti-Terror propaganda frenzy was still in full swing – a new GM disease scare touted around the Internet every week or so. The Government had said nothing that didn't amount to an evasion, and I couldn't accept what people were whispering. The alternative? To believe in monsters! Whatever the stories leaking out of Europe and the US, the whole zombie thing seemed like viral advertising for some Hollywood crapfest. I mean, the walking dead? No one was going to believe that, right? Not here. Not in Australia. We're way more level-headed than that. Probably just a nastier version of swine flu spread by insects.

I wish it was.

RFDS Base sent me out, with nurse Barry Chandish and Dr Abhijeet Kushwaha, for an emergency retrieval in Gulargambone – a nice little town about 526 kilometres north west of Sydney. I was glad of it. The interrogations we'd gone through had left me feeling like I was guilty as hell, even though I wasn't. Thought maybe ASIO'd make sure I never flew again.

You know, I reckon something happened to the naval clipper that attacked the "refugees". Don't know what or how, but my gut's telling me that's what the fuss was about. Maybe the navy guys boarded the boat and the zombies got them. Who knows? There's no point in speculating. And I guess I shouldn't be doing so here – in case there *is* someone listening. It's top secret. But will there be any Security Protocols left by the time this is over?

One thing's for sure. I reckon the naval clipper might've sunk the boat and thought that was the end of it. Guess they forgot that zombies can't drown.

God, I'm thirsty. I think I'll just shut up for a bit.

[BREAK IN TRANSMISSION]

Anyone still out there?

I'm in Gulargambone. "The place of the galahs". I can see one now, sitting at the top of a tree and squawking. Ha! There's a zombie under the tree, standing staring up at the bird. At least it's distracting the creature from coming after me.

Looking out the window westward all I can see of the landscape through the blood splatters are the tops of straggly trees and bushes lining the river course. I know the Castlereagh Highway's up there but I can't see it. Maybe if I could get to it. Fifteen minutes ago a truck roared along there, going like a bat out of Hell from the sound of it. Apart from that, nothing. The truck was headed for Gulargambone. Don't like his chances. If I went up there to thumb a lift, I'd be zombie chow in five minutes flat.

All academic, anyway. I'm stuck.

God, the air's so dusty. I need something stronger than water.

Times have been tough in the rural sector for the past decade or so. Tougher than ever now. I bet the townsfolk weren't expecting this. Though the locals had worked hard to bolster their diminishing coffers with re-development plans and tourism awards, Gulargambone's economy had been failing the same way everyone else's was, only worse. When you've got a local population that would barely fill the front rows of the Opera House Concert Hall, hard times just get harder. Even fewer are left there now. Alive anyway.

The issue at hand was an accident on a property about 50 kms out of town, something the local medical center didn't have the means to deal with. The RFDS had been called in to transport the most critical of the injured to Dubbo hospital – or even back to Sydney – as fast as possible. While we were in the air heading north-west over the mountains, Dr Kushwaha did his best to coax some useful medical details out of the vagaries of the patchy communiqués we were receiving. It wasn't easy, especially when foul weather began to play havoc with the HF radio reception. Before we got there, they went off the air completely. So as we landed we were still unsure what the nature of the emergency was. The only thing we'd found out was that a farmer and his family had been visiting Sydney and they were injured there somehow. They arrived back home okay, but then their condition got worse. Car accident? How would they have made the journey in that case? It didn't make much sense.

I'm presuming now that their "accident" had involved the Infected that came ashore at Sawtell. So when the travelers returned home, they brought Death with them. I remember reading an article a while back – 2009, I think – about a Canadian Mathematics professor who developed a methodology for estimating civilization's likelihood of surviving a fictional zombie plague in reality. He concluded that our chances were very low. The Prof reckoned that neither "cure" nor attempts at co-existence offered any hope. Only aggressive action designed to eliminate the zombies at once and on the spot would be effective, but unless undertaken immediately and violently such action would most likely fail. Within a very short time from the first outbreak, he calculated, we'd be up the spout. Would the folk of Gulargambone have been likely to go with immediate elimination of the diseased? No way. Not knowing what they had on their hands, they'd quite reasonably called for medical help. If the Prof were right (and it appears he was), that compassion spelt their doom.

No one was waiting for us when we came to a halt on the rough bush landing strip we used when visiting the area. That should have been our first warning that all was not well. Well? Ha! Things were so far from well, there's no way I would've gone near this idyllic country town if I'd known, despite the RFDS's inherent altruism.

We traipsed toward a shed built to one side for storage and as a waiting area, wondering if we'd have to walk into town to find anyone. It wasn't far, but there wasn't time to waste wandering around like tourists. Chandish tried the contact number we'd been given on his mobile. No one answered.

We argued a bit about who was at fault then Dr Kushwaha noticed what appeared to be an overturned van, tangled in the bush off the runway. When we went to investigate, we found not only that it was a rural "ambulance" – fitted out with some basic medical equipment – but also that all had not gone well with the passengers. The back doors were open and the interior was covered in blood splatter. Chandish circled toward the front and growled "Oh God!" in a low horrified tone.

As I rounded the side of the van, I saw what had provoked his horror. The body of a man lay under the overturned vehicle, crushed by the roof. Blood pooled around him. Only his legs and one arm were poking from under its dead weight. I swear one of his legs moved, as though trying to gain purchase on the slippery grass. He's still alive!, I called out.

Chandish dismissed the idea, pointing out just how much blood and gore had oozed from under the van. He said I was imagining things. We snapped at each other and by the time we'd finished Dr Kushwaha had knelt beside the mangled, half-exposed corpse. Body's cooling, he said, testing for a pulse. There was no sign of life at all.

It was clear from the skid marks on the grass and the compacted dirt of the landing strip that the van had been traveling fast along the runway, had skidded off the flat surface and overturned. Someone must have been unlucky enough to be standing right at that spot when it happened. Blood smears decorated the inside of the windscreen, too, but there was no sign of the driver. He hadn't been seriously injured then. But what had happened? I poked around and found crushed grass enough to indicate the direction the survivors had taken.

We argued some more, with Chandish keen to climb back on the King Air and get the fuck out of there. I rather agreed, but Kushwaha trumped us with his seniority and an appeal to duty. We headed on foot toward the township, making for its small ten-bed hospital. The landing strip was maintained mainly for the RFDS and other medical needs, so building it as close as possible to the available services had been a priority. Nevertheless, it was a bit of a hike in the dry heat and lumbered with all that uncertainty.

Apart from a few distant figures – moving with an odd stumbling motion, I thought – we saw no one. They didn't see us either and for some unspoken reason none of us felt compelled to yell for their attention, even if they could have heard from so far away. There was an unnatural silence and sense of desertion about the place. It made us nervous.

Bourbah Street wasn't deserted though. As we turned into it, we immediately saw a corpse spread-eagled in the middle of the road. On examination, we discovered that parts of its flesh had been torn off, eaten, the doctor reckoned, pointing out the teeth marks. A wild animal, I suggested hopefully. He shrugged. Whatever had done it left tears that looked more like the result of human-like teeth than an animal's fangs. But that couldn't be, surely? Anyway, the *coup de grace* had come from the victim's head being ripped off and the skull smashed open.

Chandish demanded to know what the hell had gone down here. I didn't speculate, but I'd started to think we both knew exactly what had happened.

The hospital was a mess. There were a few more mangled corpses in the foyer area, but nothing living – not even the four or five figures that appeared from down the corridor. Their clothes were disheveled and bloody and they all bore signs of physical damage. One of them began to scream, eyes dark and expressionless. Chandish at least recognized it for what it was. He whispered, grabbing at my arm: Remember the creeps on that refugee boat? Same look.

Dr Kushwaha moved toward them as they shuffled closer. A chill ran through me – it was terror, the emotion you feel in the presence of unnatural death. I grabbed the doctor and pulled him away. He resisted, annoyed, and I blurted out an explanation that I'm sure made no sense.

We have to help them, he said.

They're beyond help, doc, I growled at him, hard, hoping the words would impress themselves into his consciousness. They're dead, I added in case he didn't get it. He frowned.

Then he got it, suddenly, as though the barrier between the world he'd known and this bizarre new one had been breached. His eyes widened and the blood leeched from his face.

I've seen a few of those zombie flicks where ordinary blokes become superheroes and start whacking the living dead with baseball bats and the like, making bad puns as they go. Right then, however, heroism was impossible. Faced by those utterly unnatural creatures – the abysmal absence in their eyes, the inhumanity that threatens all the long-held notions you've ever had of the sanctity of life, the absolute nature of death and the stability of the existential world – any pretense to notions of heroic action simply drain away. I felt threatened at a level so deep it totally blocked both rational thought and my ability to respond. It's not like facing some guy in zombie make-up. Mere sight of those shambling metaphors for the implacable absurdity of death is debilitating beyond anything you can imagine – until you experience it. My mind turned off in self-defense.

Suddenly I felt someone shaking me, a voice yelling in my ear. Painfully, my awareness of the moment returned. A dozen victims of The Death were way too close for comfort. Luckily Chandish was dragging me out of their clutches.

He is – was – a good man, Chandish. I remember sitting around with him while out on an overnight job once, boiling the billy, eating barbecued sausages with homemade bread and drinking beer from an Esky in the middle of nowhere under the vivid outback stars. Talking about life and its disappointments. He'd never tried to flirt with me, or at least I'd never noticed if he did. That was something of a relief. Not my type, physically, so his apparent disinterest had let us work together pretty well. One time, he told me how he'd wanted to be a doctor but hadn't had the patience when he was young. Life had seemed too urgent to spend it studying, he'd said. He found it odd that he'd ended up studying anyway, though to become a nurse. Seemed like a cop-out. Nurses are as important as doctors, I said. He shrugged. Reckoned one day he'd have a go at upgrading his qualifications. I'd understood then that it was unlikely. Now Death has made it impossible.

I can see him from where I sit, a few 100 metres behind and to the right, impaled on a splintered fence post. He's still, thank god. I keep looking back at him from time-to-time, even though seeing him like that is painful. I can't help but wonder what I'd feel if his corpse began to move. Luckily I can't see the details of his injuries . . .

[HERE THE TRANSMISSION BREAKS UP]

Something happened there. I managed to receive some hysterical chatter, but it was too incoherent and too brief for me to work out the who or the what-the-hell of it.

Back to the story.

In those first endless minutes, as we ran along the street after our encounter with the dead in Gulargambone

Hospital, I still held a humanistic sense of hope that we could escape this absurd nightmare. I'd had no idea how fucked we really were. Later as we came upon more and more of the zombies, their slowness and the damage they'd sustained before they'd been infected and come back to infect others encouraged a sort of desperate complacency. For a while we ran and avoided contact as much as possible, but had Buckley's chance of avoiding it forever. The dead might be slow and awkward, but they don't stop and were likely to be waiting, often in packs, around any corner.

Why didn't we go back to the plane immediately? Fuck knows! I think, at first, we'd simply run, mindless, not noticing where we were going. Thinking we'd find others to help us. By the time we realized that whatever others there were weren't in a position to help themselves let alone us, we'd been cut off or were too disoriented to think straight.

Gulargambone had reportedly had a population of about 580 people, plus whatever visitors happened to be there that day. Now, I reckon, it had a population of a handful of living – and doomed – citizens and a few hundred zombies. Assuming some of the population had driven out of the place once it became obvious what was happening – and assuming there were survivors somewhere. The lack of cars suggested that many did drive away. Probably they helped the disease spread.

But some had remained, for whatever reason.

At one point, a four-wheel-drive came careering out of a side street and accelerated erratically along the road. With the dust and the glare of the sun on its windscreen I couldn't tell if its driver was alive or dead. The quality of the driving gave bugger-all indication. At first it seemed to be coming to our assistance. It plowed into a group of zombies that had just noticed us and had turned in our direction. One of the zombies – a stereotypical Country Woman's Association type – got caught on the front bull-bars. Her arms and head flapped around, spraying the last of her blood over the hood and windscreen. The other went under the wheel and even at a distance I could hear its skull crack as the rear wheel ground it into the road surface.

The Pajero kept coming, turning now and heading straight for us. We yelled and scattered. It swerved sharply, at which point whatever control the driver might have had was lost. The car overturned, rolled several times and crashed into the display window of an arts-and-crafts store. It didn't explode in flames, but as the dust and debris settled, I noticed fuel leaking over the ground around it.

Dr Kushwaha insisted we stay where we were – a spot relatively free of zombies at that moment – while he checked on the driver. I thought it was a fucked idea, but this time there was no gainsaying his Hippocratic insistence. We watched as he pulled open the car door as best he could and reached in. While he was checking for vital signs, the CWA zombie who'd been jammed onto the front of the wagon appeared from inside the ruins of the shop. She was moving stiffly, one leg snapped and useless, and her belly ripped open, leaking gore. Chandish yelled a warning. Kushwaha pulled out of the wreckage and backed away fast. But not all the way. He stood, teasing the zombie to come closer. I realized it would have to pass right over a puddle of spilt fuel. Anyone got a match? he yelled. Chandish was a smoker – a once-dying breed whose addiction now seems less suicidal, given the human race's prospects for the future. He ran toward Kushwaha, pulling a lighter from his coat, and in a single fluid movement tossed it onto the pool of petrol. For a moment nothing happened, then it caught. With an oxygen-sucking whoosh the fire ran across the puddle and into the car. Kushwaha and Chandish both turned and ran.

There was no explosion though. The zombie kept coming, picking up a few flames as she passed over the thin veneer of fire. Her dress began to burn, with surprising vigor. Must've been some old-fashioned über-flammable synthetic. She ignored the burning, even as it licked over a dragging intestine. She was intent on reaching Kushwaha and Chandish, who swore at her and at the world's failure to live up to proper Hollywood standards for exploding cars. We ran on and she . . . it . . . followed.

It. How should we refer to the infected? Are they victims? Monsters? Seems wrong to be casual about it, to just dismiss them. This unnatural corpse had been a person once. Maybe still was. Who am I to say? There should be compassion. But the neutral pronoun makes it possible to do whatever needs to be done. Frankly, if any of us had had a can of petrol on us at that moment we would've tossed it over the zombie without a thought. Make it *really* burn. Incinerate it to a heap of helpless blackened bones. Maybe it would've kept coming anyway, even looking like a pillar of fire. Wouldn't have stopped until the flames burned through tendons and it lost control of its limbs and collapsed. Maybe even then it would have clawed its way toward us . . . until . . . until someone caved in its head.

The horror of these plague victims was making me physically ill. Makes me ill now, thinking about them, about what I did. Only that mind-wrenching nausea let me overcome the paralyzing effect of seeing them that I mentioned before. We were passing a hardware store and the door was open. I went in and grabbed the first weapon that came to hand – a spade. Kushwaha and Chandish had followed. The zombie dragged itself after us, smoldering, trailing curlicues of smoke. I went out and bashed in its head before it reached the door. Kept hitting it while it twitched and growled. Wasn't until I'd buried the spade right into its skull, hitting hard and splitting the bone, that it went quiet. Even so, I kept hitting it.

Chandish was shocked. He looked at me as though I'd lost my mind. Maybe I had. How else could I have done that? But it was only for a moment. I looked down at the bloody mess the woman had become and . . . and, fuck it! I cried. Couldn't help it . . .

Hang on! Hear that? Someone's trying to get through on the radio. Thank god! At last! I think I would've gone ape-shit mad for sure, talking to myself like this—

[BREAK IN TRANSMISSION]

You are what you eat.

It was one of my mother's favorite maxims, as she fed us tasteless vegetable mush night after night, in the pursuit of some elusive health she herself never found.

Died of disappointment, I've always thought. Not the bacterial endocarditis that was supposed to have done her in. Disappointment about me, her life, and the irrational and random nature of death. Maybe that's why my father didn't cry over her. Maybe that's why, after she'd gone, he stopped talking to me altogether.

Neither of my parents was ever very happy with me – and the lack of self-worth I learned from them has stayed with me even when I'm at my most arrogant. They weren't even proud of me when I earned my pilot's license and joined the Royal Flying Doctor Service. *I* was proud. I thought I'd done a righteous thing. Though I was earning a living, I felt as though there was something selfless about it, too – something worthwhile. I'm foul-mouthed and self-opinionated and loud, but seeing the welcome, the gratitude, on people's faces as you come into their isolated lives bringing care and even salvation is . . . was . . . a real joy. My parents merely saw the pilot's license as unacceptable for a woman and, if I had to be a pilot, the job as regrettable, a failed opportunity.

God! Why's it so hard? – life, I mean. The only way I could have pleased them was to get married and give them grandchildren. But what use would there have been bringing children into the world of Death that lies in our future now?

I wonder if my father's dead? Really dead. Maybe he's become the zombie he'd always aspired to be.

I'm babbling, aren't I? Falling into self-pity. I can feel myself fading, getting more and more introverted, angrier with everything, with myself. Once I start using metaphors, you know we're in trouble.

The radio call that finally came through didn't last long. The connection had been dodgy to start with, but then – Shit! I think they were all killed while I listened. I'd been right: The Death is everywhere. I'm not sure where the transmission originated, but I think it was the RFDS Control Center in Canberra. Sounds like the national capital has gone to the same Hell as Gulargambone, only on a larger scale. I wouldn't have thought that politicians and public servants would be gourmet tucker, but clearly the dead aren't fussy eaters.

But the lesson is, if the ACT's gone, the zombies have got to be everywhere.

Maybe now I can accept the truth. No one's going to come and rescue me. Still, I need to keep talking . . . to be heard . . . in case . . . in case there's still hope.

I can barely remember what happened after I went nuts and mashed the CWA zombie into the road – and it doesn't matter now anyway. If anyone's listening to this, I'm sure you've experienced your own version of the near-misses, the violence, the running, the deaths.

We headed toward the landing strip – to make an attempt to get out of there, I remember that. Even Kushwaha had given up the idea that helping this town was still possible. But somehow we lost our way, diverted by packs of increasingly ravenous zombies.

The monsters are so slow you can duck and weave around them when they're alone, but in a group they're unrelenting. And once they know you're there, once they realize you're alive, they gather like hyenas to a rotting carcass, the crowd getting larger and larger. Life attracts them, so you have to be invisible – and if not, then evasive as hell. But sooner or later you'll trip or mistime a move. Or one of the buggers will reach out of an unnoticed shadow. It happened to Kushwaha. We were passing a crashed truck and suddenly there it was – a big one, with bad skin and dead eyes and teeth that bit into the doctor's arm, right through the sleeve. Chandish got to Kushwaha and pulled him away and I used the spade I was still carrying to smash in his attacker's face.

Hours went by. I know because the light changed, fading into dusk. We met a young bloke, little more than a boy. He was with us for a while, but I think he was killed when he panicked and got trapped by a group of zombies, who tore him to pieces. At least he didn't become one of them – wasn't enough of him left. During some of those grim, relentless hours we were hiding, exhausted and scared shitless – I forget where. It was dark and smelt of compost. We discussed how to get back to the plane, but it was meaningless. None of us were willing to take any more risks. We were too demoralized. Kushwaha became sick, weakened by the attack made on him. The infection had taken him by the throat and was slowly squeezing the life from him. We knew where it would lead.

Eventually they found us, and Chandish and I were running again. We had to leave Kushwaha behind – he was dying and too heavy for us to move. We'd known for some time that we had to make a decision: was the greater mercy to kill him now while we had the chance, rather than let him become one of the ravenous dead? But we'd been cowardly and had hesitated, excusing our inaction by waving rags of false hope. When we were forced to run, not having to commit ourselves to unwanted action came as something of a relief, despite the guilt I then had to carry. How could we have done it? As we dodged away, I looked back, thinking that the horde would tear the poor bugger to pieces and eat him. But they didn't. They ignored him completely. He was dead already and they knew it.

The dead don't eat their own.

Then we ran into a huge crowd of them, after which it got a bit fucking crazier. I lost sight of Chandish. I think I ended up in a scuffle with a pair of zombies in an upstairs room, where I'd hoped to hide. Desperate to avoid getting bitten or even scratched by them, I jumped out of the window and tumbled to the ground and into a deepening twilight. A dirty, unkempt figure leaned over me, face impersonal in a mask of shadows. He reached toward me. In my last split second of consciousness, I felt grateful that it was over now and that I wouldn't have to deal with any of the absurdities any longer.

I woke to the smell of roasting meat cooking on a barbecue. It was so ordinary, so fundamentally Aussie, that for a brief moment it pushed the hours since we'd landed in Gulargambone out of my mind and re-set their harsh parameters to something kinder and more mundane.

It was a stupid fantasy.

Yet this is the important bit. At least I *think* it might be important. I don't know any more. At the time I was too hysterical to appreciate how significant a discovery it might be, but now, sitting trapped in the wreckage of my King Air, I can see the possibility of human salvation in it – a dark and degrading survival maybe, but humans will do anything to survive, right?

As I groaned into consciousness, a shadow materialized out of the darkness, side-lit by a flickering lightshow emanating from a rough brick barbecue. I watched a column of smoke drift over me into the sky. I growled out a curse, thinking the shadow was a zombie come to chew my head off. But it wasn't. The grizzled, unshaven face that leered down at me was alive – as indicated by a breath that smelled of grease, tomato sauce and beer.

He introduced himself as Al Bachmeier. He'd grabbed me off the street when I fell out of the window and brought me to this place of safety, as he insisted it was. I glanced around at the almost suburban backyard – paling fence on three sides and a fibro cottage behind. There was even a tool shed and a Hill's Hoist clothesline further down the back, with a cracked concrete path leading to it. I was lying on a tacky fiberglass sun lounger in the shadow of an umbrella and a famished wattle tree.

"Thought you'd like to wake up under God's heaven," he said.

About then I registered that there was a bright morning sky above me, not the growing gloom of evening I'd fallen asleep to. Apparently I'd been out of action for about fourteen hours.

I asked about the zombies, rather hesitantly as I was half expecting that he'd tell me I'd been dreaming. But no! He simply said not to worry as I'd be safe enough here. But we were completely exposed, I argued.

He smiled – and told me what I needed was some food.

By which I figured he meant the meat that was turning to charcoal on the barbecue. It seemed very odd to me right at that moment – this determined normality. How could we laze around eating over-cooked meat and drinking beer – a can of which he shoved into my hand before going to attend to the steaks sizzling on the warped metal grill – when people elsewhere were dying and a hundred carnivorous corpses could appear at any moment, insisting they had a reservation for lunch?

Well, why not? I hadn't eaten a thing for about twenty hours and I was, in fact, starving.

Bachmeier handed me a hunk of blackened meat stuck between two thick, rough-cut slices of what appeared to be bush damper. I took a bite. Not bad, if a bit gamey. I reached for the sauce bottle and slapped a few squirts of the red stuff on it. I asked him what sort of meat it was. It had the texture of pork. He looked evasive. He claimed it was local wildlife.

I assumed he meant kangaroo and chewed on another mouthful. I'd had 'roo before, but never this good.

By the time I had finished that steak sandwich and a second with some lettuce and a slice of tomato, I was feeling a little nauseous. The after-effects of fear and stress, I figured. I began to wonder what had happened to Chandish and questioned Al about him. He commented that if he were still running around through the town, his chances weren't good.

I asked Al if he had a wife and kids.

He said he used to have, as he scratched sadly at the stubble on his chin. "The bastards got 'em," he added in a monotone.

I said I was sorry.

"Found out about the meat too late," he said.

Right at that moment a wave of nausea hit me. I doubled up, retching. A flush of heat sizzled up from my guts.

"Try not to up-chuck," he said. "I got you to eat some last night, but you need to digest as much as possible."

Digest what? I asked.

"The zombie steaks," he said. "What you've been eating."

As you can imagine I took a fit. He had to be out of his fucking mind. I yelled and screamed and hoped like hell he was kidding me. But deep down I knew he wasn't. I'd sensed there was something off about him from the moment I woke up. That'll teach me to follow my gut instincts! I slugged him one, but he was a strong bloke, spun me around and pinned down my arms from behind. I felt his whiskers on my neck and gagged at the greasy funk of his breath as it drifted into my nostrils.

Once he calmed me down, he explained that he'd got real mad with a couple of zombies when they ate his wife and son, had gone crazy, he reckoned, watching them chew the flesh from their bones. He'd attacked with the first hunk of wood he could get his hands on and busted a few heads real quick. Somehow, by luck rather than planning, he'd avoided getting scratched or bitten, but when he found himself wrestling with the last of them as it tried to eat his arm, a sort of berserk mania overwhelmed him. He smashed its head open then kept beating at it even when it had gone still. Like I had – only more. Beating at it, screaming and finally chewing its face off. By the time he came 'round, he'd swallowed a lot of its flesh. When he realized what he'd done he recoiled with horror, just like me, but then found that it had somehow made him immune from attack.

He told me to watch, and let me go. He went to the garden shed, opened the door and stood aside as a woman came out. She was bloody and awkward and obviously dead. Her shoulder bones were visible under her torn dress. Behind her, in the gloom of the shed, I thought I caught a glimpse of bodies with large slabs of flesh cut off them.

He said the zombie woman was Martha, his wife. "She's dead," he growled.

I was speechless, unable to move. He held out his arm to her. She sniffed at it, but then turned away and headed for me, grumbling low in her throat.

He claimed they weren't interested in him because of the zombie meat he'd eaten. They don't attack each other, he explained, and now they thought he was one of them.

I knew he was crazy. It was obvious to me that she was ignoring him because something in her recognized him as the man she'd loved – or, more likely, because he already had the virus and was all but dead. Now the mad bastard had infected me with their diseased flesh. How long did the disease take to kill you, I wondered, and turn you into one of them?

As she approached me, uncertain, sniffing at the air, I grabbed a barbecue skewer off the table, warning her off. Al told me to leave her be. When she came within reach, I jabbed the skewer into her eye, pushing it hard, right through to her brain, I hoped. She screeched and stumbled away. I ran. Scrambled over the fence. Ran some more. Kept running.

That was the beginning of the end. My end.

Sun's going down again outside. A zombie has stumbled down the embankment, trudging with an appearance of dispirited boredom toward Chandish's impaled corpse. Surely, it's not going to eat him. He's dead.

[Off mic] Hey—!!!

Oh, shit. I was nearly going to shout out, curse the bugger and tell it that Chandish was no longer its concern. But that would only draw its attention to me – and if it came for me, I wouldn't be able to escape it, pinned here in my seat as I am. Fuck it! Maybe I could cut my leg off. But it's not numb, I can still wiggle my toes, even though it hurts. If I did, I'd just bleed to death. Anyway, how could I cut my leg off? Chew through the bone and gristle with my own teeth?

Wait, it's okay. The zombie has left Chandish alone and stumbled off back toward the highway. Thank god! I couldn't have sat here watching him get torn to bits, even though he's dead already. That would've been too much. Way too much.

[BREAK IN TRANSMISSION]

I should end this, now, while I still can. I'm tired. I could broadcast forever – probably I'll have to, until someone comes for me, if they're ever going to. But I've had it for now. I've still got one bottle of water within reach – with another emptied already. Luckily I'm a bit obsessive about having drinking water handy while I'm flying. I have to conserve what I have. But my throat's dry and scratchy. I can barely talk.

God, I'm hungry. What I don't have is food. Haven't eaten since . . . well, you know.

No sign of the fever yet. For a while I thought I'd caught The Death from Al Bachmeier's insane catering. Felt my skin heating up – I was trembling badly, sweating a river . . . but it went away until all I felt were the normal pains that come from having been in a plane crash. So I stopped worrying. Maybe I didn't catch it. I'd made myself vomit after escaping from Al Bachmeier, though not much meat came up – just bile and tomato sauce. But maybe it helped. I might work for the Flying Doctors, but I'm no medical expert. I don't know how The Death works. Its virulence might be diminished when ingested via cooked flesh. I don't know. Maybe it just takes time. Kushwaha took quite a while to die.

What would've happened, I wonder, if I hadn't found my way back to the landing strip? Certainly I wouldn't be here now, vainly chattering into the airwaves while the world dies around me. Probably the dead would've gotten me eventually, out there among them, on foot. I don't know and it doesn't matter. Starve to death or die of infection, even if you stay on your feet? Who cares? It's all darkness.

[BREAK IN TRANSMISSION]

Sorry. I had a bit of a bawl, off-air. But I'm over it. Got my shit together again – enough to end this anyway. The story.

After frantically dodging infected corpses for god knows how long, I found myself back at the plane, more by luck than through the agency of a brain that was working at peak efficiency. The King Air looked untouched. With a great sense of relief, I climbed on board, so desperate to be gone that I didn't even think to check if anything nasty had taken up residence. So when a human shape came at me out of the familiar spaces in my peripheral vision, I shrieked and started swinging the tree branch I'd picked up somewhere along the line. It was thick and had a gnarled, knotted end, like a club.

But it was only Chandish. Relief mingled with suspicion – and after we'd both determined that neither was certifiably dead, we hugged as though we were long-lost lovers who'd found each other again after a decade apart. Finally I pushed him away and made some distancing quip about boobs and octopus tentacles.

He explained that he'd only just arrived himself, moments before. He'd been holed up in some sort of tourist center, alone with pamphlets extolling Gulargambone's attractions and waiting for a gang of zombies outside to lose interest and wander off. Eventually he'd fought his way out. He'd been eating chips and drinking coke out of a dispenser. Lucky him. I said nothing about *my* culinary experiences.

We both knew what we wanted to do. Without further discussion I headed for the cockpit and started up the engines. I'd already positioned the plane for take-off so before you could say "Get me the fuck outa here!" we were bouncing along the rough landing strip and lifting into the air.

The wheels were barely off the ground when I was distracted by a ruckus behind me, the sound of scuffling punctuated by the familiar growls of one of the infected. Chandish shouted a warning.

Where had it come from? I don't know and didn't have time to think about it. I grabbed for my club as the creature's foul presence loomed from behind, but my strike missed and I hit the controls instead. The plane banked to the right, throwing us about. We were still low to the ground. I think the wing clipped a bunch of trees.

Chaos took over. At this point I lost all sense of what happened and why. I was too busy grabbing at the yoke to wonder what Chandish and the zombie were doing. All my efforts were futile, however. The King Air lost whatever minimal altitude it had gained, bypassing some houses, missing the highway and planing across the tops of bushes and trees at the edge of the Castlereagh River before crashing down its western embankment. When it finally came to rest, one of the propellers was crushed, a tree had smashed through the cabin wall and the main column had been forced down onto my legs, pinning me where I sat. I was dazed and numb.

I have no idea how the plane's rear door came to be open or how Chandish and the zombie were thrown from the aircraft as it plowed into the Castlereagh, but by the time my consciousness clicked back on, the interior of the King Air was quiet and Chandish was dead. The zombie had wandered off into the distance, having decided Chandish's corpse wasn't on the menu. It was Kushwaha, I realized. There must have been enough of his living consciousness at work to send the dead version of the doctor back to the landing strip looking for escape transport. Had it had some plan in mind? Who knows? I had apparently been forgotten now.

And that's it, I guess. What happens to me in the future is anybody's guess, but the prospects are grim. At any rate, you probably won't hear about it from me – you, that non-existent listener somewhere out there in Australia's Deadlands. No more from me or Chandish, who's found peace in death at least—

Holy shit! He's gone. I can see the darkness of the blood that pooled at the spot where he was skewered, but no corpse. Can't see any fucking zombies around or any other wildlife. Did he turn into one of them after all? Shit! If so, why did it take so long? Has he been alive all this time, slowly creeping closer and closer to death? It'd be a stupid fucking irony if he could save himself from the pole that had killed him only *after* he was dead.

I wonder if he's—

What's that?

[SCRAPING SOUND, GRUNTING]

Oh fuck, it's one of them, clambering up through the door. Yeah, it's Chandish all right. He's got a huge hole through the middle of his gut.

Bazza! Bazza . . . Chandish, you fucker, it's me, Russo. No, oh shit . . .

[GROWLING AND GRUNTING. RUSSO SCREAMING ABUSE. THUMPING SOUNDS. MORE GROWLING]

What the—?

[HEAVY BREATHING SOUNDS]

[BREAK IN TRANSMISSION]

Shit. I don't believe it! Chandish was dead but he didn't attack me. What he did do was . . . Bloody hell! I'm not sure I believe it. What does it mean? He came down the length of the cabin, growling and snarling, and leaned toward me, sniffing at the air. Then he grabbed at the branch that was forcing the torn yoke column onto my legs. I was hysterical . . . When I realized what he was doing – what he'd done, I dragged myself out. He let the branch fall and turned. Just turned away and stumbled back down the length of the plane and out the door. He's gone. Wandering away. Indifferent. What the fuck?

He freed me. Why? Did he remember that we'd been friends? No. I've thought about it and I think . . . I reckon he smelled The Death in me and freed me because he thought I was one of his kind.

Maybe I *am* one of his kind.

[BREAK IN TRANSMISSION]

I've made a somewhat disturbing discovery. I'm hungry as hell. Starving. I forced my wounded body to carry me down the plane to the food locker. Oddly, considering the damage that has been done to them, my legs don't hurt much. Strange. One of them looks fractured.

Anyway, fuck that! That's not important. The long and the short of it is I fetched some chips and an apple from the locker. But you know, I couldn't eat either. They . . . the taste of them . . . was making me sick.

Oh god. I hate to admit this. But what I feel like, what I really crave deep down in my belly, is meat. Zombie flesh.

I guess I'll have to go out and hunt.

Ha! There's irony for you. You are what you eat indeed. More or less, anyway. Bloody universe has validated my mother yet again!

[PAUSE]

No way I'll be hunting Chandish. Dumb sentiment, I know. But what can I say? There are standards we have to adhere to. Loyalty, at the very least.

Don't we?

Sure we do.

[PAUSE]

Well, we'll see. For the time being, that's it from me.

Perhaps I'll catch up with you around the traps sometime.

Whoever you are.

Whether living or dead.

[TRANSCRIPTION ENDS]

[LIVE ONLINE WEBCAM EXCHANGE]

Honeybunny: Jase? You there?

Doctorfrankenstein: You betcha – been waiting for you. Where are you? I see you're on the plane.

Honeybunny: Yeah. Bad seat, though – aisle. Anyway, we're in the air and clear of Kennedy.

Doctorfrankenstein: Honey, that's great. What's the ETA?

Honeybunny: I'll be down at Akron at 9:11. Will you be there?

Doctorfrankenstein: Silly question. How's it been?

Honeybunny: Don't ask, Jase. Not good. The Brits took out most of London. You hear that? Unbelievable.

Doctorfrankenstein: Yes, I just saw the news. Where's it going to end?

Honeybunny: Who said it's going to end?

[PAUSE: THE WOMAN IS LOOKING AT SOMETHING OVER THE CAMERA]

Jeff okay?

Doctorfrankenstein: Yeah. He's writing. I can hear him muttering in his room.

Honeybunny: He using my dad's Dictaphone?

Doctorfrankenstein: Yeah. It's a new story. He says he's going to bring The Death to the Falls.

Honeybunny: Ugh. What a thought.

B *I* U ☺ Arial ▼ 10 ▼

Doctorfrankenstein: Well, it'll happen, honey. Sooner or later. We just have to be ready.

Honeybunny: How's that going?

Doctorfrankenstein: Slow. Right now, the stuff we're coming up with is no more effective than paracetamol.

Honeybunny: Keep at it.

Doctorfrankenstein: You bet.

Honeybunny: I'm gonna sign off now. Maybe watch a mov—

[PAUSE: THE WOMAN IS NOW CRANING HER NECK]

Something's happening up front.

[SOMEONE SHOUTS OUT]

Doctorfrankenstein: What? Problem?

Honeybunny: Honey, I'm signing off.

Doctorfrankenstein: You okay?

Honeybunny: See you on the ground.

[the woman is reaching for the "clear" button on her screen, looking at something behind the camera]

Doctorfrankenstein: Love you.

Honeybunny: Love you, too. Bye.

[SCREEN MESSAGE: HONEYBUNNY HAS JUST LEFT THE BUILDING]

B *I* U ☺   Arial ▼   10 ▼

[Transcript of Videofile 01.mp4 from USB stick]

Note: transcription is rough in places. Some was originally transcribed by hand, some by voice-to-text software

10:04 am, 07/06

> Looking out windows of residential high rise at several people camped on rooftop of nearby lower building. Abruptly camera swings right and refocuses on Hudson River.

Female #1 – "Angela":
"Oh my God, am I seeing things or is that another miracle on the Hudson?"

Male #1 – "Tom":
"Holy shit!"

> Several excited exclamations from others in room as camera finally focuses on a passenger plane that has just landed in the Hudson River. Camera zooms in, refocuses.

Female #2 – "Emily"
"Somebody hook up the feed to the TV!"

Male #2 – "Clay"
"Workin' on it. Turn off the lights. *All* the lights. Save some juice."

Female #3 – "Louise"
"But it's sunny. We don't have to worry about the solar panels running out."

Female #4 – "Georgia"
"Someone else explain the wisdom of not using everything all at once to her this time."

Male #3 – "Alan"
"Louise, not using everything all at once is wise."

Male #4 – "Nate":
"Here, Tom, use the tripod."

> Camera swings around wildly for a few seconds, then steadies and refocuses on plane in river. The emergency exit is now open and the emergency chute has inflated and become a life raft. Passengers in lifejackets are gathering at the exit; the camera has zoomed in close enough to show they are all reluctant to get into the raft.

Tom:
"No, don't hook the feed up to the TV – use one of the laptops. That's good enough."

Clay:
"I've already got it connected."

Nate:
"Then leave it, it's easier for everyone to see anyway."

Emily:
"Stupid apocalypse. I'll be glad when it's over."

Nate:
"Silly girl, it's not gonna be over. Not like a hurricane or an earthquake is over. When it ends, we'll all either be dead or zombies."

Alan:
"Tomahto, tomayto."

Nate:
"You mean tomayto, tomahto. And it's really more like tomayto or head blown off."

On camera, some people have finally begun to get into the raft; others have climbed onto the wing. As the plane bobs and drifts slightly in the water, it's possible to see that the same thing is happening on the other side.

Georgia:
"Hey, you think that's the same pilot that landed in the Hudson that last time?"

Tom:
"I highly doubt it."

Emily:
"I thought they were going to close all the major airports after what happened on that flight to Ohio?"

Alan:
"Guess not."

Nate:
"I don't think this was a scheduled flight."

Someone detaches the chute from the emergency exit, allowing it to drop down into the water to become a raft. Immediately, all the people in the water try to get in, pulling at the sides. Several people attempting to get in at the same spot pull the side down enough to submerge it briefly and make the raft take on water. There's a brief flurry as some people who have managed to get into the raft try to force those people to let go, apparently afraid they'll sink the raft. That side submerges even more and a couple of the people in the raft fall back into the water again. Now the people in the water are fighting each other; most of them have let go of the raft and it rights itself with no problem. Two people still in the raft lean over the side and begin helping people in one at a time. The inflated lifejackets make the job difficult; one of the helpers removes his so he can move more freely.

All the people in the water finally get into the raft. The people on the wing show no sign of wanting to join them, but a woman in the raft wants to get up on the wing. Paddling with their hands, the people in the raft maneuver the craft close enough to the wing so the people there can reach down and lift her up. Once up on the wing, she also removes her lifejacket and tosses it into the raft.

Tom:
"I can't see anyone who looks like a stewardess or a flight deck officer."

Angela:
"Me, either."

Alan:
"So? Is that supposed to be significant?"

Angela:
"It means Nate's right – it's an unscheduled flight."

Alan:
[saying something, but Angela talks over him]

Angela:
"I mean, it looks like a bunch of people commandeered a plane."

Alan [faint laugh]:
"Maybe they already had tickets and didn't want to waste them. Hey, think about it. You've got this vacation planned that you've been looking forward to for months and then, all of a sudden, they cancel all flights because of a fucking zombie apocalypse. What would you do?"

Angela:
"Alan, The Comedy Store also cancelled open mike night. Try to commandeer us as an audience and you might end up in the Hudson, too."

Alan:
"You call that heckling? Pretty lame."

Georgia [a bit far from the camera mike]:
"I knew we should have gone to the airport."

Lots of incredulous exclamations, some laughter.

Tom:
"You'd rather be swimming right now?"

Georgia:
"No, we should have gone when there were still flights. If we had, we probably wouldn't be watching this right now."

Angela:
"Honey, you saw the news before the networks went down. I don't think most people could even get *into* the airports. And the ones that did, I don't think most of them ended up on planes."

Georgia:
"But if we'd gone to Newark . . ."

Emily [speaking at the same time as Georgia]:
"I never realized there were so many cemeteries in Queens. Or how many people were buried there every day."

Alan:
"Not anymore. Those that are still in one piece will either be shuffling west toward Manhattan or following the L.I.E. east for some juicy Great Neck brains."

Angela:
"Stop it."

Georgia:
"If we'd just gone to Newark. Early, when it all started."

Alan:
"I hate to break it to you, Georgia honey, but Jersey has cemeteries, too. Not to mention plenty of dead people waiting to be buried. Of course, some of them have jobs in Manhattan. Ba-dum-ching!"

Tom:
"Give it a rest."

Georgia:
"If we'd just gone to Newark—"

Tom:
"You, too, Georgia. That's not helping."

Emily:
"Why are all those people just standing on the wing?"

Clay:
"Maybe because they don't want to be in the water? Just guessing here."

Emily:
"So why don't they get in the raft?"

Tom:
"Too many of them. Probably why the plane went down – it was too heavy. Too many people got on."

Emily:
"Oh."

Some of the people on the wing have turned toward the New York shore and are waving their arms. A couple of men are trying to climb up on top of the fuselage. A woman near the tip of the wing loses her balance and falls into the water. The people closest to her kneel down and look for her. One of them points; two arms reach up out of the water, the hands flexing, fingers clawing the air as if desperately trying to get hold of something. Someone moves toward them, but the others pull him back. For a moment he seems to fight them and then suddenly everyone is drawing back from the arms, which have drifted close enough now to find the wing.

People are backing away as someone clambers up onto the wing. It's not the woman who fell in. This person seems to have been in the water for a very long time.

Tom:
"Oh, *Jesus.*"

Emily:
"Why don't they just push it off into the water?"

Tom:
"Because they don't want to get bitten."

Georgia [voice fading]:
"I'm not watching this, I'm going [unintelligible]."

More arms are reaching up out of the water – many near the raft and all around the airplane, which has begun to sink.

Angela:
"Oh my God, they're pulling it down. They're pulling the plane down into the river. But how did so many people get in the river? So many dead people, I mean. Where did they come from?"

Clay:
"You have any idea how many people drown in that river every year? Murders. Suicides. There must be hundreds of dead bodies down there. Or they might just have fell in or just walked in when they attacked people on the boats or near the shore."

Angela:
"But wouldn't they float?"

Clay:
"Don't ask me. Zombies obviously don't swim. Who knows how many of them are down there underwater trying to shuffle along looking for brains to eat. Hell, maybe a bunch of them *are* shuffling along the bottom."

Angela:
"That doesn't make any sense—"

Alan:
"You're arguing about sense when there are fucking *zombies?*"

The dead are clawing at the sides of the raft; there are so many of them that they actually claw themselves into the raft with the living people, where they go into a feeding frenzy. The blood excites the ones still in the water who try harder to get at the people in the raft. Suddenly the raft begins to deflate.

More of the dead are clambering up onto the wing. Many just fall off again, but when they come back up they grab the wing and hold on. The plane is sinking faster and the water around it foams with the thrashing of both living and dead.

Angela:
"Oh, God, I can't watch this. Why are you still shooting?"

Tom:
"Because there ought to be some record."

Angela:
"What?"

Tom:
"You see any Eyewitness News helicopters flying around? No one's witnessing this, no one but us."

Clay:
"You'd have to be some kinda freak to wanna watch that, though—"

Tom:
"I didn't say anyone would *want* to watch. I said there ought to be some kind of record. To show what happened."

Nate:
"Sure, sure. I'm just not sure there's gonna be anyone left to appreciate that thought."

The raft has disappeared. Some people are trying to swim away but they are all pulled below the surface of the water. The plane is going down faster as the dead swarm over each other to get at the living.

Tom [under breath]:
"Shit, there really *are* a hell of a lot of stiffs in the Hudson. Where the fuck did they all come from?"

The camera zooms in a little closer on the nose of the airplane, which is the only part remaining above water. Two women are sitting back to back on the area just in front of the windshield and kicking the dead away from themselves. Finally, a zombie grabs one woman's leg and manages to keep hold of it. More pull themselves up over that zombie and throw themselves on top of her. They all tumble into the water a few seconds before the nose disappears beneath the surface.

There are a few seconds of silence, broken by the sound of someone vomiting.

Alan:
"I bet that never happened to Walter Cronkite." [pause] "I'll get something to clean the carpet. Otherwise it's gonna smell."

Tom [coughs]:
"I can do it."

Alan [voice fading]:
"Forget it, I'm already in the [unintelligible] [voice fades back in] " . . . ink Nate's right. I don't think there'll be anyone left to appreciate your hard work at record-keeping."

Emily:
"And *I* think we've got to take a more positive approach to surviving, if we really do want to survive."

Alan:
"Yeah, well, I'm re-thinking my position on that."

Emily:
"Fine, but *I'm* not. I don't want to just give up, I *want* to live through this, I *want* to survive and I'm *going* to."

Alan:
"Yeah, OK, whatever. As the kids say."

Angela:
"I don't think the kids say that any more."

Alan:
"Oh, right, they all got eaten, didn't th—"

[FILE ENDS]

[Jolene_06-11.rtf]

Man, the last thing I expected was I'd be in the middle of the fucking end of the fucking world and I'd still be able to access the fucking *web*. How the fuck does that work?

Maybe I better not look a gift-horse in the mouth or I'll jinx it. I pulled the file labeled Videofile 01.mp4 out of some online storage site. It wasn't password protected or anything but considering the name of the folder – SCENES FROM MANHATTAN ZOMBIE APOCALYPSE – I'd say whoever put it there wants other people to find it.

It feels like a month since the subway but it's only nine days. Maybe someone else from my unit made it out but I may never know – my radio isn't merely dead, it's really most sincerely dead. And unlike things of the organic persuasion, radios don't reanimate or reactivate or whatever. It's probably stupid to carry it with me but I can't bring myself to dump it; if I actually do make it out of Manhattan and back to base, I want to be able to show them that I didn't lose my fucking radio, it fucking broke. No idea why I think this is important, considering this is probably The End of Everything. Or The End of Most of It, at the very least.

I broke into a store – well, I didn't really break in, the front windows were smashed already – and swapped my uniform for cargo pants (the kind with all the pockets) and a T-shirt, and found a non-military looking backpack to carry my gear. After I made it out of the subway, I got this overwhelming sense that I should get into civvies ASAP and hide any trace of being with the Army. Don't know why, exactly. Well, I sort of do, except I can't figure out how to explain it. I mean, it *is* like I'm behind enemy lines but with this particular enemy, it doesn't matter what I'm wearing or even if I'm stark raving naked. I'll only be fooling the people I was sent in to protect, which seems kind of weird. But every instinct I've got is telling me it's the best chance I've got of staying alive. I'm going to have a hard time explaining that when I get back to base.

If I get back to base. *If* base is still there. *If* they haven't pulled out.

I'm pretty sure they lit up Long Island with white phosphorous by now. It's a complete Scorched-Earth policy for zombies. Jesus, I can't believe I'm using that word. I can't believe *anyone's* been saying *zombies* like it was *house* or *tree* or *car*. Like this is a world where corpses trying to eat you alive is one more bad thing that can happen to you along with car accidents and getting mugged. Where it's more of a problem now than global warming.

This must be what it's like for people caught in a war or a disaster like a tsunami or an earthquake – like they're being run over by things that can't really be happening. I remember reading about when the US developed the atomic bomb and one of the scientists – I forget which – said, "I am become Shiva, destroyer of worlds." Well, buddy, you'd like it even less if you had to go through it as plain old Nobody Special. You're better off as the destroyer than the destroyee. Although I guess if you destroy worlds, you'll end up as the destroyee eventually anyway. Still.

When they showed us the classified video from England, a lot of us thought it was actually part of a new, very elaborate drill. That's the thing about being in the Army in peace-time – you spend a lot of time in what are basically role-playing games. They're stripped down, but you can tell the ones that have been thought up by someone who used to play – or, hell, who still plays – Dungeons & Dragons or World of Warcraft. You got to find some way to keep your Army sharp and wargames are it. We got a lot of terrorist scenarios – Al Quaeda this, jihad that, fanatic the other thing. Right after I got out of basic, I took part in this training exercise where Nazis took over the UK and Canada and attacked, with agents already on US soil. It was really complicated; my unit had to deal with a situation involving multiple hostages and human bombs. None of us knew why it had to be fantasy Nazis when we've got Al Quaeda for real. Maybe someone just felt like a change from the Middle East to the Teutonic. Anyway, we all thought that was pretty farfetched. England's got their white supremacists just like us, but I don't think there's anywhere near enough of them for a *coup d'etat*. But what do I know? I just signed up so I could go to college on the G.I. Bill. Now if I live long enough to muster out, will there be any point to college? Hell, will there be any colleges to go to?

I know how ridiculous that last sentence would be if I hadn't seen London getting nuked. By its own government. Jesus. I always wanted to go there. I always wanted to see Europe, too. The video of London getting nuked was the last anybody's heard from that part of the world.

The CO had us watch it twice through. It was South London, the part below the Thames River, that took the actual bomb. But that part of England's going to glow in the dark for who the fuck knows how long. Big Ben, Parliament, Buckingham Palace, Piccadilly Circus, Carnaby Street, that big Ferris Wheel the watchamacallit – no one'll get near those for, shit, centuries, I guess. Like I said, I never got there, but I saw it on TV and in the movies and on the web so much it was like it was part of my life. To think there'll never be anything coming out of there ever again, music or movies or TV shows, I feel like I've lost something. Or like I'm on the wrong planet.

Yeah, that's it. So how the fuck do I get off this shitball?

After we watched the video, this scientist named Mary Munroe who says she's on the President's panel of something or other gets up and starts talking about, of all things, the Black Death, bubonic plague – how it was spread by flea-carrying rats and the fleas were so thick that they actually moved people's bodies. There was some stuff about how nobody really knew how many people died across Europe because the records aren't reliable. Like, if people died of what their families *thought* was the plague but they were actually infected by these fleas, they'd have been taken away for burial but later, they'd have started moving around. So they'd have had to be killed again – head chopped off or crushed (delightful idea) – which would mean they'd have actually been counted twice.

I never heard anything like that in history class. Well, I heard about the fleas and the rats spreading disease but nothing about fleas making the dead move. I read that over and it still sounds fishy to me, even though I've seen fucking zombies grab my buddies and sink their teeth into their shoulders or faces or legs or necks and chew while the blood runs down their

OK, that's better. My stomach's been queasy all day and I was actually trying to make myself throw up, just to get it over with. All I had to do was think of Tommy McManus, falling backwards with that thing on top of him: when I ran over and pulled it off, most of Tommy's face came off with it. And he was still able to shoot the one about to put the bite on me from behind. He got it right between the eyes, blew its brains right out the back of its head. Sprayed right in Linda Washington's face, though and she got some in her mouth – she was spitting and retching while she used her bayonet.

We shouldn't have been down there in the subway. A bunch of us wanted to argue with the order. The sarge said there were a bunch of civilians hiding in the tunnels and they needed rescue more than the ones that had barricaded themselves up high, on rooftops and in the high-rises. Sarge said unless they were actively chasing live meat right in front of them, zombies wouldn't climb stairs; it just wouldn't occur to them. Nothing occurred to them except eating live people alive. Zombies didn't hunt on their own initiative and they didn't explore. They just wandered or stumbled or crawled around till they got a whiff (or something) of the living and then they went after them. And man, can those stiffs run. The ones that *can* run, anyway. Some of them are too busted up but if there's something alive near them, they try scrambling for it however they can. I saw one thing using its *chin* to try to drag itself along the sidewalk.

Anyway, the sarge said zombies going *downstairs* was different. They'd fall down a flight of steps, then pick themselves up and keep going. Anyone hiding underground, like in a parking garage or in the subway, could end up trapped.

Linda Washington leaned over and whispered in my ear that we could end up getting trapped with them. Corporal Chang looked like she was thinking the same thing but she didn't say a word. Before we got on the transport, some of us tried to get her to talk to the sarge, but she wouldn't. Well, yeah, of course she wouldn't. She couldn't. I've tried to put myself in her place and think how I'd have reacted if a bunch of grunts came up to me wanting me to tell the sarge their orders sucked and they'd rather not comply. Except I can't. If I'd been corporal, I think I would have said something. Hell, if I'd been the sarge I'd have found some way to get around the orders and do something else. Because we all saw the video of the cemeteries. I mean, *shit*.

I wonder if *that* video's online somewhere. If I can get into the Army site, maybe I could find it and put it up on the web myself. Or at least store it in the folder where I found the video of the plane in the water.

I've got to get off this rooftop and head north, uptown, see if I can get back to base. No, see if base is still there. Because I know that if command can't get on top of this and squash it, they'll go to Plan B, like the Brits did.

I'm actually having trouble deciding if I'll be better off hooking up with command before that happens or not. First London, then New York, then—? What will the world be like? Maybe not the kind of world anyone would want to live in. Maybe it'll be the kind of world where the best thing you could do for yourself was figure out where Plan B was going to hit and make sure you were there to meet it.

[END OF FILE]

[Transcript of Videofile 02.mp4 06-12]

Looking out of window of residential high-rise again at the same rooftop as at the start of Videofile 01.mp4

Half-a-dozen people are camping there. They have small tents as well as mattresses and sleeping bags in the open, also some barbecues probably liberated from the same stores where they got the tents and sleeping bags.

Alan:
"—why they never invite us over for a cookout?"

Georgia:
"What's going on?"

Nate:
"Doesn't look like a cookout."

Tom:
"Oh, Jesus—"

Four people, three men in shorts and T-shirts and a woman in a jogging suit are forcing a fourth man down on his knees. He is wearing only black bikini underpants that seem a bit too small for him. Something white is hanging off his shoulder and flaps as he struggles to get free. A second woman comes over, rips the white thing off and throws it down. It's a bandage; now the dried bloodstains are visible, as is the wound on the man's shoulder. It looks like a bite from a large animal.

The second woman lifts her T-shirt and pulls a large handgun from the waistband of her baggy pants.

Georgia:
"Oh, no. *No, NO!*" [continues yelling but voice fades as she runs from room]

[Other voices talking in distance]
Emily:
"—going on, Georgia's hysterical." [pause] "Oh, *Christ.* How can they *do* that?"

The wounded man has been forced to lie face down on the roof by the four people holding him and they sit on him to make sure he stays there – one on his legs, three on his back, two holding his arms up and back at an awkward and probably painful position. The woman with the gun puts her foot on the back of his neck, braces herself, and then aims the gun two-handed at the back of his neck.

Tom:
"What choice do they have? Obviously he got bitten and he was trying to hide it."

Emily:
"All right, then how can *you* film it?"

Tom:
"Because someone ought to witness this."

Emily:
"*This?!*"

Tom:
"People witness executions in states that have the death penalty."

Nate:
"Only because they're barbarians."

Tom:
"Because it matters. It matters if someone gets executed."

> The woman with the gun fires. The man's head explodes; blood, bone, and tissue splatter her trousers and the bottom of her shirt as well as the man sitting closest. He jumps away, pulls off his shirt and scrubs at his flesh with it, then throws it aside and removes his shorts.
>
> The others get up and move away while the woman who has just killed the wounded man sets the gun down. She undresses calmly but carefully. She eases off each shoe and as she steps out of her trousers, she looks at each leg for any sign of blood. Rolling up the bottom of her T-shirt a couple of times, she holds it firmly while she slips one arm and then the other out of her sleeves, then pulls the shirt over her head without the spattered part of the T-shirt getting near her face. She tosses it away, takes off her bra and underpants, and then bursts into tears.
>
> The other woman and two of the men put on overalls and rubber gloves before rolling the dead body up in a tarp or canvas and throwing it off the roof. One of them pours a gallon of what appears to be bleach on the blood and gore left on the roof. The naked woman continues to cry until one of the men comes to her with a blanket. He wraps it around her and leads her to a mattress where she curls into the fetal position and doesn't move for a long time. Another man uses a mop handle to pick up her discarded clothing and drop it off the roof.

Emily:
"They didn't have to do that."

Angela:
"They did and you know it."

Tom:
"This is one of those times when I feel the need of something from the medicine cabinet. Ange, you have the key."

Angela:
"What do you want?"

Tom:
"What would *you* want?" [pause] "We got any of that left?"

Emily:
"I meant throwing the body off the roof."

Tom:
"What?"

Emily:
"They didn't have to throw the body off the roof. They shouldn't have done that because that's like they don't care any more. And if they don't care any more, why don't they all just shoot themselves in the head right now?"

| Long silence.

Tom:
"Maybe they're trying to work up to that."

Emily:
"*We* aren't, are we?"

[END OF FILE]

[Transcript of Videofile_Jolene1.mp4 06-14]

Private Jolene Lindbloom:
"I uploaded the log I wrote on the phone to the storage where I found those two videos, and sent copies of it and the videos to every email address I could think of, including the White House. I figure they'll reach at least one live recipient." [sharp fumbling noises] "Then I thought why not do videos myself instead of going cross-eyed trying to use the keyboard on the phone. The phone's got a camera but not enough capacity so I did a little, uh, shopping and found this all charged up and ready to go in one of the electronics stores. They've all been smashed in but none of them's as looted as I would have thought. I guess a lot of looters got eaten, or left before they got eaten, I don't know."

> Point of view swings from street to the face of a young woman, early twenties. The camera is slightly too close and the lens can't focus completely.

"Yeah, that's me, all right. Private Jolene Lindbloom, US Army, serial number blah-blah-blah, who cares. Sorry, I've tried to stay disciplined but I'm losing it already. I went into this intending to be a good soldier, really, and look at me now. I forget everything they taught me at the drop of an apocalypse."

> Point of view swings from face to street with scaffolded building. Camera pans left to subway entrance and then down so we can see iron gates pulled closed, chained, and padlocked.

"This is an example of my handiwork. I got a Mr Microphone and used it to hail anyone alive in the station – I wasn't about to go in, no way in hell. I think if anyone had been in there to hear me, they'd have yelled to let me know. I'm saying this because I *do not want* to think I might have locked any live people in with zombies but I also know there's a possibility. If I did, I hope they can blow their brains out or figure some other way to destroy their own heads so they don't have to come back. I mean, when you die, you're entitled to *rest in peace,* just like God himself said. Now we got a regular zombie population explosion, responsible people don't want to make it worse. It's like—" [smothered giggling] "—you got to spay and neuter your pets, and make sure your head's crushed or cut off when you die. Otherwise—"

> Camera swings left and refocuses on a sidewalk across the street where a human-looking figure is moving awkwardly, dragging one foot. Literally – it's scraping the pavement at a right angle to the leg. This was a young man, late teens or early twenties at most; blood and tissue is crusted around his mouth and the left eye is slightly out of its socket. There is so much blood and filth on the shirt that it's impossible

to tell what color it really is. The corpse seems to look directly into the camera with its good eye and starts to drag along faster, mouth working, jaws snapping.

"—you're part of the problem. Gotta go."

[CUT]

Daylight indicates slightly later in the day, ground level. Looking down a long, wide street to what seems to be a traffic pile-up of cars, buses and trucks.

"If I had any sense, I'd delete the recording I made before or cut the sound. I'm not making myself look too good here. I thought I was going to start getting *less* shaky but I'm not. Instead of feeling like I'm getting further away from the subway, it's like it's actually sinking in more and more. Memories of what I saw keep resurfacing in my mind, just like pop-ups on a web page, and I can't stop seeing them. Tommy McManus's face ripping away. Linda Washington spitting, spitting, spitting – we're all yelling and guns are going off and the sarge is still giving orders but under all that, I can hear Linda making those disgusted sounds – *phthah, phthah, phthah!* Still trying to get the taste out of her mouth when two of them caught her bayonet hand and chewed through her arm up at the shoulder till they took it off. Blood sprayed out as she fell away and while that's hosing everyone down, what's going through my mind? This lecture from back in basic about how fast you can kill somebody if you cut the brachial artery. I can't hear Linda any more. Can't see her either under the zombies piled on top of her."

Camera pans right along a row of storefronts. Most windows are cracked or smashed. Abrupt change to face of Jolene Lindbloom, first in extreme close-up. Then she moves back, sits on chair. She is indoors; behind her is a pale green wall with a vertical crack running from ceiling to floor (probably – it goes out of frame). It's not a very wide crack but it is visible. It is not clear exactly what kind of room this is. Light comes from a window somewhere behind and to the right of the camera; it is not strong and continues to degrade while Lindbloom talks. By the end of the file, her shadow is barely visible.

"OK. So I was saying, about Linda and . . . that. Right then I decided to bug out. Saying it like that makes it sound like I thought it over and said to myself, 'OK, time to get the fuck outa here.' I just *bugged.* I turned around and started clubbing, punching, shoving, ducking, whatever it took to get *out.* Some of the ones I hit must have been my buddies. I couldn't see too well and I didn't really care at that point. I just kept punchin' and pushin' and kickin' and then I was running and running and running and I didn't stop until my legs gave out. I don't know exactly where I was but I wasn't in the subway any more."

"Dream about it almost every night, several times a night. Sometimes I dream that I watched Linda Washington bug out while a bunch of zombies piled on top of me, other times I dream that I woke up the next day and found a big bite on my leg. Or that I wake up and find Tommy McManus standing over me saying, 'Thanks a lot, buddy,' enunciating perfectly even without most of his face. And there's this part where I see the sarge lying on his back, struggling to get the barrel of his sidearm positioned just right under his chin before he fires; he's having trouble because of the zombie chewing through his belly. That shows up in every dream. I don't know exactly where but I remember it so vividly every morning. And I know it's a dream because each time, I see it from the vantage point of some distance away, as if I'd stopped to look back when I was bugging out. And I sure as hell don't remember doing that. I wouldn't let myself. Ergo, it's a dream. Or part of a dream.

"Last night, I slept on a roof with some other people. I climbed up ten floors in this apartment building I thought was empty. Two floors before I got to the roof level, I came face-to-face with these guys with guns. And I mean they had an armory. That didn't bother me so much as their faces. Actually, their eyes. They had crazy eyes. That's the only way I can describe it: crazy eyes. You find yourself looking at someone with crazy eyes and you don't know what they're gonna do, except it won't be pretty.

"If I'd had my sidearm handy instead of in my backpack, I think I'd have shot them just by reflex, before they could shoot me. Instead I just froze with their semi-automatics pointed at my head. Sometime later, one of them lowered his weapon and said, 'If you're looking for a safe place to sleep, you can stay here as long as you can prove you aren't infected.'

"I was still frozen. The other one said, 'You gotta strip, show us nothing bit you.' He turned around and hollered up the stairs: 'Female up!'

"This plump woman about forty came down, looked at me and told the guys to turn their backs. I could take off my clothes and let her see I didn't have any bites or I could find another place to spend the night, no problem either way. I obliged her. What the hell. All the time, she was telling me about how they were mostly people from the neighborhood in the beginning but they'd lost a few and picked up some others looking for a safe place to rest. She and some of the others including the two guys planned to stay put and wait for National Guard or the Army or whoever was supposed to come and get them. They were sending emails and trying to make contact with other people and sometimes even Twitter was back up and they hardly ever lost the wireless signal. I was putting my clothes back on when I realized that at some point, I'd stopped listening because I was crying. She didn't pay any attention.

"The guys went through my backpack and of course they found the sidearm. One of them knew enough about weapons to know it was military issue. I'd have told him I'd found it if he'd asked but he didn't. To my surprise, they let me keep it. Because I only had one, the woman told me as I followed her up to the roof. If I'd had two or three or more, they'd have taken them for the stockpile. But they weren't going to take my only self-defense. Things weren't that bad. Yet.

"There were about thirty people with sleeping bags or blankets getting ready to bed down. I found a spot near the center, between an older man and his granddaughter and a black-haired woman about my age with vivid tattoos running the full length of her skinny arms and a curved upholstery needle through her left eyebrow. I noticed she was putting studs and rings in her nose and cheeks and ears rather than taking them out, which seemed pretty weird. She caught me watching and said she didn't wear any of her jewelry when she was out because the zombies could grab her by it but she didn't want the holes to close up.

"I didn't know holes closed up but all I said was 'Good thinking' or something like that. She introduced herself as Cal (short for Calla Lily). The older man was Rodrigo, the granddaughter's name was Graciela. Then a chubby guy showed up with a teapot and cups on a tray and asked if anybody wanted some herbal tea. I felt myself start to shake. Just a little but I knew it was gonna get worse so I asked where I could go to the toilet. In the apartments one floor down, they said and the policy was not to flush except solid waste.

"The apartments had all been broken into and stripped of anything useful. Very practical and organized bunch, I thought, as I locked myself in a small bathroom with a shower stall rather than a tub and a sink about the size of soup bowl, and had hysterics.

"Or maybe not hysterics, exactly, because I didn't scream or wail or anything. I just shook, because I couldn't do anything else.

"I wanted to leave. I wanted to take my stuff and run for it but I was too tired. There was the prospect of something close to a good night's sleep; I couldn't resist that. But first thing in the morning, I was bugging out.

"Where did these people think they were? What did they think was going on? Well, yeah, obviously: they thought the cavalry was coming; they thought the Army or the National Guard was on the way to scoop their asses up and take them to safety. I was so glad I'd ditched my uniform. And I know I was being a coward not telling them about the subway or about what they'd decided to do about Queens and Long Island. Or Plan B.

"But at least they didn't know it. As far as any of them were concerned, I was just one more person who'd been looking for a safe place to sleep. The lie went with their guards and the courtesy of having a woman to inspect other women for zombie bites and the offer of herbal tea. There's this expression I heard once: *cozy catastrophe.* You see a lot of that in movies and TV, where the world ends and a little group of congenial survivors balance off the disaster part by being able to take anything they need or want – everything is free and nowhere is crowded or noisy and all the issues and neuroses anyone ever had about their day-to-day life just melt away.

"If I stayed just one more night there, I was gonna think I was in something like that, one of those *cozy catastrophes.* All we have to do is hang out, shop for free, and wait for our ride to pick us up before the herbal tea runs out or the zombies run in, whichever comes first.

"So could I sleep? Could I *fuck.* I got a couple of hours at most, not before the sky started to get light. Tattooed arms and Grandpa and his granddaughter were still asleep when I packed up and got the hell out. A guy and a woman were on guard duty when I came down. They didn't try to stop me from leaving but the woman made me take a card with a hand-drawn map of how to find the building – not a lot of detail and definitely not to scale but clear enough. I didn't want to, but she insisted. I stuck it in one of my pockets intending to throw it away later.

"From there, I went west but it wasn't long before I started crashing. Not enough sleep. I dragged around till I found this empty health club with a third floor Pilates studio. I barricaded the door and didn't so much fall asleep as I just passed out. Slept all day, I guess, because when I woke up it was pitch black. And totally silent. I couldn't hear a thing. I didn't know whether it was really that quiet or I'd gone deaf. Every other night, I've heard gunshots, screams or yelling, sometimes an engine, a very small one like a motorcycle, in the distance but close enough to keep me alert. I figured the more I got into the city, the more I'd hear. Well, not then. Anyway, I just went back to sleep, I was that tired still. And what the fuck, you know? If everybody in Manhattan had really cleared out or if I was deaf, what could I do about it?

"Next time I woke up, it was day. Actually, what woke me was the sound of rain hitting the windows. It was such a *normal* sound. It didn't make any sense – rain on the windows, in a world where we have zombies? And not just rain, but thunder and lightning, too."

"I stayed low and took a peek outside. First thing I see down on the street are these three fucking zombies struggling along, crawling on their hands and knees. They have to crawl because they only have three feet among them. One of them is completely naked and chunks of hair and scalp have been yanked out. The skin on his back has split in places and the backbone is showing through. Another is wearing the remains of a tuxedo and there's a dress shoe on his left (and only) foot. The third one is wearing a rubber wetsuit.

"So I'm crouched there watching this and suddenly I hear myself say, 'Only in New York.' I was just thinking, I didn't mean to speak out loud. And of course, that gave me away. I don't know how they didn't sense me before then – I don't know how they sense the living, I don't think anyone does – but me and my big mouth did it. Their heads came up like dogs getting a scent – zombie dogs with serious motor difficulties – and they started crawling in circles for a few moments before they aimed themselves at the building where I was.

"I got out of there at Mach 2. It wasn't that I didn't think I could outrun them. It's just that with zombies, there's never just one, or two, or three. If even just one homes in on you, suddenly a whole pack of them come outa nowhere and then you're in the shit. And vice versa.

"This is enough for now. It's getting dark, I gotta find some place to—"

[END OF FILE]

[Transcript of Videofile_Jolene1.mp4 06-15]

> Daylight, early to mid-morning. Looking down the same long, wide street to the pile-up of cars, buses and trucks. Camera movement indicates person shooting the video is walking toward the pile-up.

Private Jolene Lindbloom:
"I think we'll investigate what's going on here. I want to know if they're actually driving cars. Sounds like it. I wonder if they cleared the street. Plenty of other streets have cars and buses blocking them—"

> Cut to vantage point directly in front of pile-up. Cars and light vans are stacked on top of buses lying on their sides. Camera pans up to show the top of a crane with dangling hook visible behind the motor vehicle barrier.

Man's voice:
"I said, identify yourself and state your business! What do you want?"

> Camera pans left to a man leaning out of a wrecked police cruiser, aiming a rifle directly at the lens.

Jolene:
"Excuse me, I'm not from around here. Where am I?"

Man:
"This is 14th Street. What are you doing here?"

Jolene:
"Trying to get to a safe place."

Man [still aiming rifle]:
"Yeah? Any luck?"

Jolene:
"You tell me."

Man:
"OK, but first turn off that fuckin' camera—"

> Cut to low vantage point, looking up from about waist level at what could almost be a standard street scene B.Z. (Before Zombies) Many storefronts are open and people are out on the sidewalks but there is no motor vehicle traffic and many armed people obviously on patrol, talking into radios from time to time.

Jolene:
"Is that – is that guy selling *pretzels?*"

> Camera swings to standard street-vendor cart.

Woman [later identified as "Claudia"]:
"You like pretzels?"

Jolene:
"Sure. Who doesn't?"

Claudia:
"Five bucks."

Jolene:
"You guys use *money?*"

Claudia:
"What else would we use?"

Jolene:
"I don't know. Barter?"

Claudia:
"The rest of the country uses money and it's still out there."

Jolene:
"Have you heard anything? Like from the government or—"

Claudia:
"The web's still up. If the web's still up, the good old US of A must still be in business."

> Camera turns to look down road again. A small boy on a red tricycle pedals directly toward the camera, which is at the level of his nose. Just before he would have hit, it lifts, swings briefly to give a view of the pavement; rustling noises drown out any other sound briefly before camera returns to the same point as before.

Claudia:
" . . . suggest they keep 14th Street pedestrian-only after this is over. We all kinda like it."

Jolene:
"It's, uh, almost cozy. Not what I was expecting when I saw all those buses and everything piled up."

Claudia:
"Oh, yeah? What did you think?"

Jolene:
"Honestly? It looked kinda Mad Max to me. No offense intended."

Claudia:
"None taken. It can get kinda Mad Max for troublemakers. More than kinda."

Jolene:
"What do you call troublemakers?"

Claudia:
"Zombie lunch."

Jolene [nervous laugh]
"I mean—"

Claudia:
"I know what you meant. Anybody who breaks the law is a troublemaker. This is a crime-free zone. No looting, no violence, no breaking the perimeter, stay out of any zone you're not authorized for, observe the curfew, do your assigned job."

Jolene:
"What assigned job?"

Claudia:
"We've got to clean our own streets, collect our own trash, keep the generators going, produce food, keep an accurate head count, and make sure the perimeter's secure. Among other things. So whaddaya think – you want to stay?"

Jolene:
"I, uh . . . no, not really."

Claudia:
"I didn't think so. How much money you got on you?"

Jolene:
"What?"

Claudia:
"How much money you got on you?"

Jolene:
"I don't know – I'm not sure I've got any – well, not much—"

Claudia:
"Whatever you've got'll be fine. Hey, we don't let people in here for free and we sure as hell don't let them out for free, either."

[Coins clink and paper rustles]

Claudia:
"Good. If you need any more yourself, try further uptown on Fifth Avenue. Just be careful not to get too far east. Plenty of zombies from the Queens cemeteries made it across the bridges before the Army blew them—"

[END FILE]

JolLindBlm06-16.rtf

Stupid fucking camera battery went flat and I didn't notice for most of a day. At least I got most of Mad Max Goes to Manhattan. Jesus Christ. How the fuck did they get themselves organized so fast? Who are they, some kind of militia? I really wonder. Tax protestors and white supremacists are alive and well everywhere and I remember hearing about some group in upstate New York a while back. Except I didn't see any swastikas or white pride shit. I don't know. They all just gave me the creeps. There was something off.

Or it could just be me. I'm off. I sure feel off. Maybe it's just because I keep breaking into people's apartments to find a place to sleep. Last night, I found a place that had already been broken into and picked clean. I bedded down in the closet. All night, I could hear gunfire and sirens in the distance – it would wake me up but I was too bone-weary to get and investigate, even if I'd wanted to. I mean, sirens would seem to indicate there's some kind of organized, official authority working somewhere. Or it might only be people playing with sirens.

[END FILE]

Sound of helicopter. Camera sweeps across gray sky back and forth till it finds the helicopter.

Private Jolene Lindbloom:
"Holy shit, it's really there! Hey! *Hey!* Down here, down here!"

Camera set down at ground level; looking at flat tire of parked car.

Jolene (slightly distant):
"Down here! Look down here, you son of a bitch! Down here! Look at me! No, no no – don't fly away, goddammit! *Goddammit!*"

Camera picked up, aimed at helicopter growing smaller in the distance as the sound fades.

Jolene:
"Shit. I shoulda been in uniform."

Cut to low POV near ground, along side of building, looking down sidestreet; camera zooms in and refocuses on a man with a very large machete. Four people are lying on the ground, hands and feet tightly bound. The man with the machete is standing over a fifth, one foot on the person's chest, machete raised, obviously about to behead him.

Jolene:
"Aw, shit—"

Camera set on ground; falls over onto side. Rustling noise then sound of gunshot, very loud and very close. The man with the machete falls over.

Jolene:
"Stay down. Stay down, you son of a bitch—"

Cut to man lying on his back on the street; chest wound. He is dying. Camera pans to the bound people, struggling. They are all zombies. They haven't been dead for very long but close up there is no mistaking them for living people.

Man [with an effort]:
"Really . . . fucked up, didn't you . . . lady."

Jolene:
"Oh, Jesus . . ."

Man:
"Now you're . . . gonna . . . haveta do it."

Jolene:
"I—"

Man [crying]:
"Put down that fucking camera and do it! Me, included!"

⊪ Camera set down on ground; man's bloody chest heaving up and down

Man:
"OK, use both hands, bring it down . . . hard as you can . . ."

⊪ Chopping sound, scrape of metal on pavement.

Man:
"One down . . . five . . . to go."

⊪ Another chopping sound.

Jolene:
[Wordless gagging noise]

Man:
"*Again!* You gotta . . . *all* the way through."

⊪ Sound of metal hitting pavement, following by retching.

Man:
"Don't stop! *Don't!*"

⊪ Chopping noise, then metal on pavement. Coughing.

⊪ A fourth chopping noise, following by shrieking.

Jolene:
"He got looѕe!"

Man [in terrible pain]:
"Never mind that! Get his fucking head all the way off!"

Jolene:
[Hollering wordlessly; three chopping sounds]

Man:
"OK, you got it done. One more and you can go."

Jolene [crying]:
"Oh, Jesus . . ."

Man:
"Hey, you *owe* me . . . your fault! Come on, I'm suffering! Get 'er done, lady! Get 'er done! Get 'er—"

⊪ Jolene screams.
⊪ Chopping sound; man's body goes limp.

[END OF FILE]

[Transcript of Videofile_Jolene1a.mp4 06-17]

> Camera on Jolene's face in semi-dark; bright lights in various colors from somewhere behind camera shine on her.

Private Jolene Lindbloom:

"I almost deleted that. I fucked up so bad. I made it here and crashed out and I was gonna delete it when I woke up. But then I saw this."

> Camera picked up and turned around. Looking out a restaurant window onto Times Square. Many of the lights are still on. Only one of the giant video screens is lit up; it's showing Videofile1.mp4, the plane in the Hudson. This is near the end of the video.

Jolene:

"I don't know who's doing it. I don't know how they're doing it. Or why. Maybe because if it's filmed, it's gotta be shown."

> Videofile1.mp4 ends. Screen goes blank white for a few seconds, then words form in black capitals:

1 HOUR AND 45 MINUTES LEFT TO EVACUATE. IF YOU ARE READING THIS AT ANY LOCATION BELOW 50TH STREET, IT IS IMPOSSIBLE FOR YOU TO LEAVE MANHATTAN BEFORE ZERO HOUR. YOU SHOULD GO TO ONE OF THESE HIGHLIGHTED AREAS ON FIFTH AVENUE:

[a line drawing of Manhattan appears showing the traffic grid, with only 5th Avenue and certain intersections identified]

ANY LIVING THING AT THESE POINTS WILL NOT SUFFER.

IF YOU ARE ABOVE 110TH STREET, YOU HAVE PLENTY OF TIME TO REACH ONE OF THE CHECKPOINTS WHERE YOU CAN BOARD TRANSPORT AND BE TAKEN TO A SAFE PLACE.

DO NOT ATTEMPT TO BRING WEAPONS OR ANYTHING THAT COULD BE A WEAPON WITH YOU. YOU WILL BE SUBJECT TO A PHYSICAL EXAMINATION. ALL THOSE WHO REFUSE WILL BE EJECTED AND REFUSED TRANSPORT. ANYONE WITH AN OPEN WOUND OR A WOUND THAT HAS RECENTLY HEALED WILL BE SUBJECT TO FURTHER EXAMINATION BEFORE APPROVED FOR TRANSPORT.

Screen goes blank white again. Then more black letters appear:

ACTUALLY, THERE'S NOT THAT MUCH ROOM ANY MORE AND YOU'RE PROBABLY GOING TO END UP DEAD ANYWAY. SO YOU MIGHT AS WELL STAY HERE AND DIE.

Blank screen again; then a video of the Triboro Bridge blowing up in slow motion, with bodies flying everywhere.

Jolene:
"That message appears after every video. I don't know if it's true – if the Army's gone to Plan B and they're about to bomb Manhattan – or if someone's just having a sick laugh. Or rather, I'm pretty sure the Army's going to bomb Manhattan. I just don't know if there's actually any time left to get out of New York or not."

Camera pans down to the street below the screen. Many figures are roaming aimlessly around.

Jolene:
"They were here when I woke up. I don't know if it's me they smelled or whether there are other live people here, too. Maybe. But I'm so tired. And so tired of being so tired."

Camera set down on table, still aimed at crowd in Times Square.

Jolene [slightly distant]:
"I don't think I dreamed about the sarge after all. I think I saw it. OK, right under the chin."

Gunshot.

Camera continues to run for 45 minutes until battery dies.

[END FILE]

Note attached to package:

[signature illegible]

Tony–

You're right.
We might as well.
Tell the pilots to
saddle up.

▼

The Longest Distance Between Two Places
by Will Halloway

I didn't go to the moon, I went much further –
for time is the longest distance between two places.
> — from *The Glass Menagerie*
> Tennessee Williams (1911–1983)

MY MOTHER'S FINAL DAYS were long things, as still as bedclothes in an empty room and as quiet as dust settling on hardly used furniture.

▼

Friday, 10:08 pm

Mom called from New York this afternoon. Turns out things down there are not too good, with folks from this plague thing – they're calling it "The Death", which sounds totally dire to me: needs to be something like "The Rapture", though I think that's been done already. Maybe "The Big Sick" like a riff on that old Bogart movie. Anyway, folks with "The Death" are wandering around Manhattan taking chunks out of people. I still find it hard to . . . Hang on, the Leaf has arrived. She's just come into her bedroom, turned the light on. I think she glanced across here – my light is on as well, just the one on my desk where I'm writing this journal. She knows I'm here, I'm sure of it. She's come across to the window and opened the small one. Now she's pulling the curtains. Let's see if . . . Yes, now I'm sure of it. She's pulled the curtains closed but the right-hand one has shot across and left about two feet un-curtained, so I can still see into her room. Can't see <u>her</u> now, though. I think maybe she's gone to the bathroom or something. Anyway, dad said for mom to come back as soon as she can and not hang around Manhattan. The news shows and the papers are full of talk about "the final solution". When I asked dad about what that might be he just stalled and says they're considering ring-fencing New York like that old Carpenter movie but I'm not stupid. I may be only fourteen – next month, anyways – but I know they're talking about maybe nuking Manhattan, like they did in London. Leaf has come back into her room. Jesus God! She's just got her bra on and a short skirt. The bra is . . . Dad just called up. He's going out. That's good. I can get down to this now. The bra is blue, a light blue as far as I can make out. The skirt is white or maybe cream. She's just unzipped the skirt and dropped it down. Oh Christ – matching pants, deep ones. She's standing right in front of the uncurtained piece of window, folding her skirt. Totally full on. Now she's turned around – oh, that <u>ass</u>! – and walked across to a chair. She's just laid the skirt on the chair. I need to get dad's binoculars and keep them here in my room. No, he'd want to know where they were. But no again, there's too much going on with The Death for him to bother about his binoculars. The Leaf has just pulled the curtain closed. I'm wondering if maybe she saw me lying across my desk with my face up against the window. I hope not. I need to start the new story. I just hope there's going to be a world left for me to write in. It's going to be a zombie story that's what they're calling them . . . the folks with The Death: <u>zombies</u>. It's going to be about a sales rep for a national company who catches The Death and brings it to a small town. Like maybe "The Death from a Salesman". Still no movement from the Leaf's window. More tomorrow.

▼

Okay, here's the story. It's called "Something Undead This Way Comes:" So, "Something Undead This Way Comes" by Jeffrey Douglas Willson
  [clears throat] First of all, it was July, a rare month for a small town.
  School was out and the dread days of September were a whole summer away. But there wasn't much call for smiling faces. Truth was it wasn't a good year anyplace,

and especially not for the small town of Cuyahoga Falls, Ohio - type that up as just "OH" - a suburb of Akron and Cleveland and the pride and joy of Summit County.

In the 2000 census, the Falls came out at just a lick shy of 50,000 folks - six years later the records had it around 50,400 - with most of them good people, God-fearing people. And the Town Fathers wanted to keep it that way. So Mayor Robart had posted militia on all the roads leading in and out. And he'd strung them across the Cuyahoga Valley National Park, a long thin line of stern men with guns — and machetes — who were not afraid to use them. Basically, the word was that if you went out then you stayed out. Only a few brave souls made the decision to do just that, their pickups and flatbeds stacked with whatever belongings they considered essential. The thing was there weren't all that many things people considered essential any more, just their health. But while the Falls was considered very healthy and safe, the lure of family trapped outside the city limits was just too powerful for a lot of folks and they decided to run the risk. The trouble was, in the hot summer lined up for that year, most towns had cordoned themselves off the same way as the Falls had done. So good healthy folks who had come out of the safety of their hometowns suddenly found themselves aliens in their own country, and no matter what their skin color or their religion or their sexual preferences, they were not welcome anyplace.

Jeff? Jeff, you up there?

Okay, that's it for now.

[From the computer records of William Halloway. File name: "STORIES IN PROGRESS"]

▼

THE END OF INNOCENCE
by Will Halloway

SCHOOL WAS OUT and the dread days of September were a whole summer away.

Dear Jeffrey

You're reading this because I'm no longer around to say the words to you myself. A regret but, as we know, these things happen. Death and taxes, my boy. How I envy you that neither has played a significant part in your life - at least, not until today. And for that, I apologize.

Ah, words... what delight they have given me over the years. And what delight it looks as though they will give you. I only wish I were there to see it. But don't be sad. Who knows what's waiting for us just around the corner - you know, I have to say I'm rather excited.

In fact, I'm particularly excited knowing that at least someone in this heathen family of ours is going to keep up the great tradition of wordsmithery. Your mother was never one for the arts, preferring to bury her head in books of equations and formulae. Just like your father. Neither of them seems to appreciate that there is a magic in the sound of the wind in the trees and the sight of a bird swooping through the sky and the smell of freshly-mown summer lawns... a magic that can be neither explained nor translated by any number of textbooks. And the appreciation - or even the recognition - of this magic cannot be learned or taught. It's either there, in your soul, the very second you draw breath. Or it's not. We know it's there in you. I have always known that.

So take this gift and use it well and often. I have included a few batteries and a nice shrink-wrapped bundle of new cassettes, plus some old ones to re-use. I suggest you stock up on them - with all this iPod, Twitter and download malarkey,

I wouldn't like to venture a guess as to how long it will be before they're a quaint relic of a bygone day.

I searched for the instructions but I fear they're long gone. But it's simple enough: start, stop, pause, record, rewind and fast forward. Hard to go wrong, really. I'm sure you won't.

In closing, I'll say this: my life has been a constant joy. Not always a huge success but always enjoyable. My books and my stories have been generally well received if not massive moneyearners. But so what. The thing to aim for is the enjoyment. Plus maybe a few dollars to pay the bills, put some food on the table and maybe take a vacation at the beach every now and again.

So good luck to you. I have no real advice to give you except for this: be true to your characters as you are to yourself and they will always be true to you. Do not make them do or say anything you know they wouldn't want to. If your readers care about your characters - really <u>believe</u> in them - then that is what will drive them.

And one more thing. Short stories is (are?) the way to progress and hone your craft. Leave the long-haul of the novel until such time that you've honed your craft. (Sorry, I see I already wrote that but I'm too tired to re-do this page and too fussy to cross through the first one.)

Time to go, I think. I shall watch your progress with great interest. And, of course, with the deepest affection.

Forgive scrawly writing.

With all love and best wishes for the future,

Your grandfather
William Halloway

▼

Okay, where we were: skin color or their religion or their sexual preferences, they were not welcome anyplace.

But, you know, no matter how secure you think something is, well, there's always going to be a way to get around that security. And so it was in the summer of this particular year, with the world on the very brink of going to Hell in a hand-cart, when a small Ohio town got a surprise guest [no, sorry, "visitor" . . .], when a small Ohio town got a surprise visitor.

He was a salesman of sorts, but the only commodity he was selling was death. *The* Death, to be more precise.

Once upon a time he was Arthur Melville Bennett, a sprightly 53-year-old with a spring in his step and a smile on his face, always ready to help someone when they were down. And that was his problem right there. The person he had decided to help over on East Avenue, staggering dazedly from his Camry late the previous evening, had a problem. *His* name was James deFentos and he sold linoleum flooring for LinoleumFloor.com, a subsid of Eco Products Inc., operating out of Boulder, CO. And, though James too was a decent fellow – leastways up until just a couple minutes before he hit the tree, when he suffered a massive coronary – he was . . . [Hold it: the Leaf has arrived, ladeez and gentlefolks. More later. Work to do.]

▼

Saturday, 4:20 pm

Christ, I don't even know how to do this. Mom is dead. Turns out one of the passengers on the plane from Kennedy totally freaked. Before they were able to put him down (the co-pilot had a taser so even walking corpses must have some kind of working nerve system and dad says that's a good thing – yeah, right!) the guy had taken a chunk out of a stewardess's arm, the lower jaw of a man from Cleveland who had just given his notice so that he could be away from danger and safe with his family, and the entire left hand of a little four-year-old boy with Down's Syndrome. He also managed to swipe his nails at mom's arm and drew blood. The authorities terminated the stewardess, the man and the little boy when they touched down at Akron – turns out the Cleveland guy had already come back but they had him tethered down on a row of seats. Dad had mom taken to the lab at the General Med Center where old man Foley had gone on ahead and was ready for them. But dad says she didn't make it. When I asked him for more info he just said, Jeffrey, I said she didn't make it. Then he apologized and we both hugged and wept. But since then I've gotten to thinking how it maybe all ended for mom. I didn't want to ask dad for any more. I'm in my room now playing music on my iPod. I don't like to think about those final few minutes over at General Med.

["The News Hour" on NewsChannel 5 WEWS, Cleveland, Ohio, 6:00 pm June 8]

[A man and a woman – their names are on screen: LEON BIBB and ALICIA BOOTH. The station ID along the bottom of the screen is NEWSCHANNEL 5 WEWS. The man is nodding as he turns to the camera and moves a sheet of paper on the desk in front of him.] "Thanks, Alicia. And yesterday, The Death reached its bony fingers deeper into the mid-west with the tragic death announced of Marianne Willson, the wife of noted Ohio bio-chemist Jason Willson and daughter of the much-loved Illinois author, Willam Halloway." [Cut in a photo of a dark-haired woman wearing a wide smile. It could be a High School Achievements Book entry save for the fact that the woman appears to be in her mid-thirties.] "Jason Willson is a key figure in the President's attempts to find a cure for the plague that has so decimated Britain's population and that of other European countries." [Cut to shot of a man getting out of his car and walking to a glass-doored building. We follow him. The constant glare of flashbulbs is like the Fourth of July. The anchor continues.] "Following the incident on yesterday's American Airways flight from New York's JFK airport to Akron, Mrs Willson was taken to Akron General Med but she had sustained wounds from which – despite her husband's frantic attempts to reverse the infection – she later died. Mr. Willson had this to say just a few hours ago." [The man stops and turns to face the reporters. His face is drawn and his voice cracked.] "Marianne put up a fight, a brave fight, but the time that had elapsed between the original infection and our treatments had been too long. We were left with no option but . . . but to end her misery. My son Jeffrey and I are devastated, of course, but my determination is undimmed. In fact, it is increased. We *will* find a cure to this blight on humanity. So, if you'll excuse me, I have work to do." [We cut back to the anchors. Alicia Bibb shakes her head sadly.] "Yes, and it's more bad news, this time for sports fans and ball players alike as one of Minor League baseball's finest teams today announced the apparent suicide of Akron Aeros pitcher Cleve Breitenbach." [Cut to video of a smiling young man wearing the Aeros uniform, making some practice pitches to teammates . . .]

[The diary of Jeffrey Willson – entry for Saturday June 8]

▼

Saturday, 8:15 pm

Now that's the strangest thing of all. The Leaf just came into her bedroom holding her face in her hands. She made it over to just in front of her window – I think there must be a chair or something there – and then she looked right over at me. I kid you not, dear diary. She looked right across at our house and specifically at my bedroom. Then she waved and she blew me a kiss. Then, just as she was about to pull the curtains, her mom came into the bedroom in her wheelchair. The Leaf looked suddenly guilty and she quickly pulled the curtains closed. But this time there was no overshoot. The curtains ran from right over at the left to right over on the right. I waited for a while (it's now ten before nine) but she ain't coming back. Not tonight, anyways. I've had to turn up the volume on my iPod cos I can hear dad crying. Even with the plugs in my ears. I envy the Leaf sitting up there in her bedroom with her mom. I wish mom was here now. Even in a wheelchair.

▼

Okay, back to it. So . . .
 And, though James too was a decent fellow - leastways up until just a couple minutes before he hit the tree, when he suffered a massive coronary - he was cheating on his wife of 27 years. But that didn't matter because Gloria deFentos was also shtupping it to Carlos Bennault, the deFentoses' gardener and odd-job man over on State Route 343 in Yellow Springs. And Carlos had been across to Oxford, England, to stay with his sister, Merryl . . . while Merryl had been having a fling with a married guy from the savings and loan office where she worked [check that: I think they're called building societies over there, not savings and loan]. Also need to check with dad to see just how this thing can be passed on: saliva - we know blood - semen, breath.
 DeFentos who wouldn't do harm to anyone, stepped over the spread of disarrayed 13" square linoleum tiles in Blue, Gray, Green, Sunset, and Neutral and out of his wrecked Camry and looked around for someone to share his problems with. In the end, he shared his problems with Artie Bennett. Just because he didn't know better. And even Artie making it back to his own vehicle in time to get his Smith & Wesson out of the glove compartment and find a home in Jimmy deFentos' head and chest for three of the five slugs he fired in quick succession, just wasn't enough. Not enough even with young-no-more-but-simply-and-finally-dead Jimmy lying with his face transformed into something that resembled

the meatfeast platters they served up in A Pizza the
Action over on Eastwood Avenue.

And to give Artie all credit due, he did consider
putting the still warm barrel of the Smith & Wesson
into his mouth and fire the last round up through his
upper palette and all the way to his brain. But even as
he was looking at the weapon, he started to shake
uncontrollably. He pitched backwards, still holding the
gun, and was both dead . . . and alive once again
before he hit the ground.

The gun stayed down there a few feet away from him as
he rose unsteadily to his feet.

[Note extract from the laboratory of Dr Jason Willson]

▼

The reaction of the zombie on the plane to the taser is the first
suggestion that we could have a route towards achieving some kind
of viral clamp. At the Med, I worked on Marianne. A type of
excitatory synaptic transmission which is novel for the vertebrate
brain was found in the ner neuron (M-cell) by means of the passive
spread of their action currents across the synaptic membrane. After
stimulating the ipsilateral eighth cranial nerve, an excitatory
postsynaptic potential (EPSP) appeared in the M-cell with a latency
which is very brief (about 0.1 msec) and which probably represents
a negligible synaptic delay. This response can only be attributed to
the club endings: there were steep gradients of potential along the
lateral dendrite of the M-cell during activity and the early EPSP was
maximal in the distal part of the dendrite where the club endings
predominate. Potential changes in the M-cell spread (passively)
backwards into certain eighth-nerve fibers (probably club endings)
indicating the presence of special low-resistance connections between
them and the M-cell. In short, we could be on a breakthrough for

treatment here by somehow introducing a reactive agent into the synaptic reflexes of the neural complex. But it was too late for Marianne.

[Telephone conversation recorded from Jason Willson's private number to Professor Jacob Zeitner in Saratoga Springs, New York, Saturday June 8]

▼

Jack?

Yes, Jack Zeitner here. Who's this?

Jason. Jason Willson.

Jason! Oh, shit, Jase . . . Kath and I were so sorry to hear ab—

Yeah. Thanks, Jack.

You okay?

Okay? Well, you know.

Yeah. Oh, Christ, Jack, I'm so sor—

Hey, I need to pick your brain.

Go ahead.

The guy that took out Marianne? The guy on the plane? They flattened him with a taser.

A taser?

Yeah. He went down like a sack of coal.

And?

So, I'm wondering if maybe we could introduce or induce some kind of electrical charge in the victims?

You mean . . . like zap 'em?

Uh uh. Tried that.

You *tried* it?

[Silence.]

Who'd you try it on?

[Silence.]

Jase, who'd—

You know who I tried it on, Jack. Let's not piss around here with protocols. I'm asking you a fucking question. Help me out, okay?

[Pause.] Okay.

So?

Well, maybe you don't need to *introduce* something.

Huh?

Maybe you just need to·*enhance* something that's already there.

Sure, something that'll . . . that'll increase the electrical activity in the nervous system.

By boosting the neurotransmitters?

By boosting the neurotransmitters.

Like, serot—

Like serotonin, yes.

▼

THE PREMATURE BURIALS
by William Halloway

TUESDAY, 18 JUNE 1946

The tall man removed his hat as Alice opened the door.

She nodded at him. "Matthew," she said, the word so soft that, even though he knew what she had said, Sheriff Matthew Modine felt a need to lean forward so that he might pick up a residue of it. A vapor trail, perhaps, of something so mightily fine shooting right on by, a meteor maybe, or a comet, shooting across the sky oblivious to him and to her and to every other damn thing watching it.

▼

Sunday, 4:20 am!

Can't sleep. I can hear dad moving around in his room all the time. And he's taken to talking – to mom, I'm guessing. I can only hear a dull mumble and I don't want to get close so that I can hear the actual words. The Leaf has been keeping her curtains drawn for a while now, day and night. I'm sitting here at my desk staring at the damn things, willing them to open. But still they remain closed. I think I know why – she just can't bear to see me or let me see her. I think she maybe thinks it'll somehow cheapen mom's memory . . . me seeing her (Leaf) in her underwear – cos I'm almost sure she knows I watch her. I wonder if dad's thinking of how mom used to look in just her underwear . . . if that's what he's saying to her right now . . .

▼

Hi, Mr Willson. It's Alex.

Hi Alex.

Hey, I'm really sorry about Mrs Willson.

Thanks, Alex.

[Silence]

You want Jeffrey?

Please.

Okay, hold on.

[Pause]

Hello?

Jeff, it's Leaf.

Oh, hey.

My dad said to let you know he and mom are going on a sponsored walk later today. He wondered if you felt like coming along.

Oh. Tell him thanks, but I don't think I'd be much company. You going?

If you go, yeah. Otherwise I'm just gonna chill.

Well, thanks for the offer but I'm writing.

Yeah?

Mmm. New story. Monsters come to town.

Maybe I'll see you later.

Yeah?

Well . . . you know.

[Pause] Oh, right.

Good luck. With the story, I mean.

Thanks. Tell your dad thanks.

Sure. Take care.

Uh huh. You too.

[Recorded cassette in the Dictaphone of Jeffrey Willson – Part Four]

▼

```
Okay, back to it once more.
  He looked at the gun, tilting his head first to one
side and then the other. To anyone watching, it would not
have been clear that the man recognized it for what it
was. His interest, such as it was, was fleeting, brief.
```

[End of weather report on NewsChannel 5 WEWS, Cleveland, Ohio, 1:57 pm June 9]

▼

"Thanks, Dick.

"Hey folks. Go get your walkin' shoes ready cos we're steppin' out!

"We'll be meeting at the corner of East 4th in front of Flannery's Irish Pub in Downtown Cleveland at 4:00 pm. We'll be traveling down the newly revitalized East 4th Street pedestrian alley, and we'll shoot the decorative neon signs and unique architecture of the East 4th restaurants and then head down to Euclid and take in some of the impressive architecture of Public Square. Then it's on to the Tower City building with its large beautiful open spaces. Then on to West 6th, to Lakeside Ave, to Willard Park and a view of the Rock and Roll Hall before heading up East 6th to Rockwell through the Library Garden and a walk thru the Hyatt hotel and Arcade and back to Cadillac Ranch for libations and pixel peeping. Bring your cameras and good shoes. Pray for good weather. And tune in to WEWS tomorrow because I plan to review the entire walk and make sure we have the best Cleveland has to offer photographically. So if you're coming, bring your cameras.

"Back to you, Dick."

"Thanks, Ronnie. It's the top of the hours here on WEWS, two o'clock in the afternoon. Here's Rosie with today's headlines. Rosie . . ."

[Radio conversation between Lorain County Sheriff's patrol car and Cleveland Police Department Central Dispatch, Sunday June 9, 7:11 pm]

▼

Ange?

JJ?

It's not good.

Casualties?

Yeah. Fourteen dead, two more on their way.

What the hell were they all doing there?

Some kind of organized walk.

Not good timing.

[Silence]

Charlie okay?

He's okay.

You get everybody? Everybody I mean who's—

Nope. A guy and a woman. Charlie's gone after the woman – shouldn't be difficult [gunshots]. Ah, might be okay now. She was in a wheelchair.

And the guy?

No idea. He lit out while we were dispatching the others. Looks like something out of *The Texas Chainsaw Massacre* here. Fucking heads everywhere. And Ange?

Yeah?

The heads keep on – you know, after we've . . .

After they're severed?

Yeah.

Keep on what?

The mouths keep on opening and closing, like they're trying to speak. And their eyes keep blinking.

Mmm.

What's that supposed to mean? Mmm?

I don't know what el—

Charlie's back. He's got the woman's head. Jesus.

What about the guy?

What about him?

You going after him?

It's a needle in a haystack, Ange. He could be anyplace. Anyplace at all.

[Telephone conversation made from Jason Willson to Professor Jacob Zeitner in Saratoga Springs, New York, Sunday June 9]

▼

Me again.

Shoot.

The serotonin won't work.

You tried it already?

No, I did the math. There's no way we can build up a big enough charge, even amalgamating it with another component – say, tryptophan – it doesn't compute. The virus is too aggressive.

So?

"So?"

I mean, so what next?

Yeah, right. What next.

[Newsflash on NewsChannel 5 WEWS, Cleveland, Ohio, June 9]

▼

"We got some bad news here, Rosie."

"Go ahead, Dick."

"We're getting reports of a major outbreak of The Death right here in downtown Cleveland. And it's happened on the walk."

"The Big Walk?"

"Yes ma'am."

"What do we have?"

"It's sketchy but from what I can make out, it's all over."

"And fatalities?"

"Fourteen fatalities."

"And . . . is it contained?"

[The man shakes his head] "I'm afraid not, Rosie. They have all but one of the infected people and those unfortunate souls have been neutralized."

"And the last one?"

"There is one man unaccounted for."

"One of the walkers?"

"We're going to have to check that out. It's a mess down here."

"Keep us in the loop, Dick."

"You bet."

"Meanwhile, elsewhere in town there are roadblocks at ev—"

▼

Sunday, 8:55 pm

The curtains are still pulled back over at the Leaf's place so I'm just going to keep on waiting. I've seen her out in the yard and then back in the house but . . .

▼

Hello?

Hi Mr Willson. It's Alex. Again. Is—

I'm here, Leaf. I got it dad.

Leaf?

It's her name, dad. The middle one.

I guess I'm getting older than I figured. Say hi to your mother and father, Alexandra. [click]

Will do.

Hey.

Hey. What's up?

My mom and dad. They're not here.

Where are they?

On some kind of walk.

Oh yeah, you said. [Pause.] But like, you know where they are, right?

They're late.

It's only nine.

No, my mom's medicine. She should have taken
her medicine.

When?

Around six, seven o'clock.

Oh . . .

Hello?

Sir, how can I help you this evening?

We got a prowler.

Where are you calling from, sir?

From 2211 Eastwood Avenue.

Is that in Cleveland, sir?

[Pause.] It sure as hell ain't in Des Moines, lady.

I mean what county is that, sir?

Cuyahoga.

Thank you, sir. The prowler. Is he in the house?

No, ma'am. He's outside.

In the street?

He's back on the street, yes. I'm watching him. He's staggering.

You say he's back on the street. Where was he before?

Staggering through the yard, knocking over the trash and setting off
my Subaru alarm. It's on right now—

I can hear it.

Well, it can run itself down all I care. I ain't goin' outside,
that's for sure.

I'll send a car, sir. May be a while.

Well, like I said, we ain't goin' nowhere.

▼

Go back inside the house.

You're watching me?

I saw you go outside. I can see you now, Leaf.

Why'd you call me that?

[Pause.] Don't you like it?

I didn't say I didn't like it. I said—

Well, do you or don't you like it.

[Pause.] I don't know. [Pause.] You okay?

Yeah. I'm okay.

Your dad?

He's okay. We're both of us okay.

Will?

Yeah?

Can you come over?

[From the computer records of William Halloway. File name: "STORIES IN PROGRESS"]

▼

OTHER LIVES
by Will Halloway

"HONEY?"

"Yes?"

"I have a confession to make."

Jacob's face looked drawn when Sheila glanced across at him, her husband fresh into the kitchen, with the smells of bacon under the grill and fresh coffee brewing, the radio weather announcer proclaiming, in a chirpy voice, that the cold front heading down from

Maine was likely to freeze your saliva in your mouth, talking to Sheila and Jacob as though he knew them, knew the both of them and had done so for all of his life. It had seemed like a normal morning and yet now, suddenly, it wasn't normal at all. Not at all. But maybe she had already known something was up, something Sheila hadn't been able to put her finger on when she'd gotten out of bed, emptied her bladder and washed her face, gone into the kitchen and turned on the Mister Coffee and the radio but now, with Jacob's opening line . . .

I have a confession to make – what the hell did that *mean*?

[Radio conversation between Lorain County Sheriff's patrol car and Cleveland Police Department Central Dispatch, Sunday June 9, 9:22 pm]

▼

Ange?

We have a complaint about a prowler.

Yeah, what's he doing?

[Pause.] Like, prowling maybe? How the hell do I know what he's doing?

Ange, a prowler is low man on the old totem right now.

Give it a look.

[Sigh.] Where is it?

[Recorded cassette in the Dictaphone of Jeffrey Willson – Part Five]

▼

It was getting dark.
  Artie Bennett moved slowly, sluggishly through the darkening – no, not darkening: I already said it was dark – through the lonely streets. Who's to say he recognized anything that he saw. It was simply a matter of putting one awkwardly placed foot in front of the other, with only the slowly burgeoning sense of needing to eat providing any kind of motivation.

Somewhere off to Artie Bennett's right, a dog barked.
Then again. Without stopping, Artie turned his head in
the direction of the noise, stumbling but failing to
put out his hands. He fell face forward onto the
sidewalk, glancing his head against a shin-high picket
fence. The damage - if there was any - didn't seem to
phase him. He just got to his feet again and carried
on.
  One intersection in front of him was his house.
  Was that where — [large clattering sound in the
background][long pause; rustling]
  Huh? That's Mr Spaulding. Shit.
  [the sound of telephone buttons]
  Pick up, Leaf, pick up . . .
  Leaf, it's me. Leaf, listen to me. Your dad's
outside. No, wait a minute . . . wait a minute, Leaf. I
think he's . . . he's . . . Leaf, get out! Leaf, your
mom isn't with him. Leaf . . . *Leaf!*
  [the sound of a door opening] Jeff, what's—

[Telephone conversation between Jeffrey Willson and Alexandra Leaf Spaulding,
Sunday June 9, 9:47 pm]

▼

Dad?

Leaf, it's me.

They're still not home, Jeff.

Leaf, listen to me. Your dad's outside.

Wha . . . oh that's—

No, wait a minute . . . wait a minute, Leaf. I think he's . . . he's—

Jeff, what's going on? [distant clattering sound]

Leaf, get out.

You said dad – is my mom with him?

Leaf, your mom isn't with him.

Jeff, you're frighten—

Leaf, just get—

▼

—happening?
 [clattering sound overwhelms the voice] Spaulding.
He's in the house. Leaf's in there. He's one of them,
dad. And the phone's gone dead. [clatter]
 What? [pause] I can't see anything.
 Dad, he's already in there. We have to—
 Wait, I see him - or I see somebody. In the kitchen.
 Oh, Leaf. Look. She's in her bedroom.
 What's she doing? She do that all the time?
 Dad, we have to go over there.
 [sounds of banging, doors slamming, feet racing, fading away]

[Radio conversation between Lorain County Sheriff's patrol car and Cleveland Police Department Central Dispatch, Sunday June 9, 9:58 pm]

▼

Ange. I'm at the prowler call now. There's a guy
and a kid running across the street. The kid's waving me down. I'm
going in. I'll get back to you.

Steve, you need back-up? [Door slams.]

Kid, what's going on here?

Steve?

[Muffled voices.]

Sir, stay back. Sir, I'm asking you to—

[Screams – woman or girl]

Steve—?

[From the computer records of William Halloway. File name: "STORIES IN PROGRESS"]

▼

THE DISTANT SOUND OF HUNTING HORNS
by Will Halloway

Memories are hunting horns
Whose sound dies on the wind.

> —Guillaume Apollinaire (1880–1918)
> from *"Cors de Chasse"*

It was a time when only the dead smiled,
happy in their peace.

> —Anna Akhmatova (1889–1966)
> from *"Requiem"*

I HADN'T SEEN MELVIN STOCKARD since the days at the bank and I was astonished at how he had changed. I waved to him from my table, half standing up, and at first I thought he'd seen me and the lack of response was that he couldn't place me – he was looking right in my direction. But it wasn't me he was looking at, it was something behind me. I didn't know what it was . . . at least not then.

[Incident report filed by Deputy Sheriff Steve Prather, following the confrontation on Eastwood Avenue, 10 June, 11:16 pm]

I and the kid and his father, from across the street, made straight for the house.

When we got inside, the perpetrator – the girl's father – had made it to the staircase. The girl was already on her way down and the guy caught her. Simple as that. The guy from across the street – his name's Willson – he tackled the perp but they just have too much strength. I pulled the kid back – he was about to have a go himself [I think he has the hots for the girl, name of Alexandra but he calls her Leaf]. I got my gun out of the holster. No Miranda rights. I pushed the kid out of the way, moved to one side – my right – and fired two shots. One hit the perp – the girl's father – in the small of his back, maybe five, six inches above his pants line. The second shot got him in the back of the head. There was no appreciable time lapse between the two shots. The first one did not seem to have any effect at all.

The second one took him down. Unfortunately, the perp had broken his daughter's skin, on her calf, right one. She was trying to get back up the stairs once she realized her father had been contaminated but she just wasn't fast enough and he managed to get his mouth to her leg. It wasn't a big wound – I managed to stop him before he could make any significant damage – but the skin was broken and the girl was traumatizing. She went almost immediately into . . .

[Note extract from the laboratory of Dr Jason Willson]

▼

. . . shock, unable to control her movements. It was clear that we did not have much time. Alexandra's mother suffers from MS and I knew there was a likelihood of serotonin being on the premises. I left the Sheriff calling for an ambulance and Jeff tending Alexandra while I went downstairs. I found the pills, but seeing them in my hand I was suddenly struck by how feeble was my attempt to reverse or at least slow the viral infection. There had to be a better . . .

[From *Giving Thanks* by Jeffrey Douglas Willson (unpublished mss.)]

▼

. . . method," he said to the empty kitchen, his eyes darting to and fro looking for inspiration.

"Better hurry, doc," the cop shouted from upstairs. "She's going."

That was when he saw the screwdriver.

"What are you going to do with that, dad?" Tom asked his father when Jerry Douglas reappeared at the head of the stairs carrying a metal screwdriver and a roll of brown adhesive tape.

Jerry crouched down next to the deputy and reached out to feel the girl's pulse. He nodded. "It's weak but it's there. Fading though. We're going to have to move quickly." Jerry looked around.

"Help me get her over there by the wall."

The deputy and Tom helped move Martha across the carpet, each of them providing little assurances that everything was going to be okay. The truth was, none of them thought that, deep down.

"Okay," Jerry said. He lifted Martha's left hand and placed the screwdriver into it, closing the girl's fingers and then running brown tape to keep it secure. Then he pulled the plug attached to the air-cooling fan and wedged the screwdriver between the points.

Martha's eyes were rolling back now, almost completely white. And she was shaking and lurching.

"Is she dying, dad?"

Jerry nodded and rolled more brown tape tightly around the screwdriver and the plug.

"Okay. Move back."

"Dad! What are you doing?"

"I'm not sure about doing—"

"We don't have a choice," Jerry snapped at the deputy.

The deputy pushed Tom back away from the twitching girl and the pair watched in a kind of fascinated horror as Jerry took the plastic plus and jammed it into the wall-socket. Then he too moved back . . . and he flicked the rocker switch beside the socket.

[Incident report filed by Deputy Shoriff Steve Prather, following the confrontation on Eastwood Avenue, 10 June, 11:16 pm]

▼

There was a flash and the girl arched up with her head and her heels still touching the carpet. Flames broke out around the socket and I had all on to keep the boy where he was. Then Mr Willson reached over and flicked the switch again.

[From *Giving Thanks* by Jeffrey Douglas Willson (unpublished mss.)]

▼

Jerry pulled the girl's arm clear of the socket and removed the tape and screwdriver. "Okay," help me get her blouse off," he said.

Tom watched as his father and the deputy tore open Martha's blouse exposing the light blue lace of the brassiere he had admired across the space between their houses. It looked so delicate and her breasts so milky white . . . though Tom was shocked to see steam rising from Martha's body. No, not steam – smoke.

"She isn't breathing," Tom said.

Jerry straightened the girl's arms out on the floor and he thumped her hard on the chest, both hand clamped into one big fist.

Tom watched.

The deputy watched.

Nothing.

Jerry did it again. And again.

Still nothing.

"Is she dead?" Tom asked.

Jerry didn't say anything. He lifted his hands high and then, just as he was about to bring them down once more onto Martha's chest, the girl coughed. And then farted.

Tom promised himself in that moment that, no matter how long his life might be from that point forward, he would never tell Martha about that little involuntary explosion.

She looked at first one and then the other of them, and moved her hands to cover her breasts. Wincing, she lifted her left hand and stared at it. "I burned myself," she said.

[From the computer records of William Halloway. File name: "STORIES IN PROGRESS"]

▼

THE WONDERFUL COUNTRY
by Will Halloway

Fortunate too is the man who has come to know
the gods of the countryside.

— Virgil, *Georgics* no. 2

The past is a wonderful place – I go there often.

— Nick Hassam, *Chop Suey Days*

"HERB?"

Herb Lemann turns around from the window, squinting at the gloom after staring at the bright sunshine outside, and sees Annie's familiar outline framed against the kitchen door. "Yeah?"

"You okay?"

The darkness of his wife's figure and face fills in with color and expression, as though airbrushed by some unseen artist, and Herb sees a momentary frown of concern etched on her brow. "I'm fine." He turns back to the window and the spring fields beyond. "Just fine."

[From *Giving Thanks* by Jeffrey Douglas Willson (unpublished mss.)]

▼

Dedicated to Leaf:
thanks for falling for me.

—J

ERNESTO NERUDA:

When the first of the zombies was seen in the streets of Mexico City, it appeared in the *barrio* of Tepito. This famously chaotic area, with its sprawling illegal market, where anything can be bought – drugs, firearms and especially pirated goods. It is said that everything is for sale here, except dignity. The people of Tepito are deeply proud of their autonomy, and their alternative mode of life in the urban inferno. But it is also here that the heart of the *Santa Muerte* cult of worship is to be found, with dozens of shrines. The cult has been associated with the area around the market where all sorts of criminal activity has taken place in the past, and which the police have tried in vain to eradicate several times.

Marguerita Pinedo was an eyewitness to the appearance of the first zombie, and here is her account, in her own words:

MARGUERITA PINEDO:

I was serving a customer his order of *tacos de pancita* when I saw what looked like an injured man. His face was familiar, although I did not know his name. He often came to our restaurant in the market, and liked to eat here. There was blood on his lips, and I thought he had cut himself. His face was a yellow color, like corn. He was in a daze, bumping into tables and stalls. Perhaps, I thought, he is drunk. But it was still morning. Too early for drinking unless one is an alcoholic. I had not seen this man drunk before. And he came to eat here many times. He had a stall selling pirate films and music. Like many of us, he kept a statue of *La Poderosa Señora* at the back of his stall. He was making a nasty sound, grinding his teeth together. His eyes did not blink. And then he attacked one of the customers, and tried to bite him on the throat. There was much screaming. Tables were turned over. The crowd overpowered him, but several of them were scratched or bitten. The *federales* came and took him away, his mouth covered with duct tape, and his hands cuffed. They told us to say nothing of it, and then they took away the ones who had been bitten or scratched by the man. Father Hernández said the man had got the plague, but that *La Poderosa Señora* had brought him back to life.

ERNESTO NERUDA:

This story is typical of the first accounts that came out of Mexico City. Of course it was scarcely surprising to outsiders that the notorious Tepito would be amongst the first parts of the city to suffer an outbreak of the plague. Sanitary conditions in that labyrinth of overcrowded alleyways and streets have been poor for decades. There is no modern sewage system available and instead latrines and septic tanks are used. All this is a consequence of, in the 1960s, the autonomous community obtaining a freeze on rents payable. There are often seven or eight families living in the same premises. Several attempts have been made to modernize Tepito and offer its residents brand new homes outside or on the outskirts of the city, but they have resisted all attempts at relocation. When the people inside Tepito require more living space it is often their practice to break down a wall and take possession of an unoccupied adjacent room. The *barrio* is infested with vermin of all kinds, its ever-burgeoning population of rats and cockroaches being the principal carriers of disease. Here is Manuel Vásquez, a resident of Tepito, describing the situation from our archive recordings dating to before the outbreak there:

MANUEL VÁSQUEZ:

We are proud to be Tepiteños. The government hates us because we are independent, right under their noses here in D.F., the capital of Mexico! The politicians call us criminals, but they are the most corrupt ones of all, with their rigged elections and picking the pockets of the poor for decades! Like the Zapatistas in the State of Chiapas, they want to stamp us out because we are beyond their control. We are mostly Indios, outside of their system. We are indigenous folk. We want nothing more than what is ours by right. And yes, that is why we continue to live in the ruined buildings, along with the rats and the cockroaches. We prefer to. They say our Tepito is a disgrace, but they only want it for themselves, so that they can raze it to the ground and put in new shopping malls or offices. But this is our *barrio*. Even the company of rats and cockroaches are better than crooked politicians!

ERNESTO NERUDA:
Some of the more extreme commentators called not only for the containment of Tepito, which was attempted, with disastrous results, but also its complete destruction.

FRANCISCO NOYES (PAN delegate)
speaking outside the Ministry of the Interior:
These people are criminals. Everybody knows it. They deal in drugs and weapons, and the area is the home to gangs of narcos. They have been indulged for too long. The Tepiteños live in squalor like animals, in housing that should have been cleared decades ago, but which they have protected like cornered rats in their lair. Given the nature of disease, why should anyone be surprised that Tepito has turned out to be the source of the outbreak? It is folly to try and contain the zombies within the area, because it is only a matter of time before the entire *barrio* is overrun and everyone inside is a flesh-eater. How then can it be contained? No, containment is not an option. The only answer is extermination.

The streets around Tepito should be evacuated and the army brought in to shell the infected area with artillery. The soft-headed will talk of innocent casualties, but that is what they always say. It is their excuse for doing nothing, each and every time. There are no innocents in Tepito, only criminals and the dregs of our society. The bleeding hearts say "what of the children?", but they will have been the first to be attacked by the zombies, being the weakest. I doubt that there are any children left alive in that hellhole. And even if there were, remember that these are the children of criminals, and would have become like their parents in the end! I sense a gasp of outrage at this statement, but it is a hard fact.

Let us see matters clearly. We cannot afford to be sentimental when the very survival of Mexico is at stake. We require the use of force right now, it is the only thing that will stop this infection spreading.

Tepito must be razed to the ground and reduced to rubble without delay.

ERNESTO NERUDA:

Noyes's call for Tepito to be shelled was not carried out, mainly due to the swift actions of left-wing protestors who surrounded the *barrio* street by street with a human chain. Violent clashes with the army resulted and produced a confused situation on the ground. Here is Pilar Morales, who joined the protest.

PILAR MORALES:

We came in peace, to protect the rights of innocent people from a state that had decided to commit mass-murder. There was no democratic vote on this action. The people were not consulted. The curfew was by then in place, of course, but the President had not declared martial law, although we knew it was just a matter of time before the complete clampdown. We had received information from within the *barrio* that there were people still trapped inside and under siege from the zombies. The poor victims were streaming video over the Internet and producing text updates pleading for assistance from within the quarantine area. They were holding out, just, and relying on help coming from outside in order to rescue them from the zombies. They had no idea, until we told them, that the government plan was to annihilate them all by flattening Tepito to the ground, as happened recently with half of *Londres*!

It's true that some of them were followers of the *Santa Muerte*, but many of them were not. The religious aspect was exaggerated out of all proportion. Remember how we saw something similar with Islam after 9/11, with Bush the war criminal and his crusade against the Muslims?

I never heard of any Tepiteños deliberately hiding zombies who had been friends and family members in their ramshackle houses, in the cellars or attics. The government, I believe, spread this lie because it suited their agenda. They wanted people to believe that the proletariat of Tepito had brought this destruction upon themselves, and were entirely to blame. These statues of *Santa Muerte* can be bought everywhere, in shops and markets all over

Mexico City, and were even popular with tourists I believe. They are often just decorative – ownership does not prove anything, you know.

We were there to defend the dispossessed and the downtrodden from the actions of what was rapidly becoming a neo-fascist state! Perhaps they had been taking lessons from the Israeli Government. And all this was taking place here in Mexico, the country that had once given sanctuary to Leon Trotsky himself!

At first we thought our protest successful, for we had arrived before the *federales*, and they were supposed to have secured the area before the army came in to set up their artillery for the bombardment. I believe that there were more than two hundred thousand protestors there that day, and the human chain that we formed around Tepito was unbroken. The *federales* tried to break our line, first with riot-shield charges and batons, and then with tear-gas. The government must have instructed them to use extreme force.

Let's be clear. They attacked first. Not us.

They alone were responsible for the carnage that followed. They were determined to smash the protest at all costs and massacre the Tepiteños.

It was mayhem all around the perimeter of human beings we'd formed.

The clashes between ourselves and the *federales* must have drawn the zombies away from attacking those who had barricaded themselves in their homes. They were now the more difficult prey. We were an easier meal.

Do you know what the first thing is you notice when a horde of zombies is on its way? It's the smell of their rotting flesh carried on the wind. The groaning sound follows close behind, but it's the *stench* that alerts you. It turns your stomach and makes you want to retch. Once, when I was a little girl, someone had dumped some vats of ice cream in the alleyway behind my parents' apartment. There must have been some still left in there. It had turned sour in the heat. Ice cream is mostly dairy fat you know, and it decays much like human fat, producing the same rancid *stink*. I never had another ice cream as a child after that. And the smell of zombies was just the same. Cloying, sickly and nauseous.

Any flesh-eater that was out on the streets of Tepito made its way towards the sound of the battle, that is, they made straight towards us and the fascist *federales*. It was all the government's fault. Had they left us alone, and not tried to initiate wholesale slaughter, the breakout might not have happened.

The zombies attacked protestors and *federales* alike. Within a few minutes the streets were awash with blood and vomit, and such a sound of screaming! I hope never to hear such screams again. Of course the *federales* were in body armor, riot shields, batons and firearms. Those police could defend themselves, but we protestors were scarcely armed at all. They made no move to defend us, but simply backed off and let the carnage happen. All they were concerned with was saving their own skins. Okay, so most of them had seen nothing like it before, and were as scared as we were, but they sacrificed us, there's no getting away from that fact.

Political protest died that day in Mexico.

All that remained was primal and bloody chaos.

ERNESTO NERUDA:

Doubtless every Mexican listening to this broadcast is familiar with the spread and growth of the *Santa Muerte* worship phenomenon, which has been a feature of our culture now for more than fifty years, but which had attained incredible popular support since the crazy events in London and New York. Perhaps, having a long history so soaked in blood, corruption and darkness, it was only in Mexico that the adoration of a skeletal horror dressed up in the finest of fabrics, and paraded in the streets as a Holy Queen, could have developed. Some say that *Santa Muerte* is a modern-day continuation of the old Aztec death goddess *Mictecacihuatl*, the guardian of bones and flesh-eater. She goes under many names, and *La Flaca, La Poderosa Señora, La Comadre,* and *La Santa Niña Blanca* are just a few examples. Some say that she is the true face of the Roman Catholic Church in Mexico, with its mask of false piety torn away. Perhaps she is a combination of the two. Others say that she is an entirely post-modern object of worship, and one much more suited to these apocalyptic times.

I have here in the studio Father Ignacio Hernández of the Old Mexican-Catholic Church. Let us begin with some background information if we may, Father. You have been involved with the cult of *Santa Muerte* for how many years?

FATHER IGNACIO HERNÁNDEZ:

We are not a cult, Señor Neruda. We regard ourselves as good Catholics. The veneration of saints is a feature of traditional Catholic practice. *Santa Muerte* is Our Lady of Death. We ask for her intercession and the favor of her miraculous powers. I have been a priest of the Old Mexican-Catholic Church since 1969.

ERNESTO NERUDA:

The official Catholic Church has long denounced this worship, has it not? They describe it as a cult centered around murderers, drug-traffickers and other criminals.

FATHER IGNACIO HERNÁNDEZ:

That, I deny. It is true that Our Lady of Death accepts all men and women without judging them, anyone who comes to pray for her intercession, her help, whatever the nature of their crimes. Even the so-called crime – in this corrupt value system we hold – of being poor. Too often the rich and powerful elements of the Church have turned their backs on the desperate and the needy. And who amongst us is without sin?

ERNESTO NERUDA:

You deny the murders that have taken place, here in Tepito? The chopped-off heads of murder victims placed by Narco dealers on roadside altars built to honor *Santa Muerte*? Put there as offerings? This has been going on for many years.

FATHER IGNACIO HERNÁNDEZ:

Misguided people have sometimes tortured and killed in the name of the Church. This has been true throughout its history.

ERNESTO NERUDA:

Do you believe that resurrection is possible only through Jesus?

FATHER IGNACIO HERNÁNDEZ:
The resurrection of the soul, and final salvation from Hell, yes. These are only possible through Our Lord Jesus Christ.

ERNESTO NERUDA:
And the resurrection of the body? Is this too possible only through Jesus?

FATHER IGNACIO HERNÁNDEZ:
The body and the soul are not of the same essence.

ERNESTO NERUDA:
Father Hernández, do you agree with those who say that *Santa Muerte* is the Queen with all power over death, and over the body, and that Jesus saves only the soul?

FATHER IGNACIO HERNÁNDEZ:
The answer to that, I imagine, is self-evident. Our Lady of Death, *Santa Muerte*, the Sacred One, the Queen of Queens, has rewarded the Faithful with such wonders as the men of science declared impossible.

ERNESTO NERUDA:
You believe then, that the bodily reanimation of the dead is a demonstration of the power of *Santa Muerte*?

FATHER IGNACIO HERNÁNDEZ:
What else could it be? I too have heard the tales of the godless English, saying that it was caused by a mutation of the bubonic plague carried by fleas, but these are fables of the scientists. They give something a name, and think antibiotics are the answer. But this is the will of God, expressed through the incarnation in all men of a new stigmata. Not in the form of the wounds of Christ Jesus, but the form of La Flaca, Our Lady of Death, *Santa Muerte*. Let even the scientists bow down before her. Those faithless men who have thought themselves the masters of the world, with their biological and nuclear weapons. They talk of DNA and the control of human disease, even as they destroy millions of the unborn innocent across the globe.

ERNESTO NERUDA:

What do you say to those who claim *Santa Muerte* is evil?

FATHER IGNACIO HERNÁNDEZ:

This is not true! To those who betray her, she can be cruel, but to those who pay tribute, she is generous. One cannot pray to *Santa Muerte*, then have that prayer granted, and expect there not to be a price. Constant devotion is that price. It is not an onerous price to pay for those who are willing to do so.

ERNESTO NERUDA:

Can you control these zombies?

FATHER IGNACIO HERNÁNDEZ:

Could I control all my flock when they were alive, ha, ha?

ERNESTO NERUDA:

It is claimed that you have conducted obscene Masses in which zombies were present with their arms tied behind their backs, and their lips stitched together, have you not? These zombies have been brought to the ceremonies by grieving relatives, who have refused to give them up for proper disposal by cremation.

FATHER IGNACIO HERNÁNDEZ:

Who told you this?

ERNESTO NERUDA:

I have the photographs.

FATHER IGNACIO HERNÁNDEZ:

Such photographs are fakes. No one from our church would provide such things to the atheistic media. If there are such photos they were produced by interlopers, who cannot be trusted and who deny the power of *Santa Muerte*.

ERNESTO NERUDA:

Some of the people in your congregation claim that you preach the doctrine that, one day soon, the souls of the departed will return

to these dead bodies and take them over again, once they have
served their time in purgatory and expiated their sins.

FATHER IGNACIO HERNÁNDEZ:
Tell me Ernesto, *how long do you think* it takes for a man or woman
to atone for their sins in the afterlife?

ERNESTO NERUDA:
I believe that the official doctrine of the Catholic Church is that it
may be a matter of centuries or even thousands of years, should
one die in a state of sin.

FATHER IGNACIO HERNÁNDEZ:
But here we are dealing with the Eternal. Pah! You reveal your lack
of understanding in these end days. It may indeed be centuries or
millennia to the unfortunate sufferer, but only the blink of an eye
to someone else. Interior and external time, you see?

ERNESTO NERUDA:
But this is an interesting point, I mean, it is revealing, in general,
Father Hernández, because you seem to believe it is possible that
the souls of those in purgatory will return to occupy their bodies
again. And this could happen at any time.

FATHER IGNACIO HERNÁNDEZ:
Through the grace of *Santa Muerte*, all things are possible.

ERNESTO NERUDA:
And what of Heaven? Listen, I do not understand why you think the
souls of the departed do not go on to Heaven, instead of returning
to the rotting bodies of these zombies? And what awaits those who
have no corpses to return to?

FATHER IGNACIO HERNÁNDEZ:
Perhaps those who died in sin, without bodies to return to, will find
themselves in Hell, perhaps for the others, they are required to
prepare for the Kingdom of Heaven here on Earth.

ERNESTO NERUDA:
And all this is determined by *Santa Muerte*?

FATHER IGNACIO HERNÁNDEZ:
Who brings men closer to God than Death?

ERNESTO NERUDA:
And your church, the Old Mexican-Catholic Church, opposes cremation on the grounds that a soul, without a corpse or body to return to, is in danger of Hell?

FATHER IGNACIO HERNÁNDEZ:
This was the position of the Vatican itself until the twentieth century. Cremation was forbidden. They abandoned the position as a consequence of muddled modernist thinking. The reformers have been shown to be wrong. The traditionalists shown to be right. These so-called "zombies" are not mere empty shells. They are vessels awaiting the return of what has been lost to them, the return of souls that are elsewhere and being judged and purified by the Living God.

ERNESTO NERUDA:
Wait, are you suggesting that this outbreak, all these terrible events taking place throughout not just Mexico, but the whole world, are a prelude to the establishment of the Kingdom of Heaven here on Earth?

FATHER IGNACIO HERNÁNDEZ:
They are necessary, they are part of a process that can only be achieved by *Santa Muerte*, and I urge all your listeners to understand this quite clearly. There is no room for doubt in these times of miracles and no room for doubters. The moment requires men who are believers to the core. All the words of the heretics, the atheists and the false believers are as naught. Science is a lie.

ERNESTO NERUDA:
I regret that we are out of time Father Hernández, and will have to end the interview.

FATHER IGNACIO HERNÁNDEZ:

But I . . .

[sound of a microphone being switched off]

ERNESTO NERUDA:

I have with me now Professor Miguel Leopoldo of UNAM's human biology department. Welcome Professor.

PROFESSOR MIGUEL LEOPOLDO:

Thank you. I am glad to be here.

ERNESTO NERUDA:

Can you give us the scientific perspective on the cause of this reanimation of the dead?

PROFESSOR MIGUEL LEOPOLDO:

We know that the disease is spread only through direct contact, via the saliva in a bite or even through a scratch that breaks the surface of the skin. It is closest, in its genetic make-up, to *yersinia pestis*, or the bubonic plague. We are familiar of course, with this disease, which still occurs in parts of Africa and can be treated with antibiotics. One of the consequences of infection by the bubonic plague is necrosis of the living tissues. That is to say – the body begins to decompose despite the victim still being alive.

ERNESTO NERUDA:

This is not, however, the bubonic plague, is it? These people are dead but nevertheless functioning.

PROFESSOR MIGUEL LEOPOLDO:

It is a variant strain, we believe, but one totally resistant to both wide and narrow spectrum antibiotics. We knew that this might happen eventually, given the amazing capacity of bacteria to adapt and become resistant. What we did not expect was a variation so startlingly unusual, and which appeared for the first time centuries ago.

ERNESTO NERUDA:

It's not a virus then?

PROFESSOR MIGUEL LEOPOLDO:

No, it is not a virus.

ERNESTO NERUDA:

But isn't the bubonic plague an old disease, one that has been studied?

PROFESSOR MIGUEL LEOPOLDO:

The variant that swept England in 1665, nicknamed "The Black Death", has not been studied until now because it has not been seen for centuries. There is no record, or rather no modern scientific study, of it available to the medical profession. All we have are historical records and not all of these are actual eyewitness accounts. For example, Daniel Defoe's famous account was written around twenty years after the events he described in his "Journal of the Plague Year".

ERNESTO NERUDA:

Perhaps you can explain this in layman's terms, Professor. How is it possible for a *dead body* to still function?

PROFESSOR MIGUEL LEOPOLDO:

It is true that the usual human life signs are absent. The victim, if you like, is dead. No heartbeat, no respiration, no pupil dilation, minimal EEG activity – and even this aspect mostly confined to the cerebellum and the brain stem. You see, the body, the original organism, has passed into becoming another type of organism: the bacterium has taken it over completely. The human corpse becomes in effect, just a vehicle. In some manner we do not yet fully understand, this particular bacterium is even able to oxygenate muscles in the body despite the cessation of a bloodstream, which is the normal mechanism for this process.

ERNESTO NERUDA:

Forgive my ignorance, Professor, but why should bacteria need to adapt in this fashion?

PROFESSOR MIGUEL LEOPOLDO:

The primary genetic function of all organisms, even at the most basic level, is self-replication. By some process that I cannot yet explain, the bacterium involved in the reanimation of the dead has mutated precisely in order to replicate itself via this inefficient method.

ERNESTO NERUDA:

Inefficient?

PROFESSOR MIGUEL LEOPOLDO:

Certainly, when seen from a genetic perspective. The disease would have been much more effective had it simply been airborne and not spread only through bites or scratches. Transmission by flea bites can be easily prevented with repellents.

ERNESTO NERUDA:

But it seems quite effective to me, Professor! A disease that not only kills people but brings them back to life, making them spread the condition to anyone they encounter by attacking them!

PROFESSOR MIGUEL LEOPOLDO.

It is strange indeed. This business of the fleas. They may have been the carriers, but now it's the dead themselves. Perhaps the, ahem, so-called zombies bite, not in order to feed, but in order to spread the contagion. Perhaps the bacterium tricks the host body into thinking it is hungry. Again, I say: this is not a virus like the flu or the common cold. I really cannot begin to explain all the complex factors required in order to re-animate a corpse, even at the most basic level. Reanimation of the human organism is not merely a by-product of the bacterium, it operates too precisely for that. It is unique in my experience and those of all my fellow experts in the field. As yet, we have not been able to fully explain how it interacts with the human body in such a way as to, umm, give the appearance of biological reactivation.

ERNESTO NERUDA:

You heard Father Hernández earlier, before he left the studio?

PROFESSOR MIGUEL LEOPOLDO:

I did.

ERNESTO NERUDA:

What did you make of his explanation for the events? That they have a supernatural cause, that *Santa Muerte* is the power behind all this?

PROFESSOR MIGUEL LEOPOLDO:

I will say this: the first duty of the scientist is to dismiss all thoughts of the supernatural. There will be no solution to this problem from any church or from any so-called mystic. Only science can save us. We must keep faith in science and the power of reason. If we do not, mankind will slip back into the Dark Ages. This cult of *Santa Muerte* is a throwback to superstition. It is nothing more than voodoo. If we start giving superstitious nonsense serious credence then hundreds of years of progress will be lost.

ERNESTO NERUDA:

Professor Leopoldo, thank you.

PROFESSOR MIGUEL LEOPOLDO:

My pleasure.

ERNESTO NERUDA:

We now go live to our correspondent in Tepito, Carlos Villa, who has managed to get inside the quarantine zone, and he speaks to us now from the infected area. Carlos, can you hear me?

[sounds of gunfire in the background]

CARLOS VILLA:

Yes, Ernesto, I am broadcasting from the top floor of a three-storey house on Calle Aztecas. The fighting is still going on all around me in the streets. I can see *federales* shooting at zombies and residents indiscriminately. They're wiping out everything that moves. This has been described as a "moping-up operation", but it is a massacre! Calle Matamoros is on fire. Over there, they are using flame-throwers in order to flush out of buildings the zombies they say are being protected by the people in here.

[huge crashing sound]

A building has gone down! It's collapsed into a mass of rubble, dust and smoke. It stood five hundred yards away from here. They are planting explosives, I'm sure.

ERNESTO NERUDA:
Carlos, what's the situation with the helicopters? Is it true they're offloading chemical weapons?

CARLOS VILLA:
There are four of them circling the area . . .

[sound of more gunfire drowns out the voice]

. . . too dangerous for that. No way to control the effects of it. The gas would disperse over too wide an area, carried along by the wind. Perhaps it's the huge amount of acrid smoke from the burning buildings here that's given rise to that rumor. No gas, no. Gassing the zombies wouldn't work. I don't know if those things need to breathe anyway. I've heard them making sounds like breathing, that hideous gasping. An eternal death rattle of the damned, as the poet David Huerta put it. But I don't know if it's more than an instinct left over from the time when they were alive. Perhaps Professor Leopoldo can answer that, if he's still there in the studio with you Ernesto.

ERNESTO NERUDA:
He is. Professor, do these things need to breathe?

PROFESSOR MIGUEL LEOPOLDO:
My research would indicate not. As I said earlier, the process of oxygenation of the tissues seems to be present but is not the same as

in a living human being, and does not operate via the lungs and bloodstream, but through some other mechanism as yet not identified.

ERNESTO NERUDA:

Back to you, Carlos.

CARLOS VILLA:

I am now descending the staircase of this building on Calle Aztecas. I hope that you're still able to hear me. Earlier I met with some locals who told me that a group of *Santa Muerte* devotees have locked themselves away in the cellars that run beneath the road. They have their own shrine down there. Let's see just how accurate is Father Hernández's claim that zombies play no part in their religious ceremonies. This will be a Radio 93.2 exclusive, as I don't think even the *federales* know yet about the presence of this underground enclave. The walls on the stairway are smeared with bloodstains, as if violent attacks have taken place here. The marks seem to indicate that people have been dragged down, in some fierce struggle, towards the basement. There is more going on than has been admitted by the likes of Father Hernández.

[sound of footsteps descending the stairs and of Carlos Villa's labored breathing]

I can smell something rotten, a foul stench. It's something we've all come to know and dread – the zombie stench, since it means *they're* close by. Funny that I didn't notice it before but, then again, I didn't explore the ground floor when I first entered the building. Here we go, the entrance to the cellars.

ERNESTO NERUDA:

What's going on in there, Carlos? Can you hear anything?

[muffled sounds – which could be living humans in pain, or the senseless moaning of zombies – but the noises are too indistinct to make out clearly and therefore to determine which of the two possibilities is the more likely]

CARLOS VILLA:

Hope you picked that up back in the studio. I just put the mike boom close to the door. It's locked, I think – and from this side, the outside, that is. I'm going to force it open. The reinforced jamb is on the outside. This thing's been put there to keep people, or *things* (ha!ha!), from breaking out. Not to stop someone, like me, breaking in. Whatever's going on down there now is at the heart of what Father Hernández and his twisted followers are up to, and may reveal the secrets they want to hide from the media – and from the public of course. They're the important ones. I am determined to expose the wickedness of this evil cult, in the name of the people, so we finally get to the truth. *When the last king has been strangled with the entrails of the last priest* – as my good old university tutor used to say!

ERNESTO NERUDA:

Are you okay, Carlos? You sound odd.

PROFESSOR MIGUEL LEOPOLDO:

The boy seems not to realize that this is scarcely the time for levity.

**[sound of wooden panels splintering and cracking,
and a muffled grunt of satisfaction]**

CARLOS VILLA:

I've broken in, and am now inside, looking down into a stairwell. It's lit by candles, tea lights, two on opposite sides of each step. They've been placed all the way down into the cellars.

**[sound of the stairs creaking and, in the background, the
moaning noise is closer and louder]**

CARLOS VILLA:

Here it is, the underground catacomb where they worship. They've erected a subterranean church here. It's lit up with a hundred church candles, and there's an altar over on the far side. It's an altar to *Santa Muerte*! Here's where they've come to congregate, to pray to her, to pray to this filthy thing. The skeleton, an obscene Madonna, is draped in a bright blue robe, her grinning skull like a yellow moon. The worshippers all have their backs to me, and they're praying to their goddess.

[the moaning is rhythmic now, like a repeated chant of pain]

ERNESTO NERUDA:
Carlos, what's that sound? Can you see any zombies tied up by the Tepiteños?

CARLOS VILLA:
Doesn't look like it. Wait! I've been spotted. This looks bad.

[sound of scuffling and chairs being overturned and
Villa's voice rises to a terrifying crescendo]

They're all dead, they're all dead, they're all dead! Not a single person alive! *All dead, all dead, all dead, dead, dead, dead . . .*

[Villa screams repeatedly]

ERNESTO NERUDA:
Get out of there, Carlos! Carlos, can you hear me? Get out of there!

[sound of rending and feeding, as the screams continue, and then
a final howl of despair]

CARLOS VILLA:
La Flaca! La Flaca! Oh Thin Lady, have mercy! Have mercy!

[the microphone goes dead]

ERNESTO NERUDA:
I . . . I apologize, we seem to have lost contact with . . . there is a . . . and my producer is telling me, now the government are closing us . . . off air until . . .

[the broadcast terminates and is replaced by a monotone test signal]

DEPARTMENT OF RECONSTRUCTION
INTER-OFFICE MEMO # 249
RE: YOURS OF THURSDAY

Attached please find an E-mail chain recovered from Server#117 (Los Angeles/San Fernando Valley). Chain re-ordered to oldest first for convenience. Please advise re: deletion.

From: upstartcrow117@aol.com
To: ScottC@NewRidgeEntertainment.com
Sent: Wednesday, June 19th 3:27 PM
Subject: Already rollin'!

Hey Scott,

Excellent meeting yesterday! Too bad Larry couldn't be there himself, but I understand. And it was great to meet with you and Craig anyway. Exciting ideas! I love the way you guys are always thinking ahead of the curve.

So listen: I was really jazzed by some of the shit we were throwing around and – couldn't help it – I hit the keys the second I got back.

Now we both know that my agent would kill me if I went ahead and attached any actual *pages* before we have an actual *deal*, so please regard the stuff pasted in below as just thoughts. Random thoughts. Really specific random thoughts. Really specific, sequenced, structured random thoughts. The sort of sequenced and structured random thoughts that a casual observer might understandably mistake for, you know, the opening seven pages of a screenplay or something. But which absolutely aren't the opening seven pages of a screenplay. Not At All. Because that would be wrong. ;-)

ZOMBIE BITCH GOT GAME
Not a Screenplay
By
Cliff Brightwell

FADE IN:

EXTREME CLOSE UP: An EYE staring out at us.

Wide open. Unblinking.

Is there a thought there? An emotion? Maybe fear? We don't have time to guess. Because, suddenly ...

... the eye EXPLODES outwards in a viscous shower of blood and membrane. Right at us. <u>Right</u> at us. Like if it was 3-D, we'd be trying to wipe the cum-like gunk off our horrified faces.

Chasing the blood'n'slime out of the cavity of the socket comes the tip of the nine-inch RAILROAD SPIKE that did it.

CUT TO WIDE to reveal that the eye had belonged to a ZOMBIE – some undead motherfucker all gray-pallor, open-wounds, and rotting clothes – who's now twitching galvanically like a freshly-zapped steer in a slaughterhouse.

The railroad spike twists professionally in the eye-cavity like it's making a clean bore and – after a couple more nauseating seconds of its spastic death-dance – the Zombie collapses, revealing behind it ...

JACK STUYVESANT – 26, handsome, cool, totally ripped – who pulls the spike from out the back of the Zombie's head and wipes it clean on his wife-beater.

He looks across to the girl who he's just saved from being the Zombie's lunch.

This is CLAIRE GALLIGAN. Claire's our leading lady, which means – in case you've been too busy splitting the atom or curing cancer to have watched any movies in the last fifty fucking years – that she's 21 and hot. No, I mean <u>really</u> hot. Megan Fox hot.

JACK
You all done shopping?

Claire looks around at the derelict CLOTHING STORE in which they're standing.

> CLAIRE
> Red is <u>so</u> last year.

The store is a BLOODBATH. <u>Gallons</u> of blood paint the walls and floor, some of it dried and rusting, most of it new and running.

Despite its abattoir-chic overlay, the store is still full of whatever was in style the week the world ended.

It's also full of CORPSES. They're everywhere, some human, some Zombies.

A free-standing CLOTHES RACK is immediately behind Claire. Twenty ZOMBIES dangle from it, hooks through their skulls. Most of them have gone where the good Zombies go, but two or three are still twitching.

Without batting an eyelid, Claire pushes two twitching Zombies apart on the rack to get at a tiny TUBE-TOP between them.

> CLAIRE
> But <u>this</u> is cute.

Slipping the tube-top from its hanger, Claire peels off her blood-and-gore-soaked T-shirt.

Though every guy in the theatre has just decided he's had more than his ticket-money's worth, there's no reaction from Jack as he watches Claire change tops. Because he's, you know, <u>cool</u>.

Claire wriggles into the tight-fitting top. As she smoothes the fabric over her belly, leaving enough midriff eye-candy to keep the rest of us happy, she looks up at Jack.

> CLAIRE
> That's better.
> (beat)
> Duck.

Claire grabs up her hip-mounted SPIKE-LAUNCHER – a kind of zipgun-on-steroids fitted with an oversized revolver-style cylinder loaded with ten Spikes – and fires one directly at Jack ...

... who drops instantly into a crouch ...

... as the spike slams unerringly into the forehead of a FAT FEMALE ZOMBIE whose blubbery arms were about to grab Jack from behind.

As the Zombie hits the ground, quivering into death, Claire cocks her head and gives it a quizzical look.

> CLAIRE
> Right. Like they have <u>your</u> size in stock.

Jack straightens up and nods at Claire.

> JACK
> Thanks. Where the hell d'ya think <u>she</u> came from?

> CLAIRE
> (looking past Jack)
> Probably the same place they did.

Jack spins around to see that, at the back of the store, a set of double FIRE DOORS have been slammed open ...

... and countless ZOMBIES are pouring in like bargain hunters on a day-after-Thanksgiving sale. And Jack and Claire appear to be this year's tickle-me-fucking-Elmo.

Claire glances down at her Spike-Launcher. Suddenly its nine remaining Spikes seem woefully inadequate. She looks up to meet Jack's eyes.

> JACK
> Don't worry, I called us a cab.

BAM!! The entire side wall of the store explodes as a CLASSIC BLACK LONDON TAXI smashes through it, hurtles forward twenty feet, and screeches to a halt right in front of Jack and Claire.

The cab's window cranks down and the driver leans out. Meet KEVIN. Your classic sidekick. A just past college-age overweight schlub. Over-educated. Under-achieving. Way too fond of STAR TREK. Never been laid.

[Scott – is Jonah Hill too expensive?]

Kevin looks at Jack and Claire and then at the scores of Zombies heading their way. He calls out to Jack in a mockney-accent that is every bit as bad as your classic MARY POPPINS Dick Van Dyke.

                              KEVIN
         Gor Bloimey, Guv'nor. This better be a bloomin' big tip.

Kevin brings his arms up out the driver's window. Each one holds a double-barreled Spike-firing CROSSBOW.

As Jack and Claire clamber hurriedly into the back of the taxi, Kevin takes out the first four Zombies with a skill and accuracy that almost lift him out of nerd status.

As he reloads the crossbows from a QUIVER of Spikes dangling from the rear-view, he shouts over his shoulder.

                              KEVIN
                              You in?

                              JACK
                    (slamming passenger door)
                          Just drive!

                              KEVIN
         Stone the bleedin' crows, mate. No need to get stroppy.

THWACK!!! Taking out another four zombies, Kevin floors it in reverse and does a stunning rubber-burning one-eighty to face the front of the store ...

... and the taxi stalls.

The remaining Zombies race to close the distance, undead arms scrabbling at the back of the cab, rotting mouths chomping in anticipation.

                              CLAIRE
                              Fuck!

                              KEVIN
      Ooh-er, missus. And there was me finkin' you was a proper lidy.

> JACK
> Move!
> (beat)
> And drop the accent.

> KEVIN
> (plain American)
> Geez, Jack. Just tryin' to give you some local color.

SLAM! A Zombie has clambered onto the trunk of the cab and is flailing at the rear window.

As the zombie's putrescent face presses hungrily against the glass ...

... Jack snatches Claire's Launcher and, pressing it tight against the window, blasts a spike right through it and directly into the Zombie's forehead.

The taxi's engine stutters back into life.

> KEVIN
> (chatty, informational)
> Hey, did you know these things run on Diesel?

> CLAIRE
> (shut the fuck up)
> Kevin!!

Kevin revs it and the Taxi jets forward, clambering Zombies flung from its trunk as it races toward the store's big PLATE GLASS WINDOW ...

> KEVIN
> (calmly professional)
> Please buckle up for safety and comfort.

CUT TO: EXT. HARRODS, PICCADILLY CIRCUS – SUNSET

The front of Harrods, London's famous department store.

We get about half a second to take in its olde worlde splendor ...

... and then its main front window explodes as Kevin's Taxi comes flying through the air to land in the middle of Piccadilly Circus.

At the far side of the Circus is LONDON BRIDGE, its famous towers bathed in the setting sun. SHAMBLING SHAPES are silhouetted as they shuffle their way over the Thames river.

The Circus is totally overrun by marauding Zombies. Hundreds of them. The various London THEATRES are derelict, their neon signs long-dead and their posters peeling. Even the famous CAVERN CLUB, home of the Beatles, is a lightless hulk.

But it's ST PAUL'S CATHEDRAL that seems to be ground zero for the hordes of the undead. Beneath its famous dome, its doors are open and spilling thousands of Zombies into the Circus.

The landing of Kevin's taxi hasn't exactly gone unnoticed. Every zombie starts shambling toward it.

> KEVIN
> I hate fucking Zombies.

> CLAIRE
> Then stop fucking them.

> KEVIN
> Easy for you to say. You can get dates.

> JACK
> Give me a crossbow.

Jack hands her launcher back to Claire as Kevin tosses him one of the crossbows.

> JACK
> Let's go.

Claire and Jack lower their windows and start firing at the Zombies as Kevin starts the Taxi up.

> KEVIN
> Little road music?

He punches the cab's radio into life as he accelerates. Some long-dead Glam Rocker starts warbling instructions to ride a white swan like the people of the Beltane as the taxi plows forward mercilessly,

Zombies falling beneath its eager wheels like so much undead road-kill.

As the cab sweeps past the doors of the cathedral, the spewing ranks of Zombies pause and part, to reveal a single figure standing on the steps.

Their leader.

He's all dolled up in moldering MADNESS OF KING GEORGE drag – you know, britches and silk, doublet and hose and shit – and his long ringleted WIG looks particularly bizarre over his pockmarked cadaverous face.

There's something odd about that face. No, I mean odder than the standard-issue undead look.

It's the eyes.

Unlike the glazed and cretinous hungry-and-nothing-more expression shared by every other back from the grave shambler, this fucker's eyes gleam with a kind of malevolent intelligence. Like it knows what it's doing, and likes it.

This is NICHOLAS HAWKSWORTH. Master Architect. Black Magician. King Zombie.

> [Hey Scott, it is "Hawksworth", right? That church-builder guy you mentioned? Google's down again, and I'm fucked if I'm driving to the library to check this shit right now. Once you *pay* me, I'll do my research ;-). Anyway, where were we . . .]

Hawksworth points dramatically across the distance at the cab and stares, his eyes locked on Jack and Claire and tracking them as they move. His mouth opens – revealing a strange SWARMING BLACKNESS within it – and a wordless ROAR of challenge echoes over the Circus.

At the eerie sound of their master's voice, the other Zombies fling themselves with renewed rage at the Taxi, as if intending to stop it by sheer weight of numbers.

Claire, grabbing something out of her purse, leans out the window and meets the Hawksworth-thing's eyes, an I'm-so-over-your-bullshit look on her drop-dead face.

Her thumb is poised elegantly at the top of her lipstick ...

                    CLAIRE
                Eat me.

Claire depresses her thumb.

Not a lipstick.

A <u>detonator</u>.

BOOOOOOOOOOOOMMM!!!!!!!!!!

The BIGGEST FUCKING EXPLOSION you've ever seen in your entire movie-going life. Suck on it, Michael Bay. Kiss my white ass, Roland Emmerich. Go eat at the kids' table, JJ Abrams.

The Cathedral – fuck it, the whole of Piccadilly Circus – ignites into a FIRESTORM that makes Dresden look like a sparkler and Nagasaki like a roman candle.

As the flames entirely fill the frame, DEBRIS comes hurtling toward us: Bricks, mortar, body-parts ...

... culminating in Hawksworth's severed head spinning right at us.

Just as the head "reaches" us, its eyes flick open and its undead mouth opens in a silent SCREAM ...

... and the head EXPLODES into a TSUNAMI OF PLAGUE FLEAS. Hundreds of the little bastards. Thousands. Fucking <u>millions</u>. Writhing, twitching, jumping, biting ...

SMASH TO BLACK and crank up the Metallica Cue.

RUN OPENING TITLES

        There it is.
        Whaddaya think?
        You wet? Cause I'm hard.
        Let's *do* this mofo, beyotch!

        Cheers,

        Cliff

P.S. Don't crap your pants that I've killed off our lead villain in the pre-creds. What I'm figuring is that the surviving now-we're-*really*-pissed Zombies find the reconstituted head, skewer it on a stick for safe-keeping, and later insert it into another Zombie body which is then animated by Hawksworth's undead intelligence. New body doesn't even have to be a human one. Who says this plague is limited to homo sapiens? Zombie wolf body. Zombie gorilla body. Whatever we want. Cool? Damn straight.

From: ScottC@NewRidgeEntertainment.com
To: upstartcrow117@aol.com
Sent: Monday, June 24th 2:59 PM
Subject: RE: Already rollin'!

Cliff –

Sorry for the delay. Couldn't get to your pages until the weekend. But I'm stoked, bro! Love the energy of this! Look, I can't get into a full response right now – Larry's just back from Mexico and we got a big meeting at 3 to talk about the entire slate – but four quick things:

1. Your geography is *totally* wack. I know London's the third fucking world but come on, crack a book or Google Earth or something.

2. It's HawksMOOR. And if you'd read the research material Craig got for you, you'd know he's not really the guy anyway. But I'll give you a get-out-of-jail-free on that one on the grounds of i) poetic license and ii) needing a cool-looking villain ;-)

3. Don't know if we can actually use the Plague Fleas. I know, I know. It blows. But apparently that info's like classified or shit.

4. Metallica? Really? Dude, the eighties called – they want their soundtrack back.

Just busting your balls. This pretty much rocks. And you know what, I bet we *can* get Jonah Hill – I heard SUPERBAD IV just fucking *died* at a test screening.

Scott

From: ScottC@NewRidgeEntertainment.com
To: upstartcrow117@aol.com
Sent: Tuesday, June 25th 11:47 AM
Subject: RE: Already rollin'!

Bad news, brother. I said I liked it and I was so not bullshitting you. I
still like it. But – don't hate me – I ran a drive-by verbal past Larry
and truth is he didn't really spark to it. Nothing to do with your take,
just that he really thinks that action-adventure isn't the way to go with
this material. I guess his trip to Mexico really made an impression on
him. He's thinking high-road more than popcorn now. When I get a
better read on what he's planning for us, I promise to bring you back
into the loop. Okay?

Bestest,

Scott

Sent from upstartcrow117@aol.com
To ScottC@NewRidgeEntertainment.com
Sent: Tuesday, June 25th 3:33 PM
Subject: RE: Already rollin'!

Sure, sure. Not a problem. Larry didn't break all those Box Office
records by *not* reading the zeitgeist well. I'm sure he's right about
the approach. But look. Let's not be too quick to spike this one in the
head. If it's *tone* that's the problem, we can reposition. Forget the
gags and the explosions. Look at the set-up and structure. How about
– just spit-balling here, go with me – how about if we made Claire a
documentarian (think Christiane Amanpour with a rockin' bod)
commissioned by Congress to capture on-the-ground footage of the
European situation. Yeah? And Jack is a former Black Ops guy
brought out of desk-job exile to keep her out of trouble? Maybe even
get an ersatz father-daughter vibe going between them? But sexual
tension, too, of course. Think Viggo Mortensen for Jack and for Claire
. . . shit, what's her name? That English Oscar-hottie? Carey Mulligan.
Think about it. Whole different movie now. Popcorn schmopcorn.
This is pure high road. Viggo all brooding and existentialist, Carey all
oh-the-humanity. C'mon, bro, don't tell me *that* doesn't play.

Cliff

Sent from ScottC@NewRidgeEntertainment.com
To upstartcrow117@aol.com
Sent: Friday, June 28th 12:01 PM
Subject: RE: Already rollin'!

Cliffie, you are a tryer. Gotta give you that. But I still think you're on a different page. You know what's big now? Reality.

Scott

Sent from upstartcrow117@aol.com
To ScottC@NewRidgeEntertainment.com
Sent: Friday, June 28th 4:52 PM
Subject: RE: Already rollin'!

>>You know what's big now? Reality.<<

Alright. We can work with that. (You mean TV, right? And a series, not a special?) Check this out:

Who's for Lunch?
Reality/Competition
By
Cliff Brightwell

Thirteen competitors. In a cage. Single walkway to a podium (think witness-box – whole set is like a Kafka courtroom). Beyond the podium, two doors. One marked EXIT, the other marked KITCHEN. Tribunal of judges. You know – your classic Simon, Randy, Ellen set-up. But dig this. The judges are *Zombies*. You've heard they're talking now, right? Seen that amazing YouTube thing? Can't find the link, but just go to their search window and type in *ZombieGirl15*. You'll lose your lunch. But you'll smell the money. Anyway, so here's the twist. Our competitors *don't* want to be picked. Their gig is to present their cases for why the judges shouldn't eat them.

Sent from ScottC@NewRidgeEntertainment.com
To upstartcrow117@aol.com
Sent: Saturday, June 29th 11:28 AM
Subject: RE: Already rollin'!

Can't believe I'm in the office on a Saturday fucking morning. I should be watching *Hannah Montana* reruns and trying to make the girlfriend believe I'm there for the comedy not the jailbait. But Larry's got us all in here around the clock right now. He's like a new man since he got back. He's making some changes around here and things are getting wack. Which is one reason I need you to be patient about your reality show idea. We're all learning to be careful about what we put on Larry's plate. Don't want to present it wrong and piss him off. Tell ya, the way he reacts these days, he makes Joel Silver look like a frigging pussycat.

Anyway, the good news is I think you're onto something here, young Clifford. It's an envelope-pusher, for sure, but since when was that a bad thing? Hang tough for a few and let me play with it, get the right spin. I wanna tweak it right, make sure Larry bites.

More as soon as I know.

Scott

Sent from upstartcrow117@aol.com
To ScottC@NewRidgeEntertainment.com
Sent: Tuesday, July 2nd 3:13 PM
Subject: RE: Already rollin'!

Scott. Just checking in. Haven't heard back from you on Larry's reaction to the reality show proposal. I'm cool with working it up a little more if that helps, but you have to let me know yay or nay. Fact is, my agent's up my ass to go directly to Fox with it, says they're desperate for a new franchise and that my idea could play as a ballsy response to the "unfortunate incident" on that last X FACTOR out of London. God's honest truth, I'd much rather work with you guys than those assholes but, you know, trying to make a living here . . .

Sent from upstartcrow117@aol.com
To ScottC@NewRidgeEntertainment.com
Sent: Tuesday, July 2nd 5:59 PM
Subject: RE: Already rollin'!

Hello?

Sent from upstartcrow117@aol.com
To ScottC@NewRidgeEntertainment.com
Sent: Wednesday, July 3rd 9:01 AM
Subject: RE: Already rollin'!

What, are you guys dead, you don't answer your fucking e-mails?

Sent from ScottC@NewRidgeEntertainment.com
To upstartcrow117@aol.com
Sent: Wednesday, July 3rd 9:06 AM
Subject: RE: Already rollin'!

Cliff,

Come in for meeting. Door always open. Eager to pick your brains.

Scott

[A phenomenon of the YouTube era was the "zombie novelty track" – altered versions of popular hit songs which provided the soundtrack to the so-called "Zombie Apocalypse". Most of these ephemera are lost to time, but the following tracks survived on a flash-stick found in the stomach of a big music fan post-mortem]

Here we come . . . lurching down your street
Get the funniest shrieks from . . .
People that we eat . . .

Hey Hey we're the Zombees
People say we're back from the dead
But we're too busy eating
To take a bullet in the head . . .

We're just horribly hungry
We've got to rip, rend and slay . . .
We're the last generation . . .
And we're not going away!

Talking to myself and feeling cold
Sometimes I'd like to die
Nothing ever seems to fly
Hanging around, nothing to do but frown
Rainy days and zombies always get me down

What I've got they used to call the blues
Nothing left half-alive
Feeling I don't want to survive
Walking around some kind of lonely clown
Rainy days and zombies always get me down

Funny but it seems I always wind up here with you
It's nice to know somebody wants me
Funny but it seems that it's the only thing to do
To run and find the one who'll eat me

What I feel is come and gone before
No need to scream it out
We know what guts are about
Hanging around, nothing to do but frown
Rainy days and zombies always get me down.

Z is for the Zillions of you out there
O is for the Offal that you munch
M is for the Mass outbreak of panic
B is for the Brains you want for lunch
I is for the Idiot I am for tripping up
E is for my Entrails dragged away
Put them all together they spell . . .
ZOMBIE
You made me what I am today!

Everybody's doin' a brand new dance now
(C'mon baby do the zombie-motion)
I know you'll get to like it
If you're stuck in a trance now
(C'mon baby do the zombie-motion)
My little baby sister can do it with class
It's easier than chewing off your grandma's ass
So come on, come on,
Do the zombie-motion with me

You gotta drag your foot now
Come on baby, grab guts, hmmm chole back
Oh well I think you got the knack . . .

Now that you can do it
Let's grab a chainsaw, bud
(C'mon baby do the zombie-motion)
Chug-a chug-a motion like a swallowing brains or blood
(C'mon baby do the zombie-motion)
Do it nice and easy now don't lose your head
A little bit of rhythm and to waken the dead
So come on, come on,
Do the zombie-motion with me . . .

You gotta swing your axe now
Come on, relax,
Do the zombie-motion with me
Yeah . . .

Break into a house in a zombie-motion
(C'mon baby do the zombie-motion)
Eviscerate some pets if you got the notion
(C'mon baby do the zombie-motion)
There's never been a dance that goes right to your head
It even makes you hungry
When you're ten days' dead
So come on come on do the zombie-motion with me.

THE WHITE HOUSE
WASHINGTON

My fellow Americans –

I speak to you tonight from behind a hallowed desk within the most important building of the greatest nation on Earth to report what many of you already know, what each of you must surely by now feel in your bones, without the necessity of me even having to say the words aloud.

And that message – one which has been long awaited, much anticipated, and frustratingly elusive – is this.

The recent difficulties which we have endured as a nation are near an end, and our long, national nightmare is almost over.

We come together on this July 4th both to observe a victory of the spirit and to share in a celebration of freedom, for the battles which in recent months have raged between the living and the dead have dwindled, and the stability and peace which we have enjoyed as a people but which has lately escaped us has been restored. That restoration is not yet complete, for we are not yet what we once were, but the victory is close enough at hand that we as a people should feel license to rejoice.

What we gather in utmost gravity to observe today is both a beginning and an end, a renewal of hope made concrete in a people. We continue to be, as we have ever been, the last best hope of the world.

The citizens of our great cities – Los Angeles, Chicago, even what remains of New York – have already experienced the fruits of our peacekeeping efforts, and we thank them for their heroic sacrifices, which continue even today. Clean-up operations are being completed as I speak. Much blood was shed in these towering metropolises on behalf of us all, and for that we are grateful.

To those of you hearing this in our nation's suburbs and rural areas, in the small towns and hamlets, I am aware that you do not yet fully share in the bounteous good fortune already gained by the rest of us. But I promise that you, too, will soon enjoy what we have traded our blood to earn. I pledge that I and the members of my newly formed cabinet will work tirelessly on your behalf until the order which has for too long escaped you been enforced.

As long as one American lives in hunger, all Americans live in hunger. You have my word as one of you that this will stop.

I speak also tonight to our foreign friends, especially those whose will was tested by the twilight struggle up to the New Festival of Britain, for if these trying times have taught us anything, these United States cannot be isolationist. I say that we are here to aid you in any way we can as you attempt to rebuild your countries as we have rebuilt ours. We pledge to strengthen the bonds which have been so recently tested. United, there is little we cannot do together.

As I speak to you now so that future generations may understand how there came to be future generations for them to be a part of, I am well aware that you have not chosen me as your president with your votes. I have achieved this high office more through Divine Providence than through any deliberate will of the people. I am as amazed as any of you that it has fallen upon me to report to you tonight on these truths, for while I always had faith that someday one of us would tell the story of our survival, I had no faith that it would ever be me come before you to tell it.

No man may know the hour of his passing, and I had not expected the timing of mine to allow me to lead you. I feel humbled before the Higher Power which has brought me, brought all of us, to this day.

If I had been asked at the start of the great civil war in which we were so recently engaged, one which tested both our nation and the world, whether I thought that Destiny would lead me to a moment such as this, I would have responded that I had expected to end up like so many of us whose daily lives revolved around the White House.

Despairing. Defeated. Destroyed.

But I am none of these things. I have survived. And so instead, I am astonished, grateful, and determined.

I have not sought this enormous responsibility, but I will not shirk it. And so, in the spirit of healing and reconciliation, I will share my thoughts, on this day, at this time, on where I came from, how I got here, and where I am heading. Where all of our fortunate race is heading, now that the bloody storm which threatened us has nearly passed.

It is important for a people to know who their president is. There are days when even I do not recognize the great transformation which has overtaken us all, as the torch is passed to a new generation of Americans, born in this century, tempered by war, having just reached a hard-won peace.

And so, let me tell you my story, the path which I have trod to reach this place. It is a uniquely American story, one which could have only happened here, a nation both melting pot and pressure cooker, a place where the low can be raised high.

Can be reborn.

As I lay before you my thoughts on the recent unpleasantness, you will likely be surprised to learn – it surprises me still – that though I now hold the exalted office of the President of the United States, I did not begin my working career seemingly within reach of such an celebrated position. I was born of modest beginnings, unlike most who have in recent decades been called upon to lead this nation, which still, even after all we have endured, is the last, best hope for man on Earth.

I was never a congressman, or a senator. I never served as a cabinet member. I have never held an elective office, nor did I ever, until now, feel myself qualified to do so. When I woke each morning, I never aspired to do anything more than, as is true for so many of you, provide an honest day's work for an honest day's pay.

And so my function here in this place was as one of the lowliest of the low, a nearly invisible cog in the machinery of politics.

I hope that these unprepossessing origins do not disturb you. But I have nothing left to hide. On this momentous day in history, no truths should remain hidden, for I believe truth is the glue which will bind us together, not only as a government, but as a people.

And so when I tell you that before the onset of the months of terror, I spent my days mopping floors, unclogging toilets, and other similarly menial tasks, I do that in the spirit of such truth, to illustrate that in our blessed country, anyone can work his or her way up the food chain and rise to occupy the highest office in the land.

In fact, I was attending to the second of those duties when the sirens went off. I was down on my knees feeding a metal snake through the pipes.

I had been trained what to do if I ever heard such an alert, but I must admit I wasn't as smart then as I have become now. Recent experiences have made all of us wiser. But then I didn't take it that seriously. Yes, I had been hearing tales of the dead come back to life, just as you had, and I even heard more than that, for those in the White House were not immune to gossip, and so I had overheard the whispers of those for whom I toiled. But I lived in a bubble of sorts, and never thought the plague would reach to this spot, to breach the walls of this historic building.

The old me was foolish, I admit it, and I look back on who I was and the decisions that I made as if I was a different, distant person.

But I felt safe in this building. I worked among the smartest men and women in the world, surrounded by brilliance, by those whose brains worked at a level far beyond that which I could then conceive. I had thought that they could, if anyone could, figure out a way to keep us safe. I was stupid then, I guess. But I assure all within the sound of my voice that I've become much smarter now, for I have been lucky enough to absorb all the best and brightest had to teach.

But that is now. Let us return now to the beginning of things.

Confident in my safety, rather than drop what I was doing and rush to one of the many protected areas for the lockdown, which we had often rehearsed, I simply continued unclogging the pipes. I believed this to be just another drill, one of the many we'd had to engage in since the aftereffects of the unearthing of the plague pit in Great Britain, and the rediscovery of what has become popularly known as "The Death."

So I slowly and carefully retracted the metal snake, and stepped back, feeling a certain satisfaction at a job well done, even one such as that. I take pride in my work. And then I stepped out into the hall and headed back to my workstation to return my tools. With everybody but me locked away in the many safe rooms, there was a quiet to the building I'd never heard before. I allowed myself to enjoy that peace. Until I heard a thudding, thundering sound, and turned a corner to find—

Well, you can guess what I discovered. You know. I don't have to describe it to you. I came face to face with someone dead reborn. I did not know who he had been or where he had come from. I did not pause to wonder how he had breached the defenses and made it so far. I only turned and ran.

I did not get far. I almost immediately felt a tugging at my arm, and my sleeve ripped from my work shirt and fell away.

The dead that walk, as you know, are faster than any at first thought. Everything the movies had taught was wrong, as humanity quickly learned. I turned and twirled the snake, and the coiled metal caught my attacker at its ankles. It tripped, falling back from me as it went down, but though its fingers slapped at my skin, I was able to make an escape. As it rose to its knees, I raced to the nearest safe room, and I began hammering on the door, begging to be let in, shouting out my code name – for, yes, even I had a code name – as I prayed for them to realize I was still one of the living.

And let me in they did, the two statisticians who were huddled within the small chamber. If they hadn't opened up their hearts to me, I would not be here with you today to help lead you through these trying times. Overcome with emotion, I crumpled in a corner, and shook, and listened to men much wiser than me try to make sense of a future they never thought would arrive.

As they talked of us and of them, and the great war that was to come, a war unlike any ever fought before, I felt a great peace settle over me, and their words faded away.

At some point, a moment beyond conscious thought, I realized in my soul that I had too much of discussion. The time for it had passed, and I had an undeniable urge to act. It had become time, in the words of the poet, to strive, to seek, to find, and not to yield.

And that is what I did.

That is what all of us did.

That is why we are here.

Having taken from them all I could of value, invigorated by a sustenance of body and buoyed by a sustenance of spirit, I left them behind, and moved on to the next such chamber, knowing somehow in that place beyond knowledge that only through digesting the wisdom of the greatest minds of our generation could I become who you needed me to become for us to move into a new, more serene, more peaceful future.

For are we not a new people?

My rebirth came with a scratch, unnoticed until I cowered in that corner, not realizing that a new hunger was being born, a hunger that would make me greater than I had once been, much like the hunger for freedom felt by those who founded this country.

You who hear these words, who have also been remade into better selves, may have been reborn with a bite or the loss of an arm. These are not scars. Do not mourn for any of them, for these are our medals, evidence of our admission to a greater age of peace.

Those of you who are within the sound of my voice and have not yet joined us, our ancestors, know that we welcome you into our ranks. Embrace us.

Let us embrace you.

We are stronger than you. We are wiser than you. We are the citizens of a new America. A new world.

Ask not what this new world can do for you, but what together we can do now that we have achieved freedom from man.

As you go forward this blessed day, remember – as we resolve that those dead shall not have been reborn in vain – we are what you eat.

Be wise in your feasting. Grow wiser in your feasting.

But feast. And feast well.

May the God who has reanimated us bless each and every one of you.

And God bless these newly United States.

—James Moreby,
President of the United States of America
July 4th

December 25th

*E*ach year that passes seems to have its own character. Some leave us with a feeling of satisfaction, others are best forgotten. This has been a difficult year for many, in particular those facing the continuing effects of the return of deceased subjects as semi-mindless vermin with an insatiable hunger for human flesh. Even more, our hearts reach out to those of our subjects who, while no longer living, remain full citizens of Great Britain and have urgent dietary requirements which must somehow be accommodated.

I am sure that we have all been affected by events on the streets of our cities and in the squares of our market towns, and saddened by the casualties suffered by our forces serving there. Our thoughts go out to their relations and friends who have shown immense dignity in the face of great personal loss. But we can be proud of the positive contribution that our servicemen and women are making, in conjunction with our allies. And many of our casualties are up and about again, putting a brave face on the loss of higher cerebral function and carrying on and making do in that great Great British tradition.

I myself lost a son, who is returned to me now and sits at my feet and may still one day inherit my throne. Just as his reanimated lawful wife, mother to future kings, is once again at her place by his side.

It is little more than sixty years since the Commonwealth was created and today, with more than a billion of its members still alive and free of the anthropophagous pestilence, the organisation remains a strong and practical force for survival. I am speaking to you, not from my home at Balmoral or my London residence in Buckingham Palace, now sadly little more than a radioactive ruin, but from a bunker which recently hosted the Commonwealth Heads of Government Meeting in Trinidad and Tobago. I understand how important the Commonwealth is to recently deceased yet active people. New communication technologies allow them to reach out to the wider world and share their experiences and viewpoints. For many, the practical assistance and networks of the Commonwealth can give skills, lend advice and encourage enterprise. It has been said that all humanity needs to soldier on is a healthy surplus of brains. Never has this been more true than now.

In many aspects of our lives, whether in sport, the environment, business or culture, the Commonwealth connection remains vivid and enriching. It is, in lots of ways, the face of the future. If it is to be a mouldy, blotched face, drooling bloody spittle, then so be it. And with continuing support and dedication, I am confident that this diverse Commonwealth of nations can strengthen the common bond that transcends politics, religion, race and economic circumstances. And find the brains!

We know that Christmas is a time for celebration and family reunions; but it is also a time to reflect on what confronts those less fortunate than ourselves, at home and throughout the world. Some have no brains to eat. No entrails. No human muscle tenderised by servants with hammers. These are poor indeed, and to be pitied.

Christians are taught to love their neighbours, having compassion and concern, and being ready to undertake charity and voluntary work to ease the burden of deprivation and disadvantage. But what of our neighbours? What duty do they have? If we, as Christians, love them, should they not, as neighbours, return that love with some gratitude. Perhaps with the gift of a small, relatively juicy child. Or two. We may ourselves be confronted by a bewildering array of difficulties and challenges, but we must never cease to work for a better future for ourselves and for others.

I wish you all, wherever you may be, a very happy Christmas.

–H.M. Queen Elizabeth II

ACKNOWLEDGEMENTS

Many thanks to Duncan Proudfoot, Pete Duncan, Dorothy Lumley, Nicola Chalton, Pascal Thivillon and all the contributors for bringing the Zombie Apocalypse to, er . . . life. Special thanks to H.P. Lovecraft, for those who know . . .